ONLY ONE

Stacy felt Cord's hand touch her shoulder lightly as he moved away from her to the horse vans. The warmth of his touch radiated as she visualized the imprint of his hand on her shoulder. Not thinking of much else, she walked over to the others, conscious that her whole attention was now focused on the retreating figure of Cord. Throughout the meal, she involuntarily watched for him. What kind of man could make her want to be with him and dislike him at the same time? Only one. Cord Harris.

from "No Quarter Asked"

BOOK YOUR PLACE ON OUR WEBSITE AND MAKE THE READING CONNECTION!

We've created a customized website just for our very special readers, where you can get the inside scoop on everything that's going on with Zebra, Pinnacle and Kensington books.

When you come online, you'll have the exciting opportunity to:

- View covers of upcoming books
- Read sample chapters
- Learn about our future publishing schedule (listed by publication month *and author*)
- Find out when your favorite authors will be visiting a city near you
- Search for and order backlist books from our online catalog
- Check out author bios and background information
- Send e-mail to your favorite authors
- Meet the Kensington staff online
- Join us in weekly chats with authors, readers and other guests
- Get writing guidelines
- AND MUCH MORE!

**Visit our website at
http://www.kensingtonbooks.com**

Texas Kiss

JANET DAILEY

ZEBRA BOOKS
Kensington Publishing Corp.
http://www.kensingtonbooks.com

ZEBRA BOOKS are published by

Kensington Publishing Corp.
119 West 40th Street
New York, NY 10018

All Kensington titles, imprints, and distributed lines are
available at special quantity discounts for bulk purchases
for sales promotion, premiums, fund-raising, educational, or
institutional use.

Special book excerpts or customized printings can also be
created to fit specific needs. For details, write or phone the
office of the Kensington Special Sales Manager: Attn.: Special
Sales Department. Kensington Publishing Corp., 119 West 40th
Street, New York, NY 10018. Phone: 1-800-221-2647.

Zebra and the Z logo Reg. U.S. Pat. & TM Off.

ISBN-13: 978-1-4201-0665-7
ISBN-10: 1-4201-0665-1

First Printing: July 2009
10 9 8 7 6 5 4 3 2 1

Printed in the United States of America

Contents

NO QUARTER ASKED

Chapter 1

Stacy stared out the window at the traffic rushing through the streets below. The simmering heat of Dallas in summer was held at bay by air-conditioning that made her feel cold all over. The somber gray and brown tones of the towering concrete buildings were oppressive, a reminder of the depression that had weighed on her ever since the unthinkable had happened. A little sigh escaped her as she let the curtain fall back in place and turned to face the older man behind the large walnut desk.

"Mr. Mills, you were Daddy's friend. You should understand more than anyone why I have to get away by myself to sort things out. It really doesn't make any difference if I'm in a city or a cabin in Texas."

"I don't agree, Stacy. As your father's attorney and closest friend, I wish you'd think it over a little more." Carter Mills took off his black-framed glasses and wiped them absently with his handkerchief.

She studied him for a long moment before replying. "Look, I'm not trying to run away or anything." Stacy ran a hand nervously over her bare arm. "I just need time to see where I fit in again."

"I can understand that." But Mills frowned. "Even so, a complete change of scene might do you good—"

"If you mean going someplace like Europe, the answer is no. I'd rather stay in Texas."

The attorney shook his head. "You don't have to. You're independent now and you don't need to worry about money."

Tears welled in her eyes. "Maybe not. But I wish—" She was too upset to finish the sentence but she was damned if she'd cry. Stacy fought silently for self-control.

"The death of someone dear always involves a difficult adjustment," Mills said gently.

"Tell me about it." Her remark was too softly spoken to be rude.

"Maybe I shouldn't say this, but you've always been headstrong," Mills went on. "All the same, I still don't see why you insist on hiding away out in the country."

Stacy Adams looked hesitantly at Carter Mills, Sr., wondering how she could make him understand why she had to go. Her father, Joshua Adams, had respected this man and trusted him. *Her father.* The words caught in her throat. Stacy glanced down at her hands clenched tightly in her lap. In a blue suit, she was the picture of respectability, but her life didn't quite match the image. Her mother had died shortly after Stacy was born, leaving her globe-trotting husband with the unfamiliar task of raising a child. Refusing kind offers from relatives to care for his little daughter, Joshua Adams had filled one of his suitcases with disposable diapers and cans of formula and carted the year-old baby off on his next foreign assignment. Life for father and daughter had been one long world tour with brief respites in big cities to catch their breath before starting out again, as he built his reputation as a freelance photographer. Foreign bureaus of newspapers and magazines were based all over the globe; Joshua and Stacy had been too.

But the Internet had changed everything about his business—except Joshua Adams's spirit of adventure.

Loving memories whirled through Stacy's mind—most vividly, her seventeenth birthday three years ago when her dad had smuggled a puppy into a plush New Orleans hotel. Cajun, he'd called the pup, in honor of his backwoods birthplace. The wiggling, playful puppy had grown into a huge German shepherd, devoted to his young mistress. Her father had predicted that Cajun would protect Stacy better than any guardian angel.

She had to wonder if her father knew how right he'd been, because it was Cajun who'd pulled her, unconscious, from the wreckage of the chartered plane before it burst into flames. The pilot and her father hadn't made it.

As she tried to blink back the tears that clouded her eyes, Stacy raised her head to meet the lawyer's affectionate gaze. Her brown eyes grew misty with tears as her mouth curved into a painful smile.

"I take it back, Stacy. Maybe going out in the wilderness will help you think things through. Joshua loved the West and never turned down an assignment that would take him there." Carter Mills rose from his chair and walked around to where Stacy was seated. "But remember, you're still a young woman, barely twenty, with your whole life ahead of you. He wouldn't have wanted you to miss any of it— not the good and definitely not the bad."

Stacy took the hand he offered and rose, her tailored suit enhancing the curves underneath. "I hoped you'd understand why I have to do this."

"Well, it's your decision. But there's a young guy I know who's rather upset about you leaving," Carter Mills said. "And I can't blame my son for wanting to treat you to the best clubs and nightlife that Dallas has to offer. Not that you need to have anyone pay your way, not with the inheritance your father left you."

She never could have imagined that it would come to as much as it had. But the rights to Joshua Adams's photos were worth a lot, although it was her father's creative legacy that meant the most to her.

"I'm afraid I haven't accepted the idea that I have money of my own yet," she told him. "Before, I was happy just to be with my dad, traveling wherever the wind blew—maybe I inherited his wanderlust."

"I think you did, Stacy."

"Anyway," she continued, reaching for her purse, "out there with just Cajun, Diablo, and miles of sky, I should be able to decide about the future."

Carter Mills shook his head. "Are you taking that fool horse, too? I had hoped you'd sold him long ago," the lawyer exclaimed with no attempt to hide his concern. "I have to say that I think you're making a big mistake taking him."

"Oh, Diablo isn't all that out-of-control. He's high-strung. There's a difference." Stacy smiled. "And you know very well that I'm an excellent horsewoman. Dad never would've allowed me to have Diablo if he didn't think I could handle him."

"I realize that, but I'm sure it never occurred to him that you would be taking that horse out to the back end of nowhere with you," Carter replied gruffly.

"No. I'm sure Dad probably hoped that I would settle down and take my place in society, so to speak. He could be really old-fashioned about things like that. It doesn't interest me much," she said, then added, "I like living simply."

Carter Mills nodded. "What are you doing with the apartment while you're gone?"

"I decided to just lock it up rather than sublet it or let it go," Stacy answered, a shadow of pain in her eyes. She didn't want to look at him.

"Just as long as you know you're always welcome at our home. And if there's ever anything you need, don't hesitate one minute," Carter Mills said.

"I won't. Carter Jr. is taking me to dinner tomorrow night for one last fling with civilization. He seems to think that I'm going to the dark side of the moon or something." Stacy smiled again, touched by the sincere concern extended by the lawyer. "Thanks for everything, Mr. Mills."

Stacy walked out of his office into the reception area. She understood his misgivings about her proposed trip. Not that she was going to an utterly remote area, but it was true enough that she would be somewhat isolated. When his son had told him about Stacy's decision to rent a hunting cabin in the Apache Mountains of Texas for the spring, the older man had immediately checked into the situation. But he honestly could find no real flaws with her plans, except that she was going alone.

Stacy entered the elevator with an illuminated down arrow above it. Mulling over her plans, she was unaware of the interested looks she received from some of her fellow passengers. The sprinkling of freckles across a too-straight nose usually meant that strangers took her for an average American girl, nothing more. But second glances noticed the gleaming brown hair framing her oval face and the dark brown eyes, more solemn now, with naturally thick lashes that gave her a wholesome beauty all her own.

On the ground floor, Stacy proceeded to the street. It must be lunch hour, she thought absently—lots of pedestrians awaited the commands at the stoplights. Swept along by the flow at the crosswalk, she let herself be led by the steady stream until she reached the parking lot where she had left her car. Preoccupied with her memories as she was, her hand caressed the steering wheel for a second before she accelerated into traffic. The cool little sports car had been the last present her father had given her.

Looking back, Stacy realized she should have recognized the significance of the gift. She'd always assumed that, although she and her father lived very comfortably, their finances were essentially dependent on a freelancer's often erratic income. She hadn't understood all that much about the rights and royalties part of it until Carter Mills's careful explanation. The discovery that her father's death had left her with the means to be independent and live well still seemed like a dream. Stacy didn't know what she would have done if that had not been the case. She possessed a smattering of knowledge about everything, but she had never enrolled in college, preferring to travel with her father, which was an extraordinary education in itself.

Arriving at her apartment building, Stacy pulled into her designated parking spot and got out. The elevator doors were not far away, a convenience her father had insisted on. Even in the digital age, professional camera equipment meant lugging heavy cases. She pressed the button for the fifth floor, then walked silently down the corridor to the apartment that was hers now. She hesitated as she reached her door. Depression spread over her as she inserted the key and opened the door. She was immediately greeted by an ecstatic German shepherd yelping his pleasure at her return.

"Cajun, did you miss me?" Stacy smiled sadly, cradling the enormous head in her hands as she looked at the adoration in the dog's eyes. "What would I do if you weren't here?"

The telephone jingled dimly, stirring Stacy out of her thoughts. Bending a knee on the flowered couch, she picked up the receiver.

"Yes?"

"Hey, Stacy. It's Carter," said a masculine voice on the other end. "Dad said I just missed you."

"I left there around noon or maybe closer to one," Stacy said, glancing at her watch as she sat on the couch.

"How's everything going?" A touch of concern warmed his light tone.

"Fine, really. I was just going to finish up the last of my packing, except for the few odds and ends that will have to wait," Stacy said, adding with a little laugh, "I even threw a couple of dresses in with my riding clothes. I'm planning to live it up in some little cow town."

"Just so long as you don't meet some tall, dark, and handsome cowboy, and ride off into the sunset with him," Carter mocked, "I won't mind."

"I wouldn't worry. They don't make cowboys like they used to," Stacy said wryly. "Our last trip west, all I ever saw were sunburned, middle-aged men with families to support."

"Are you still driving down?"

"Yeah. Just Caj and me. Diablo's going by train as far as Pecos. I'll pick him up there and go on to McCloud. The cabin's about thirty miles from town, so I'm really not too far from civilization."

"I'm glad you didn't ask me to go along. All that solitude would drive me up the wall. I don't see how you'll be able to take it for more than a week. How different can one mountain be from another?" Carter teased.

"Maybe you're right, but I have to find that out for myself."

"Can't talk you out of a thing, can I?" the voice in the receiver said. "Listen, I have a brief to work on tonight, so I won't be able to come over. We still have a date for tomorrow evening. Seven sharp, right?"

"Right," Stacy agreed.

"Okay. Take care and I'll see you tomorrow. Bye."

"Bye, Carter."

The click of the phone echoed forlornly in the crushing silence that followed. Refusing to give in to the melancholy that suffused the empty room, Stacy rose from the flowered couch to enter her bedroom. She would do every last-minute thing right now, filling the void intensified by the phone call with a bustle of activity.

The next night Stacy was just fastening the clasp on her onyx pedant when the doorbell rang. She surveyed her reflection one last time in the mirror. The sleeveless, peach-colored dress set off her skin and the golden highlights in her hair, pulled up in all its ringleted glory. Taking a tissue, Stacy blotted her lipstick and applied a little gloss for more shine before allowing a satisfied smile to light her face.

When she opened the door to admit Carter, her dark eyes were flashing with pleasure. "I didn't keep you waiting too long, did I?"

The tall, fair-haired man grasped her hands and pushed her away from him to give her a once-over. His blue eyes answered her sparkle with a shine all their own. "I would wait longer just to see you looking this good, Stacy."

"Aw, thanks."

His response was a grin. "Guess you know how good you look, huh?"

She shrugged and flung a crocheted stole around her shoulders, adjusting it as he took the liberty of brushing a light kiss on her hair.

"I made reservations for eight at the Meadow Wood country club," he said.

"Okay. Let's go." Stacy smiled up at him.

The two chatted amiably on their way to his car but once

inside the conversation pretty much stopped. Carter gave his full attention to the traffic clogging the busy highways that threaded through metropolitan Dallas while Stacy glanced now and then at his profile. He was a good-looking guy with light brown, almost blond, hair and clear blue eyes. Six years older than Stacy and just entering his father's law firm, Carter was considered a serious catch by many of her acquaintances. And it had been said often enough that they looked great together, as if they were meant to be. For what that was worth.

There'd never been any avowals of love or promises to wait between them. When Stacy accompanied her father on his travels, she'd sent Carter funny postcards of wherever she was and called him when she was back in town. Carter dated other girls when she was gone, but never anyone as regularly as Stacy. The two families had seemed pleased with the budding relationship, and she'd suspected that there had been hopes of an eventual marriage.

Stacy sighed, watching Carter competently maneuver the car into a tight parking space. The country club lot was crowded with expensive SUVs and big sedans. Gleaming, all of them. Very different from the battered but indestructible Land Rovers her father drove on assignment, rugged vehicles that were the real deal and not tricked out to impress a valet parker at a posh restaurant.

She glanced again at Carter. Their relationship could never be considered as brother-and-sister, she thought, even if it hadn't reached the heart-pounding passionate stage yet. They were both enjoying the other's company while waiting for love to come their way.

Someday, she supposed, they might marry. They would have a good life. They got along too well for it to be any other way. But not just yet.

Besides, Stacy thought, she was still naïve enough to

wish for a love that would sweep her off her feet, even if that only happened in fairy tales.

"Dreamer, are you going to get out of the car or just sit there?" Carter asked, laughing down at her as he stood there holding the car door open.

"Sorry—I was off in another world."

"Well, come back to this one. Tonight is my night and I plan to make the most of it."

He smiled as he escorted her to the entrance, his arm resting lightly around her waist. He opened the elaborately scrolled doors of the private club. Once at the bar, Carter ordered their drinks while Stacy gazed at the retro décor. The designer had gone for an exotic, jungle-type atmosphere with faux leopard and zebra skins adorning the walls.

When the waitress returned with their drinks, Stacy caught Carter looking at her with a somber expression on his face.

"Why so grim? I thought we were celebrating tonight," Stacy chided him.

"Oh, I was thinking about that vacation you're taking, Stacy. Dad isn't too happy about it and neither am I. If anything happened to you out at that godforsaken cabin, it could be weeks before anyone finds out," he said earnestly.

"Please, let's not talk about it tonight. I've made up my mind that I'm going and that's all there is to be said." She replied a little sharply because of her own apprehension. "How come everyone but me knows what's best for me, by the way?"

"Did it ever occur to you that this time you might not be right?" There was a hint of impatience in his voice. "You seem to think that because you've traveled all over the world you can handle anything that could possibly happen."

"And what's wrong with that?"

"Stacy, your father took care of everything. I have a feeling that he showed you the world from a safe distance."

"What do you mean? I was right there with him."

"I mean you saw it all through a camera lens. You have no idea what it's like to be on your own."

Stacy fumed for a few seconds before she replied. "Just because I've seen war and hunger and famine from his point of view, does that make it any less real? I know what life is about. And I have a few ideas about what I'm going to do with mine, so there's no need of discussing it any further."

"Will you stop being so stubborn for once and listen to reason?"

This was a new side of Carter and Stacy didn't like it. Just because her father had passed away didn't mean that any other man got to boss her around. God knows, Joshua Adams had never even tried. "The subject is now officially closed."

"Then let's dance," Carter suggested, smoothing over the awkward moment rather than argue with her.

Points to Carter, Stacy thought not very happily. She rose, pushing back her chair from the table. Carter held her elbow firmly, directing her to the dance floor. When he took her in his arms, both were scowling—until they caught each other's eyes.

Stacy laughed first. "Carter, I'm sorry. I really didn't mean to lose my temper. We don't have anything to argue about."

He smiled down at her pleading expression. "Okay, I'll consider the subject closed, per your imperial command. Your humble subject would like to enjoy his date with you."

Later, when their reservation for dinner was called, the couple entered the dining room and were escorted to a table for two secluded from the rest of the diners. When the final course was cleared, they settled back contentedly with coffee.

"That was a delicious meal," Stacy said as Carter passed her a small pitcher of half-and-half.

He nodded, watching her pour a liberal dose into her cup. "Think they have any skim milk?"

"Live dangerously, dude. Be like me." She wiggled two packets of sugar at him, then ripped off the corners and poured them in, stirring the rich coffee. "This is going to be even more delicious."

"No, you are."

She took a sip. "Thank you, kind sir."

He drank his coffee black, as the waiter seemed to have disappeared, and looked at her thoughtfully when they were done. "Did you want to go back in the bar and dance, or would you rather go somewhere else?"

"No, let's stay here. I really enjoy the atmosphere and, besides, I'm not in the mood for going clubbing tonight," Stacy replied.

"Good. Me neither. There's some talking I want to do and I don't want to shout over the din of a DJ."

"Please, not another lecture about my trip," she begged. "You promised there'd be no more discussion about my going to Texas."

"And I have every intention of keeping my word. This is something entirely different. And I vote for going someplace different. Okay with you?"

"I guess so, sure."

A short drive later, Stacy waited for Carter at the entryway of a lounge while he paid the cover charge. They found a table over in a corner and ordered drinks. At the beginning of a slow dance, they wound their way onto the floor. Holding Stacy a little away from him, Carter gazed down into her brown eyes and smiled gently.

"Remember after your father's funeral the comment Dad made about you being one of the family?"

"Yes," Stacy said, returning his serious look.

"I want to make it legal. I want you to be my wife," he said, their steps almost ceasing. "I'm not trying to talk you out of your trip, but while you're thinking about the future, I want you to include me. Stacy, I care about you—actually, I've begun to realize that I love you and I want to watch over you for the rest of my life. We've never talked about the future before and it's time we did—"

"Whoa," she said softly. She was *really* not ready for that speech.

"Hear me out. Before, we were both too young. I had law school to finish and you had some growing up to do."

Some? At the age of twenty, Stacy knew she was far from finished with that. But Carter didn't seem to think so.

"It's time to start planning the rest of our lives," he said firmly.

She couldn't begin to think that far ahead. "Carter, I don't know what to say. I don't know if I'm ready to settle down. I don't know—"

"Don't say anything. I know it's awfully soon after losing your father. You're bound to be confused, so I'm not asking for an answer yet. When I think you're ready, I'll ask you again properly. Until then I just want you to remember while you're out there in the boonies that I do love you and want to marry you," Carter said, gently kissing her forehead.

He drew her once again into the circle of his arms, and they continued dancing in silence while Stacy mulled the proposal over in her mind. She shouldn't have been surprised by it, but she was, despite her earlier thoughts in the same line. Returning to their table after the song was over, they sat quietly for a little while.

"You mentioned you were taking Diablo. I was going

to ask if you wanted to take my gray," said Carter. "He's definitely more manageable than that red devil of yours."

"I don't expect to have much trouble with Diablo, but thanks for offering," Stacy said, feeling a little annoyed. "Besides, he's already on his way to Pecos, so I'll just stick with my original arrangement."

"What time do you plan to leave tomorrow?" Carter asked.

"Around the middle of the day."

"Well, it's getting late. I don't want to keep you out into the wee hours. You'll have plenty to think about tonight. At least I hope so," Carter said, casually referring to his earlier proposal.

As if it was a done deal. But it wasn't.

They didn't talk very much on the way home. Stacy nestled down in her seat and gazed out the window at the gleaming glass skyscrapers of Dallas, feeling blue. Pulling into the parking lot of Stacy's building, Carter turned the engine off. Then, instead of getting out of the car, he sat looking at her. "I won't be able to come over tomorrow and tell you good-bye, so I'll wish you my good luck now," he said, drawing her into his arms.

Stacy tilted her head back and awaited his kiss. His lips were firm and gentle as they pressed down upon hers. He held her body close to his as his hands caressed her shoulders, bare under the stole. Stacy's heart increased its tempo with the growing urgency in his kiss.

"Take that with you, Stacy, and let it plead my cause," he said.

Reluctantly, Stacy stepped out of the car when he came around and opened the door for her. In silence, they walked into the building to the elevator.

"I'll leave you here. Come home soon," Carter whispered to her, looking affectionately down at her freckled nose and wide brown eyes. Softly he touched a kiss to her cheek and walked away.

Watching him depart, Stacy felt a cold emptiness chill her heart. She turned uncertainly to the yawning doors of the elevator. Quietly, she let herself into the apartment, questioning her decision to go away from the only home and friends she had, even temporarily.

As if he understood her troubled thoughts, Cajun pushed his nose into her hand and licked her palm.

She rubbed her hand dry on his big head in playful revenge and went looking for his leash. He was one of the great dogs of all time, but he still couldn't walk himself. Not in Dallas anyway.

After they'd taken their usual tour of the surrounding streets, she got ready for bed. An hour later she had fallen asleep, once again resolved to carry through with her plans to journey to the wild side of Texas.

Chapter 2

McCloud—10 miles, the sign read. Stacy arched her back, stretching the cramped muscles. Many hours of non-stop driving were beginning to tell. But she was almost there and the excitement of finally reaching her destination was starting to flow through her. She glanced briefly at her reflection in the rearview mirror. Only her eyes showed the weariness she felt from the long drive. Her clothes still looked fresh. She'd taken off her jacket before starting out and hung it over the back of the passenger seat where Cajun was sleeping, his huge body contorted by the limited space.

The two-horse trailer specially designed for the Jaguar was pulling easily. Diablo had kicked up a fuss when she loaded him in Pecos, but had settled down since then.

The afternoon sun was glaring through the windshield of her car as Stacy reached for the sunglasses lying on the dash. It wouldn't be long now before she reached the mountains. First she would stop in town to look up the Nolans so they could direct her to the cabin and then she'd pick up groceries. With luck she'd be cooking her supper by seven.

Ahead she could see the growing outline of small stucco buildings from a long time ago. In this dry climate, they lasted forever. Perfect examples of genuine Americana, something her father would have loved to photograph. Stacy lowered her speed, taking in as much of her surroundings as she could. A land that time forgot was exactly what she needed.

She pulled into a gas station on the outskirts of town. Stepping out of the black sportscar, she snapped her fingers at the waking dog to get him to follow. Stiffly and a little sleepily, he joined his mistress on the concrete sidewalk. Stacy glanced appreciatively around the station, noting the lack of litter and junked car parts. Although the building probably dated from the 1930s, it was in excellent repair.

A teenage boy came out of the office area toward her car, casting an admiring look at it and then her. Stacy barely noticed either as she surveyed the town ahead of her, shimmering in the afternoon sun.

"Fill 'er up, miss?" the young voice drawled.

"Please. Check under the hood, too," she replied, smiling inwardly. Full service gas stations were hard to find and she felt even more like she'd stepped back in time.

Cajun went off to investigate a grassy lot next to the station while Stacy walked into the office to escape the sun. Inside, it took her eyes a minute to adjust. There were two men—one, the older of the two, was dressed in an attendant's uniform. The other—well, wow, even with his back to Stacy, he looked attractive. Some men looked good from any angle and he was one, in those faded Levis and well-worn plaid shirt. His dark, almost black hair was barely visible under the brown Stetson on his head. His tall, muscular frame blocked the attendant's view of Stacy until she went over to the counter with the candy display and a rack of seven different kinds of beef jerky.

"'Scuse me, Cord. Can I help you, miss?" the attendant asked.

Stacy glanced up at him, taking in the smiling hazel eyes and his kind face, creased into leather by the scorching Texas sun. She couldn't help but return his smile.

"Yes, I'd like one of those chocolate bars," Stacy said.

The man nodded. "Sure thing." He turned toward the cash register with the coins Stacy handed him. "Don't think me nosy, ma'am, but from your accent, I take it you're not from around here."

Laughing, Stacy replied. "I never realized I had an accent, but I suppose everyone does. Actually, I'm from"—she hesitated—"well, not really anywhere in particular. We traveled a lot when I was growing up."

"I see." Perhaps he really didn't want to be nosy for he said nothing more.

"Anyway, I'm staying here this summer. I was wondering if you could tell me where I might find a family named Nolan. I rented their hunting cabin," she explained.

It was then that the second man turned to face Stacy and she was surprised by the seeming antagonism in his eyes. Puzzled, she heard him mutter a goodbye to the man behind the counter and stride out the door to a jeep parked beside the station. Turning back to the counter, she wished she could shake the feeling that the haunting expression in his eyes had given her. What had she done?

"I'm sorry, what did you say?" she asked, realizing that the attendant was talking to her.

"I said the Nolans run the grocery store in town. Used to be the old mercantile. They still sell just about everything a body might need."

"Good." She smiled at him, recovering her composure.

"Just turn right at the next block, then straight for two more, then left. Theirs is the second shop from the corner." He smiled back.

"Thank you."

"Miss, you were a quart low on oil, so I put some in. That's some car you got," the teenager commented, coming inside and gesturing to the black sports car through the window. "I'll bet she leaves everyone in the dust on the straightaway!"

"That's enough, Billy," the older man put in, taking Stacy's money for the gas and the oil. "I'm sure the lady appreciates the fact you like her choice of cars."

Stacy laughed in return. "Right now I'd better look up the Nolans or it'll be dark before I get to my new home."

"Well, you just follow the directions I gave you and you can't miss it. Molly Nolan is always there in the afternoons and I imagine she'll know where to find her husband," the attendant said as he walked along with Stacy to her car.

She was tickled by the way he dragged the first syllable out and clipped the second. *Huzzzz-bin.* She might need a guide to true Texan speech if she was going to stay here. It was nice to be in a place where the accents still sounded so distinctive and home-grown. She whistled to Cajun and waved a good-bye to the two attendants, young and old, as she drove out onto the highway. Stacy smiled to herself as she turned right at the next block. The people seemed friendly anyway. At least two of them were, she qualified. And she wasn't going to let a dark-haired stranger's rudeness spoil her first visit to the town. If he hadn't seemed so grouchy, she probably would have considered him handsome, she reflected.

He certainly had the requirements—dark hair, brown eyes, and built—but he'd acted as if she was beneath consideration herself. There really wasn't any reason for her to keep dwelling on those unfriendly dark eyes; chances were she would never see him again. His clear-cut features with the strong jaw and cheekbones gave Stacy the feeling there was no give in the man.

Reaching the corner of the second block, she spotted the

grocery store. Ahead of her was a space just wide enough for her to park her car and trailer. Cajun attempted to join her when she hopped out of the car but she ordered him to stay, leaving all the windows rolled halfway down so he got plenty of air on the hot day. He was too big to sneak out that way, but he stuck his muzzle outside as if he was considering the possibility and let his tongue loll in the breeze, panting. She glanced in the horse trailer at Diablo before continuing on her way.

The main street was quaint, covering all of two or three blocks. There was a drugstore on the corner, the grocery store next to it, a little brick post office, followed by a clothing shop and a café.

Not a big town but big enough to serve the ranch community surrounding it and holding its own, she hoped, against the lure of malls that were fifty or more miles away.

Pushing the door open, she entered the grocery store. Behind a narrow counter was a small, matronly lady Stacy guessed to be in her late fifties. Her hair was peppered with gray which made her seem more motherly. The simple dress covering her plump figure made Stacy think of a kitchen filled with the aroma of fresh-baked cakes. When the customer the woman was waiting on left, Stacy stepped forward.

"Excuse me, are you Mrs. Nolan?"

"Yes, I am. Is there something I could help you with?"

"I'm Stacy Adams. I made arrangements to rent your cabin for the summer," Stacy explained.

"Of course! How silly of me, I should have known it was you right off. We don't have many tourists stop in. You did say you'd be here in the first part of May, but it had completely slipped my mind," the older woman said. "I imagine you're anxious to get out there before dark."

"Yes. Actually I'd hoped to stay there tonight, Mrs. Nolan."

"Oh, goodness, call me Molly or I'll think you're talking to someone else." She laughed. "My husband will be here shortly and can drive out with you. We cleaned it up last week, but it's still not as welcoming as I'd like it to be."

"That's all right—"

"No, no," Molly interrupted her. "It won't do, that's all, not for you. Men, now, if they got somethin' to sit on and a place to cook food, it don't matter if there's curtains at the windows or a cloth on the table."

"I'm sure it will be fine. I hope you didn't go to a whole lot of trouble just for me," Stacy answered, realizing that the woman had noticed her city clothes and was probably concerned about Stacy expecting something fancier.

"Excuse me," a voice from behind Stacy said.

As she turned to move away from the counter, she found herself face-to-face with the broad shoulders of the man from the gas station, the one who hadn't smiled.

Her eyes met his. There was no flicker of recognition in his dark gaze, no spark of interest.

"Oh, Cord, I'm so glad you're here," said Molly, coming around the corner to take his arm.

A faint smile turned up the corners of his mouth as he looked down at the motherly woman, but he didn't say anything.

"I want you to meet Miss Stacy Adams. She's rented the hunting cabin in the foothills of the east range for the summer. Stacy, this is Cord Harris, your official landlord. The Circle H headquarters is about ten miles from the cabin."

Surprised by the unexpected second encounter with the stranger, Stacy murmured a polite reply to the introduction and managed to raise her eyes to meet his stony gaze again. This time there was no doubting the stern look in his eyes. Deliberately, he searched her face and then he looked down at her crisp new clothes. Everything Stacy'd thought of as practical for traveling suddenly seemed too chic for this rough country.

Embarrassed, she felt a growing heat burn her cheeks. Angry that Cord Harris had managed to make her feel that way, she thrust out her chin defiantly.

"I hope you won't find our part of the country too desolate for your liking," Cord was saying, a trace of sarcasm in his voice.

"I'm sure I'll enjoy my stay here. Almost everyone has gone out of their way to be friendly," Stacy replied, attempting to control the emotions that trembled on the edge of her words.

"I'm sure they have," Mrs. Nolan chirped. "Why, once the word gets out that you're staying for the summer, our young men will beat a path to your door!"

"I doubt that," Stacy said with a smile, "but it's nice of you to say so."

"Not worried about staying alone at that deserted shack, are you?" Cord Harris said dryly. "After a few nights alone out there, you'll probably welcome some company. Beats listening to the coyotes."

"Is that right," she said levelly. "I'll take your word for it. But I came here to be alone. I do intend to make friends, but I don't intend to go out honkytonking, if that's what you mean."

"Intend? Hmm," the dark-haired man drawled, meeting Stacy's annoyed glare with a cool look. "That leaves you an out to do whatever you please. But somehow you don't seem like the type to isolate yourself for any amount of time."

"Now, Cord," Molly Nolan put in, trying to ease the obvious friction between the two. "I don't think it's your place to judge Miss Adams or her plans. You apologize for your rudeness, y'hear?"

"If what I said was unfounded, I certainly do apologize."

His hand touched the brim of his Stetson, but the gesture was more mocking than gentlemanly. "I do hope you enjoy your stay here, Miss Adams, however long it may be."

Nodding a good-bye to Mrs. Nolan, the arrogant rancher picked up his sack of goods and went out the door without allowing Stacy time to reply. Her annoyance had reached the point where words failed her. Never had she met someone so full of himself. Turning to the astonished woman beside her, Stacy vented a little.

"Who does he think he is?"

"Oh, you mustn't mind Cord," soothed Molly absentmindedly. "He has a tendency to voice his opinion. Underneath all that bluster, though, he's a good guy."

"You could have fooled me," Stacy exclaimed. "I wish he lived ten thousand miles away instead of just ten. What did I do to make him mad at me? Hell. I don't care."

"Honey, he might just be feelin' ornery. Or maybe you reminded him of someone else that he—oh, I don't know exactly," the woman replied, bustling around to the other side of the counter. "Best not to waste your time worryin' about it. Now, you came in here to pick up some food, I'm sure. And as far as the cabin, my husband ought to be here soon."

She drawled the word—*huzzz-bin*—just like the older man at the gas station, and Stacy softened a little, hearing nothing but friendliness in the other woman's voice.

Still, she was fuming inwardly. Stacy took a tiny shopping cart and went down one of the narrow aisles, picking out canned goods that would last her for a while, and heading for the fresh food in another aisle.

Cord Harris might be her nearest neighbor, but she was going to make a serious effort to avoid him at all costs. There was only one drawback to that plan: she would have liked to crack his infuriating coolness somehow. And given half a chance, she would.

After picking up all the supplies she felt she would need, Stacy returned to the checkout where she found Molly Nolan engaged in a conversation with a thin, balding man. Guessing that it must be Mr. Nolan, Stacy joined them.

"Hello again. Did you find everything you needed?" Molly asked, then turned to the man by her side. "Miss Adams, this is my husband, Harry. He'll drive up to the cabin with you."

"I'm happy to meet you, Mr. Nolan," Stacy said, extending her hand to the man before her.

"Molly said you was a pretty thing, but she didn't say you was this pretty. Ya sure are going to light up this little cow town," the bright-eyed man responded, eagerly shaking her hand. "I hope the cabin will suit you all right, because it sure ain't very fancy."

"Of course it will. I'm used to roughing it with my dad," Stacy said, smiling at the man who was an inch shorter than her own five-foot-four.

"Oh, is your daddy coming to join you?" Molly asked.

"No." A flicker of pain crossed Stacy's face. "He was killed in a plane crash a few months ago."

"Oh. I'm so sorry. I didn't mean to—" Molly started.

"It's all right. You couldn't have known," Stacy said swiftly.

"What about your mother? She probably don't want you gallivantin' off by yourself," Harry Nolan said.

"My mother died shortly after I was born, so I'm pretty much on my own now. But no one has to worry about me being alone. I brought my German shepherd along with me. I'm sure he can handle any four-footed animal that would wander in and the two-footed variety as well." Stacy managed a smile, thinking of Cord Harris.

"Good dogs, them shepherds," the old man agreed. "He'll watch out for you real good."

"Well, I hope he won't have to." Stacy reached in her purse to pay for the groceries. "And I'm ready to go whenever you are, Mr. Nolan."

"Where'd you park your car?"

"Across from the drugstore."

"I'll meet ya in about five minutes with my jeep and you can follow me out." He moved toward the door.

"Now if you need anything or get to feelin' you want some company, you just hustle yourself into town. Me and my husband would love you to visit with us any time," said Molly after her husband left.

"I'll keep that in mind. But I think for a while I'm just going to enjoy the peace and quiet," Stacy replied, touched by the motherly concern.

"The folks around here are all pretty friendly and would be more than glad to help you out if you have any kind of trouble, so you just don't hesitate to ask," instructed Molly. "Peace and quiet's fine, but you mustn't shut yourself off completely. Remember that you're always welcome here and don't be ashamed to ask for help."

"I won't be. Thank you again. You'll be seeing me."

Balancing the sack of groceries in one arm, Stacy pushed the door open with the other. It was nice to feel so at home with people she'd met only a few minutes ago. With the exception of a certain rancher, everyone had been happy to help her.

Reaching the car, she put the groceries in the back, quieted the excited dog, and looked around for Mr. Nolan. In the trailer, Diablo was starting to get restless. Walking back to it, Stacy entered by the side door of the empty stall. The sorrel turned his blazed head to her and blew gently on her face.

Softly she talked to him, trying to calm him down. His ears flicked back and forth, catching her words, but his eyes still rolled uneasily.

Glancing up, Stacy saw Mr. Nolan drive up beside the Jaguar. As she emerged from the van, the old man clambered out of his jeep and joined her.

"All set to go?" he asked.

"Yes. Just making sure everything was secure in the trailer. I'm afraid my horse is a bad traveler," Stacy explained, indicating the sorrel's tossing head.

"Mighty flashy-lookin' horse," commented Harry. "What breed is he?"

"Mostly Arabian," Stacy answered, walking over to the driver's side of the sports car.

"Never cared much for them. Too flighty actin'. Give me a steady quarter horse any time," the man answered a little gruffly. "Well, we best get goin'. The road's not in too bad a shape, so you should be able to keep up with me easy." He started the jeep and moved off.

It wasn't at all difficult to follow him. They drove through a few blocks of widely spaced homes before taking a gravel road north from town. The road soon entered the foothills and finally went into the mountains. After they had gone about twenty miles, the jeep turned into a side road that was little more than a worn track. Stacy refused to let herself think about the jolts her Jaguar was taking and prayed that the low-slung car wouldn't get hung up in one of the ruts while she was trying to concentrate on the bouncing rear bumper of the jeep in front of her. She glanced anxiously in the mirror at the horse trailer behind her. Diablo would really be nervous by the time they got to the cabin.

The pine woods were so thick that she couldn't see to either side and, with the sun setting, the rays filtered through the trees only in patches. The woods thinned out ahead as she watched the vehicle in front go down a small hill into what looked like a clearing. Reaching the top of the hill, Stacy saw a luscious green meadow before her with a stream cascading through it. Off to her left against the back of a canyon wall nestled a small wooden cabin with a corral and a lean-to beside it.

Looking to her right, Stacy could see that the mountain meadow continued on into the arroyos beyond. The landscape beat any picture she had ever seen.

Harry Nolan had stopped his jeep and was standing by the cabin's porch when Stacy pulled her black sports car in front.

"It's beautiful!" she exclaimed as she got out to gaze at the surrounding mountains.

"Yep," the man replied, removing his straw hat to wipe his balding head with a kerchief. "I'll show you around the inside. I think it'll do, but my missus never agrees with me on that."

Smiling, Stacy followed him into the cabin. The main room boasted a fireplace with a mounted ten-point buck's head above it. Firewood had been laid in the hearth and there was an ample supply of more wood piled beside it in a wrought-iron holder. There was one sofa in the room and an ancient rocker. The kitchen, consisting of a few metal cupboards over an old porcelain sink with a pump-type faucet, covered the west wall. Luckily there was a propane stove to cook on; Stacy was sure she could never have managed a wood-fired range. The table with its two chairs sat in the middle of the room. She could see Molly Nolan's touch in the red-checked tablecloth and matching curtains at the window.

The motherly woman was probably responsible for the pillows on the sofa and the Indian blanket hanging on the far wall too. Harry Nolan launched into an explanation of how to light the kerosene lanterns and adjust the wick to give off the right amount of light without smoking the glass before he showed her into the bedroom.

A big four-poster dominated the small room. The bed was covered with a large patchwork quilt that Stacy knew had come from the Nolans. Pushed into a corner was an antique chest of drawers that had probably come to Texas in a covered wagon—how it had gotten up here was anyone's guess. Muleback, maybe. Behind the door was a place to hang her clothes.

"Oh, this is perfect." Stacy surveyed the two rooms excitedly. "I can't think of anything that isn't already here."

"Well, I'm glad it suits you. The missus will be happy to hear how much you like it," said Harry, his eyes glowing at Stacy's enthusiasm. "Now, if you'd like, I'll help you get that horse of yours into the corral."

Accepting Mr. Nolan's offer, Stacy practically skipped out of the house. It was better than she'd imagined, rustic and serene. Just right for one.

She maneuvered the car so the back of the trailer was over by the gate that Harry had opened. Stacy set the parking brake and walked to the back of the trailer to let the gate down before she entered the empty stall beside the restless horse. Anxiously, the sorrel pulled at the rope that held him, interfering with Stacy's attempt to loosen it. She tried to calm Diablo down, but his hooves increased their tattoo on the trailer floor as his ears flattened against his head. Finally the knot on the end of the lead rope was loose. As soon as he found himself free, the red stallion half-reared, pulling Stacy along with him out of the van. The whites of his eyes flashed menacingly as he danced down the ramp to the solid ground of the corral. As quickly as she could, Stacy turned the horse loose to gallop around.

The Arabian circled the corral warily, his flaxen mane and tail whipping in the wind. Then his attention was caught by the stranger leaning against the fence rail near his mistress. Instantly he bore down on Harry Nolan, his teeth bared and his pointed ears back. With surprising agility, old Harry leaped away from the fence and the savage attack.

"Does he do that often?" Harry muttered.

"Fortunately, no. Sorry about that," Stacy offered. She waved the horse back to the center of the corral. "Once in a while he does strike out without being provoked, though."

Studying the spirited horse pacing up and down on the opposite side, head held high into the wind to catch the smells on the mountain breeze, Harry turned to Stacy. "What's that scar on his neck? A rope burn?"

"I don't know," she answered, noting the faint white line barely visible under the full mane. "He had it when I bought him."

Eying her and then the horse, Harry demanded, "Just how the devil are you able to handle him? He could walk over you like you was air."

"We seem to have an understanding. Although sometimes I think he just tolerates me." Stacy laughed, shrugging off the concern in the old man's voice. Changing the subject quickly, she asked, "Are there many trails around here accessible on horseback?"

"Plenty. Most of them either lead deeper into the mountains or into the valley, and a few of them branch out over to the Circle H," Harry replied, gesturing toward the west.

"Where is the Circle H exactly?" Her hands shaded her eyes from the setting sun. That was one place she intended to avoid.

"This here's Cord's land that the cabin sits on. We just got a lease. It's an abandoned line shack that me and some of my friends use when we go huntin' and fishin'. But if you're referring to the ranch house, that's about nine, ten miles from here. Yep, he's got himself quite a spread. Runs it with an iron hand, he does. But the men don't mind 'cause they always know where they stand with him. He pays good money and he expects a good day's work for it."

Stacy could believe it. Cord probably rode around with a whip in his hand.

"Molly said you met him at the store," Harry added. "'Course, you know he ain't married."

Stacy made no reply as she watched the sorrel paw at some hay in the lean-to. *Who could stand him?* was what she thought.

"'Bout six years ago, we all thought he'd got himself caught, but the girl up and ran off with an oil well man. Never did much like the girl. She always thought she was so much better than the folks around here. He's better off without her." Harry ignored the look on Stacy's face as he rambled on.

Secretly, Stacy was inclined to applaud the girl who'd managed to set that arrogant cowboy back on his heels, but she didn't want to say that.

"He fixed up his grandma's hacienda on the place for her, piled a lot of money into it. He lives there alone, except for his housekeeper." Moving away from the fence, Harry Nolan started toward his jeep. "Well, if I want to get home before dark, I'd better mosey along. If there's anything you need, you be sure to let us know."

"I will, Mr. Nolan. And thanks for all you've done. I really appreciate it." Stacy shook his hand warmly.

She stood in front of the cabin and watched the jeep drive off on the faint trail into the stand of trees. The solitude encompassed her as she lost sight of the bouncing taillights in the gathering shadows. Cajun came up behind her and shoved his moist nose in her hands. Kneeling down to love him up, she rumpled the thick fur on his neck.

"I'm not alone, am I? Not as long as I have you around, huh?" Stacy smiled and looked toward the cabin door. "Let's go fix us something to eat."

Chapter 3

The sun was streaming over the meadow when Stacy walked out of the cabin door. A golden haze suffused the air and the valley was filled with the songs of birds trilling their greeting to the new day. The sun's rays were striking the rippling brook, turning it into a ribbon of shimmering quicksilver. Inhaling the brisk, clear air, Stacy gave a sigh of pure pleasure. Then, clicking her tongue to the dog standing beside her, she walked over to the corral.

Two days had passed since her arrival at the cabin. The first day Stacy spent unpacking and settling in. The tack had to be cleaned, as well as the horse trailer and the car, which was dusty from traveling over back roads. She'd taken an evening ride down the meadow to give Diablo some exercise and accustom him to the change of climate. The second day she'd explored the mountains to the east, spending most of the day away from the cabin. The scenery continually took her breath away. Never had she traveled so far without finding any trace of civilization except an occasional herd of cattle in the valleys below. Surprisingly enough, she didn't miss it. The evenings passed rather quickly. After cooking her meal, feeding the horse and the dog, she'd sat out on the porch until the evening light faded and the stars came out.

It was so restful that, for the first time in several weeks, Stacy felt at peace. Surrounded by the natural serenity of the valley, she could come to terms with her grief. Her father would have understood. Nothing mattered to her but being alive. She knew she'd done the right thing by getting away from the world. A part of her never wanted to leave here, even though she knew she would have to eventually.

Last evening, she'd written Carter a letter to tell him that she'd arrived safely and was settling in. Her cell phone didn't pick up a signal too well out here and sometimes it didn't work at all. And she sure didn't miss e-mail. The simple act of putting pen to paper had helped her think, and even sticking on a stamp felt like a minor accomplishment—she was never without a few, a traveler's habit. This morning she planned to ride along the main road to find a rancher's mailbox so that she wouldn't have to go into town to send it off. She hadn't noticed one on the drive to the cabin, but then she'd been concentrating on the road and the jeep in front of her.

Entering the side gate of the corral near the lean-to, Stacy got the bridle out of the shed and started to approach Diablo. The red horse began retreating to the side of the enclosure. Ignoring the flashing white feet and the pointed ears that kept flicking back and forth, she walked up to the horse. Snorting, the sorrel lashed out half-heartedly with his front hooves and dashed to the other side. He looked back at Stacy, tossing his head defiantly.

"All right, Diablo, don't play hard to get this morning," Stacy said, walking slowly toward the horse. "It's a lovely morning and I don't want to work up a sweat catching you."

The horse stood uneasily as she approached, talking to

him in a soft voice. He eyed her apprehensively as she stopped in front of him and extended her hand. Diablo stretched his muzzle to her hesitantly and after a little investigation, blew into her hand. Docile for the moment, he submitted to the bit and bridle and stood quietly, the reins dangling on the ground while Stacy fetched the blanket and saddle. She never knew how he was going to react to the saddle—sometimes he accepted it calmly and other times he acted like a yearling who had never seen one before. Cinching up, Stacy led the horse out into the yard before mounting. Whistling to Cajun, she started her mount toward the main road. The sorrel pranced a little as the dog ran alongside, but offered Stacy no trouble.

The sun's rays peeping through the cover of branches hit the coppery red coat of the horse. Cajun raced ahead, investigating all the sights and sounds of the trail. Sensing her horse's desire to run, Stacy nudged Diablo into a canter. They continued at a ground-eating lope until they reached the main road. Here Stacy slowed the horse to a trot, turning him in the direction of town. Diablo resented the slowed pace and began sidestepping and pulling his head in an attempt to loosen the tight rein. She was unable to admire the scenery as she fought to control him. Cajun still led the way, but checked back to make sure his mistress was with him. Stacy's whole attention was on her mount, who'd begun to rear and plunge around. It was then that she noticed the saddle slipping. The cinch had loosened during the ride from the cabin.

Pulling the horse to a stop, she dismounted. But Diablo was no longer in a cooperative mood and refused to let her near him. His hooves lashed out, keeping her at a safe distance. Stacy tried to edge her way up the reins to the horse's head only to have him pull away with strength. Concentrating on trying to control the fractious horse, she didn't hear the car coming down the road behind her until it was within a hundred feet. As she turned to see where the vehicle was, Diablo bolted past her, but was pulled up short by her quick thinking as Stacy yanked the reins hard, forcing the horse to turn in a tight circle.

Between the noise of the car and its own tendency to misbehave, the sorrel became completely unmanageable. Not looking at the car that'd stopped just a few feet from her, Stacy concentrated on preventing the horse from breaking away. In the endless open space of this part of Texas, she knew she'd never be able to catch him once he escaped. In the mood he was in now, he'd run for miles without stopping.

From the corner of her eye, Stacy recognized the dark, towering figure that climbed out of the car and walked toward her.

Of all people.

Cord Harris was the last one she wanted to see just now.

"Looks like you're having a little trouble, Miss Adams," his low voice drawled.

"Brilliant observation," Stacy said, puffing from the effort it took to hold on to the high-strung horse.

Walking up behind her, Cord took the reins out of her hands and motioned for her to move back. At the sight of a stranger on the other end of the reins, Diablo renewed his battle for freedom, but he was no match for the determined Cord. Dodging the flying hooves, Cord grabbed the cheek strap of the bridle and hauled the horse down on all four feet. Gradually the sorrel settled down, tossing his head and snorting occasionally.

Stacy gazed at the broad shoulders underneath the jeans jacket Cord was wearing and watched as he ran his hand down the horse's neck. She couldn't imagine anyone being able to win a fight with this forceful man. Just then he turned his head and met her searching gaze. As much as she wanted to, she couldn't keep from staring into the dark eyes that smoldered with a strange, deep fire. He was the one who broke the silence.

"I'd recommend that you get yourself another horse. He's more than a girl can handle."

"Thanks, but I didn't ask for your advice or your help," Stacy retorted, hating the fact that he'd come to her rescue.

"No? It didn't look to me like you were doing a very good job," he replied coldly, his mouth turning up in a mocking smile. "But then, maybe I have the wrong idea."

"I would have been able to handle him if you hadn't driven up," she said, gesturing defiantly at Cord's expensive car, "and worried him more than he already was."

"I didn't realize I needed your permission to drive down a public road," Cord said, sarcasm in his voice as his eyes flashed at her. "If your horse gets skittish in traffic, maybe you shouldn't ride him where he's bound to meet it."

"I'm sorry. I shouldn't have said that," Stacy said tensely. Cord had done her a favor and she wasn't giving him any credit for it. "He's a little temperamental sometimes, and this happens to be one of those times."

"I hope it doesn't happen often or I'll be finding you out on the range injured or worse the next time he throws you."

"He didn't throw me," Stacy corrected. "I got off to tighten the cinch."

"Oh," he said, a frown creasing his forehead as he turned to the saddle. "I apologize, then. I assumed the two of you had parted company a little more dramatically."

"No," Stacy laughed, "though I have to admit that's happened once or twice."

She walked up to fondle the horse's head while Cord proceeded to tighten the girth on the saddle. Turning back to face her, he rested his arm on the saddle horn. Self-conscious, Stacy felt his gaze on her and turned to meet it, but he turned away quickly before she could read the expression written there. When he looked back, his face revealed nothing of his thoughts and Stacy was the one to look away this time, feeling herself redden.

"Where were you heading, anyplace special?"

"I was looking for a mailbox," Stacy replied hurriedly, trying to cover the sudden unexplainable blush.

"A mailbox?" Cord chuckled. "Just where did you think you'd find a mailbox out here?"

His amusement nettled her. "Want me to spell it out?"

"Go right ahead."

"I meant a mailbox for a ranch. You know, the kind by the side of the road where the mailman picks up and delivers mail. Is that clear enough?"

"Well, I'm sorry to disillusion you, Miss Adams, but there aren't any between here and town," he said. "This part of the country lacks a few of the luxuries that city folks consider necessities."

"I didn't know," she said hotly, her temper rising, "and I don't see any reason you have to be snotty about it."

"I'm not. Just pointing out a plain fact," Cord said calmly. "And here's another one: you might be happier if you go back where you belong."

She stared at him, thoroughly ticked off by now. "You know, Cord, if you're on the welcoming committee, that must be the reason this little corner of Texas is just about empty."

He only nodded. "I like it that way."

"You—damn you!" She opened and closed her fists.

Glowering down at her from his greater height, Cord Harris seemed about to say something, but clamped his mouth shut in a grim line.

Already regretting her hasty words, Stacy felt compelled to raise her chin to emphasize that she meant business.

They stood facing off for a few minutes and then, without warning, the rancher swooped her up in his arms.

"Allow me to help you on your way," he said fiercely, his iron arms holding her against his chest.

Astonished by his move, Stacy didn't even attempt to struggle but lay in his arms, her heart beating wildly. She realized that she was playing with fire where this man was concerned.

Effortlessly, he dumped her in the saddle, tossing the reins over the horse's head. Catching them, she looked down at his blazing eyes.

"That's what you wanted, wasn't it?" he asked darkly.

Regaining some of her composure, Stacy retorted. "As I said before, Mr. Harris, I didn't ask for your help."

"You'll find folks around here don't ask—for anything. If they want to do something, they do it."

Diablo, sensing the tension in the air, began dancing about. Cajun kept a wary distance from the moving hooves, but Stacy noticed with chagrin that her dog didn't seem inclined to sink his teeth in Cord's muscular butt.

Too bad. It would have served Cord right. But the dog's presence made her feel safe enough. However, Stacy could think of no answer to his cryptic words and felt sure that anything she said would only make the situation worse. She didn't want to provoke him again. The consequences were anything but predictable.

With as much poise as she could summon up, she reined the sorrel around Cord. She could feel his eyes on her as she urged the horse into a trot back up the road she had just come down. Burning with humiliation, she longed to gallop away but her pride insisted on an orderly retreat.

Stacy had to steel herself to keep from looking back. Finally she heard the car door slam and the engine start. Immediately she kicked the sorrel into a gallop. She didn't allow Diablo to slow down until they'd reached the turnoff to the cabin.

By the time the woman, horse, and dog had reached the cabin, Stacy's humiliation had turned to anger. Cord Harris had no right to treat her like that. His overbearing manner was outrageous and interfering. He acted as if he had a God-given right to tell her what to do.

Steaming, she unsaddled the fidgety horse, flinging the saddle and bridle in the shed with an unusual disregard for their care. She stomped out of the corral, closing the gate vehemently, and continued to the porch of the cabin. The dog sensed the mood she was in and scurried off to sit in a shady corner.

Disgustedly, Stacy plopped into a chair on the porch and gazed moodily at the quiet meadow. She shuddered as she recalled Cord's arms around her. She could still smell the masculine fragrance of his aftershave clinging to her blouse. If only she had struggled or fought with him or done anything instead of just lying so passively in his arms, submitting to his will . . . she could have at least scratched those rugged features or pulled his dark hair. Never again would she allow herself to be so weak-kneed in his presence. If she ever ran into him again, she vowed, she would tell him exactly what she thought of him.

The serenity of the valley meadow failed to comfort her wounded pride. The peace she'd felt earlier in the morning was gone and the inactivity of just sitting only made her more restless. Finally she rose and entered the cabin. It was almost noon but she had no appetite. Grabbing her swimsuit, she changed clothes and, with a terrycloth coverup over her shoulder, started down to the brook that ran through the meadow. Maybe an icy dip in the mountain stream would cool her temper.

Not far from the cabin the stream widened and became

just deep enough to enable her to swim. Kicking off her sandals, Stacy waded into the water. Cajun had followed her at a safe distance and settled himself under a tree to watch his mistress. She splashed around for nearly an hour before pulling herself exhaustedly onto the bank. Propping herself up against the tree with Cajun, she chewed idly on a stem of grass. The afternoon sun started making its way across the sky, but still the two sat under the tree. The exertion of swimming had calmed her nerves, but it hadn't taken away her preoccupation with a certain extremely annoying man. She toyed with the idea of returning home, but dismissed it quickly when she remembered Cord Harris's mocking smile and the way he'd said *go back where you belong.* Never would Stacy give him that satisfaction.

"We're going to stay, Cajun, and what's more, we're going to enjoy ourselves. And we're not going to avoid Cord's ranch. If he doesn't like it, well, that's just too bad." Stacy rose to her feet. Tomorrow she would go into town and mail that letter before Carter sent a search party after her.

If it wasn't one man giving her trouble, it would be another.

The two started back for the cabin, Cajun trotting contentedly at her heels. Stacy's spirits rose as she walked. Her stride had a little spring in it and her face wore a satisfied expression. She was convinced that any future confrontation with Cord wouldn't end with her coming out second-best.

The next morning Stacy overslept, awakening only because of Cajun's determined nuzzling. Hurriedly, she dressed and made coffee. She'd hoped to get an early start into town but that wasn't going to happen. Just as quickly she fed the dog and gave Diablo some oats and fresh hay before throwing on a shirt and jeans.

Ordering Cajun to stay at the cabin, Stacy hopped into her black Jaguar and started down the trail to the main road.

She increased her speed when she made the turn toward town. This time she was able to look a little more at the view around her. The tall stone mountains seemed to rise out of the prairie as they reached for the sky, their peaks changing into a dark gray that contrasted with the tans and greens of the plains below. The panoramic view was breathtaking. An occasional greasewood tree dotted the horizon with an exclamation point.

As the car passed the bend in the road where Stacy'd had her run-in with Cord Harris yesterday, she went even faster. She didn't want to be reminded of that episode and was glad that she could hurry by it. But her spirits were dampened by merely passing the place, causing her to ignore the scenery and concentrate on driving. It was difficult to escape the memory of those dark, compelling eyes that had watched her so intently as she sat astride her horse the day before. Their sardonic gleam remained indelible along with his sculptured face and dark, almost black hair.

A little over half an hour went by before Stacy reached the town of McCloud. The streets were fairly quiet with only a few people walking from store to store. She parked in front of the post office and thought about calling Carter. She reached for her cell phone, flipped it open and checked the signal bars—looked like service was better here. No messages. On second thought, she closed the phone and put it back in her purse. She really didn't feel like talking to Carter right now—and he hadn't left her a text message or a voicemail. As she climbed out of the low-slung car, she removed the letter from her purse before walking into the brick building. Nodding a good morning to the clerk in the mailroom, Stacy dropped her letter in the outgoing slot.

She started to leave and then hesitated. Turning around, she walked back to the counter in the mailroom.

"Excuse me, is there any mail here for Stacy Adams?" she asked.

"You're the young lady that rented Nolan's hunting lodge, aren't you?" the clerk asked. "Yes, you had a letter, but I gave it to Cord to drop off for you. You've met him, haven't you? He said he knew you and since he lives closest to you, it seemed only natural."

"You gave *him* my letter?" Stacy was flabbergasted. "He knew I would be coming into town."

"Maybe it just slipped his mind," offered the middle-aged clerk. "He'll probably bring it to the cabin today. Folks are pretty neighborly around here."

"In the future, please hold my mail here until I come personally to pick it up," Stacy said, checking her rising temper. The clerk had obviously thought he was doing her a favor, so she really couldn't blame him.

"Yes, ma'am," he replied, eyeing her quizzically.

With a quiet thank-you, Stacy turned away from the counter and walked out the door. Reaching the sidewalk, she stopped for a few seconds. She decided that it would be only polite to stop in and talk to Mrs. Nolan and thank her for everything.

As she walked into the grocery store, she noticed Molly talking to a young, red-haired woman with two cute kids tugging at her skirt. When Mrs. Nolan recognized Stacy coming in, her face immediately broke into a smile that reached all the way to her eyes. The young woman beside her also turned to meet Stacy. Her smile held as much welcome as Molly Nolan's.

"Stacy, I was wonderin' how you were gettin' along," the older woman said, walking up to take both of Stacy's

hands in her own. "Cord said he met you on the road yesterday and you seemed to think you were doing all right."

"You bet," Stacy replied, biting her lip to keep from
making a caustic comment about Cord Harris. "I just
wanted to tell you that I love the cabin. Mr. Nolan told me
about all the decorating you did to make it more feminine,
and I want to thank you."

"Well, don't thank just me, thank my daughter, too,"
Molly said, indicating the redhead beside her. "I'm glad
you stopped in, because I was really lookin' forward to in-
troducing you two. Mary, this is Stacy Adams, as you must
have guessed. And this is my daughter, Mary Buchanan."

"I'm so pleased to meet you," Mary said. "Momma's
talked of nothing else but that 'lovely young girl' living all
alone in the cabin. She didn't quite do you justice." The
young woman smiled and extended a hand to Stacy. Her
kids quit fidgeting to stare curiously at the newcomer.

"Thanks," Stacy replied, feeling a little embarrassed.
"Mrs. Nolan—I mean Molly," she corrected herself, "has
really made me feel at home."

"I think she'll always be a mother hen looking after her
chicks whether they're hers or not," Mary teased, looking
affectionately at the woman beside her. "As you mighta
guessed, these two little maniacs are mine. This is Jeff and
this is Dougal."

Stacy knelt down to shake hands with the two young
boys.

"You're awful pretty," Jeff said, scrutinizing the golden-
brown hair that framed the oval face smiling back at him.
"A'most prettier than my momma."

"That's high praise." Stacy laughed. "Thank you very
much."

"You made a conquest." Mary smiled, gazing at her

oldest son with pride. "But then he always had good taste. Takes after his father, right, Momma?"

"Naturally," Molly Nolan said, "and don't you ever forget it!"

"That's my momma, always reminding me what a catch I made, as if I would forget." Mary grinned. "Are you in a hurry or anything? Why don't you come over to my house for coffee?"

"That would be wonderful," Stacy said, warming to the open friendliness. "My car's right out front and—"

"Good, we walked down here and now we can beg a ride back," Mary said happily. "We only live a few blocks away."

"You two run along then," Molly said, "so I can get back to work. Take care of these two boys. And don't let them eat all that candy I gave them."

Once in the car, Mary directed Stacy to her home, a beautiful ranch-type house with a large fenced yard. The boys got out of the Jaguar reluctantly.

"So how was that?" their mother asked. "Better than a monster truck?"

"Heck, yeah," they said in unison.

"Wish it could have lasted longer?"

Stacy laughed. "We could drive around the block if you like."

Jeff and Dougal bounced out and ran off somewhere.

"No, that's all right. But that was a real thrill for them. They'll remember that for ages." Mary got out and went to open the front door and waited for Stacy to enter first.

"I enjoyed it too," Stacy answered as she followed Mary into a spacious kitchen. "As trite as it sounds, I love kids."

"Well, I'm not going to say the usual about 'wait until you have some of your own,' because I love mine and wouldn't change them for the world." Mary started making fresh coffee for the two of them. "Moms that moan and groan about how much trouble children are almost drive me up the wall."

"I know what you mean, although I'm not too experienced on the subject," Stacy said, sitting down at the table.

"You will, I bet. So . . . do you have someone waiting back home?"

"Sort of," was all Stacy said. She was a little taken aback by the blunt question, especially when she remembered Carter Mills and his unexpected proposal.

"Sort of? You mean, he hasn't popped the question and you've come out here to make him see how much he misses you?" Mary joined Stacy at the table with the coffee. "Cream or sugar?"

"No, black," Stacy answered. "He did propose before I left, but I'm not sure if I want to get married just yet."

"Do you love him?"

Another unbelievably blunt question. Stacy hemmed and hawed, saying finally, "I suppose so. I've never dated anyone else but him. We just knew each other so well that—"

Mary nodded. "I see what you mean. I guess with the loss of your father and all, you didn't want to make any rash decisions."

"Partly." Stacy sighed, aware that Molly Nolan had obviously filled her daughter in on a few details.

"If you don't mind my saying so, maybe being apart will help you decide how much you really do care for this guy," suggested Mary.

"Maybe."

"Fortunately, there was never any doubt in my mind as to how I felt about Bill. He's the doctor here. The minute he got into town and took over old Doc Gibbon's practice, I knew he was the man I wanted to marry. I was almost twenty-two by then and had dated my share of men."

Mary wasn't shy, Stacy thought. So she might as well

follow her lead. "I wonder if that's my problem," she said. "Traveling with my father on photo assignments the way I did, I was never in any one place long enough to meet people my age." It was actually comforting, Stacy decided, to confide in Mary, a comparative stranger. "And when I got back to town, I always had Carter to fall back on. I admit I did have a crush on one of the reporters Dad worked with, though." Stacy chuckled.

"I guess everyone has those." Mary laughed. "I had it bad for Cord Harris. I used to chase him all over."

Stacy drew in a breath. "Uh—Cord Harris?"

"Yup. Every girl around here has fallen under his spell at one time or another. He used to be quite the playboy," said Mary, a sly smile on her lips.

"Him? I can't imagine Cord even being polite. He is good-looking, though."

"And he can work it when he wants to. Even if he's a little bitter, still, after that dirty deal Lydia Marshall pulled on him. But it's only a matter of time before some other woman breaks through that thin veneer of his and then you'll see what I'm talking about. When he turns on the charm, no female is immune," Mary concluded with a shake of her red hair.

"You're looking at one who is," Stacy said vehemently. "He is without a doubt the most arrogant, full-of-himself man I've ever had the misfortune to meet!"

"I see he's made a real impression on you." Mary hid a smile with difficulty. "But maybe you judged him too fast. Outside of being too handsome for his own good, you'd find he still fits the description on a Husband Wanted poster. And I'd bet anything he'd make a great daddy into the bargain." She thought a little harder. "If that isn't enough, he owns the biggest ranch around and runs it with a profit."

"That's all well and good," Stacy said, "but I still pity

the woman who ever marries him. He didn't hesitate to form a hasty opinion of me and I don't intend to turn the other cheek."

"Whew! The sparks must fly when you two get together," Mary exclaimed, amused and puzzled. "Funny, I'd think you two would hit it off somehow."

"Well, we didn't," Stacy said, hoping to change the subject. She couldn't bring herself to fess up to yesterday's encounter with Cord. The humiliation was too fresh in her mind to talk about it.

What with one thing and another, it was the middle of the afternoon before she said her goodbyes to her new friend and her rambunctious boys. She promised to stop in the next time she was in town.

In less than an hour, Stacy was back at the cabin being greeted by Cajun, wildly thumping his tail. The dog stuck close to her when she actually went in, as if he regretted obeying the order to stay.

While Stacy was poking around the kitchen for the makings of an early dinner, she noticed a note on the table. Walking over to pick it up, she saw an envelope underneath it. Quickly she read the note.

Sorry I missed you. I took the liberty of bringing your mail.

"The nerve of him!" Stacy said aloud, ripping the note into shreds and going into the next room to throw the pieces into the fireplace. "'Sorry I missed you.' Hmph!" she muttered, returning to the kitchen. "Well, I'm not!"

After eating, she took her coffee out to the porch and read the letter from Carter in the waning light.

Chapter 4

The late afternoon sun cast a long shadow of horse and rider picking their way through the rocky foothills. The red horse pranced a little as a lizard darted across their path, but responded to the quiet words from the woman on his back and didn't shy. From an arroyo on their left came the German shepherd to rejoin his mistress.

Stacy called a hello to the dog and urged the horse into a canter on the opening flatland. A smile came to her lips as she turned to survey her backtrail with satisfaction. To her there could be nothing as beautiful as this untamed land. She was glad she had finally decided to trespass on the Circle H home range. The scenery was fantastic in its undisciplined beauty. Pulling up the stallion near some greasewood trees, she dismounted to sit in their shade and gaze at the panoramic view before her.

After removing her straw hat, she dusted off her white blouse. They had been exploring since midmorning and, even though her muscles were complaining, she was still exhilarated by the wonderful country she'd seen. She glanced at her watch and knew that when she remounted she would have to go directly back to the cabin in order to make it in before sundown. After dark she might have trouble finding her way.

Her thoughts turned to the letter Carter had sent. She knew he wouldn't be so eager for her to return if he were here beside her to enjoy all this scenery. And she would have to return. She couldn't hide away from the world indefinitely. Nature in all its beauty was still harsh and the balmy days wouldn't last forever. In Texas you either got scorched or you got pounded by hailstorms or God knows what else. She'd decided during her ride that she would return in two or three weeks. She was sure that was the way her father would've wanted it. She'd grieve. Think things through. Move on with her own life.

She'd get a job somewhere, maybe something to do with travel. If not that, then animals or kids.

But marriage? No, she wasn't ready for that, she thought as she shook her head. She cared too much for Carter, when it came right down to it. But she wasn't going to just grab at the straw of escape that he offered her. When they married, or rather when she married, Stacy knew she wanted to put her whole heart into it and the family that would come. She could only hope that Carter would understand that she wanted to feel whole again before they made a life together.

Standing up, she faced the gentle breeze ruffling her long hair and smiled as she took a deep breath. Life was good and there wasn't any sense in worrying about things that hadn't happened. Crossing over to the sorrel, she picked up the reins. Remounting, she whistled to the dog and turned her horse into the mountains from which they had come.

The horse broke into an eager trot, refreshed by the brief rest in the meadow. Stacy captured his spirit and eased her hold on the reins. The horse immediately moved into a rocking lope. As they reached the boulder-strewn foothills, his gait slowed to a fast walk as he picked his way. Cajun followed not far behind. Stacy turned for one last look at the grassland she had left.

At that moment, with Stacy just a bit off-balance in the saddle, a rattlesnake resting under a nearby bush sounded his warning. Before Stacy could turn around, Diablo was screaming, rearing high into the air. His terror was beyond restraint as he shook his head violently, fighting Stacy's instant tightening of the reins. Spinning in a half rear toward the flatland, the stallion unseated his light rider completely. As Stacy lost her grip and tumbled off, the horse bolted, seizing his chance to escape.

Unable to break her fall, Stacy landed heavily on her shoulders. Her neck snapped back at the impact and her head struck a rock. Pain seared through her body. She struggled up on one elbow, catching a glimpse of Diablo streaking across the meadow with his tail high. Vaguely she recognized the huge dog racing toward her before she succumbed to the promising relief of blackness.

Frowning, Stacy shifted slightly to look where the voice had come from. With difficulty she forced herself to focus on the smiling face hovering above her.

"Where am I? My father—is he—" she started to say, then glanced around the unfamiliar setting in panic. She closed her eyes and added, "I remember now. I fell."

"Don't try to talk," admonished the doctor. "Yes, you took a bad fall, but you're going to be fine. By the way, I'm Dr. Buchanan, Mary's husband."

Attempting a smile at a name she recognized, Stacy tried to speak. "Is Mary here?"

"No, you're at the Circle H. Cord Harris found you and brought you to his ranch. You owe him, big time."

"No!" Stacy cried, feebly struggling to rise from the bed. "I can't stay here! I can't!"

"Now listen up," the doctor said, gently restraining her movement. "You need rest. The best place for you right now is in this bed."

Pleadingly she looked into his face, her eyes filling with tears as she desperately willed him to change his mind. His gaze was adamant. Involuntarily her eyes turned to the doorway that was now blocked by Cord. It was impossible to tell how long he had been there. His fierce gaze gave nothing away.

"Oh," she sobbed helplessly, "why did you have to be the one who found me?"

"Believe me, I wasn't out looking for you," was Cord's calm reply. "I found your horse out running loose and backtracked him."

"That's enough talking," Dr. Buchanan said. "It's time you rested."

Not having the strength to fight her unwanted host or her doctor's orders, Stacy turned her face from both of them and allowed the frustration and pain to sweep her away. She wasn't aware that the two men's eyes locked over her, the rancher's defiant and unflinching, the other's probing and questioning.

Dr. Buchanan motioned Cord away from the bedside and spoke in a whisper. "I think we should leave her to rest in quiet," the doctor suggested. "I'll stop by to check on her again in another hour or so. In the meantime, you know what to be on the lookout for."

It was late evening before Stacy woke again. She lay in the bed and studied her surroundings with a little more interest, even though her head hurt like hell.

The bedroom was masculine with heavy Spanish furniture and bold, definite colors. She couldn't help wondering if this was actually the bedroom that Cord slept in. It seemed stamped with the same austere quality that he had. Dark *vigas*, massive hand-hewn beams, ran the length of the ceiling, accenting the white-painted plaster between them. The strong effect was carried through in the loose-weave curtains and the handmade woven coverlet on the bed.

Stacy pushed herself into a sitting position, fighting off the wave of nausea that followed the movement. She was wearing a nightgown. The realization shocked her as she looked down at the yellow bodice. How and when had she changed? Who had helped her? Her face crimsoned as the only possible answer occurred to her: Cord. It was even her own nightgown. How had he gotten it? Maybe he'd sent someone else for her things. But he wouldn't dare have the nerve to touch her!

"Well, you must be feeling a little better. I thought you were going to sleep through the night," came a low voice from the doorway.

Stacy's head snapped up to confront Cord, her cheeks still blushing. "What t-time is it?" she stammered, unnerved at seeing the man who had been drifting through her disordered thoughts.

"After eight," Cord replied, pulling up a chair beside the bed and gazing at her intently. His voice held no trace of the sarcasm she associated with him as he asked, "How are you feeling?"

"Better," she said, echoing his assessment. But she was unable to meet his penetrating eyes. "I want to thank you for all you've done. I—"

"That's not necessary. I consider myself lucky that I spotted your horse. I hate to think how long you might have lain out there before you were found." His low voice held a gentleness that was unfamiliar to her, coming from him anyway. It did strange things to her heart. "Here, let me fix those pillows for you."

Reluctantly, Stacy allowed him to add another pillow behind her head. All too aware of his nearness, she glanced up at his face, taking in the clear cut of his jaw and soft firmness of his mouth, but refusing to look above the high cheekbones at the dark, unfathomable eyes. She caught the scent of his aftershave which she remembered so vividly from their encounter on the road. It was difficult to ignore the muscular chest and arms encased in the crisp white shirt. Stacy was sure he could hear the wild beating of her heart and silently cussed at the way his physical presence could arouse her.

"Isn't that more comfortable?" Cord said, reseating himself in his chair. A smile was showing faintly on his mouth. He couldn't fail to detect the flush growing in her cheeks as she sat silently with downcast eyes. "Maybe, Stacy, we should try to begin again." His voice changed to an impersonal tone at her continued study of a little bow on her gown. "We got off to a rather bad start. Doc Buchanan thinks it's best for you to stay here until you can get back on your feet. Only temporarily, of course. So we can ignore our personal feelings for the meantime."

Surprised at his openness about the unspoken antagonism between them, Stacy looked up into his thoughtful eyes at last.

"Well, are we friends?"

Hesitantly Stacy placed her slim hand in his outstretched palm. It was engulfed in Cord's large, tanned hand. She felt he held it a little longer than was necessary, yet the sudden way he let go upset her. His brows pulled together in a frown that seemed more like him somehow and his mouth curled in a odd smile as he rose and looked down at her. Once again his size and air of superiority overwhelmed her.

"I imagine you're more interested in getting something to eat than listening to me. I'll send Maria in with soup and crackers," he said, moving toward the end of the bed. "Oh, by the way, your dog is outside and your horse is bedded down in one of our stud pens. I also took the liberty of bringing a few of your things from the cabin. Hope you don't mind."

"No," Stacy answered, aware of the meekness in her voice. If her friends could hear her now . . . or see her.

"Good," he said, a twinkle now in his eyes. "And in case you were wondering, Maria got you undressed and into that nightgown."

Indignation rose in her as the tall rancher left the room. He really was insufferable. How could she have been taken in by that supposedly gentle tone? Just imagining how he must have been laughing up his sleeve while he was sitting there made her even more fuddled. He was right about one thing: she had to compromise until she was on her feet again. The throbbing in her head forced her to stay as calm as she could.

By the time the robust housekeeper arrived with food, Stacy's composure had returned, though she was sure her cheeks still had a high color.

"Ah, you are awake. *Bueno*." Maria placed a tray with a bowl of broth on Stacy's lap. "The head does not hurt so much now?"

"Only a little. The soup smells good," Stacy replied, inhaling the aroma of the hot broth. She was hungrier than she had thought. Thankfully, Maria left the room and Stacy was allowed to eat at her leisure. She had just finished when the housekeeper returned.

"That was excellent, Maria." Stacy smiled, handing the tray to her.

"*Gracias*. Mister Cord say my cooking is the best anywhere in Texas." The housekeeper giggled at the audacity of the claim.

"He isn't exaggerating. It was very good," Stacy assured her.

"There is more, but you get some sleep now, okay?" Maria helped Stacy settle back under the covers. "We have you up in no time. Doctor says you should keep warm and rest, but this bed is so big we might lose you. Cord says it is all right, but me, no. You should have a man to keep you warm, not a big bed."

Stacy could feel herself blushing all over again at the woman's earthy suggestion. She remembered again her impression that this was Cord's bedroom. She had to ask.

"*Si, si.*" The housekeeper laughed. "But he won't sleep here tonight. He is in office. All alone, the *pobrecito*."

The thought made Maria laugh even more as she carried the tray out of the room. Stacy found it hard to think of Cord as a poor little thing, considering the way he took up space. She glanced around a little apprehensively before switching off the light. Although fearful that she would be unable to sleep, she dropped off almost immediately.

The morning sun was dancing in patterns on the braided rug beside the gigantic bed. Maria had already brought in her breakfast and had helped her clean up. Rather than attempt to brush the hair around her scalp wound, Stacy had merely pulled it back cautiously with a scrunchie to match the T-shirt that had been brought along with her other clothes. She felt much better as long as she ignored the dull pain in her head and the sniffles in her nose. She was just examining the unusual scrollwork on the bedroom door when it opened to admit a smiling Cord Harris.

"Mornin'. Maria said you were up." His voice was cheerful. "Do you feel like having a visitor?"

"A visitor?" Stacy echoed, trying to think of who would be coming to see her. "Sure. I guess so."

"Okay, feller, come on in." Cord swung the door wider to admit a wary German shepherd.

"Cajun!" Stacy exclaimed happily as the big dog bounded to her, his tail wagging a mile a minute. With his front paws on the bed, he proceeded to give her face a thorough washing with his tongue. "Thanks for the bath— but no thanks!"

"He's happy to see you. He refused to eat this morning and wouldn't move away from the front door, so I decided the best thing would be to let him see for himself that you were all right," Cord explained, still standing in the doorway.

"He's a great dog," Stacy said after she'd managed to push the shepherd off the bed and onto the floor where he sat gazing at his mistress with undisguised adoration. "We're pretty attached to each other."

"I have some work to do around the ranch, so I'll leave the dog here for company. I asked Maria to bring you some books from the library and there's the TV. Two hundred satellite channels and nothing worth watching."

"Not even rodeo? Not even the Dallas Cowboys?"

"You like football?" he asked curiously.

"Well, I wouldn't say I like it, but I used to watch it with my dad wherever we could."

"Oh, right. You're a world traveler. Forgot about that. Well, we don't have a whole lot of luxuries and whatnot here, but if there's anything else you would like, just ask and we'll see what we can arrange."

"Thank you," she replied, wishing she could think of

something else to say. "Everything's fine, really, and I'll try not to be any trouble to you."

"You won't be—at least, not any more than I can handle," he replied. The mocking smile returned to his face before Cord left, closing the door behind him.

"He's a piece of work, isn't he?" Stacy asked her dog, wondering why Cord was so touchy around her. "I imagine he thinks he can 'handle' anything that comes along!"

A few minutes later Maria arrived with some paperbacks and magazines. Stacy noticed a couple of her favorite authors and settled back to read. The day passed quickly. With each knock on the door she half expected to see the rancher appear. When Maria came back for the supper tray that evening and Cord still hadn't come, Stacy decided that he wasn't going to come. Strangely enough, she felt disappointed. She tried to attribute it to her loneliness and lack of focus after the accident. And what was so special about Cord, anyway? Cajun was better company.

Chapter 5

With a contented sigh, Stacy rested her head against the cushion and gave the dog lying beside her an affectionate pat. Her hair tumbled around her neck. She had dressed up a little, just to improve her morale, in new jeans and a pressed shirt. Even put on makeup.

A subtle application of powder hid the slight redness around her straight nose that was the last reminder of the cold that had racked her body with chills and fever the past week.

Like she needed more problems, she thought absently. Cold formula had kicked her brain into low gear. But she was on the mend. Dr. Buchanan had stopped by when he could and prescribed his favorite remedy: tincture of time.

Stacy was so engrossed in her outdoor surroundings that she failed to hear the measured steps entering the cobblestone patio until they were a few feet from her. Instantly she recognized the deliberate walk; hadn't she listened for it enough times outside her bedroom door this week?

Cord Harris stepped into her line of sight and she looked up to meet his compelling gaze. He was wearing his usual jeans and shirt, but there was something different about him:

his manner. He could be going out on a date. She felt suddenly forlorn, until he held out a tall glass of iced liquid in one large hand. Timidly she accepted it, and caught the bemused smile on Cord's face. He pulled up a chair beside her.

"You're looking a whole lot better," he said in a kind voice, his eyes flicking over her face.

"Sorry to be such a basket case," she murmured, feeling a little like a heroine in a Victorian novel. The kind that swooned and got the vapors a lot. What had happened to her backbone?

"Hope you like the drink. I don't know if it's included in the doctor's orders, but it can't do any harm."

"Thank you. It's fine," Stacy replied, taking a sip out of the tall glass. Her senses were tingling with him being so near and smelling so good. Shampoo. Aftershave. The indefinable essence of big strong man. He was definitely in date mode.

"Must feel good to get outside after being shut in for a week."

"It really does. This is such a gorgeous view. I love your house," Stacy said, a nervous lilt in her voice. She felt an unaccountable need to keep the conversation going.

"This old house? I guess I should say old hacienda— anyway, it's still standing."

"Hey, built to last." She coughed, not about to say what she was thinking. *So was Cord.* "You must have done a lot of remodeling."

"Yup, we did. The original hacienda enclosed this patio area. It served as a fortress against attacks long ago. When I decided to remodel it, I eliminated the south and west wings. Even now there's too much room for a bachelor," Cord informed her with a smile.

"But when you marry and have children, it will be perfect." Where had that tactless remark come from, Stacy wondered. She looked anywhere but at him, mostly at the whitewashed adobe walls.

"Undoubtedly." There was a coldness and withdrawal in his tone all of a sudden and his attention was riveted on a distant mountain.

"What I meant was the size—"

"I understand what you mean, Stacy." His dark eyes were expressionless. "But I don't anticipate any of that happening in the near future."

Obviously he was referring to his star-crossed romance with the girl Mary had spoken about. "You never know," Stacy said a little more brightly than she felt. "I'm sure there are lots of women who are anxious to change your mind, Cord."

"Are you one?" A lock of black hair fell over his forehead.

He must have had one of these drinks before he ventured out to talk to her, Stacy realized. She took a fortifying sip of her own. Sweet tea. A dash of fruit-flavored liqueur. And, yes, vodka. Good thing her last dose of cold formula had worn off.

"I wasn't referring to myself," she replied a trifle indignantly.

"It's very romantic-sounding to marry a man who owns a spread this size, but the reality is different," he continued. "This is hard, demanding land even at the best of times. The hours are never-ending and the results are unpredictable at best. A wife can expect to be alone a lot and isolated. As far as entertainment, we make our own— when and if there's time for having fun. Major shopping requires a trip to San Antone or El Paso. More than a city girl would want to cope with."

Stacy's face turned red. "Hey, I wasn't applying for the position." She set her drink aside and rose from the chaise.

"Didn't say you were," he said, towering over her when he got up. Taking her arm, he steered her toward the pool, his eyes shining with amusement. "Come over here. I want to show you something."

"What is it?" Her impatience was obvious from the sharpness in her voice.

"Don't get your feathers up," Cord twitted her. "Thought you would've learned to take a little teasing by now."

"Stop me before I say something really rude, okay?"

The two had reached the opposite side of the pool and stood facing each other defiantly, his hand still upon her arm. The air between them crackled with unspoken challenge. His voice was husky as he turned to face the horizon. "Let's drop it. We both could use a few lessons in manners."

"You're half right about that," Stacy said crisply. "Now if you'll show me whatever it is you wanted me to see, I'll go back to my room."

"You wouldn't be interested."

"Try me."

"It's only an old family cemetery. I'm sure a bunch of weathered gravestones wouldn't be a big thrill," Cord said sarcastically, his back now turned to her.

"Actually, I would like to see them."

"It's not necessary," he answered, as if she'd made an attempt at an apology.

"Cord, you said we ought to be friends. Give me credit for that much. I really would like to see the cemetery. If you don't want to go with me, tell me where it is and I'll go by myself."

The biting tone of her voice made Cord turn toward her, his cool eyes studying her as if looking for assurance of her sincerity.

"It's only a little way from here, but it's uphill. I wouldn't want you to overdo it your first time out. We can go another time." At the angry denial forming on Stacy's lips, Cord went on, "But if you're sure, then let's go."

"I'm sure."

"All right then."

He started to take her arm again, but Stacy shrugged him off and began walking in the direction he had indicated. Cord followed a step or two behind as they made their way up the knoll behind the house. The incline was slight, but Stacy found herself out of breath when they reached the top. She managed to ignore the look in Cord's eyes and pushed on toward the wrought iron enclosure ahead.

The assorted crosses and gravestones were dwarfed by a large monument in the center. Years had weathered most of them, but Stacy noticed that the area was well kept. The ironwork, which should have rusted with age, still had a certain freshness to its black surface and the ground had been seeded with grass, its green blanket lovingly covering the graves in a spring shroud. Cord opened the gate and Stacy walked inside.

The two walked silently on the trodden path around the dozen headstones before coming to a stop near the center. Most of the dates were in the late 1800s and early 1900s. Four of the smaller crosses marked children's graves. One stone dated eight years ago bore only the words *Stephen Harris—Father*.

"Is that your dad's grave?" Stacy asked quietly. There was a melancholy note in her voice as the freshness of her own loss washed over her.

"Yes."

"I didn't notice your mother's. Is she buried here?"

"She's buried back east with her family." She couldn't help noticing the hardness in his eyes. "She couldn't stand the ranch and its demands on her and my father. A few years after I was born she went back to her family."

"She left you?" Stacy asked, pity in her heart for the now dead man and his abandoned son.

"My dad gave her no choice," Cord said, his steel black eyes on her face, rejecting the sympathy he saw. "I doubt if you'd understand. This is a hard land. You gotta take what's yours and then fight to keep it. My mother didn't understand that. The way she grew up, she was used to being waited on. The future he was trying to build meant nothing to her. She wanted the luxuries she was accustomed to and her demands never stopped, not on my father's attention or his money. There wasn't enough of either for her."

"And the ranch came first," Stacy murmured.

"Do you see this marker here?" Cord asked, turning to the center monument. "Elena Teresa Harris, my grandmother. She was a Spanish aristocrat who fell in love with my grandfather, who was a struggling rancher at that time with a lot of dreams. She was a real woman. He had nothing to offer her but an old adobe three-room house, a few head of cattle and a lot of land that was dry most of the time. But it didn't matter to her."

There was no denying the respect and admiration in his voice as he spoke. After a moment, he stepped forward and opened the gate for Stacy, following her out. Engrossed in their conversation, she accepted his hand on her arm as they walked to the edge of the knoll looking down on the ranch yard below. With his other hand, Cord pointed toward the western mountains, purpled in the twilight.

"The Mescalero Apaches used those mountains as a stronghold and raided settlers and ranchers at will. And the Comanche War Trail isn't far from here, either. At the turn of the century the Indians were gone or on reservations, and this western region was populated by cattlemen seeking these rich pastures where grass was so abundant. Most of the settlers ran more cattle than the land could support—

overgrazed it. That's why there's so much desert land out here today."

"Can't it be reseeded? Left alone to grow back?"

"It's too late for most reclamation. Either the wind carries the seed away or the rain doesn't come when it's needed, or it washes the seed away before it gets a chance to root. Ignorance and greed do more damage to the future than they do to the present," Cord answered grimly. "But my father and grandfather realized that. In more than one way, I have them to thank for what I have today."

"You must be very proud of them," Stacy said with a smile. "A lot of things have changed since your grandfather's time."

"He was a cattleman, tried and true. He'd turn over in his grave if he saw sheep grazing on his land." Cord chuckled.

"Sheep?" Stacy was surprised. "You raise sheep?"

"Yup. I have a few hundred head of registered stock on the higher pastures."

"You don't run them with the cattle?"

"Sometimes, usually in the summer when we move the cattle to the foothills. We also have some Angora goats, but they're in the experimental stages as far as our ranch is concerned. Quite a number of ranchers have had success with them. And there's our quarter horses. We have two exceptional studs and several young breeding prospects. I've doubled the number of brood mares in the home herd. We have an auction on the grounds every spring, selling some of the yearlings and two-year-olds that we aren't going to keep or older brood mares we want to replace with new blood."

"I didn't realize you had so many individual enterprises," Stacy mused, awed by the size of the ranch's operation. "Everything but oil wells, huh?"

"Did I forget to mention them?" Cord seemed amused at her question. "We have four on the east boundary. Only two are still in operation. Most all of the ranch property is outside of the oil-producing region."

"I'm beginning to understand what the expression 'cattle baron' means," Stacy commented, looking up at him.

The bronze face was impassive. "Don't let all that lead you to believe it's an easy life," he warned her. "As diversified as the ranch has become, it's only increased the work load and made it harder to stay in control."

Stacy frowned at his words. It was hard to imagine a moment when this powerful man might not be in control. He seemed so sure of what he wanted—nothing would dare stand in his way.

"That looks like Doc Buchanan's car." Cord was watching a station wagon pull up behind the house below. "We'd better go down. Maria will probably have dinner ready shortly, anyway."

Nodding her agreement, Stacy followed him down the slope. By the time they reached the veranda, the smiling young doctor was there to greet them. Stacy was glad his wife Mary had accompanied him. The red-haired young woman walked forward, arms outstretched to Stacy.

"You look great!" Mary exclaimed, clasping Stacy's hands warmly in hers. "Tell me, Stacy, how have you two been getting along?" she teased in a low voice. "I don't see any battle scars."

"Cord and I have buried the hatchet," Stacy replied with a wink. Glancing at the tall man standing beside the doctor, she continued. "We found a couple of safe topics, put it that way."

Only the rancher understood the oblique reference to their earlier dialogue about their opinions of each other. Coolly, Stacy met his dark gaze, keeping a smile off her lips. But Mary's matchmaking mind came up with a totally different conclusion.

"Well, this is news,' Bill Buchanan remarked. "The last time I was here, Stacy, you couldn't wait to leave." With a grin on his boyish face, he added to Cord, "Think my patient's suffering a relapse?"

"I think she's decided to enjoy herself," Cord replied easily. "With a girl as pretty as Stacy, that's as it should be."

Stacy couldn't explain, not even to herself, why she had alluded to the angry words they'd exchanged before. After all, she'd been touched by his wanting her to visit his family's cemetery and his obvious attachment to their history and that of the west. There really was no reason to remind him of the fact that they'd been wary of each other at the start—but her remark had. She felt Cord's eyes searching her face as if he too wanted to know the reason she'd done that, but she deliberately avoided looking at him.

"You know, Cord, we're not doing our duty as hosts," she murmured, trying to cover the confusion she was causing by standing so close to her. Unaccountably, her hand drifted onto his arm. "We didn't offer the Buchanans anything to drink."

Cord did a doubletake, then covered it with an affable smile at the other couple. Stacy felt a flash of guilt for putting him on the spot and dropped her hand.

"I'll have Maria bring us something. Anything special you'd like, Bill, Mary?"

"No," Bill laughed. "Anything tall and cool will do."

Cord left them for a moment to arrange for the refreshments. During that time Mary and her husband seated themselves in two of the garden chairs while Stacy got comfortable on the cushioned settee. A few minutes later Cord returned, followed by the plump housekeeper carrying a tray laden with drinks and hors d'oeuvres. To Stacy's chagrin, Cord sat on the settee with her. The other couple didn't notice her annoyance amid the confusion of accepting the food and drinks Maria offered, but the one-sided smile on Cord's lips let her know that he'd noticed her dismay.

To Stacy's relief, the conversation stayed light. Several times she was uncomfortably aware of the magnetic closeness of the male body so near her own and the outstretched, muscular arm on the back of the couch. Mary, with her naturally lively personality, regaled them with funny stories about her kids, but gradually the subject turned to Stacy and her accident.

"When Bill told me you'd been thrown, I practically insisted on bringing you to town to stay with us," Mary said. "But he assured me that it was better to leave you here where you could really rest."

"Actually, what I said was you needed peace and quiet," the doctor said with a smile. "That's something hard to come by in our house."

"He means the boys," explained Mary, "but he loves them as much as I do. Anyway, I can see how right he was. You seem to be the picture of health. Of course, with this kind of scenery, who would want to stay in bed?"

There was a twinkle in Mary's eye as she gave Cord a sideways glance. Hastily Stacy spoke up, not wanting the innuendo to go any further.

"This is a beautiful ranch," she agreed, rushing the words out. "All the land around here is fascinating. It's easy to imagine how it was in frontier days."

"Texas history is fascinating," said Mary's husband.

"Were you at the cemetery when we came?" Mary asked Cord. Without waiting for his affirmative nod, she continued, "I wish you could have met his grandmother, Stacy. She was a wonderful old woman. You never thought of her as old, though. She was much too vital and active. I was only nine or ten when she died but I remember her so well."

"Cord told me a little about her," Stacy said.

"She was remarkable. Besides her Spanish pride and blue blood, she had a pioneer spirit that just didn't quit," Mary said. "And she had a real way about her—carried her head high and those eyes that seemed to look deep inside you. My mother always said that Dona Elena was the only one able to handle Cord." In a conspiratorial aside to Stacy, she added, "He was a holy terror when he was a kid—what a temper!"

Cord chuckled at Mary's words. "You forgot to mention Grandmother's temper. I always thought she cared so much for me because I'd inherited it." In a mocking tone he added for Stacy's benefit, "Guess I learned to control it some."

"Cord, I'm afraid there've been a few times when you've caused us to doubt your words." Bill Buchanan smiled with a dubious shake of his head. "Don't get me wrong, Stacy. I'm sure the right woman would be able to tame him, but we all know he's got a wild streak."

Embarrassed by all the personal comments, some of which confirmed her sense of Cord, Stacy murmured a vague response. Thankfully, she was interrupted by Maria announcing that dinner was ready.

"You'll be joining us, won't you?" Cord asked the Buchanans.

Mary began to make an excuse, but he wouldn't take no for an answer.

"I'm feeling sociable. You have to say yes. We're not going to let you go so soon, are we, Stacy?"

He extended a hand to her which she was unable to refuse without seeming rude. Distracted by his touch, Stacy half heard the lighthearted response from the Buchanans. She felt herself being ushered into the dining room behind them, Cord steering her. Her muscles tensed as she stifled a desire to pull away from him.

You get what you give, she thought. She'd baited him about their earlier quarrel, when it came right down to it, and then made the connection between them too personal, acting as a hostess when she was only a guest. Playing the little charade had amused Stacy at first—she'd enjoyed the surprised look on Cord's face. But now she had the distinct feeling he was silently laughing at her. Somehow he'd succeeded in turning the tables, and she felt put on the spot. She wasn't enjoying it at all.

As if he'd read her mind, Cord whispered to her as he seated her at the table. "You should have checked the rules."

Stacy looked apprehensively into his eyes. His expression was pleasant enough as he seated himself opposite her at the head of the table, but his eyes held a speculative gleam as he watched her flush and turn away in response to a question from Mary. Twice during the meal Stacy was forced to dodge his look in her direction, and the dinner seemed to last so long that she was sure it would never end. But when Maria served the coffee and dessert the conversation was still on safe topics. A tide of relief washed over her, knowing that the end was in sight.

"Hey, are you there?" Mary teased, waving a hand in front of Stacy. "Didn't you hear what I said?"

"Sorry. I guess I was daydreaming."

"I was wondering if your accident changed your plans about staying."

"No, not really," Stacy replied, avoiding Cord's interested look. "I'll be staying a couple more weeks, actually. Then I'll go back."

"I'm afraid this part of the country is a little too much for her," Cord interposed with a smile. "You know what they say about Texas being hell on horses and women."

"Not if you're raised here," Mary said with spirit.

"Exactly," Cord said. "Stacy's a city girl. We all know Dallas is in Texas, but even so . . . Anyway, I can't speak for her. For all I know, she finds it boring."

"That's not true at all," Stacy retorted impatiently.

"But you couldn't imagine yourself here if you weren't on vacation, am I right?"

"Yes—I mean no," stammered Stacy, realizing that she was under a subtle attack.

"Now, Cord—" Mary began.

"Anyway, it's fair to say that the newness of the adventure has probably worn off for her," he interrupted. "After all, how many mountains do you have to see before you've seen them all? A lot of people follow the call of the wild, only to run back when the inconveniences and isolation become too much for them."

"I don't mind all that," Stacy pointed out. Just in case he was listening. "I happen to love this kind of country."

"You know, Mary, it takes backbone and grit to make it out here. Some folks have to find that out the hard way."

Stacy wasn't sure if his comments were general in nature—okay, obnoxious but general—or if he was comparing her to his mother. She knew what he would say if she voiced that thought aloud. *Spare me the amateur psychology lesson, Stacy.* So she kept quiet, crumpling her napkin on the table.

He favored her with an affable smile. Stacy sensed the discomfort of the other two at the table and decided to smooth over the awkwardness as best she could. "Is that what you think of me? But I like the simple life."

Cord shook his head. "With a Jaguar and an Arabian horse? That doesn't say simple to me."

"Got it. You disapprove of my car and my horse. Anything else? Don't forget my dog. Cajun only looks like a German shepherd. He's actually a show poodle and I'm going to dye him pink when I get back to Babylon—I mean Dallas. If that's okay with you, of course."

His eyes narrowed. "I like that dog and I didn't say one damn word about you going back to the city."

Stacy shrugged. "Can we change the subject?" She pushed her chair away from the table and left the three of them staring after her.

Mary caught up with her in the living room. "What's up with you two?" she asked.

"Basically, we just don't get along," Stacy answered, her hands clutched tightly together. She glanced nervously over her shoulder into the other room.

"You seemed like real pals when we first came. To be honest, I was hoping you two had made a match of it."

"That's impossible," Stacy said. "I mean, we manage to have a civil conversation now and then, but there's something going on with him that I just don't get. Guess I wore out my welcome. First the knock on the head, and then that awful cold—he must be sick of me." Stacy pressed her lips together. Whatever—she was suddenly sick of him, when all was said and done.

After a fraught silence of several seconds, Stacy had a sinking feeling that Cord had come into the room while she was talking and heard every word. Defiantly, she turned to face his glowering eyes. So tall and broad-shouldered that he seemed to fill the room, Cord diminished everything and everyone near him.

"Bill said they need to get back to put the boys to bed. Are you going to the door with them?"

Stacy turned without answering Cord and walked with Mary as she collected her purse and started toward the front door. Stacy's back prickled ominously—she was all too aware of the rancher walking directly behind her. Before reaching the front patio, Stacy murmured an apology to the woman beside her, speaking in a low voice. "Sorry. He just gets on my nerves, that's all. But I did enjoy your coming out here."

"Don't you worry about it," Mary admonished her. "Men are crazy. It's not your fault."

"I heard that," Bill protested mildly.

"You and Cord know it's true." Mary was not to be gainsaid.

Her husband only laughed and slapped Cord on the shoulder. "No use arguing with her, is there?"

"No use arguing with any woman," Cord muttered. "You can't win for losing."

"I second that. But you still have to make sure Stacy doesn't overdo it. Wait on her hand and foot, and agree with everything she says. She won't know what to think."

He chucked Stacy under the chin. "Professionally speaking, I want you to get another couple of days' rest and limit your activities. After that you can do as you want."

Looking up at the doctor's kind face, Stacy saw an unspoken understanding in his eyes. She reminded herself that he'd known Cord for years and could probably tell her why the rancher acted the way he did around her.

Then again, maybe she didn't really want to know.

With cheery good-byes, the Buchanans walked down to their car. A little forlornly, Stacy watched as the taillights disappeared down the winding drive. She sighed, knowing she had to face Cord, but he was gone by the time she turned around. Peering into the darkness, she made out his familiar form striding toward the stables. Puzzled and relieved at the same time, she walked into the house.

Chapter 6

For two days, Stacy took special pains to avoid Cord Harris. She succeeded, because he apparently didn't want her company either. Digging the toe of her boot into the sandy soil, Stacy looked reluctantly around the grounds. The time had come to talk to him and she wasn't looking forward to it at all. She'd fully regained her strength and wanted to make arrangements to return to the cabin. The big German shepherd padded along at her side as she wandered past the open doorway of the ranch office. A glance inside verified the inner feeling that he wasn't there. With an impatient sigh Stacy continued to the stable.

He was probably out on the range somewhere, she thought unhappily, gazing out beyond the buildings.

At the corral she noticed a horse and rider rounding one of the barns at a gallop. Not recognizing the man, Stacy waited. Her curiosity was aroused by his haste. She heard shouting not far from the stables and she craned her neck to see the reason for the commotion, but the buildings blocked her view. The rider had just reined his horse to a stop by the corral gate and dismounted.

"What's wrong?" she asked him.

"'Scuse me, ma'am, but I got to call the doctor," the man murmured, starting to hurry past her.

"What happened? Who got hurt?" Stacy cried, a horrifying picture already forming of Cord lying unconscious on the ground.

"That red devil of a stallion slipped out of the stud pen when Chris went in," he answered, hurrying toward the open office door with Stacy right behind him. "The young fool climbed on his horse and tried to rope him. Diablo went berserk and attacked him. Luckily the boss and us was headed in from the range and saw what happened. Don't know how bad the kid's hurt—can't get near him."

"Oh no!" Stacy gasped, staring at the man reaching for the phone in the office.

"The boss is mad enough to kill that horse," muttered the cowboy into the phone, not directing the sentence to Stacy.

As she heard the man reach the doctor at last, Stacy rushed out of the office toward the standing horse. She jumped on the buckskin and urged him toward the distant sound of voices. Her thoughts were barely coherent as she shouted to Cajun to follow and kicked the already winded horse into a gallop. She just knew she had to get there.

Kill Diablo. The words rang like a death knell in her ears. Confused, she whipped the horse with the reins as he bounded around the buildings and headed for the mounted men beyond. As she drew up with them, she saw a rider trapped under his fallen horse with her red stallion between him and the two riders. A rope was flying free from Diablo's neck as he eluded the lassos of the other two riders. His neck and withers were white with foam as he continued to lash out with his wicked hooves.

"What the hell are you doing here?" shouted Cord as he saw Stacy dismount. His face was contorted in anger as he swung his big bay around to face her. "Get back to the house where you belong!"

"He's my horse!" shouted Stacy, turning away toward the stallion who was lunging, teeth bared, at the other mounted rider.

"You crazy female," roared the rancher, reining in his horse over beside her, "can't you see that damn stud is loco?"

It was then that Stacy noticed the bullwhip in the angry man's hand, the end dragging in the dust raised by the bay's dancing hooves. Fire flashed in her eyes as she raised her head to meet his dark gaze.

"What do you propose to do? Whip him into submission?"

"If I have to, yes! That boy over there is hurt!"

"Get out of my way!" Stacy demanded. Pushing his horse away from her, she walked to face the red stallion.

A shrill neigh split the air as Diablo pawed the ground and shook his flaxen mane at the solitary figure in front of him. Rearing, he flashed his black hooves through the air, his ears snaked back.

"Diablo!" Stacy commanded, attempting to pierce the frenzied mind of the stallion. "Diablo, settle down!"

His ears remained flat against his head as he lashed out with his back feet at Cajun, worrying him from behind. Stacy could see the fallen horse attempting to rise, only to collapse back on its side. As the stallion started to charge at her, she called to him once again, her voice raising in authority. Stacy thought she saw his ears flicker up as he swept toward her. When he was just about on her, she stepped aside and he thundered by. Spinning around, he faced her, tossing his blazed head. Out of the corner of her eye, Stacy saw the mounted riders moving. One was headed for the injured man on the ground and the other, Cord, was coming for the stallion, the whip rolled on the saddle horn and a lasso spinning in the air in readiness.

"Diablo," her voice changed to a caressing whisper, "easy, boy, settle down. It's all right, baby. Come here. Come on!"

But the excitement and the almost forgotten memory of what had caused the scar on his neck was too much. The red horse couldn't curb the demon driving him. His well-shaped head bobbed up and down, the foam flicking off his neck. He recognized the girl in front of him, but he was filled with a new sense of hate and strength. Out of the corner of his eyes he caught the movement of horse and rider coming up behind him and danced around to face them. Stepping forward, Stacy called to him. This time he spun swiftly around and raced toward her, his teeth bared and his head low. When Stacy attempted to jump out of the way, the stallion veered into her, jostling her to the ground with his big shoulder.

Breathless but unhurt, she raised herself up to see Cord streaking after the horse. He yelled at the other horseman and both ropes encircled the red sorrel at the same time. Screaming his anger, the horse attempted to charge the other rider, only to be brought up short by the rope dallied around Cord's saddle horn.

"We got him, boss! We got him!" yelled the other rider triumphantly, as the horse struggled between the two ropes. It only took Diablo a minute or two to realize he couldn't win. Swiftly the two riders led him to the gate of the stud pen he'd just escaped from.

Dusting herself off, Stacy saw the third man who'd been sent to call the doctor kneeling beside the fallen horse and rider. Hurriedly she made her way over to them, arriving the same time as Cord. His expression was grim as he kneeled beside the pain-wracked form of the young cowboy.

"Take it easy, Chris," Cord instructed. "We'll have you out from under in no time. Doc's on his way."

"My leg's broken," groaned the young rider, gritting his teeth with pain. "Get this damned horse off me!"

"Shorty, how bad's that horse's leg?" demanded Cord, directing his words to the dusty figure trying to quiet the downed gelding. The only answer was a negative shake of the head.

Without a word, Cord rose and walked over to his bay horse and extracted his rifle from the scabbard. Stacy stood numbly watching the action, unable to move or react. The loud report of the gun as it ended the life of the fatally injured horse deafened her. She knew it had to be done, knew it was merciful and right, but that didn't diminish the shock and horror she felt. She didn't see the doctor and paramedics arrive or the boy being carried away on a stretcher. The only thing she could see was the inert form of the dead horse. The tears glazing her eyes seemed frozen too. At last her vision was blocked by Cord's dusty, sweaty form. Stiffly she raised her tear-filled eyes to his blurred face.

"Why?" she whispered, forcing the words through the lump in her throat.

"When Chris roped your horse the sorrel charged, knocking them down, breaking Chris's leg and the gelding's too. The doc says his best guess is that the boy'll be all right. Six weeks or so off the leg, most likely, and on crutches for a month or two more."

"No," Stacy mumbled. "The horse! I just wish you didn't have to kill him—oh, Cord—" It was the first time she'd seen something like that actually happen. Her mind understood that the complex structure of a horse's leg was incredibly fragile—once shattered, never mended—but she couldn't keep her eyes from straying to the animal.

Didn't matter. The deed was done. It was over. Her mind whirled, trying to make sense of it. She couldn't, just couldn't—

"The horse?" exploded Cord. "Do you realize that Chris could have died?"

His anger pierced her shock and she turned to his face again and read the distaste and disgust that filled it. He didn't understand. She was upset about the rider, but the sight of slaughter, however necessary, made her utterly sick at heart.

"But he's going to be all right, isn't that what you said? He'll be back, but the horse is dead and you killed him! As if it was nothing!" Her voice was shrill with shock and near hysteria.

"Nothing? Do you realize that I'm now without a horse and a rider? Do you think it's going to be easy to replace a man at this time of year?" He got her arm in a visclike grip. "I have you to thank for that, you and that crazy horse of yours!"

"Oh, is it all my fault?" she cried. "Well, don't worry. I'll pay for the hospital bills and anything else!"

"Damn right you will," Cord growled. His voice got even lower. "But your money won't buy your way out of this one. You're going to take Chris's place. For once in your life, you ought to see what it's like to work to pay a debt."

"What are you talking about?" Stacy asked, her body now trembling with anger.

"Let's get one thing straight. I don't want to hear any sob stories from you. I bet it broke your heart when your father died and left you all that money," he replied, scorn and contempt deep in his voice.

His words cut like a knife into her heart as the mean-spirited accusation left Stacy speechless. She lashed out instantly, not even feeling her open hand make contact with his cheek. She put all her strength into the hard slap, though. Her palm was stinging as the fire in his eyes once again focused on her.

"So that's the way you play," he murmured through

clenched teeth. "Today you can get away with it, but I wouldn't try that again if I were you. You start to work tomorrow," he stated. "And wear dirty jeans, because they're going to get dirtier. We don't hold any fashion shows out on the range."

Her feet were rooted to the ground and angry tears trickled down her cheeks as she watched Cord stalk away. Her hands were clenched into tight fists as she tried to find the words to scream after him. But her mouth refused to open and the words never came out. She stood there shaking with uncontrolled anger that gradually gave way to gasping sobs. Cord had already mounted his horse and ridden off in the direction of the ranch house before Stacy moved from her position. Slowly she made her way in the same direction, her fury at the rancher not softened by her feelings of compassion for the injured cowboy and the dead horse.

By the time Stacy reached the yards, the dust from the ranch car was halfway down the road. She headed for the hacienda, more or less oblivious to her actual surroundings. Once inside the house and in her bedroom, Stacy sat on the bed and looked at the things she'd prepared to pack up.

With one hand she wiped the useless tears away from her eyes. She knew she was still in shock—every word of Cord's seemed to echo in her head. His harsh comment about her father was the worst of all—and then another thought assailed her. How had he known about the money she'd inherited? She'd told no one, not the Nolans, not Mary Buchanan. The anger in her heart faded away and was replaced by the crushing feeling of despair. How could she ever hope to convince him that she understood what had happened and why he'd done what he had? Then again, why should she try? He'd thought of her as a spoiled princess from the get-go, obviously. He'd only been nice to her while she was recuperating because Bill and Mary

Buchanan had told him to. The confusion of her thoughts drove her to her feet and she paced the room. Now what she felt was resentment.

Just exactly how was he going to make her stay against her will? He certainly couldn't force her to work. And besides, she knew zip about ranching. Stacy stopped in front of the mirror, an idea forming in her mind. He couldn't stop her from leaving because he wasn't even here. She glanced at her watch and then quickly outside. More time had gone by than she realized. The sun was already down and Cord must have been gone for at least two hours. If she intended to leave before he returned, she didn't have much time. She swept up her belongings, stuffed them into a duffel and set it outside her room.

Naturally, he would accuse her of running away and refusing to face his challenge, but let him think what he liked. Unfortunately she'd been forced to accept his hospitality when she was ill, but there was no need to stay any longer. It was enough that she'd offered to pay the hospital for the boy and reimburse Cord for the horse. If for some reason she was unable to pay him, that would be the time to try to arrange some other way to work the problem out. There was no question in her mind that she was responsible for the damage done.

Stacy had just slipped her fringed jacket on and picked up her purse and started out of the bedroom when she heard the big oak door close. Numbly she stood beside the duffel bag and stared at the tall form standing at the bottom of the stairs. Cord's features were hidden in the shadows, but Stacy could well imagine the dark brows gathered together and the clean, hard set of his jaw, and most of all the grim line of his mouth. Her eyes were wide and darkening with apprehension as she felt her body begin to tremble.

"I take it you're planning on going somewhere?" came the low baritone voice.

"What if I do?" Stacy retorted defiantly, lifting her chin in challenge.

"Then I would suggest you forget it," was the cool reply as Cord stepped out of the shadows. There were new lines on his face that Stacy hadn't noticed before, but there was no mistaking the hard quality in his voice. His gaze flicked to the bag and then to her. "You might as well unpack."

"You can't keep me here against my will!"

He gave a slight shrug before replying, "Maybe so. But you do owe me. I ought to get to set the terms of payment."

The hopelessness of fighting this man raced through Stacy and her shoulders slumped. The fire went out in her eyes and was replaced with despair and confusion. Struggling, she made one last stand. "I will not stay in that room one more night!"

A glint of amusement showed in his eyes before he turned his face away from her.

"Suit yourself. There's a guest room down the hall. Use it." He paused briefly. "In case you're interested, Chris is going to be in the hospital for a few weeks and inactive for a couple of months."

Stacy felt the heat rising in her cheeks, furious with herself for not even thinking to ask about the injured rider. That really wasn't Cord's fault. Frustrated and as fed up with herself as she was with him, she grabbed the duffel bag and stalked into the hallway, stopping at the first doorway on her left. At the very least, she wanted to hand her paycheck over to Chris. If Cord would be so kind as to pay her. She didn't owe Cord, she reasoned. But she did owe Chris.

She was too upset to take in the furnishings of the room. Her anger was too close to the surface to allow her to dwell on anything but Cord's cool indifference. He hadn't followed her but just imagining his face irritated her. All she could do, it seemed, was make a fool of herself one way or another and reinforce his belief that she was spoiled and selfish. Stacy felt compelled to prove herself and on his terms. Quid pro quo. She was going to take the young rider's place on the Circle H ranch and that was that.

"Okay, Cord," she whispered to herself. "I can take anything you can dish out. No quarter asked."

The sun had barely touched the sky the following morning when there was a loud knock at Stacy's door. Sleepily she raised herself up on one elbow and looked out the window and then over to the clock on the dresser. It took her a minute before she remembered the previous day's events.

"Yes?"

"Time to get up," came Cord's voice from the hall. "That is, if you want coffee and breakfast before work."

He didn't wait for a reply but strode away from the door. Determinedly, Stacy clambered out of the bed. It took her only a few minutes to slide into broken-in jeans and a work-shirt and to tie her hair back at the nape of her neck. A little smile played on her soft lips as she looked at the image reflected in the mirror. If he thought she was going to look like less of a woman just because she had to work then he was wrong. She checked to make sure her riding gloves were in the pocket of her suede jacket, picked up her hat and walked down the stairs to the dining room.

Unfortunately, he wasn't there. Stacy asked Maria, who told her that Mr. Harris was already out giving instructions to the men. Maria was plainly confused by the turn of events and kept giving Stacy puzzled looks. When Stacy finished her toast and coffee, Maria finally said that she was to meet Cord out in the yard.

Gratefully Stacy realized that most of the men had already gone. It would have been embarrassing to be subjected to the rancher's orders in the presence of all his men. As it was, he was still talking to two of them, but his back was to her. He couldn't see her approach, but Stacy was sure he knew she was coming.

The two men with him attempted to ignore her. One was only a few years older than Stacy and looked as though he felt awkward. She wondered what Cord had told them—the kid kept his head down, his hat preventing Stacy from seeing his expression. The other man was much older and wizened. Working under the hot sun had made his skin so leathery that Stacy was unable to judge his age. When she came closer, the older man met her gaze, sympathy etched in his face and kindness in the eyes that squinted in the morning sun. It was a comfort to recognize an ally here.

"About time you got here, Adams," Cord said, turning his head toward her. "I want you to go with Hank and Jim today to gather the stock cattle in the winter range." He cast only a glance at the petite figure beside him, then looked back at Hank. "Any questions?"

The older man shook his head.

"Okay, mount up."

Stacy started to follow the two others as they walked to the horses standing saddled on the opposite side of the corral, but was called back by Cord. She turned around to face him, taking her gloves out of her pocket. She began putting them on, hoping to stave off the nervousness she felt in his presence.

"Yes," she said, looking boldly into his face, her voice matching the crisp tone he'd used earlier. She was unable to read his expression.

For a minute he didn't answer, then he said, "Hank will show you all that needs to be done."

"All right," she replied, disliking the searching eyes that seemed to probe deep inside her. "Anything else?"

"No. Good luck," His tone was indifferent and didn't match his words.

Briskly Stacy walked to where the two mounted riders waited. The one named Hank handed her the reins of a short-coupled bay pony. Silently she mounted and turned her horse to follow the other two.

Shortly after leaving the ranch yard, the younger of the two men rode ahead, leaving the wizened old cowboy alone with Stacy. Normally she would've enjoyed an early morning ride, but today's circumstances made her conscious of the humiliating position she was in. Pride forbade her to look at the silent, hunched figure beside her. For a time the two horses moved along at a slow, shuffling trot until the rider beside her pulled his horse into a walk and Stacy's pony automatically matched the pace.

"Miss Adams," came the rough, questioning voice, "now it ain't none of my business and you can tell me to shut my mouth, but if we're going to be riding the range together, it gets mighty lonely if all you can talk to is your hoss. And it ain't in me to question the boss's orders, but I want you to know that me nor none of the boys hold you responsible for what happened the other day. It's gonna be a long day in the saddle, specially for a dude like you, but it sure does make the day go faster if there's a bit of jawin' goin' on."

Stacy had the distinct impression that this was the longest statement the man had ever made, and she smiled at his thoughtfulness. He was trying to put her at ease, and himself as well, in his own clumsy way.

"Thank you, Hank. I appreciate it more than you know."

"Well, I been workin' on this spread ever since the boss was in knee britches and I seen some strange things. But I gotta admit this is the first time we ever had us a lady wrangler. An' the boss says you gotta pull your own weight." He shook his head in confusion.

"I intend to," Stacy replied, a set look on her face. "I don't know anything about ranching or cows but I can learn. At least I can ride and I'm in fair shape."

"Well now, miss, I reckon you can ride all right, but you gotta relax a little more. Ya ain't in no hoss show, so you don't have to worry 'bout how you look," Hank said with a slight smile. "An' I'd watch what you call cows. Safe thing is to call 'em cattle."

"Okay, cattle it is." She laughed. "Tell me, Hank, exactly what are we doing today?"

"We're gonna be rattlin' the brush for bunch-quitters, mostly, an' gettin' the herd ready for movin' to the summer pasture. Most of the men trucked their horses to the far end of the pasture an'll be workin' toward us with the main herd."

"Trucked their horses?" Stacy asked quizzically, studying the cowboy's weathered face.

"Yep. It's a modern West you'll find. Rather than spend a lot of time ridin' to where the herd is, now they jus' load up the horses in trucks or trailers and haul 'em as close as they can."

"It's a miracle they don't use jeeps or ATVs for roundups," Stacy exclaimed half to herself, half in amazement.

"Been done," Hank replied. "A few years ago when we was really tryin' to gather all the scrub bulls and strays, the boss even ordered a helicopter to search 'em out. Yeah, things have changed," he muttered. "Reckon we ought to catch up with Jim?"

The brisk morning air was beginning to warm with the rising sun. Already the morning dew was rapidly vanishing from the undergrowth wherever the sun's rays probed through the shade. The distant hills were cloaked in a golden haze that cast its shimmering glow upon the grassland stretched out below it. The morning air offered no breeze and the stillness was broken only by the shuffling trot of the three cow ponies and the occasional call of quail. The three riders traveled several miles before arriving at the first barbed wire fence. They rode along the fence until they arrived at a gate. Stacy and Hank waited astride their horses while Jim maneuvered his horse into position to unhook the gate and open it for the other two. After they had passed through, the young cowboy followed, closing the gate behind him.

"This is where we start to work, miss," Hank said, indicating the land spread out before them.

"But I don't see any cattle." Stacy looked at the vacant pasture.

"That's the general idea. If they was right out in plain sight it wouldn't be quite so much work. But they seem to know every ravine and bush on the spread and that's where they plan to stay."

"But I thought that you raised domestic cattle, a Hereford cross or something like that." She was plainly puzzled.

"We do, but they been left alone. They're just about as skittish of humans as the old longhorns that used to graze this land. Only difference between the two is these ain't half as ornery as them." Hank squinted, surveying the land. "We usually split up a bit here, but you stick close to me for a while, miss."

The riders loped off; the younger cowboy moved fifty yards to their left and they all began scouring the brush. It was hot, dusty work for horse and rider, and it wasn't long before Stacy removed her jacket and tied it to the back of the saddle. Between the heat of the sun and the exercise, Stacy began to sweat. They scared up a couple of head of cattle as they worked their way along. By midmorning they had about fifteen head driving in front of them. Hank

instructed Stacy to keep them going while he and Jim
added other strays with them.

At first she thought they were giving her an easier job until
she began breathing in the dust that the cattle were kicking
up. She wasn't even able to relax on the horse. Every time
she allowed her attention to wander from the herd, that was
the precise time that one of the animals decided to make another break for the open bush. The little bay instinctively gave
chase and cut it back into the herd. Quite a few times Stacy
was positive that the horse was going to spin around and send
her flying in the other direction. Her legs were so weary from
gripping his sides and her body so covered in dust and grime
and sweat that she was sure she wouldn't make it through the
rest of the morning, let alone the whole day.

Each time one of the cowboys added another steer to the
herd, Stacy could hardly stop from sighing out loud. She'd
learned for every steer in the herd her horse had to cover
twice their distance.

Her mouth was dry and gritty, but she was afraid to sip
out of her canteen for fear that one of the herd would
decide to bolt. She was happy to see Hank ride up alongside, but trying to smile a hello was an effort. He didn't
look at her directly, but Stacy could make out a ghost of a
smile on his leathery face.

"Mighty dirty work, ridin' drag on a bunch of scrubs,"
he murmured in the air. "We're comin' up on the water
tank where we'll meet up with the chuckwagon for lunch.
Reckon maybe you could do with a rest, huh?"

"I don't mind admitting that I do, Hank," Stacy replied,
feeling her lips crack as she spoke. Giving the little bay an
affectionate pat on the neck, she added. "I think he de-
serves one too."

"The remuda will be there. His work is done for the day,"
the cowboy answered.

"Oh, look!" cried Stacy, swiveling left. "Isn't that Jim coming? Looks like he's got a little baby calf across his saddle."

The younger cowboy joined them with a new white-faced calf lying crosswise on his saddle with the mother alongside, lowing soothingly to her youngster.

"He's so cute!" Stacy exclaimed. "How old is he?"

"Just a couple of days," Jim replied, the shyness still evident in his unwillingness to look directly at Stacy, but proud of her interest in his find. "I found them out in the brush. The calf wasn't able to keep up, so I thought I'd give him a ride to the calf wagon."

"The calf wagon? What's that?" Stacy asked, her attention diverted from the snow-white face.

"There's usually a bunch of these latecomers that are too little to keep up with the herd, so we have a trailer we put 'em in until we reach the night's holdin' ground and then we mammy 'em up," Hank replied, amused at Stacy's concern for the calf. "Take the little critter on in, Jim, we'll be there shortly."

"Isn't that what you call a dogey, a baby calf?" Stacy asked, watching Jim as he rode on ahead.

"A dogey is really a calf without a momma, but a lot o' people call all calves dogies," Hank answered.

"The cattle have settled down a lot. It must be your being here. Before, every five minutes one was heading in a different direction," Stacy commented, enjoying the conversation with the knowledgeable cowboy.

"Nope, it's not me. They smell water. We just happen to be going the same direction as them."

The cattle and two riders topped a small rise in the ground and came upon a high plateau covered with tall stands of pampas grass and creosote bushes. Ahead Stacy could see the large water tank and windmill. Beyond that was a station wagon and several pickups and trailers. A look of surprise lit up her eyes.

"That's the chuckwagon?"

A dry chuckle escaped the old cowboy's throat. "I told ya the old West was gone. They bring the food from the ranch house and trailer the remuda to the noon stop." The old man smiled. "You go on and ride ahead. These cattle ain't goin' nowhere 'cept to that tank. Rest while you can. We're gonna be hittin' the saddle for another long afternoon."

Gratefully, Stacy reined her little bay out around the herd and set him at a lope for the parked vehicles. She rode over to where a cowboy waited by the trailers. There were already several riders over by the station wagon; some were eating and some were just getting their food. Behind the trailers Stacy noticed a couple of Mexican ranch hands cooling off some cow ponies with replacements picketed along the trailers. Slowly she dismounted. Her bones and muscles were so sore that she stood for a minute to adjust to the solid ground beneath her feet. Now that she was on the ground, she wasn't so sure she could walk. She took a few careful steps in the general direction of the wagon and realized that she was going to make it all right, so she joined the men where they were dishing out food from the rear.

The good-natured grumbling and bantering going on stopped when she arrived, and Stacy became uneasy. She'd been so comfortable with the old cowboy, and so tired and hungry from the skimpy breakfast, that she didn't think about how the seasoned cowboys and hands would react to a new person—let alone a woman.

With a red face and a trembling hand, she accepted the dish of stew and beans with a thick slice of bread from one of the cooks and a steaming mug of coffee from another. Nervously she turned around to search for a shaded place to have her meal. All eyes were on her. Some looked away while others eyed her boldly.

"Ma'am," came a hesitant voice from her right. Stacy turned to see Jim, the young rider who'd found the calf. "If you like, you can join me. Not many shady places left."

"Thank you," she said, looking for the first time into the hazel eyes of the young cowboy. "I guess I must look a little lost."

"Well, don't mind the men. They aren't used to seeing women around camp, not even in this day and age," he said, removing his hat to run his fingers through straw-colored hair. There was a boyishness about his face but she guessed he was in his middle twenties.

In between bites of food, Stacy asked, "Have you worked here long?"

"Off and on since forever, I think. Got out of the service a couple years ago and went to college, but I work here in the summers for tuition money." A serious look crossed his young face.

"What are you studying?"

"Forestry, conservation," was the quiet answer.

"Are you planning to be a park ranger?" Stacy asked.

"Yep. Mr. Harris suggested I come back to the ranch but I think I'd rather not. Initially I was going to be a vet, but I discovered that I was more interested in the agricultural and ecological side," he answered, enjoying the interest Stacy was taking in him.

"I wouldn't let Mr. Harris's wishes interfere with what I wanted to do," Stacy said, a trace of bitterness in her voice as she stabbed at a piece of beef in the stew.

"No, of course not," said a low, mocking voice.

Stacy jerked her head up and practically choked on the piece of meat as she stared into Cord's face. Jim scrambled to his feet.

"We were just discussing my college plans, sir," he stated, his jaw clenched tight, defending Stacy from the sardonic smile of his employer.

Swiftly Stacy got to her feet to save Jim from having to rescue her. It was humiliating enough to have to look up at Cord, but to be seated at his feet was too much. Cord Harris shifted his gaze from the young cowhand to the hatless girl before him. Boldly she met his gaze, conscious once again of her dust-covered clothes and face.

"Maybe you'd like to go check on your horses for Miss Adams, Connors," Cord said with a definite tone of dismissal.

The cowboy cast a wavering glance at her. Stacy smiled at him with a great deal more confidence than she felt. Her pulse was racing at an unsettling pace. Reluctantly Jim Connors left her and Cord alone beside the trailer.

"You seem to have gained an admirer."

"Don't be ridiculous. He was only being polite. He's obviously been taught some manners—which is more than I can say for some people," Stacy said scathingly.

"Uh-huh. I see you've managed to survive the morning in fair shape." Cord ignored her insult and leaned against the side of the trailer to light a cigarette. He held the match until it was cool, all the while his gaze traveling over her dirty face.

"Yes, I did. Surprised?"

"Nope. I imagine you could do anything you set your mind to," he replied. "I only wonder if you have the staying power."

"Hey, boss, is that the filly you picked up at the sale last week?" Hank walked up beside them, his attention fixed on a chestnut sorrel at the far end of the trailer. The horse didn't like being tied up and pawed the ground impatiently while pulling at the reins. "Sure is a nice-looking thing."

Cord's eyes never left Stacy's face. "Yes, she is."

Stacy could feel herself begin to blush, but she couldn't break away from the compelling eyes.

"Do ya think she's gonna be able to settle down to ranch life?" Hank asked, and then addressed his next remark to Stacy, not noticing that she was paying little attention to him. "She was raced a few times and she's used to a lot of fuss and bother. Spoilt, you might say."

A mocking smile crossed Cord's lips as he watched the discomfiture registering on Stacy's face. "It's hard to tell, Hank."

"Sure seems awful fractious. It'll take a lot of patience to change this one's way of thinkin'." The old cowboy shook his head.

"Yes, it will." Cord gave a husky laugh. "It most definitely will. Okay—can't keep you two from your work any longer. See you later."

With no more than a brief nod to Stacy and a friendly slap on the back to the cowhand, Cord strode to where the filly was tethered, the secretly amused expression still on his face. Untying the reins, he swung his tall frame into the saddle as the spirited horse danced beneath him. He didn't even glance in their direction as he reined the sorrel over to a group of riders chatting over their last cup of coffee. Stacy couldn't hear what was said, but gathered it was an order to mount up, because shortly after they dispersed and went over to where their ponies were tied up.

Out of the corner of her eye she saw Jim walking up leading two horses. He handed her the reins to a big buckskin. Stacy could tell that Jim was embarrassed about leaving her to Cord, but at this moment his tanned face was plainly visible in her mind and a very male laugh was still echoing in her ears. Silently they mounted and rode over to join Hank and get to the afternoon's work.

Chapter 7

Stacy had thought the morning long and arduous, but by six o'clock that evening she knew the true meaning of bone-weary. She yearned to give a shout of joy when she saw the windmill that indicated the night's holding ground for the cattle.

She hadn't shirked a moment of work, and that alone gained her both Hank and Jim's respect. Several times they would have taken over for her, but she wouldn't let them. It would have been easy for her to burst into tears and give up, and she hadn't. They would've cut her all the slack she wanted, in spite of their employer's order.

Hank suggested that she ride on ahead and get a cup of coffee for each of them, but she declined, saying with a tired attempt at a laugh that she was going to need help getting off her horse. At the moment it seemed almost too true to be funny. A short time later they merged their small herd with the main one settling down for the night about a hundred yards from the camp.

A sense of peace cloaked the riders as they rode back into the camp, where the odor of gasoline and oil mixed with the smell of sweaty horse, cattle, and humans. Good-naturedly

Stacy accepted the helping hand of the younger cowboy as she dismounted. She felt no self-consciousness as she limped her way to the station wagon and the promising aroma of coffee. Hank had arrived before them and was talking to the riders who'd gathered around the lowered tailgate.

"Hank," Stacy groaned, looking into his gray eyes, a weary smile on her face. "I think you're looking at the very first bowlegged lady wrangler. I'll never be able to walk straight again as long as I live, let alone be able to sit down!"

That got sympathetic laughter from the group and, more importantly, acceptance. Cheered up by the warm-hearted joking around, Stacy was presented with a hot cup of what the cook called "the best java west of the moon." After inhaling the steam rising from the cup, she gave a huge sigh of appreciation.

"Charlie, this is going to hit the spot, but there's one more thing I need: a hot bath. Will someone please tell me where I can get one?"

That got another round of guffaws.

"Why is that funny? Don't tell me you all never take a bath—"

"Twice on Sunday," one of them replied, and laughed at the expression of mock disbelief on Stacy's face.

"Spare me the details and help me find a way to sit down!"

Several of the cowboys stepped forward, including Jim Connors, and with exaggerated care lowered her to the ground. Despite her aches and pains, Stacy was beginning to enjoy herself and so were the men. There had seldom been a woman in their midst and definitely none that had joined in making fun of herself and her situation. With a sparkle in her eyes, she started to make another comment to the men, only to notice that they had gotten very quiet and were looking beyond her. Still in a giddy mood, she turned to focus on the object of their attention.

Cord Harris. Of course. She should have recognized the long shadow he cast over the group. His expression was a study of amused interest in her and the surrounding cowboys. Stacy couldn't say why or how she had the nerve to say what came next.

"Oh, honcho grande, please allow this lowly peon to stay seated in thy great presence, for I vow I couldn't rise if you commanded me."

There was a sudden stillness as the men waited for their boss to answer. Stacy regretted her silliness, but it was too late to retract her words. Besides, if he couldn't take a joke, then he really was too self-important to live. The low chuckle that finally came relaxed everyone, Stacy most of all.

"Charlie, give me a cup of that brew of yours while I sit down beside this señorita," Cord directed with a grin at the cook.

Someone had started a campfire, and Stacy fixed her attention on it rather than the disconcerting man beside her, trying to ignore the sensual chill that ran through her at his low laugh. The sun was beginning to set now, casting richly colored shadows on the landscape, while the two sipped their coffee in silence. The cook brought them each a plate of beefsteak and beans.

"Well, what do you think of the cattle drive?" Cord asked as they began eating. "Is it what you expected it to be?"

"No," Stacy replied with a smile, "not to complain, but it's a lot harder work than I thought."

"So far you've come through with flying colors," he said.

"So far. Meaning you don't think I'll last?"

"Meaning I have no opinion except that you've done very well." There was an edge of annoyance in his voice. "You really should do something about that temper of yours. You're a little too quick to take offense."

"Maybe there's a good reason for that," Stacy said, looking into the flickering campfire.

"Touché." Cord smiled, his eyes observing her face. "I imagine you're pretty tired after today's work. The remuda hands will be heading back to the ranch house shortly. You can catch a ride with them, or wait a little longer and I'll take give you a ride back."

"Is everyone going back?" Stacy asked curiously. "You mean you just leave the cattle unattended to stray all over?"

"No," chuckled Cord, "most of the men will be staying and taking turns at riding herd. They've brought along their bedrolls," he added, indicating places where some of the men were already getting ready for the night.

"Then why am I going back to the ranch?"

"Because you didn't come prepared for staying overnight and because a woman spending the night out here on a trail drive is asking for trouble."

"Don't you trust me to behave myself?"

He didn't answer that question, saying only, "You've been out of a sickbed for just a few days. Overdoing it isn't smart."

"But I'm just one of the boys, aren't I?" Stacy's brown eyes flashed bright sparks, magnified by the burning embers.

"During the day," he qualified.

"I'm staying the night here." Stacy's voice was low and determined.

"You will be returning with me."

"Then you'll have to carry me back, Cord. And that would make a scene. But you seem to like them."

"You're forgetting that you have no place to sleep," Cord stated. "It gets cold at night in this country. Real cold."

She waved a hand airily. "I'm sure I can borrow a blanket or something from someone."

"Or maybe share a bedroll?" was the sarcastic reply. "I'm sure you'd have plenty of offers."

"You have a dirty mind!" Stacy exclaimed, forgetting her exhaustion and bounding to her feet. Her fury showed in her face as she waited for Cord to join her. "Anyway, I wouldn't take them!" Her voice raised as she struggled to keep control of herself. "I don't have to listen to that kind of talk from any man!"

Cord grabbed hold of her arm, preventing her from running away from him. Shaking with emotion and fatigue, Stacy stopped, not attempting to pull away from his strong grip or turning to face his cold, dark eyes.

"Hoping one of your knights will come to your rescue?" he asked in a mocking whisper that she just barely heard.

Unable to reply, she stood immobile. Finally she heard a sigh leave his lips at the same time he released her arm.

"Maybe I overreacted," he said.

"That's putting it mildly."

"If you wanted to give me the benefit of the doubt, we could call it being overprotective."

"Either way, you're a pain in the—"

He coughed. "I believe an apology is in order. Sorry about what I said, but—"

"*Sorry, but* just doesn't work for me, Cord," Stacy snapped.

"You want it on a silver platter? Okay, I apologize for the insinuations made and will make accommodation for you to spend the night here," Cord said quietly.

Still Stacy didn't turn to face him. There were hot tears in her eyes as she felt his hands touch her shoulders and slowly turn her around to face him. With a gentleness she didn't expect, his large hand cupped her chin and raised it up so that he could see her face. His own expression was hidden by the shadow of his Stetson.

"I guess we're both a little tired and on edge," came the familiar deep voice. "Get a good night's rest." Cord heaved a sigh and gave her one last, long look and then he up and left.

She was conscious of a feeling of emptiness as the chill of night stole over her shoulders where a moment ago his hands had been. The anger had vanished, leaving Stacy staring off into the dark after him. Uncertainly, she turned back to the flickering campfire and the silhouetted figures of the ranch hands.

Jim Connors walked up to her from behind one of the trailers carrying a bedroll and a blanket. He must have heard it all—there wasn't a whole lot of privacy on a trail drive. Probably all the men had heard her and Cord.

His questioning eyes searched her face, but Stacy only accepted the bedding with a muttered thanks and stumbled over to the other side of the fire. Dully she watched some of the hands loading horses into vans and start pulling out. Without even wanting to, she looked among them for Cord and strained to hear the quiet conversation for the sound of his voice, but with no success.

She slipped into the bedroll and stared up into the dark blue sky, plagued by a variety of emotions—hurt, anger, humiliation, resentment, but most of all wonder and mystification about the unpredictable Cord Harris. It occurred to her that her dad would have liked him, probably would have said something about Cord being the real deal. It was easy to imagine them shaking hands and even agreeing that Stacy was, ha ha, certainly a handful . . . At last her tiredness hit her all over and, scarcely aware of the hard ground and rapidly dropping temperature, she drifted off to sleep.

* * *

She was sure she had just barely fallen asleep when a hand began gently shaking her shoulder. Her eyes fluttered open to a starlit sky. Stacy had difficulty focusing on the man beside her in so little light. At first she thought it was Cord, but then she recognized the smaller build of Jim Connors.

"It's time to get up."

"It's dark yet," she muttered, sleep heavy in her voice.

"It's four o'clock," the young cowboy answered lightly. "We rise extra early out here. Breakfast is almost ready. Better get washed up."

A moment later he was gone. Painfully Stacy struggled out of the bedroll, her muscles crying out for her not to move. It was all she could do to stand up. Stiffly she walked over to a basin of water warmed by the rekindled fire. She splashed the water on her face, enjoying the clean sensation it gave her skin. Awake now, she glanced around the camp with interest.

Everywhere there was activity. Horses and riders were walking along the outside of the camp and others were mumbling sleepily over their coffee and flapjacks. Over to the east, the sky was beginning to lighten with the coming dawn.

While she was eating the enormous breakfast Jim brought her, Stacy saw the remuda trucks coming in with a load of fresh horses for the day's work. Since Jim had already finished his breakfast, he offered to get her a mount for the morning. A few minutes later he returned, leading a big, rangy sorrel and a smaller pinto. Stacy finished off the last bite of breakfast and carried the plate and mug over to the station wagon. Several of the riders had already left when she returned to the waiting cowboy. Hank had joined him, mounted on his horse.

"Ready for another day, miss?" he asked, a grin spreading over his tanned face. Watching her slip her hat on, he added, "Now a real cowboy puts his hat on as soon as he gets up."

"I'm still learning." She laughed in return, taking the pinto's reins from Jim. "What's the agenda for the morning?"

"Gotta sweep the east side of the main herd for strays," he replied, swinging his pony in that direction.

A groan passed Stacy's lips as she mounted her horse. It was a mixture of dismay at the orders and the rebellion of her sore muscles at returning to the saddle.

"Is Cord joining the drive today?" she asked.

"Oh, he stayed up last night and took one of the watches," replied the older cowboy. "Imagine he's headin' the herd up now."

"Oh," Stacy murmured. The idea that Cord had spent the night in camp was oddly disquieting to her.

"It's a gorgeous morning," she exclaimed as her pony danced beside Jim's mount as if in emphasis of her words. The sun was climbing the sky now, chasing away the last vestiges of the night's shadows.

"It's spring," the young cowboy replied, capturing the enthusiasm of the pretty woman at his his side.

"And it's a beautiful country to be in in spring!" She laughed. "It makes you feel great just to be alive!"

"You really like it here—on the other side of Texas, I mean?"

"I love it," Stacy answered, not noting his qualifying words. "There's room to breathe. I mean, you feel free. No one's crowding you. It's hard to describe."

"I know," Jim replied, studying her face. "Let's ride over this way. I'd like to show you something."

"What is it?"

"You'll see," he said, looking ahead as they altered their course to the left. "What brought you here anyway?"

For a minute Stacy didn't answer, but there was something about the young man with the open face that made her want to confide in him.

"My father was killed in a plane crash several weeks ago," she answered softly. "We were very close. You see, my mother died a few months after I was born, so it was always just my father and me."

Jim looked at her quietly but didn't interrupt her.

"He was a freelance photographer, quite famous in his field. From almost the time I could walk he took me with him on his assignments. I was never in one place long enough to make any real friends. Oh, there were a few that I always got reacquainted with when we returned from one trip or another," Stacy added, her thoughts turning to Carter Mills, "but it really boiled down to him and me. Dad had chartered a plane to fly us to Washington after a trip into Tennessee. Over the mountains we developed engine trouble and crashed."

There was silence for a time while Stacy fought to control the lump in her throat. Staring in front of her, she began to speak again. "Cajun, my German shepherd, was along. I was knocked unconscious, but somehow he managed to pull me out of the plane and a little while later it burst into flames. My father was still inside."

"Your father was Joshua Adams," said Jim.

"Yes," she answered, a whispered hoarseness creeping into her voice. "Afterwards, I was confused. A lot of dad's friends and colleagues offered to help, but I didn't really know what they could do." A stilted laugh came from her lips. "He always loved the West. I guess I came out here for two reasons: to be close to him and to find what I wanted out of life."

"You've been here before?"

"Not here specifically, but Dad had assignments in El Paso several times and various other places in Arizona and

New Mexico," Stacy answered, then added with a laugh, "I really didn't expect to spend my time chasing cattle!"

Understanding that she was trying to shake off the sadness that talking about her father had brought to the surface, Jim Connors joined in with her laugh.

"No, I don't imagine you did. Hank and I were along with the boss when he found you that morning on the range."

"You were?"

"Cord was fit to be tied when he found your horse," Jim said, smiling at her. "He was the first one to spot your dog and reach you. None of us had ever seen him in such a state before. He was snapping orders around so fast that—well, in the end he wouldn't let anyone else near you but him."

"He was probably afraid I'd sue him for allowing that rattlesnake to be on his property," Stacy said ruefully, ignoring Jim's inquisitive glance.

"You two don't get along very well," Jim commented.

"It's not my fault. I think he just dislikes women in general."

"No, I don't believe that," the cowboy said with a dubious shake of his head. "After his engagement to Lydia, I don't believe he trusts women all that much anymore. Or maybe it's himself that he doesn't—"

"Whatever his problem is, it's not mine," Stacy said firmly.

"The place I wanted to show you is right over here," Jim said, turning his pony abruptly to the right toward a small hill. "I was in a lecture class where your father was a guest speaker. I think you'll appreciate this."

The two riders topped a small rise to view a meadow covered with a sea of blue flowers. They paused briefly on the hill as Stacy gazed awestruck at the beauty of the multiple blossoms waving brightly in the morning breeze. Mother Nature had covered the hill in a luxurious blanket of deep blue. In the distance they could hear the songs of birds bringing the earth alive on that hill.

"It's beautiful, Jim. What are they?" Stacy exclaimed at last.

"Bluebonnets."

"Such a beautiful blue, almost purple." Her gaze remained on the flowers. "They put the sky to shame."

"Shall we ride down?" he asked.

Stacy didn't answer, but touched the pinto's flank with her heel. Single file, they rode down the hill to the meadow, stopping in the middle of the indigo profusion. Jim dismounted before Stacy and helped her off her pony, ground-hitching both of them. His hand remained on her elbow as they walked companionably amongst the flowers. Stacy couldn't resist picking a small bouquet and inhaling the sweet fragrance.

"I'm so glad you brought me here," Stacy said, turning to face the young cowboy. She only had to raise her eyes a few inches to look into his hazel ones.

The hand that had been on her elbow slipped up to her shoulder, and the cowboy's other hand moved to rest on the opposite side. The bouquet held in Stacy's hands was the only thing separating them when they both heard the sound of an approaching horse. Simultaneously they turned when the hoof beats came closer. It only took Stacy an instant to recognize the rider sitting so straight in the saddle and the blood began pounding in her heart. Cord Harris reined his horse down the hill toward the couple, stopping just short of them.

"Am I interrupting something?" Not giving either one a chance to answer, he rested an arm on the saddle horn and said, "Then let's get back to work and save the flowers for off-duty hours."

Both Stacy and Jim mounted their ground-hitched

horses with a certain amount of chagrin, fully conscious of the accusing dark eyes. Once on their way again, the rancher nudged his horse between the pair as if separating two naughty children. Stacy's lips set into a tightly compressed line, resentful of the way Cord was treating them. He was unmindful of her displeasure. After they had left the meadow of bluebonnets, Cord turned his head slightly toward the silent cowboy riding on his left.

"I want you to ride back to the main herd and help Jenkins on the point, Connors. I'll accompany Stacy back to where Hank is holding some strays," ordered Cord in a tone that defied a negative answer.

The young cowboy reined his pony abruptly away from Stacy and his employer, dug his spurs into the horse's flank and was away at a gallop. Stacy glared at Cord.

"You had no right to reprimand him. It was as much my fault as it was his."

"I'm glad you see it that way. It's just what I was thinking too," Cord replied, an amused smile on his lips, but flashing fires in his eyes. "However, if it's any of your business, I was looking for him to tell him just that before I found him with you."

Stacy was more than a little taken back. She had naturally assumed that Cord was checking on Jim because of Jim's interest in her. She felt a flush of embarrassment heat her cheeks.

"But that doesn't mean I approve of you bewitching my men to such an extent that they forget to do their job."

"I don't know what you're talking about," Stacy muttered. *Bewitching?* She never would have expected him to say something so ridiculous.

"You surely don't expect me to believe you were looking for strays on foot in that field, do you?"

"No, I don't!" answered Stacy exasperatedly.

"Then there really isn't anything more to be said, is there?"

"Yes, there is! Cord, you don't have the right to tell me who I can be friends with."

"Listen up, Stacy. Right now you're working for me." There was a noticeable edge in his voice. "Meaning I have a say in what you do during those hours."

"So far it seems to be a twenty-four-hour-a-day job. Are you telling me I can't ever speak to Jim?"

"I'm telling you that you will not distract my men. I don't want them to get any romantic notions about you. Is that plain enough?" Cord flashed.

"Perfectly!" she retorted, and kicked her pinto into a canter.

Fuming, the two silent riders hadn't traveled very far from the meadow when they came in sight of the wizened cowboy driving half a dozen steers. With a wave of his hand toward Hank, Cord wheeled his horse away from the pinto and headed back across the range as Stacy fell in beside the wrangler.

Shortly before noon the small band joined up with the main herd. Stacy searched the riders around the main herd for some sign of Jim, but only caught a glimpse of Cord, which deterred her from looking more closely. She wasn't in the mood for another run-in with him. Quietly she followed old Hank to the encampment where they ate lunch and changed horses. Hot and tired, Stacy sat silently astride her horse in the noonday sun and waited for the veteran to join her. He ambled over to the ground-hitched pony beside Stacy and mounted.

"We'll be stayin' with the herd this afternoon," he stated. "The two of us will be ridin' the right flank."

Several times that afternoon Stacy caught sight of Jim but only once did he acknowledge her presence with a wave. Stacy felt guilty for possibly getting the young cowboy into trouble; she only hoped Jim wouldn't hold it against her. Of course he couldn't very well rush over when he saw her—after all, he was working. Twice, she found herself looking around for Cord Harris, but if he was taking part in the afternoon drive, he escaped Stacy's eyes. Instead of feeling relieved that he wasn't watching or participating, she felt empty.

At four o'clock the herd arrived at a stand of cottonwood trees that marked the course of a rushing stream. This was the night's encampment. They drove the cattle across the shallow water, bedding them down on the opposite side. As Stacy followed Hank back over, she looked wistfully at the swift-running water, longing for an opportunity to wash off some of the grit and grime.

All the hands had gathered around the cookwagon where the coffee was fresh and hot. Stacy and Hank dismounted at the remuda trailers and joined the others. By tomorrow morning the herd would reach the summer pasture and the drive would be over until fall. Stacy stood and sipped her coffee while listening to the boasting and grumbling of the veteran cowhands. Supper would be dished up soon and she wanted to go down to the stream before them. She finished the last of her coffee and handed the cup to the cook. None of the group paid any attention to her as she walked away toward the cottonwood trees.

Stacy strolled leisurely, following the little river uphill. Five hundred yards from camp where the stream widened around a bend, she stopped. This was the perfect place to bathe, far enough away from camp to ensure privacy and far enough upstream for the water not to be muddied by the cattle crossing. An obliging tree had a low-hanging branch on which she could hang her clothes. Happily she swept the brown hat off her head and pulled out the scrunchie holding her hair. Freed from confinement, the long chestnut hair fell caressingly around her shoulders as she sat down by the edge of the water to remove her dusty boots. Her toes wiggled happily on the coarse sand as she gazed blissfully at the beckoning water, sparkling with reflected sunlight. Stacy hopped to her feet and took one last look around to make sure there were no uninvited two-legged visitors before shedding her blouse and jeans.

Clad only in bra and panties, she waded into the water. A small shudder ran through her at the unexpected cool-ness of the stream. She hummed merrily as she rubbed away the dirt and grime of the drive. Carried away by her enjoyment, Stacy failed to hear the muffled sound of hooves in the sand. A horse and rider came to a halt beside the cottonwood where Stacy had hung her clothes.

Still humming her happy tune, Stacy entered the shal-lower water and began wading toward the bank. Glancing at the tree, she stopped in the now waist-deep water, stunned by the sudden appearance of the horse and rider. Her sur-prise was quickly replaced by self-consciousness. She wasn't wearing much and the water made her underwear see-through. Swiftly she lowered herself into the water.

"You could have had the decency to let me know you were there, Cord!"

"I missed you at camp and came looking for you," the deep voice replied, ignoring her embarrassment.

"Well, now you've found me, you can leave so I can get dressed."

"Don't be so huffy. I've seen women in their underwear before. No big deal."

She seethed inside at the last comment. Too bad he wasn't close enough to splash.

"I'll wait for you over there," Cord said, smiling as he indicated a group of trees where his view of her would be obstructed. Amusement was all too visible on his face as he reined his horse around and left.

Stacy clambered up on the bank, chagrin and resentment hampering her. Trying to dress quickly, she struggled to put the clothes on over her wet body. The sleeves of her blouse clung to the damp skin of her arms and with fumbling fingers she managed to get it buttoned and tucked into her Levis. The boots slipped on easily even over the damp socks. She removed her hat from the tree and began running toward the place where Cord waited.

He stood silent beside his horse, watching her push the branches this way and that to get to him. The haste with which she dressed and rushed to meet him had pinked her cheeks and made her brown eyes bright. Stacy stopped a few feet in front of Cord and hesitated. Her eyes searched his face, desperately trying to read his uncommunicative expression.

"Come on," he said, "I'll walk you back to camp."

A little breathless, she fell into step beside him as he led his horse in that direction. His composed face never once turned toward her as they walked in silence. The strain was too much for Stacy. With her free hand she ran her fingers nervously through her damp hair.

"I was hot and dusty from the drive." A hint of defiance was in her voice.

"The water certainly looked inviting," Cord commented, refusing to take the bait of the unvoiced challenge she had made. "To be honest, I was tempted to jump in there with you." He looked at her, his eyes traveling from the damp tendrils of her hair around her forehead down her straight nose and coming to a halt at her moist parted lips.

Stacy knew they were very close to camp now. In her side vision she could make out the moving forms of the cowhands. If they caught sight of her and Cord—well, they wouldn't say anything but they sure as hell would think it. So was she—basically, she was only aware of the broad shoulders and the strong face of the man beside her. He must have read the confusion and bewilderment in her gaze as she tried to fathom this change in his attitude toward her, for he abruptly released her arm and began their course once again for camp.

"I've never known a woman yet who could turn down a chance to freshen up," Cord teased. For some reason that she could not or would not acknowledge, Stacy felt safe with their accustomed game of mocking banter.

"I can't be a seductress if I go around smelling like a cow," she said, a new lift in her walk and swing to her head.

"You have a very good point," Cord agreed as they walked into the camp area. "Go grab yourself a bite to eat, girl. I'll see you later."

Stacy felt his hand touch her shoulder lightly as he moved away from her to the horse vans. The warmth of his touch radiated as she visualized the imprint of his hand on her shoulder. Not thinking of much else, she walked over to the others, conscious that her whole attention was now focused on the retreating figure of Cord. Throughout the meal, she involuntarily watched for him. When he failed to come she was depressed. Usually she dreaded his presence and here she was looking forward to it. What kind of man could make her want to be with him and dislike him at the same time? Only one. Cord Harris.

The cottonwood trees surrounding the camp hastened the darkening purple of the setting sun. Shadows had begun casting their black forms through the camp. The flickering fires seemed to grow increasingly brighter. On the other side of the flames she spotted her riding companion of her bluebonnet morning. Jim seemed to be looking for someone as he stood studying the various clusters of ranch hands and cowboys. Then he saw Stacy and made his way around the campfire to where she was sitting apart from the others.

The serious hazel eyes crinkled in a smile. "Hi. Been looking for you."

"Work hard today?" Stacy asked.

"Not too. I'm sorry I had to leave you in the lurch like that today," Jim said, squatting down beside her.

"Cord and I didn't come to blows, if that's what's worrying you." Stacy laughed. "I didn't mean to get you into trouble, Jim."

He took a deep breath and shook his head. "No, I wasn't. But—Stacy, I like you. You know that, don't you?" Jim asked in a low voice. When she failed to reply, he added, "Are you, um, seeing someone or anything like that?"

"No." Stacy avoided the head so near her own. She should have felt pleased by his honest affection, but she found herself regretting the turn the conversation had taken. "I like you too, Jim. You're a very good friend."

"That's the way I feel too," he replied. "I hope I'll be able to see a lot more of you."

"I hope so myself," Stacy said. "I've never had too many friends."

"Stacy . . ." A callused but very gentle hand raised itself and the fingers caressed her smooth cheek, "you're really something. I bet you could turn a man down and make him feel happy about it!"

Chapter 8

"Connors!" snapped a very male voice.

With a guilty start, Stacy and Jim separated as Cord stepped out of the shadows. Part of his face was still hidden by the darkness, but there was no doubting the tightly controlled emotion in the set of his jaw and the furrow in his brow. His dark eyes narrowed as he stared at the young cowboy.

"You have a unique talent for turning up when you're not expected," Stacy said accusingly, not liking his dictatorial manner.

"Obviously." Cord's penetrating gaze flicked briefly to Stacy and returned to Jim.

"Well?" he demanded.

"I have nothing to say, sir," Jim answered, his chin jutting out as he met the stern gaze of his boss.

Stacy could feel the resentment burning inside her. The way that Cord was treating Jim in front of her was just too much. The young cowboy was being taken down a peg—several pegs. Why? And why should it concern Cord that she had been talking to Jim?

Jim regarded Stacy silently. Finally he said an awkward

good-night to her and walked away. Furious at Cord, Stacy turned to face him, her brown eyes glowing with righteous wrath.

"Just who do you think you are, Cord?" she cried. "Do you get a big thrill out of constantly bossing everyone around? It's just plain wrong the way they all defer to you."

"All but one."

"That's right, Mr. Big Shot. I don't and I won't. But you still haven't answered my question."

"I don't see where it's any concern of yours what my reasons are," said Cord, his voice still fierce with controlled emotion.

"Typical of you," Stacy said vehemently. "You consider yourself a law unto yourself, responsible to no one. Well, you're not my boss when it comes to my—my friends."

"Friends or lovers?"

"Oh, please." She shot him a disgusted look. "But if you think you've succeeded somehow by making Jim feel small, you didn't. Yeah, he's younger but he's more of a man than you are, that's for damn sure."

"Is that right," was all Cord said.

"Yes! And deep down inside you probably know it—"

"Stacy, don't tell me what I know. You don't have a clue," Cord retorted, a muscle in his jaw twitching.

"Whatever. But I don't like what I know about you, Cord Harris—in fact, I dare you to show me one thing that's worth liking—*hey!*"

The thread of his self-control snapped. He grabbed Stacy's arms and drew her close to him as she struggled uselessly against his muscular chest. He was much too strong for her. As one large hand curved around her waist, the other cupped her head until she had to look into his face. She stared into the coal-black eyes, almost hypnotized by the intensity of his gaze.

"I've been told I can kiss like no one else," he said softly. "Want to find out if it's true?"

Heaven help me, she thought wildly. *I actually do.*

"Yes or no?"

She nodded, an almost imperceptible motion. His arm tightened around her and his face lowered to hers. He claimed her lips in a searing kiss that kindled a fire of passion in her body. Sensual and consuming, it went on and on—the throbbing of her heart seemed to echo in her ears. When Stacy felt he would never let her go, Cord stepped away. The suddenness of his release jolted her off balance and she fell to the ground.

He extended a hand to help her up. An ordinary gesture and a thoughtful one—but somehow it made her realize that she was vulnerable where he was concerned. She smacked his hand away.

Cord only shrugged. "Suit yourself. Can't say I wasn't a gentleman."

"You're not, you never were, and you never will be any such thing," she flashed, scrambling to her feet and dusting off her butt. What an ignominious end to a glorious—she almost didn't want to admit it, but it was true—glorious kiss. Even so, she wasn't going to put herself in that position again. A kiss *was* only a kiss.

"Oh, well." He didn't seem to even care that she'd as good as said outright she despised him. There was no sign of softening in Cord's eyes. As he stood there, he silently searched her face—for what, Stacy didn't know.

"Hell." Cord finally sighed. "Come on, we'd better join the others."

"Is that all you've got to say?"

"Yeah. That's all. What were you expecting, a heartfelt avowal of love? How about a moonlight serenade to go along with it?"

His caustic words stung like a slap.

"You make me sick, Cord. If that's how you talk to women, it's no wonder you got kicked to the curb."

Cord's impassive face turned to stone at her reply and his eyes bored deep inside her. Uncomfortably aware that she'd trespassed onto well-guarded territory, Stacy hung her head for a second, then looked at him again.

"I don't know what you heard about Lydia and me, but whatever it was, that's none of your business," his cold, hard voice replied. "I think we should both consider the subject closed."

Stacy couldn't speak. The soul-shattering kiss seemed to have opened up a gulf between them, not brought them closer together—not in any way other than physical. She didn't know what to think.

Bewildered, she offered no resistance when Cord took her arm and guided her back to the campfire. Several times she stumbled on the uneven ground, but he never hesitated in his stride. Nor did he even glance her way—only the hand on her arm verified that he acknowledged her existence.

When they reached the campfire he released her and walked on into the circle without her. Grateful to be away from him, Stacy slipped over to her bedroll, praying no one would speak to her or see her tear-rimmed eyes in the glowing firelight. Hiccupping silent sobs, she crawled into her covers. Trying not to remember the extraordinary feeling of being held so close by him, she snuggled inside the warm cocoon for comfort, but it was no use. Her body and mind retained a vivid memory of the strength of his arms, and the fire in his kiss. Stacy rubbed her lips with the back of her hand, but the sensation was indelible. It took a while for sleep to blot it out.

* * *

The morning sun shone brightly down on Stacy astride the little bay horse she'd ridden the first day. She took no interest in the surrounding country as she rode along the flank of the herd. Listless, she slouched in the saddle and let her gaze blur in the multitude of cattle.

Last night in her dreams she had relived Cord's embrace, but this time it was filled with passion and desire. The dream was more disquieting than the actual kiss. Afterward she had clung to him, driven by a desperate feeling that he would reject her. She felt she'd somehow betrayed herself in that dream. She hated Cord Harris and everything he stood for. The shame and guilt she felt for the imagined kiss far exceeded the strange emotions the actual kiss had filled her with the night before.

The pounding of approaching hooves snapped her out of her brooding thoughts. Looking up, Stacy saw Jim Connors astride the galloping horse. He waved and rode by to pull up beside Hank. The men exchanged a few words in low voices, making Stacy feel uncomfortably warm as she wondered if they were discussing her. If it had been one of the other days, she would've dropped back to join them, but she was afraid to face them. Stacy knew the fear they would read in her face regarding the events of the night before. It was irrational, but she couldn't dismiss it. A few minutes later Hank rode up beside her.

"We'll be reachin' the pasture in the hour," said Hank. "The boss told Jim this morning that as soon as we get to the summer pasture you were to go back to the ranch house."

"Why? Did he say?" Stacy asked, dreading the prospect of seeing Cord again.

"Nope. One of the hands will be there with a pickup and you'll ride back with him. And the boss wants you to go to his office as soon as you get there," Hank replied. He looked thoughtfully at her. "You had another go-round with him last night, didn't ya?"

Stacy started to deny it, but knew she couldn't fool the sharp-eyed old cowhand and nodded affirmatively.

"You two do rub each other's fur the wrong way." He smiled with a shake of his head. "Jim said the boss come up on you two last night."

"I suppose he jumped all over Jim this morning," Stacy remarked bitterly.

"Jim figured he would, but he didn't say a word about it. In fact, he even put Jim in charge of one of the brandin' crews." Hank waited for her reaction.

"He did?" The amazement was written on her face. Probably his way of apologizing, she reasoned to herself.

"I imagine you'll think I'm an ole gossip, but are you sweet on Jim or somethin'?"

"No," said Stacy, a hint of a smile appearing on her face. "We're friends. He knew my father a little—they met at one of my dad's lectures."

"Good." The old cowboy grinned with a satisfied gleam in his eyes.

The one-word response startled her. "Good? Why?"

"You ain't Jim's type. You need someone stronger to hold you in check. Fire and fire always makes a bigger flame."

"I didn't know you mixed matchmaking with philosophy, Hank." She laughed. "Tell me, do you have someone in mind?"

"I do but I ain't tellin'. You'll know soon enough," Hank answered mysteriously. Kicking his horse, he added over the din, "Better get back to work."

Smiling, Stacy joined him, the gloom of the morning fading in the wake of the sagacious cowboy. When the last steer had been chased through, Hank motioned toward a waiting pickup, indicating that it was the one Stacy would be taking back to the ranch house.

She rode over to the remuda trailer and dismounted. Dodging the milling horses and riders, she made her way to the truck. The driver opened the door for her and motioned her inside. Stacy exchanged a few pleasantries with him, but the growing anticipation of meeting Cord after last night's kiss gradually silenced her. Her imagination had all sorts of reasons for him wanting to talk to her. If she was lucky he might want to put an end to the bargain they had made.

Driving into the yard, Stacy noticed an unfamiliar gold Cadillac parked in front of the hacienda. Even though she wasn't familiar with all the vehicles of the surrounding neighbors, she was sure she'd never seen a car like that around here in her short stay. An odd sense of foreboding filled her as the pickup stopped at the house gates to let her out.

Tired and nervous, Stacy walked with her bedroll and hat in one hand and suede jacket in the other. As she opened the door she wished she had a chance to clean up and change before meeting the formidable Cord Harris, but knew that he expected her as soon as she arrived. Resentment flared briefly within her as she realized that he wanted her at a disadvantage. How could she seem to be in control if she looked like a dirty urchin?

Stepping inside the cool interior of the entryway, she became aware of voices in the den. Uncertainly she stopped before the closed door and tried to recognize them, but the thick oak door muffled the sounds.

Maybe he was busy and didn't want to see her now. Fine with her—but then she thought she might as well get it over with. Resigned, she placed the things in her hands on the bench outside the room, gave a few brisk brushes at the dust on her jeans and blouse, smoothed her long hair back to where it was caught at the neck, squared her shoulders and knocked at the door.

"Come in," was the muffled reply.

With more confidence than she felt, Stacy opened the heavy door and walked into the room. Cord stood directly in front of her beside his desk. There was a nonchalance and ease in his carriage that intensified her nervousness.

"Come on in. All the way," Cord instructed with a slightly imperious wave of his hand. His eyes flicked over her disheveled clothes and he added, "I see you just got here."

"I understood you wanted to see me right away," Stacy said defensively, looking him in the eye. "If you're busy, I can come back later."

"No, that won't be necessary." His gaze left her to light casually on the tall-backed chair in front of the desk. "You don't mind waiting a few minutes, do you?"

For the first time Stacy looked around the room, remembering the second voice she'd heard outside. Intent on meeting Cord, Stacy had momentarily forgotten her curiosity about the owner of the Cadillac outside. A movement in the chair got her attention.

The oversized leather chair with its back to Stacy had hidden its occupant from her view. Now she saw the slender legs in high heels and the polished nails of a feminine hand. As the graceful figure rose from the chair, Stacy felt the quiver of a premonition flow through her. The woman was strikingly beautiful. Her hair was jet black and drawn away from her face in a chignon, emphasizing her high cheekbones and creamy skin. Her eyes, as they took in Stacy, were as black as her hair and sparkled with a subdued fire. She was several inches taller than Stacy and managed to give the impression that she was looking down that graceful nose at her. The other woman seemed faintly pleased, if anything, at Stacy's bedraggled appearance.

"You are going to introduce us, aren't you, Cord?" the strange woman asked in a clear, melodic voice.

"Of course," he replied, his eyes never straying from Stacy's blushing face. "Lydia, this is Stacy Adams. She's been helping me around the ranch here, as you probably can tell. Stacy, this is Lydia Marshall, a very old friend of mine."

Not old. And not a friend, either. Stacy murmured an incoherent hello. So this was the woman Cord had been engaged to. Not sure why Lydia had appeared at the ranch, she flashed a questioning look at Cord. His face was imperturbable. The gleam in his eyes that she'd attributed to her untidy appearance held something more. Maybe they were back together again, but what about Lydia's husband? A thousand questions raced through Stacy's mind as she tried to concentrate on the conversation between the two, but the only thing that remained implanted in her mind after Lydia left the room was the silky voice of the dark-haired woman.

Stacy stared at the closed oak door trying desperately to calm the sinking feeling in her heart.

"I said would you like to sit down, Stacy?" the deep voice repeated in a slightly louder tone.

"Of course—I'm sorry," Stacy mumbled, embarrassed by her inattention. She walked over and sat in one of the straight-backed chairs beside the desk. Cord had already seated himself behind it and was shuffling through a few papers.

"She's really beautiful. Did her husband come with her?" Stacy blurted out before she realized it.

"No," Cord replied. Even the one word conveyed satisfaction. But why? Stacy braced herself. "It seems Lydia is getting a divorce."

"Oh," Stacy said in a very small voice. Okay. That happened—a lot. Why did it upset her that Cord and Lydia were obviously getting back together?

"Now to get at the reason I called you in here," he started briskly. "It's quite clear that our previous arrangement isn't going to work, at least not the way I planned."

"I'm still willing to write you a check for any of the damage my horse caused," she volunteered, perching on the edge of her chair. "I get it—you'd like to get rid of me now. Believe me, Cord, the feeling is mutual."

"Don't jump to conclusions," he said, raising one eyebrow. "I still think you should work your debt out. What's obvious is that you can't take the place of one of the men or even half of one. Therefore I propose that you tackle something easier than chasing uncooperative cattle."

"I don't understand."

"As I mentioned once before, each spring I have an auction where I sell some of my registered quarter horse stock, Texas-style. That means a barbecue and a party." Cord smiled as he watched the dawning comprehension on Stacy's face. "You don't like to be told what to do, so I'm guessing that makes you pretty good at telling everybody else what to do. I'm sure you'll be able to organize this year's activity, which will leave me free to take care of the ranch."

"What?"

Cord let his gaze linger on the grubbiest parts of her. "'Course, you will have to take a shower. Swimming in the creek got the worst of the mud off you, but I expect you to look presentable for this gig."

"Okay. I clean up pretty good." Stacy decided to take the challenge he was not so subtly handing her. She was not only going to take a shower, she was going to transform herself into a certified knockout.

Lydia had the corner on smooth and sophisticated, of course. Stacy was going to go for cowgirl chic in tight jeans.

"How many people will be here?" Stacy asked. "When is it going to be?"

"Before the day's over, I imagine, oh, several hundred people will attend. The date is set for June the ninth, almost four weeks away," he answered, studying her face again. "Now, if you think it might be too much for you—"

"Not at all," Stacy said defensively. "But I have to admit I'm curious why you didn't ask Lydia to act as hostess for you."

"That's none of your business. I've already said that I wanted you to work off the debt and this seemed like an easier alternative." His voice had grown cold at her mention of Lydia, she noticed.

"Anyway," he continued, "Lydia's having a time of it and I can't ask her to put together a shindig like this, considering the pressure she's under. And it would be—not exactly proper for Lydia to work for me right now. Maybe you're too young to understand why."

Stacy wanted to smack him. "No, Cord, I actually get it. I'm not that incredibly naïve."

"Glad to hear it."

"But I didn't realize that other people's opinions bothered you." The masterly way he was protecting his former fiancée grated on Stacy.

Cord only shrugged. "I generally don't. But where you're concerned—"

"If you're making some subtle reference to me, just speak your mind," Stacy said crossly. "You seem to have the ridiculous idea that I go ga-ga over every man I talk to. So . . . let's see. That would link me romantically to Hank, despite a, what, forty-five year age difference? And—"

"Spare me the sarcasm, okay?" Cord said in a dangerously

low voice. "I don't care who you talk to. And if you're referring to anything that happened last night, it's best forgotten. Most women would have the sense not to take a single kiss so seriously."

"I don't happen to be most women!" Stacy retorted, rising agitatedly from her seat to clasp the back of it with her hands. "Evidently you want me to forget it."

"Actually, I don't care if you do or you don't. Unless you want a repeat performance."

"That's the last thing I would ever want from you!" Guilt flooded her as she remembered her response to his kiss in her dream.

"Let's drop it," he said, turning his attention to the laptop in front of him. She'd been out here in the sticks so long the thing hadn't registered with her. He pulled up a screen and moved the laptop so she could see what he was working on. "Here are some of the arrangements already made for the sale. Get familiar with everything. The user name is Cord, and the password is cowcatcher."

She was taken aback that he trusted her enough to tell her the password. Cowcatcher, huh? That was . . . pretty catchy. He did have a sense of humor underneath it all.

"You can use this den. I won't bother you since I do my paperwork in the office and have another computer there. Most likely you'll want to go over the details with me at some point. Let me know." He looked at her calmly. "I believe that's all."

His cool tone of dismissal froze the angry words in Stacy's throat. She stood by the chair for a moment, but he was looking into the laptop.

She turned on her booted heel and strode out of the room, giving the heavy oak door an added impetus, otherwise known as a hard bang, as it closed. Gathering her things in the foyer, she stalked up the stairs to her room, where she flung her bundle down on the floor and stared at her glowering reflection.

An hour later, as Stacy was walking out of the bathroom after showering and changing her clothes, she met Cord in the hallway.

"I forgot to give you the keys to your car," Cord said. "It's in the garage." His dark eyes taking in the freshness of her appearance and, she noted with silent satisfaction, her tight jeans and fitted top.

"I had one of the men bring it over from the cabin," he was saying. "You'll need it."

"I thought it was already here," Stacy said. "I didn't think to ask." She tapped her head where the lump from her fall off the horse had finally gone away. "I took quite a whack, remember?"

"Yes. I do."

She couldn't resist. "I think it explains a lot of things."

"Such as?"

What could she say? *Like why I find you so sexy, for one,* she thought. *Despite your all-around obnoxiousness.* "How thoughtful of you," was what she said.

"I also had a printer installed in the den. I assume you know how to hook up a laptop—"

"If not, I'll ask your computer cowboy for help. I assume you have one."

Cord's mouth twisted in a smile he didn't seem to want to make. "You can ask me. I believe that covers everything you need."

"I'm sure it does." She started to brush past him. But his muscular arm shot out and blocked her passage. Stacy's flashing eyes looked up at the darkening face.

"You don't have to give me that bratty look," Cord said. "Unless you want a spanking."

"Shut up, Cord. And spare *me* the innuendoes." She didn't flinch under his penetrating gaze. "Now, get out of my way and let me by."

Seething inwardly, she pushed his arm out of her way and walked fast down the stairs. At the bottom of the steps stood Lydia Marshall, her dark eyes icy cold as she watched Stacy walk past her. The coldness vanished as Cord made his way down the steps behind Stacy.

"There you are!" said Lydia in a saccharine-sweet voice. "I was beginning to wonder if you'd forgotten me. I fixed us a drink. I hope I've remembered how you like them."

Lydia's voice was effective man-bait, but Stacy didn't wait around to hear Cord's reply. Hurrying into the den, Stacy leaned against the closed door and waited for the pounding in her heart to return to normal. Why did only Cord arouse her this way? The most ordinary interaction with him and things got a little out of control.

He never acted the same way twice to her. Sometimes he was teasing and friendly, as when he'd found her dipping in the creek, and sometimes he was warm and sexy—oh, that kiss! And then . . . sometimes he was proud and cold. Today he was making sure she knew where her place was.

Which undoubtedly had to do with Lydia, his ex-fiancée. As far as Stacy was concerned at the moment, he deserved to get worked over by someone who appeared to be a world-class bitch. Oh, how Stacy wished right now for the steadiness of Carter Mills. She was growing extremely tired of turning herself into a barometer that only registered Cord's emotions.

Discouraged and weary from the last three days of riding, she crossed over behind the desk and flipped open the laptop, entering the user name and password, then settling into a chair as it booted up.

She told herself not to forget the Eleventh Commandment: *thou shalt not check the browser history of others.* But even with that in mind, it was clear that the laptop was used for ranch business and nothing but ranch business. Absently she pulled up folder after folder relating to past cattle auctions and looked through them, then opened up a file labeled Party Planning until all its details began to sink in.

Help me. Feeling a little overwhelmed by the magnitude of the task he'd assigned her, she sunk lower in the swivel chair and went over the details once more. If he hadn't been so snotty, she would have explained that she'd never even given a dinner party in her life. What was she going to do now? The memory of his mocking smile flitted in front of her as she saw herself trying to explain that to him.

Oh, how he'd love it, Stacy thought. It would probably even amuse him to see her screw it up. Well, that wasn't going to happen. She'd have to work a lot harder than she thought, but if she was lucky, he'd never see the few mistakes she'd make.

With renewed confidence, Stacy tapped out a to-do list as she began to sort out a plan in her mind.

Chapter 9

The red sorrel tossed his flaxen mane in the air and snorted his displeasure at the firm hand curbing his pace.

"Easy, Diablo," Stacy quieted him, but he continued to pull at the bit.

Maybe a good gallop would release some of her tension, Stacy thought. The quarrel she'd had with Cord earlier that afternoon had taken its toll on her patience. Two weeks had passed since he had put her in charge of the sale festivities. The coordination of all the various elements was a full-time job and a real pain for someone who'd never done it before, despite the assistance from the wives of the permanent hands. Stacy had been pleased with the job she'd done so far. She also had the feeling that Cord was satisfied with her work.

Not that it really mattered what his opinion was, she told herself. But this afternoon when she was going over letters and e-mails with him about the preparation of the auction itself, Cord had asked her for the printer's proof of the sales catalog. Stacy knew nothing about it and had to confess as much.

She could still see the expression on his face when

he heard her admit it. She burned at the memory of his disapproval. If only she'd been able to explain her inexperience—well, it wouldn't have mattered. The man was so callous he couldn't possibly possess anything that remotely resembled a heart.

Cord had been gone almost every day since the initial meeting when he'd turned the preparations over to her. Sometimes, he took time to confer with her during the day but their talk was limited to the auction. Stacy didn't know if the ranch work was pressing or if he was merely avoiding spending too much time with her.

Lydia breezed in several times looking for him, occasionally condescending to ask about Stacy's whereabouts. Stacy was pretty sure he was advising her on the technicalities of her divorce, although what qualified him to do that, she didn't know. But Lydia hung all over him no matter what. Usually she found him somewhere, since Stacy often saw them from her window, Cord's head bent low to catch some confiding remark the raven-haired woman made, her arm resting possessively on his.

Stacy normally turned away, feeling as guilty as if she'd been caught in the act of eavesdropping, even though she couldn't hear a word they said. Other times she watched until they were out of sight before returning to work feeling oddly depressed.

She was positive that Cord's continued absence in the evenings was because of Lydia. Strangely enough Stacy found herself either missing him or dreading his arrival. She really didn't want to get into the reasons for her conflicting emotions.

Several evenings, Jim Connors had joined her on the veranda and they'd chatted away, discovering many common interests. Stacy enjoyed the easy companionship of the young cowboy with his ready laughter and undemanding company. It was a vast difference from her tempestuous relationship with Cord Harris.

With Jim she felt comfortable and relaxed, not worrying about every little word she said and how he was going to interpret it. The friendly feeling she got with Jim reminded her of the way she'd relied on Carter Mills.

Carter. Now there was someone who seemed very far away. Had it only been a short time ago that she'd been with him? His last e-mail had been fun to read, mostly news of mutual acquaintances. But it also held an undercurrent of concern that Stacy couldn't ignore. She knew he was waiting for an answer from her, one she couldn't give. Just recalling exactly what Carter looked like wasn't a snap—all she could summon up was a blurred image of short, sandy hair and basic blue eyes, an image so unclear that it could have been Jim she was picturing and not Carter.

Maybe the resemblance between the two was the reason she was so drawn to Jim. Stacy really couldn't say. But she had no desire to think on it. She probably would have been better off if she had never come out here, but then she never would've fallen in love with this wild, rugged part of Texas. Even in her present circumstances, Stacy enjoyed the demands of the unforgiving but uncommonly beautiful country. No overcrowding, no smog, and no endless blare of traffic. Instead, there was open space, fresh air, and enough room for all God's creatures.

With a glance at the sinking sun, Stacy remounted the rested horse and turned him toward the ranch house. Her wandering thoughts were brought up short by the knowledge that she had to return before the sun was too far down.

All too quickly they reached the stables. Stacy dismounted and led the sorrel through the fence gate to the stable area. Humming contentedly, she didn't hear Hank come up.

"You sure are mighty cheerful," Hank said behind her.

The sudden voice startled her. "Hank! You shouldn't do that!" she scolded him with a shaky laugh. "You practically scared me out of my boots!"

"You looked so happy and contented, I had to say something. Sorry." He grinned. "Didn't mean to make such a pretty girl jump like that."

"You did too. That sounds like Texas bull to me," she teased, a sparkle lighting up her brown eyes.

"Pshaw! Ain't nothin' wrong with tellin' a girl she's pretty when all she has to do is look in the mirror an' see."

Warmed by the affection of the gnarled man beside her and the caressing rays of the fiery sun, Stacy had a tremendous urge to spread her arms and envelop the great, untamed land that had captured her so completely. Instead she raised her face to the gentle breeze and inhaled the fragrance it carried.

"I love this place!" she exclaimed, ending in a regretful sigh. "I'm going to hate leaving all this behind."

"I thought you didn't like it here," Hank commented, turning his head away to hide the twinkle in his eye.

"I've never seen anything like it. At times it's so harsh and desolate, but the beauty is still there. No, Hank, I don't like it. I love it."

"Humph! If you're so fond of this place, why leave? Why don't you just move right around here somewhere?"

"It wouldn't be the same," Stacy replied with a gentle shake of her chestnut hair.

"What's so special about the Circle H?"

"It's a hundred different things. The sun wouldn't set quite the same. The hills wouldn't be the same color," she explained hesitantly.

"The sun sets the same anywhere," Hank snorted. Then

he turned to her rapturous face, not even trying to hide the gleam in his eyes and added, "What about the boss?"

"What do you mean?" Stacy knew he meant the boss with a capital B—Cord Harris.

"Ain't he a part of all this?"

"Of course not! He's—"

"He's the only reason why you're wantin' to stay here at all." Hank grinned, hurrying on before Stacy could voice the protest forming on her lips. "Quit kiddin' yourself that you're only here to work out the trouble your horse caused."

"Cord won't let me go," Stacy cried.

"You won't let yourself go," Hank answered. "Face it, girl, the only hold he has on you is your heart. You love him. I've known it for a long time."

"No," Stacy said weakly as the gruff words sank in.

"Reckon it's about time the cat was let out of the bag. If you got any guts at all, you'll admit it to yourself."

Hank tipped his hat to her and retreated. Stacy stood there, speechless.

In love with Cord Harris? Impossible. In fact, he was the most impossible man she'd ever known. What she felt for him would be better described as . . . okay, *hate* was too strong. But *dislike* was too tame.

Memories came back to her—the racing of her pulse when he entered a room, the annoying effect of his mocking smile, the way she blushed sometimes when he caught her looking at him . . . Stacy groaned, remembering the black hair with wayward locks that fell onto his forehead and the dark, flashing eyes that had seemed about to consume her with their fire. And that face—the finely chiseled cheekbones with a shadow of beard, the mouth that kissed hers with such sensual skill and all the time she spent daydreaming about being in his arms, seeking him, wanting him . . .

Impatiently the stallion turned and whickered to her.

She led him to his corral, stumbling several times, unable to focus on anything but the vivid picture of Cord etched in her mind. Hank was right. Never argue with an old cowboy.

It *was* love.

As she set the sorrel free in his paddock, Stacy allowed the realization to wash over her. How could she have been so blind as to not have figured it out by herself?

A feeling of elation filled her as she walked to the hacienda. A flush filled her cheeks, a glow lit her brown eyes, and a smile spread across her face with the warming knowledge of her discovery. Maybe you had to get away, far away, to figure out where you were supposed to be all along. She'd never found that place in her young life. Or that man. But now—

Stacy Adams loved Cord Harris. She wanted to shout it to the world, carve it in a tree, jump for joy—breathlessly she threw open the heavy oak door and rushed into the silent hall.

The emptiness stopped her. He wasn't here. He had left with Lydia this afternoon after Stacy had quarreled with him. A sense of utter loneliness swept over her. How could she have forgotten about Lydia?

The divorcée had picked a fine time to return to Cord and accept the love he'd once laid at her feet. It was Lydia he cared for, not her.

Get hold of yourself, she scolded, fighting the self-pity that seemed about to swallow her. *Your father didn't raise a quitter.*

If Cord thought she was a reckless girl without an ounce of sense, he was wrong. And she would have to show him before it was too late that he was wrong. The least she could do was fight for him, and give that raven-haired witch a run for her money.

With steely determination, Stacy set aside her doubts. First things first: she had to wash off the dust from her ride and then she'd dress for dinner. Tonight she'd wear her backless jersey dress. It did amazing things for her.

A spark of combat gleamed in her eyes as she undressed swiftly and got under the refreshing spray of the shower. She thought of an exercise in mental focus a friend of her father's had taught her. It was simple enough: name it, claim it.

"Cord," she said aloud. She let the name roll lovingly from her lips. It had the sound of a real man, the tensile strength of a whip cracking overhead. The rugged land of Texas had bred him, and he was more than a match for its harsh terrain—he could conquer it. Remembering the strength of his hands, the steel of his arms and the solidness of his broad shoulders, she felt a wave of passion surge over her. If only she could look into his dark eyes and see a desire and a love for her there . . .

By the time she had stepped out of the shower, she was giddy with renewed feelings for him. Briskly she rubbed the rough terry towel over her body. Sighing happily to herself, she returned to the bedroom where she proceeded to dress with much more care than ever in her life.

Finished, she stood before the large dresser mirror inspecting her reflection with a critical eye. The brilliant blues and greens of the dress set off the light golden tan of her arms and the delicate sun streaks in her hair. Giving herself a final once-over, she winked at her reflection and left the room.

Her heart fluttered as she descended the stairs, and she stood up straighter and walked slower to counteract it. Maria was setting the table in the dining room. Stacy's confidence took a little dive when she saw only one place setting. She almost asked Maria when Cord was expected home, but pride wouldn't let her concede the possibility that he wouldn't be returning early. Her questions to that effect on previous evenings had always been met with a negative answer and she couldn't bear to hear one tonight.

"*Ay, señorita*, you look lovely tonight," Maria said with her usual wide smile. "You have a date with Jim, maybe?"

"No." Stacy smiled as she tried to steel herself against her growing nervousness.

She seated herself at the empty table but only picked at the dishes set in front of her. The anticipation that consumed her didn't leave any room for food even though she tried valiantly to show an interest in the fruit salads and cold cuts that Maria had set out. Finally, after taking a few bites of a pineapple confection for several minutes and not tasting a bit of it, Stacy pushed herself away from the table. It was no use. The tension and apprehension of waiting had stolen her appetite. She was just too excited to eat. She got up and began pacing by the table.

"Do you not feel well?" Maria asked, standing in the doorway of the dining room.

"It was really a very good meal, Maria. I just don't have any appetite," Stacy apologized, not wishing to hurt her feelings.

Maria seemed to accept Stacy's explanation and began clearing away the dishes. Stacy watched for a minute, trying to summon the courage to ask Maria if she knew where Cord was.

"Perhaps you would like coffee outside and not in here."

"Yes, that would be nice," Stacy murmured absently. She started to walk from the room, then stopped and in a nonchalant voice asked, "Do you expect Cord home early tonight?"

"Oh, no. He went to a cattlemen's dinner. He will be late." Maria bustled off to the kitchen.

Dejectedly Stacy walked through the living room to the large glass doors that led on to the veranda. Her high hopes had dissolved by the time she slid the glass doors open and stood outside.

Loneliness washed over her. Restlessly Stacy went farther out and leaned against a pillar supporting the balcony above. She struggled against the swift change in her mood, looking out at the pool that shimmered darkly in the dim light, a hint of ominousness in its depths. She gazed in the direction of the family cemetery on the gentle rise above the house, hidden from direct view by the adobe walls.

Silently she whispered a prayer to Dona Elena, Cord's grandmother. If she understood how much Stacy loved this country and her grandson, maybe her ghost would intervene on Stacy's behalf.

But no. That only happened in dreams. Wishing Cord by her side didn't mean it was going to happen.

Stacy heard the sound of steps on the patio. Assuming it to be Maria with her coffee, she remained leaning against the pillar, not wanting the housekeeper to guess how upset she was.

"Just put the coffee on the table, Maria. Thanks. I'll serve myself in a minute." Stacy's voice was low and emotional.

"The coffee's already here. You don't mind if I help myself before it gets cold, do you?" came the reply.

"Cord," she whispered faintly. For a moment, she was afraid her legs wouldn't hold her. In that brief moment he rushed to her side.

"Stacy, are you okay?" His hands seized her shoulders.

"Yes, yes, I'm fine. You startled me," Stacy replied shakily, refusing to look into the dark eyes for fear they would see the love in hers. Wasn't her generation supposed to be casual about all that? She wasn't. She couldn't be.

"For a minute there I thought you were going to faint. You're so pale. Are you sure you feel all right?"

His concern and his nearness combined to overwhelm her. She was so conscious of the black elegance of his cattleman's formal suit, and his face just inches from hers, that she couldn't look up. She couldn't let him see what he was doing to her. Her eyes concentrated on his left hand, the strong fingers, the dark, curling hairs peeping out from the cuff of his shirt.

"Don't!" Her body threatened to sway against the massive chest that was so close.

"I'm sorry," Cord said, moving away from her, a briskness returning to his voice. Stacy glanced up but his eyes were hidden in the night's shadows and she was unable to determine his reaction. Did he think she was a total city girl, afraid of the dark?

"I didn't realize I was holding you so tightly," he finished.

Stacy got hold of herself. She couldn't act like a schoolgirl. After all, this was what she wanted, a chance to be alone with him. The trouble was . . . hard to say what it was, exactly. It ought to be easy to tell him she loved him.

"Let's get some light out here. It's getting dark." Cord took a long match from a metal container on the table, and struck it, lighting a tall pillar candle in a shaft of glass. The sudden flare of the little flame illuminated the rough features of Cord's face, outlining the tired lines around his mouth.

"Maria said you wouldn't be back until later. So how was the cattlemen's dinner? Did you eat?" she asked, trying to keep her emotions from showing in her voice.

"Yes."

"Are those dinners usually over this early?" Stacy asked, desperately trying to keep the conversation going, hoping he wouldn't notice her nervousness.

"No, it was still going on when you I left." His reply was abrupt and gave Stacy the impression that he didn't feel like talking.

"I guess you must be tired. Would you rather I left so you could relax?" she suggested, willing the pain to leave her heart.

"You're awfully polite tonight," Cord replied, an eyebrow raised quizzically in her direction. "Yes, I am tired, but no, you don't need to leave. I'll take a cup of coffee, though."

Without replying Stacy walked over to the table. As she stood bathed in the light from the living room, Cord's low voice carried to her. "You look great in that dress."

"Thank you," she murmured, trying not to get foolishly excited over a minor compliment.

"Were you expecting company tonight?" His voice had changed from a more or less indifferent tone to the familiar mocking one.

"No," Stacy said too swiftly, hoping she didn't sound as embarrassed as she felt. The only person she'd wanted to see was him, but she didn't necessarily want him to think that. "I just felt like being feminine."

Cord walked over into the light. She handed him his coffee, her dark eyes flicking up to meet his.

"I was hoping you'd be up," Cord said, moving out of the light where she couldn't study his expression.

"Oh." Stacy cursed inwardly at the breathlessness in his voice.

"I wanted to apologize for this afternoon. You're doing an excellent job on the barbecue and I shot my mouth off about the catalog not being ready." He seemed to hesitate as if waiting for a reply, but no words came from her lips. "Anyway, no harm done. I should have been more clear about what I expected."

"No," Stacy rushed, "I should have realized that—"

"Whoa!" Cord laughed. His warm, deep-voiced mirth thrilled her. "Let's close the conversation before we start a mutual admiration society."

But that's just what I want to do, Stacy thought as she joined in with his laughter.

She felt rather than saw the tension ease out of him as he moved over to the pillar where Stacy had been standing when he'd arrived. She wandered a few feet to the other side of him, her own cup of coffee held caressingly in both hands, enjoying the feel of its warmth in her palms.

"Oh, the stars are out!" she exclaimed as she looked into the velvet sky at the brilliant array.

"Hey, you've seen stars before," Cord said with a smile in his voice.

"Yes, but when I was out here earlier, there were only one or two little ones and now there's thousands," Stacy explained, radiant with enthusiasm. "It seemed so lonely with no moon and just a couple of stars, but now it's magnificent."

"Tell me something, Stacy," he said, leaning lazily against the pillar, his dark gaze surveying her supple figure in the dress. "One minute you're a dewy-eyed girl looking at a flower or a moon or something, another time you're hot-tempered and fighting me, then you're a cool, sophisticated chick in a satin dress. Which one is the real you?"

"Will the real Miss Stacy Adams please stand up?" She laughed, not wanting to face his serious eyes. But when he failed to join in, Stacy added as truthfully as she could, "I suppose you could check all of the above."

She tried to read his expression, but his face was hidden in the shadows. He stood quietly for a time until the silence became too much for Stacy and she nervously walked over and placed her cup near the coffee pot.

"Stacy?" There was a hesitation in the way Cord said her name that made her feel just as unsure.

"Yes?"

"Would you come here a minute?"

If only she knew what made his voice seem so different. "I'd like to ask you something, if you don't mind."

Stacy's heart beat wildly as she moved beside the tall figure leaning negligently against the white column. He didn't turn to look at her but continued to gaze out into the night.

"How can a man go about asking a woman who's had every material thing she's ever wanted and whose beauty ensures her all the attention she could ever desire . . . to share her life with him?" Cord's voice was controlled but deeply emotional, and the hidden depths in it wrenched at Stacy's heart.

With difficulty she suppressed a gasp. *Oh dear God,* she thought, *he's asking me about Lydia.*

"What can I offer her? A life in country that's too harsh for her? A monotonous existence?" he went on thoughtfully. "Just exactly who does the giving and who does the taking in that kind of situation?"

"I—I think offering her your love would be enough," Stacy stammered.

He twisted to scrutinize her face.

"Would that be enough for you?" his low voice asked, but he didn't wait for a reply. "And just how would you let your man know?"

"It would be enough for me if the right man asked," Stacy answered, a calmness settling over her, knowing his love would be all she would ever desire. A serenity radiated from her face as she added. "And if he loved me, he'd know."

He reached out a hand and pulled her over to him. Her

breath came in rapid gasps as the dark, fiery eyes bored into hers.

"If he was unsure, how would you go about telling him, Stacy?" Cord's voice vibrated near her hair. She felt his left hand slip behind her waist, coming to rest on the bareness of her back, its contact searing through her body. His right hand released her wrist and traveled up to caress the side of her neck just below her ear. She knew she had only to lift her head slightly to his face, but she couldn't. Very gently, his thumb slid under her chin, forcing her head up. Stacy looked only at the mouth that was slowly descending upon her own.

At the first touch of his lips upon hers, she stiffened, not wanting to give in to their gentle demands. But soon, as Cord's ardor intensified, she succumbed—begging silently, then demanding, passion coursing through her body at the answering hunger in his embrace.

She never would have dreamed that Cord would kiss her like this. Lydia, yes, but not her. *Lydia* . . . With a start Stacy came to her senses. Cord wasn't kissing her, not with this much passion. He had to be working off his sexual tension, that was all. She broke free from his arms, ashamed of what he had to have guessed. His face was soft at first as he looked down at her until the panic-stricken expression on her face registered. Cord's eyes blazed as he turned away, his broad chest rising and falling with his deep breaths.

"Looks like we got carried away by our conversation," he said roughly.

With an audible sigh of relief, Stacy realized he was willing to dismiss the kiss.

"Luckily we both know what we feel for each other, so there's no need to be embarrassed," he added, refusing to look at the unmoving girl beside him.

"No, thank goodness," Stacy replied with a shaky laugh. "It could've been very awkward otherwise."

She moved a step away from him, her body still trembling, the initial magic of the sensation destroyed by the knowledge that she was probably a substitute for Lydia Marshall.

"Well, it's getting late," Cord said thoughtfully. "I suppose we ought to be turning in."

"I am pretty tired," Stacy said, grasping the straw he offered. "I'll see you in the morning."

With as much poise as she could muster, she walked out of the veranda into the living room. Cord followed a few paces behind, but as he entered the living room, the phone rang. At the bottom of the stairs, Stacy heard him answer it.

"Harris Ranch, Cord speaking." There was a brief pause. "Yes, Lydia, I left the dinner a little earlier than I'd planned. I intended to call you but—"

Stacy didn't wait to hear more. With the softest of cries, she rushed up the stairs. It was going to be difficult enough to face him tomorrow without increasing her pain tonight.

Chapter 10

Three days had passed since that fateful evening with Cord. There were faint circles around Stacy's brown eyes and a drawn look to her full mouth, indicating the sleepless nights and tension-filled days. Cord had repeatedly ignored her, no longer checking with her every day as he had done before. In fact, twice when Stacy had been out walking and had seen him in the distance, he had changed direction to take himself out of her path. A crushing sense of defeat had closed in on her as she realized that he couldn't even stand to see her.

Abruptly Stacy rose from the desk, refusing to let the melancholy within her interfere with her work. The sale was only a week away and there was a great deal still to be done. She was grateful that her time would be so occupied with the auction that she wouldn't be able to dwell on her own problems.

There was a light rap at the door to which Stacy called out to whoever was there. "Come in."

The oak door swung wide to admit Lydia Marshall.

"I'm not interrupting you, am I? Because if you're very

busy, I'll just stay a minute." The perky tone in her voice made Stacy cringe inwardly.

"No, not at all," Stacy said, taken aback by Lydia's unexpected arrival. "What can I help you with?"

"Nothing really. I just thought you might have time for some coffee and a little chat."

"Sure," Stacy said, wondering what in heaven's name they were going to talk about. "Just a minute and I'll ask Maria to bring some coffee. Would you care for a roll or anything?"

"I hope you don't mind, but I already asked her to bring some on the chance that you'd be free," came a quick reply that grated on Stacy.

"How nice of you," Stacy answered with a smile that didn't quite reach her eyes. She'd never attended a traditional high school, had no idea how the Mean Girl dynamic worked. But her instincts told her that Lydia definitely was one. Seating herself in the chair behind the desk, she continued, "I don't often get a chance to take a coffee break. So, thanks."

"I thought so." Lydia rose from her chair as the housekeeper entered the room carrying the coffee service. "I'll take that, Maria. I didn't ask for any sweet rolls. Did you want any, Stacy?"

At the negative nod of Stacy's head, Lydia dismissed Maria with a curt thanks.

Lydia's take-charge air irked Stacy, and she didn't really want the steaming cup of coffee that was offered to her.

"Oh, before I forget," Lydia exclaimed, reaching down beside her chair for her purse, "I was by the printer's and I remembered Cord mentioning something about needing the proof for the catalog so I picked it up. I hope you don't mind. He mentioned how hard you were working and I thought I'd save you a trip into town."

"Thank you," Stacy said coolly, accepting it. "Unfortunately, I still have to go into town for some other things. I'm sure Cord will appreciate it, though."

"Well, I knew how upset he was over it," the smiling Lydia went on. "I hope he didn't get too difficult. I know what a temper he sometimes has."

Her overly familiar tone and the way she pursed her red lips left no doubt that she wanted Stacy to know just exactly how friendly Lydia was with Cord. An anger slowly began to burn within her.

"Naturally, he was upset," Stacy said firmly, "I was, too, but everything's under control now. A minor breakdown in communication."

"I'm glad to hear it." An icy look appeared in Lydia's black eyes. "I offered to help with some of the work, but Cord assured me that it wasn't necessary. He seemed to think you were doing an adequate job."

Stacy's cheeks flamed at the emphasis on the word "adequate." Just knowing that she'd been casually discussed during one of their conversations made her feel a little sick. The solicitous tone of Lydia's words didn't cover up the coldness underneath.

"Cord did say you probably wouldn't want to do much, considering what you're going through right now," Stacy murmured, wondering where she found the voice to speak at all.

Lydia's dark eyes narrowed as she smiled and said, "Then Cord did explain a little of the problems we face." With a disconcerted sigh, she went on, "It's common knowledge how we've always felt for each other, despite my foolishness that got me into this mess. I wonder now how I could have been so naïve as to trade in all this for a sun that shines the same on the Riviera as it does here. I assure you, Stacy, it's a crushing blow to discover that to your husband you're no more than another possession to be dressed and displayed like a trophy. If I hadn't known that Cord had promised he'd always be here, I don't know how I would have made it through. I guess it's knowing my future is once again secure with Cord. And it's just a matter of time until it will all be official."

Stacy didn't know if she could take much more of this conversation. She didn't want to know one thing about their plans. Why was Lydia discussing this with her at all? Aloud Stacy managed to say something about how wonderful it was that everything was working out for them.

"Yes, it is," Lydia replied, studying Stacy, who felt increasingly flustered. "I'm so glad you see it that way. A lot of girls in your place would've developed a huge crush on Cord, you know."

Her needling words were meant to annoy, Stacy realized. Best not to react. "Oh, Cord and I only talk business." There. She'd succeeded in keeping the emotion out of her voice. "I'd have to have an overactive imagination to read anything into that."

"You do understand I would hate to see you get hurt in any way. I know Cord feels a certain responsibility for you, and I wouldn't want to see you interpret it the wrong way." Lydia smiled smugly as she rose to place her coffee cup on the tray. "Well, I really shouldn't keep you from your work. I know you have a lot to do, and if I can help you in any way, please call me."

"Of course," Stacy replied, the smile on her lips covering up the pain she felt. Lydia was the last person she'd go to for help, ever, and she had the distinct impression that Lydia knew it.

Glumly she stared at the catalog proof in front of her. She leafed through the pages on auto-pilot, her mind racing back to Lydia's words. *Cord feels a certain responsibility for you, and I wouldn't want to see you interpret it the wrong way.*

If only she could. If only she could read more into his actions than what they were. Responsibility? He'd generally acted as if she was a liability. It was a miracle he considered her at all.

Shaking off the troublesome thoughts, Stacy began rummaging though the drawers of the big oak desk looking for the copy of the proof supplied to the printer. She finally found it in one of the lower drawers and began the task of proofreading the long list of quarter horses complete with their registration numbers, sires, and dams. It was tedious, but at least it required her full concentration and her thoughts of Cord couldn't distract her.

Flipping one of the pages over, Stacy gave a start. Mixed in among the papers was a piece of stationery with the letterhead of Lindsey, Pierce & Mills, Attorneys at Law. The words fairly leaped off the pages at her. Shocked, she glanced at the signature at the bottom of the letter. *Carter Mills, Sr.*

What was a letter from Mr. Mills doing in Cord's desk? Drawn by the unexpectedness of the familiar letterhead and signature, Stacy read without thinking.

It was addressed to Mr. Cord Harris, Circle H Ranch, McCloud, Texas.

Dear Mr. Harris,

Stacy Adams, the daughter of a client, has rented a cabin located on your property. In writing this letter, I am stepping out of my sphere of authority. I would like to impose on you by asking that you keep a close watch over her.

The recent death of her father, a close personal friend, has left Stacy without any living relatives. Her father left her a very substantial income so that she is financially secure for the rest of her life. It was her

*decision to retreat to western Texas, and unfortu-
nately, her cosmopolitan upbringing didn't prepare
her for that. She was unwilling to consider the dan-
gers of going it alone, and has refused to discuss the
length of her stay, insisting that it is indefinite. I would
appreciate it, Mr. Harris, if you could persuade her to
return. If she will not, I have enclosed a check which
should cover any unforeseen eventualities.*

Sincerely,
Carter Mills, Sr.

"No!" Stacy whispered, staring at the scrawled signature at the bottom of the page. Carter Mills had definitely
overstepped some kind of boundary by writing a letter like
this.

But it explained a lot. Why Cord had been so hostile the
first day they met, advising her that she should return to
the city life she was accustomed to. Why he had felt so responsible when she'd taken that fall off Diablo and insisted
that she stay at his ranch to recover. And when she was
well, the episode with Diablo had conveniently given him
an excuse to keep her here. It was also the reason he was
so concerned about one of his ranch hands taking advantage of her. It was all so clear now. He'd undertaken the
role of guardian, more than a little misled by the old
lawyer's interfering. What she'd seen as caring or even
loving behavior was most likely motivated by fear of a
lawsuit.

Lydia's words washed over her again. *Cord feels responsible for you.*

Oh, God, Stacy thought. He must have told Lydia too.
Her humiliation grew. Shamed and hurt, Stacy rose from
her chair and made her way out the front door. Tears
weren't going to fix the awful feeling inside.

She wasn't a child, but she'd been treated like one from the start. Once outside, she stared numbly at the buildings and surrounding hillsides. A hesitant breeze lifted the tendrils of her chestnut hair as she stood there, immobile.

A hand touched Stacy's arm. "Are you okay?" the housekeeper asked with concern.

Slowly Stacy turned around and managed a weak smile before she replied, "Yes, I'm fine, Maria. I just needed a breath of fresh air, that's all."

"You don't look so good." The Mexican woman shook her head as she followed Stacy into the house. "Maybe you should take a little siesta."

"I'll be all right." Quietly she added, "I'm fine, really. It was just a bit stuffy in there."

Pride and a sense of fatalism squared Stacy's shoulders as she went back inside, opened the door of the den, and entered. An unnatural calm settled over her, walling off the pain. If she could maintain control over her emotions, she would be able to face the long week ahead. At the first opportunity, she would announce to Cord that she'd be going back home as soon as the auction was over. That would release him from any false sense of responsibility he felt and remove her from his life forever. Bleakly she replaced the lawyer's letter in the lower drawer and began mechanically rechecking the catalog proof.

That evening Stacy was on her way down the stairs when she saw Cord talking with Maria in the foyer. The starched freshness of his blue shirt and the sharp look of his new blue jeans indicated his plans to be gone that night. Still in the odd mood that had possessed her earlier, she walked up to him. Poised, she stood waiting until his conversation with the housekeeper was finished.

"Did you want to speak to me?" Cord asked.

"Yes, if you can spare the time," Stacy said crisply, ignoring the uncontrollable racing of her heart.

His dark gaze rested inquiringly on her pale, drawn face. "What's up?"

"I just wanted to let you know that I'll be returning home as soon as this auction thing is over," Stacy answered.

The expression on his face hardened noticeably. "That's rather sudden, isn't it?" Without waiting for her reply, he added, "I take it you're not asking my permission."

"No."

"I see." The coldness in his reply sent an involuntary shiver through Stacy. "Well, I didn't expect you'd last this long."

The morning sun was high over the mountains before Stacy woke up the next day. She had cried herself to sleep the night before, but with sleep had come the endurance to face tomorrow. Mechanically she took off her clothes, crumpled from being slept in, showered, dressed again, and went downstairs for breakfast. As she gazed out the window of the dining room, the distant hills beckoned her.

It was the weekend and there wasn't much Stacy could do for the auction. She decided to spend the day riding the hills. She wasn't up for another confrontation with Cord and that would be by far the easiest way to avoid him. She went into the kitchen to put together a cold lunch for herself and a few minutes later she was walking out of the front door, her hat swinging from one hand, her food in the other. There was no lightness in her step but her stride was firm.

Reaching the stables, she went to the paddock where the sorrel was. Diablo danced forward to meet her and nibbled playfully at her arm as she put on his halter.

She waved a greeting to Hank riding by the stables, thankful he was busy and didn't stop to chat. The old cowboy was far too observant and she didn't want to be put through another ordeal. Her sense of defeat was far too painful to talk about.

Diablo was full of fire, prancing and side-stepping in defiance of her efforts to hold him at a walk. Four people came around the corner of the stable. Stacy's attention was concentrated on controlling her spirited mount and guiding him to the pasture gate, but she glanced in their direction.

Two ranch hands were walking in front of Cord and Lydia. A stifled oath came from Cord as he pushed past the hands and ran toward Stacy and Diablo, but the sudden movement spooked the sorrel into a half rear as he tried to turn in the direction of the approaching figure.

Before Stacy could protest, Cord was by her side, grabbing her by the waist and pulling her off the horse while he got a grip on the reins of the panicking stallion. Setting her roughly on the ground, he ordered one of the hands to hold the horse.

"What in the hell do you think you're doing, girl?"

"I was going for a ride, if it's any of your business!" Stacy retorted, her own temper flaring at the undignified treatment she'd just received.

"You're damn right it's my business!" Cord raged, grabbing her wrist to draw her closer to him. "Isn't one fall enough for you? Or are you looking to get killed?"

"That was an accident. It could've happened no matter what horse I was riding." Her eyes flashed with anger. "I own that horse. He's mine, and you have no right—"

"I have every right in the world as long as I'm responsible for what happens to you while you're on this ranch," Cord interrupted coldly, releasing her wrist with a scornful sweep of his hand. "And I'm telling you not to go near that devil!"

"Good thing I won't be here long!" Stacy retorted sharply. Her anger was reaching a point where even Cord couldn't intimidate her. "And you'd better think of a way to keep me away from Diablo, because he's mine and I intend to ride him any time I please!"

In the background Stacy happened to notice Lydia Marshall's contemptuous expression. Too bad, if Cord's ex didn't like what she saw, Stacy thought furiously. She'd had it with the rancher's dictatorial ways and his overworked sense of responsibility.

Thoroughly steamed, she barely noticed the tall man in blue jeans coming out from the hacienda. There was something familiar about his walk, but Stacy's attention was directed back by Cord's voice.

"I'll lock you in the house if I have to, but you're not riding this horse. There's plenty of other mounts available if you want to ride," Cord answered, his voice lowering in an attempt to curb his anger.

"No thanks," Stacy said sarcastically, turning on her boot heel to walk in the direction of the dancing stallion.

The raised voices and angry tones had incensed the hot-blooded horse and his flashing white feet drummed the ground in a staccato rhythm. A rolling white eye glanced back to catch a flicker of movement. Pulling at the lead rope held by the ranch hand, Diablo reared slightly and just as swiftly came down and lashed out with his back feet at the unidentified person behind him. Just as quickly, Cord reacted, pulling Stacy away from the menacing hooves.

Holding her back and shoulders tightly against his broad chest, he muttered in her ear, "You are the most stubborn woman I've ever known!"

The sudden and unexpected physical contact with Cord swept Stacy's breath away. She felt her knees trembling and her heart racing from his nearness. She could only hope he would attribute it to the close call she'd had with the spirited horse.

Stacy was too weak to step away from him, cherishing the strength of his arms and the mild aroma of cologne from his freshly shaved face. Cord turned her around, keeping his hands firmly on her shoulders. His expression was serious as he studied her face.

"I've never met anyone in my life who needed a good spanking more than you," he growled, releasing her and turning to the waiting group.

"Hear, hear!" came the laughing agreement of the man standing beside Lydia.

The happy baritone voice broke through Stacy's preoccupied mind and the mist of tears in her brown eyes cleared. Of course! She should have recognized him. With a shake of her head, she rushed away from Cord to the waiting man.

"Carter, Carter! I'm so glad to see you!" she cried, throwing herself into his arms. Her voice was slightly muffled as she pressed her head against Carter's chest, but her unexpected greeting had brought Cord up short.

"Hey there, honey," said Carter, surprised at the affectionate welcome he was receiving. He stroked her hair. "If I'd known I would be welcomed like this, I'd have come a long time ago!"

Sniffing up more stupid tears, Stacy stepped away and looked into his blue eyes. The suddenness of Carter's appearance combined with the unsettling contact with Cord had robbed her of her self-control. She realized that Carter had misinterpreted her welcome, but she was too relieved at having someone she could depend on here. His presence represented a refuge of sorts from her mixed emotions. Although, she scolded herself, the world didn't actually revolve around her and her emotions.

"I take it you two know each other," Lydia commented dryly, breaking the silence that had settled over them all.

Embarrassed now, Stacy blushed before turning to introduce Carter. She stammered Lydia's name, not liking the smug smile on the other woman's face.

Lydia offered a smooth, beautifully manicured hand to Carter, favoring him with an intense look while Cord stepped forward to complete the circle. His dark eyes were icy cold as Stacy started to introduce Carter to him, but Carter interrupted before she could get past first and last names.

"Hey, Cord, I'm glad to meet you," said Carter, grasping the rancher's right hand firmly. "I never thought I'd see the day that anyone would be able to refuse to let Stacy ride that horse and make it stick. I want to thank you for myself and for my father for looking after her so well."

That rankled. Stacy glared at him.

"I won't mislead you by saying that it was an easy job. Stacy's a strong-willed girl," Cord said dryly. "So, will you be staying long?"

"Only as long as it takes to convince Stacy to come back with me." Carter smiled, glancing tenderly down at her. "Hopefully, as my fiancée."

Chapter 11

Stacy had been covertly watching Cord's face, feeling protected by the man standing beside her, but at Carter's statement. Cord's eyes flashed at her.

"Wow. Isn't that wonderful, Cord?" Lydia gushed, her gaze flicking briefly over Stacy before she smiled up at Cord and took his arm. "What a romantic conclusion for a reunion! It's really just perfect, isn't it?"

"Yes, it is," Cord agreed, but his voice sounded husky, as if he was trying to control his emotions.

No one seemed interested in Stacy's answer to Carter's public, de facto proposal, not that she was ready to offer one. But it grated on her that everyone seemed to assume she was going to automatically say yes.

"Carter, I'm in charge of the Circle H's annual sale of registered quarter horses this coming Saturday. Will you be able to stay until then?" Stacy asked, anxious to change the subject.

"Oh, Stacy, don't let a little thing like that get in your way," Lydia inserted quickly before Carter could answer. "I'm sure it would be perfectly all right if I stepped in for you. After all, it would be an emergency of sorts."

The last remark was directed more or less at Cord. Stacy had the distinct impression that Lydia was only too anxious to get her out of the way and the sooner the better. It was all Stacy could do to keep a sigh of relief from escaping her lips when she heard Cord's reply.

"It's too late for that. The sale took a lot of organizing and I don't want any last-minute confusion. I don't believe it's vital that Stacy leave the ranch right this red-hot second," Cord answered, his cold eyes surveying Carter as if daring the other man to disagree.

"No, of course not." Carter added hurriedly, "As a matter of fact, Dad gave me a week to persuade you to come back with me. We'll just call it a little vacation." The young lawyer exchanged a conspiratorial smile with Stacy before turning back to Cord. "Is there a motel around here where I could stay? I'd like to get settled in."

"There's nothing in town," Lydia began.

"No, you can stay here," Cord interrupted, silencing the polite protest Carter had started to make with a wave of his hand. "There's plenty of room at the hacienda. If you'll excuse us, I have some work to do, and I believe you mentioned that you were having lunch with a friend, didn't you, Lydia?"

With a firm hand on Lydia's elbow, Cord maneuvered her away from the standing couple. Silence descended over Carter and Stacy as he surveyed her quietly.

"You never did answer my question. It wasn't exactly a question, though, was it?" Carter asked. "Don't answer it now either. I'll ask it again later when the mood is a little more romantic. Right now you can direct me to my room and tell me all the tall Texas tales you've learned."

With a nervous laugh, Stacy joined hands with Carter and began to fill him in. Eagerly she related the happenings since her arrival, many of them taking on a humorous aspect on their recounting. Going into the house, she brought him to the spare room down the hall from hers, after suggesting that he meet her at the pool in half an hour.

Stacy was floating lazily on her back in the pool when Carter surfaced from his dive beside her. They swam around for an hour before pulling themselves up on the side, happy and exhausted.

Stacy studied Carter's buff body through her lowered lashes. His light, almost blond hair was still wet from the swim and his smooth, unlined face seemed a little too young somehow, compared with Cord's sculptured ruggedness. Soberly, Stacy realized Carter wasn't as indomitable as he had seemed before, but she fell easily into their old friendship, unable to let him know the change that had taken place in her, the difference in her thinking. But there was something they definitely had to talk about.

"Hey, Carter," she said softly. "You should know that I found that letter your dad wrote to Cord before I came out here. Maybe he meant well, but it threw me for a loop."

He turned red. "You understand that Dad was concerned about you," Carter said after a little while. "As it turned out, we can be glad he was. I didn't know anything about it until after you were hurt." Turning to study Stacy, he asked, "What made you stay here at the Circle H? The auction?"

With as little detail as possible, Stacy explained the incident with Diablo, glossing over Cord's antagonistic attitude toward her. Mischievous amusement spread over Carter's face when she finished. "Imagine you out there chasing cows! That's too much," he chuckled.

"Well, it wasn't too funny at the time," Stacy retorted, unable to keep from bristling at his teasing. "You don't exactly have a choice when Cord Harris issues an ultimatum."

"I got that impression this afternoon," Carter said

calmly, but there was still a gleam in his eyes. "I don't think patience is one of his virtues."

"Hardly," Stacy replied. "And he certainly doesn't have any patience where I'm concerned. I still think your dad shouldn't have written that letter, especially without telling me. When I remember what I said and did because I thought Cord was an arrogant tyrant who enjoyed ordering people around—"

"You mean he doesn't?"

"No. That is, um—" She struggled to find the right words to explain her change of attitude without giving her true feelings away.

"Never mind." Carter only laughed and rose to his feet. "I don't care what he says or does. He managed to pretty much keep you off that horse and in one piece until I could collect you. For all I care he could be Billy the Kid. Now I'm going to go change before this West Texas sun turns me into a lobster."

The following night, as Stacy dressed for dinner, she dreaded the evening to come. She'd hoped with Carter here that she would be able to put Cord in the back of her mind, but Cord had very successfully squashed that. Since her brief conversation with Carter alone the previous afternoon, Cord had been around constantly. If he didn't actually take part in their conversations, he was in an adjoining room. Either way his presence thwarted any attempts to find privacy that Stacy and Carter might have made.

Carter had jumped at the dinner invitation when Stacy passed it on to him. His enthusiasm coupled with her earlier agreement left no way for her to back out. Being so near to Cord was sure to make her wonder if she was getting something she wanted out of this uneasy triangle. She ought to just pack and go. Each day that went by brought her closer to the time when she would leave for good, and every glimpse of Cord was likely to turn into a memory she'd never be able to shake.

Willowy and delicate, like something out of a misty dream, Stacy descended the stairs to where Carter Mills and Cord Harris waited in their white dinner jackets. Carter didn't speak but the admiration in his eyes was a more eloquent compliment than words. Hesitantly Stacy looked into Cord's face for an affirmation of Carter's approval, but the dark eyes were as masked as his expression.

Regretting that she'd even wanted to know what was on Cord's mind, Stacy turned back to Carter. "Are we ready?"

"And willing." Carter smiled, possessively clasping his hand over hers, resting on his arm.

A sleek and shiny luxury car was parked in the drive. Stacy slid into the back seat behind the driver and waited nervously for Carter to walk around the car and join her. She glanced into the rearview mirror at Cord sitting behind the wheel, but the rancher quickly looked away.

Carter got in and Cord started the motor and maneuvered the big car out of the driveway. The conversation was sketchy on the way to Lydia's, with Stacy too conscious of the man behind the wheel to do anything but pretend to be interested in the scenery racing by.

"You're very quiet tonight," Carter commented after they'd parked and Cord had gone into the house to collect Lydia. "Is something wrong?"

"No, of course not." Stacy was grateful for the concern in Carter's eyes. How could she explain that Cord's presence in the car upset her? "I enjoy looking at the land, especially when the sun is about to set. It gives everything a mysterious peace."

"That's my girl," Carter said with a shake of his head.

"Sitting beside a guy who's traveled two hundred miles to see her and she's admiring the scenery."

"Oh, Carter, you know I'm glad you're here." Stacy laughed, fully aware of the comfort his presence was to her.

"But I wonder if you're glad only because I'm an old friend." A sad, serious expression in his eyes made her begin to protest, but she thought better of it when Cord approached with Lydia clutching his arm.

Stacy felt a pang of jealousy constrict her heart. Lydia looked great, unfortunately. Her raven black hair fell loosely around her neck, accenting the sensuous décolletage of her lilac satin gown hanging precariously by slim rhinestone straps.

Pleasantries exchanged and small talk made, Lydia glanced at Stacy's ring hand and then looked inquiringly at Carter. "I thought we were going to have something to celebrate tonight. Or did you forget to bring a ring along to make the announcement official?"

Carter managed a joking, noncommittal reply which escaped Stacy, whose attention was caught and held by Cord's intense gaze in the mirror. She felt the color rising in her cheeks at the derisive expression in his deep brown eyes.

Unwilling to take part in the conversation between Lydia and Carter, Stacy again forced her attention elsewhere. She managed to keep her strong emotions fairly well hidden, or at least she hoped so.

Arriving at their destination, Stacy was enchanted with the rambling two-story building nestled in a sylvan setting of pine trees and lush greenery. As the foursome entered the restaurant area, the host greeted Cord by his first name and ushered the group to a secluded table.

Carter held out the chair on Cord's left for Stacy, his hand lingering briefly on the filmy silk covering her shoulder. The reassurance of his touch made her a little less nervous. She raised her champagne glass with the others as Carter proposed a toast.

"To Texas."

"And to a happy reunion for those who've been separated," Lydia added, her gaze taking in Cord possessively.

Stacy was relieved when the dinner was served and over. At least in the lounge the entertainment would keep conversation to a minimum. Leaving the table, Stacy and Carter followed the other couple into the lounge. Stacy's eyes were riveted on Cord's dark hair curling above the collar of his white dinner jacket. As if conscious of her inspection, he turned, gazing mysteriously into her startled brown eyes before speaking.

"I hope you won't be too disappointed with the band. They play a lot of great old mariachi songs, not like a regular bar band, if that's what you were expecting."

Inwardly Stacy flinched at the not-so-subtle censure in his tone. His opinion of her was so low already that it seemed useless to defend herself, if that was what *he* was expecting. Without replying she and Carter followed them to a table. As soon as the cocktail waitress had taken their order, Carter asked Stacy to dance. She was more than happy to leave the disconcerting company of Cord and Lydia. Three guitars played the strains of an old Spanish ballad to the gentle tempo of drums. As she matched the familiar patterns of Carter's steps, a little of her confidence returned. But only a little.

"What's the matter with you tonight?" Carter asked suddenly. "I have the feeling that you're afraid—or hiding something."

Startled by his unexpected frankness, Stacy missed a step. Her throat tightened as hundreds of protests flashed through her mind, but before she summoned one, Carter went on.

"I don't think I want you to answer me. I think you'd lie or maybe not tell me the whole truth." His tone was serious. "It would hurt me too much either way. Stacy, if you ever want to tell me what's wrong, I'll be here no matter what."

"Carter, I——" Stacy took a deep breath, vowing not to cry. Not to allow herself so much as a miserable sniffle. Her makeup would be conspicuously ruined, and she couldn't just go around bursting into tears all the time.

"Ssh! We won't talk any more. Maybe later when we're alone, but not now," he whispered in her hair, and drew her close into the comfort of his arms.

When the last notes of the ballad faded away, the group struck up a bouncier tune and the young couple remained on the floor. The knowledge of Carter's affection buoyed her up and she was able to return to the table with a more sincere smile on her face.

But despite Carter's invisible support, the evening dragged. Cord's mocking tone whenever he addressed her made Stacy nervous again, and the triumphant look in Lydia's eyes only made it worse. The envious lump in her throat swelled whenever she watched Cord dancing with his sultry black-haired ex.

Toward the end of the evening, Carter asked Lydia to dance, leaving Stacy alone with Cord.

"They look good together," Stacy commented with an attempt at nonchalance as she watched Carter and Lydia fall into step. Cord gave her an amused smile that flickered briefly with an emotion Stacy didn't quite recognize.

"Jealous?" he asked in a low voice. "Lydia is a very beautiful woman."

"No, of course not," Stacy replied, but there was a catch

in her voice as she spoke. She was jealous of Lydia, but not for the reason Cord was thinking.

"Shall we dance?" Cord rose and stepped behind her chair.

She ought to refuse. Why punish herself when it was so obvious who he really wanted? Dancing with him would give her nothing but more heartache. Yet not a word of disagreement passed her lips as she found herself in his arms on the dance floor. There was no retreat now.

The glow that radiated from her upturned face had nothing to do with her unspoken reluctance. The firm hand on the small of her back was strangely exciting and the brown eyes that looked down at her made her heart race with uncontrollable happiness. At this moment it didn't matter whether he was dancing with her out of pity or courtesy. Her hand tightened imperceptibly in Cord's and with a gentle smile on his mouth he drew her closer to his broad chest until her head nestled against his shoulder. Not hearing the melody the band was playing, the muted conversation of the dancers around them, oblivious to anything but the nearness of Cord, Stacy danced in silence, capturing the sensation of the rhythmic sway of his hips, the gentle pressure of his body against hers, the firm clasp of his hand and the caress of his breath on her hair.

The dance over, as if by previous arrangement, Cord immediately suggested calling it a night. Torn apart by the emotions that threatened to surface and the hopelessness of her love, Stacy seconded it.

The ride home had been a silent one. Looking back on it two days later, Stacy tried to analyze the reason. Carter had been unusually quiet. In the past they'd often spent hours together without talking, but this time there was an uneasiness about him, as if he was grappling with a problem he didn't know how to handle. It'd been a huge relief that night when the car finally turned into the ranch drive and Stacy escaped to the sanctity of her room.

Carter had been his old self the next morning, laughing and joking as before. After volunteering to help Stacy with the auction, he'd pitched in with his usual gusto, running errands into town, checking with Hank regarding the yearlings, and taking some of the more time-consuming tasks off Stacy's hands.

Cord, on the other hand, had reverted to his habit of unexplained absences. The last two days he'd practically avoided Stacy and Carter, joining them only for dinner Monday evening and leaving right afterward. He hadn't mentioned where he was going, but later that evening Stacy had seen a light burning at the ranch office. Lydia hadn't been over there, though, which surprised Stacy as the divorcée had almost become a fixture at the ranch since her return.

Staring absently into the laptop screen, Stacy forced her thoughts to return to the business at hand. Her morning had been consumed with last-minute requests for e-postcards of the auction particulars. The one that had just popped up was, she hoped, the last. She hit SEND and closed the laptop lid. If she was lucky she would have time for a cup of coffee before she had to meet with the ranch hands, male and female, to go over various details they would be responsible for during the barbecue.

Leaving the den, Stacy walked toward the kitchen. But Maria appeared in the archway between the dining room and living room carrying a small tray with a steaming cup of coffee and a sweet roll on it.

"You're psychic." Stacy smiled. "I was just going to the kitchen to get myself a cup."

"I should fix another one. For Lydia."

"Lydia?" Stacy's tone was puzzled.

"*Si.* She just drove up." Maria nodded toward the front of the house.

"I don't know—" Stacy began but she was interrupted by the opening and closing of the door.

"Stacy, good morning. I'm so glad to see you're not busy." Lydia entered the living room as Maria left. "I was hoping to chat with you today, but I was afraid you'd be all tied up with the auction."

"I do have to run," Stacy said, not anxious to "chat" with Lydia now or ever. Their previous discussion had been unpleasant enough.

Gracefully Lydia seated herself in the chair opposite Stacy, smoothing the skirt of her elegant sundress before speaking. "I don't see any engagement ring. Haven't you put that poor guy out of his misery and said yes by now?"

"If you mean Carter," Lydia said coldly, incensed that Lydia was meddling in something that was none of her business, "I—we—have been pretty busy. There's no rush, is there?"

"I wouldn't let him get away if I were you."

"That's the point, though, isn't it? You're not me."

Lydia's cold eyes flickered ominously for a moment at Stacy's words.

"That's true," she said, "but you might find my take on the situation useful. Maybe not."

"Why don't you come to the point?" Stacy was thoroughly irritated by the phony concern that Lydia was attempting to project. "We could talk in circles all day. Fortunately I have better things to do."

Surprised by Stacy's unexpected audacity, Lydia rose from her chair, walked behind it, then turned to face her haughtily.

"You're quite right. There's no love lost between us, so

why pretend? My point is really quite simple—you should answer Carter. Don't hope that Cord will come through with a better offer, because he won't. Do you think that Cord is so blind he doesn't realize you've fallen in love with him?"

"Afraid of a little competition?" Stacy retorted. "Or is your hold on Cord so shaky that you can't take the chance?" She stood to meet the glare in the other woman's eyes.

"Don't be ridiculous!" Lydia exclaimed. "You're still too young to tell the difference between affection and pity. You moped around all Sunday evening and then lit up like a Christmas tree the minute Cord danced with you."

Stacy wanted to tell Lydia to shut the hell up but decided to hear her out.

"Can't you tell that he feels sorry for you?" Lydia went on. "His overactive sense of responsibility forces him to do things like that. I don't know where your sense of pride is or whether you haven't grown out of that cow-eyed teenage stage yet, but either way your presence has managed to get in the way of the plans that Cord and I have made. Believe it or not, he doesn't feel he should make his true feelings known for fear of hurting you."

"Please. Don't do me any favors, either of you," Stacy said heatedly. "I'm leaving right after the auction. With Carter. So that's that, and in a few more days I'll be out of your lives forever and you and Cord can do whatever you like. In the meantime, I'd prefer that you leave this house now and stay out of *my* way in the future." Stacy's voice trembled with controlled anger. But the truth of Lydia's words cut deep.

The triumphant click of heels echoed through the living room as Lydia left. Numbly Stacy heard her satisfied tone as Lydia exchanged greetings with Carter, who'd just entered the house. Walking into the living room, he studied Stacy for a second, noticing the clenched fists at her sides.

"What just happened?" he asked. "Lydia looked like she'd just tried on the glass slipper and it fit."

"Really?" Stacy remarked with unnatural bitterness. Sensing there were more questions to come, she hurried on. "I have a meeting in a sec. There's some mail that has to go out today. Would you take care of it?"

Gathering her notebook, she stormed out the door.

The following evening Stacy and Carter went for a late ride after dinner. On their return Stacy chattered away happily with Carter refreshed and relaxed from the sunset ride.

"If you don't mind, I'm going to wash off this precious Texas dirt," he said as they reached the front door of the hacienda. "I'll meet you on the patio for a drink in half an hour."

"Deal." Stacy smiled, preceding him upstairs to her own room.

A short time later she joined him outside. He was sitting down, rubbing the ears of the German shepherd abstractedly as he stared off into the deep ebony of the night. Seeing his mistress, Cajun padded over to meet her. Stacy took the hand Carter extended to her and let herself be drawn down to the settee beside him.

"It didn't take you very long." Carter smiled. "I thought I'd be able to sneak an extra drink before you got here." He indicated a tray of tall glasses on the side table.

"At least you saved one for me," Stacy teased, cradling an icy drink in her hands as she gazed at the dark sky. "It's a gorgeous night. I wonder where all the stars are."

"Mind if I get corny and say they're all in your eyes?"

"Oh, Carter!" Stacy laughed, leaning back against the cushion.

Tenderly he cupped her chin in his hand, his face somber as he studied her expression.

"I wish you took me more seriously sometimes," he said at last.

Stuffing his hands in his pockets, Carter walked over by the pillar and gazed into the distance. Stacy fidgeted a little, watching him, not sure what to say. His statement brought back in a rush all the feelings she'd been trying to subdue.

"Do you know how I've planned for this evening ever since I've arrived?" A strange, bitter quality was in his voice that Stacy had never heard before. "Here we are, all alone with not a soul to bother us. The setting is perfect, the black night shutting out the world, a couple of stars winking encouragement, and a beautiful girl whose eyes are filled with anticipation at the words that are to be said." He turned to look back at Stacy. "Only your eyes aren't filled with anticipation, are they?"

Salty tears trickled down her cheeks to her tightly pressed lips as she looked away from his accusing gaze.

"I was going to do it all properly tonight—get down on one knee and say, 'Stacy, I love you and I want you to be my wife," said Carter, his voice almost a monotone. "Even more corny, isn't it? I love you, but I'm a proud man. I don't want to possess something that doesn't belong to me. You know, there are guys who would've asked you anyway and taken the chance they wouldn't be turned down. I'm not asking for an entirely different reason. I'm afraid you might accept and I couldn't live with knowing that you're in love with some rancher from Texas."

Stacy's shoulders shook when she thought about what she'd done. Rousing from his self-pity, Carter looked at the silent, sobbing form and walked over to where she sat, a hand moving toward her head.

"Oh, Stacy, why does it have to be this way?" His voice choked as he swept her off the chair into his arms.

"Carter, I wanted to tell you but I couldn't," she moaned into his shirt. "I couldn't hurt you, not when I knew what that pain was like."

"It'll be all right." His expression was resigned. "You know what they say. It only hurts for a little while."

"I wouldn't have said yes. I wouldn't have done that to you."

"No, I think I knew that." He held her away from him as he wiped her moist cheeks with his hand. "You're too tough for that."

"You will stay," Stacy asked, "and take me home after the weekend?"

"Of course. Don't you know, honey, that you can use me any time?" Carter grinned, his smile taking the sting out of his words.

"I don't know what I would've done if you hadn't come when you did. I didn't have the pride to leave or the strength to stay," she confessed, nestling under his arm as they walked toward the light from the glass doorway.

A troubled sigh echoed her words as Carter stepped forward to open the door. Hesitating just inside, Stacy turned to wait for him. He had stopped behind her, his attention riveted ahead of her. The brittle iciness of his blue eyes startled her and she turned to where he was looking. Cord was standing slightly to her right, a book in one hand and a glass of whisky in the other. His dark eyes were narrowed.

"You two are turning in early," he said with a noticeable edge in his voice.

"It's been a hectic day," Stacy murmured, starting to go to the stairs.

"Are all the arrangements going smoothly for the sale on Saturday?"

"Of course. If you'd like to go over them now—" Stacy began, stung by the indifference of his tone.

"No, that won't be necessary," Cord interrupted. "There's time enough in the morning." The dismissal was curt.

"Good night then," Carter said to Cord, a little sarcastically.

"Yes, good night, Cord," Stacy chimed in. Cord cut her a look she didn't like.

"Good night." His voice followed them out of the room.

Chapter 12

"Hello!" came the call from the hill.

Stacy looked up in answer to see Carter coming down, his long legs moving fast. "Hi yourself," she replied with a grin.

"I should've known I'd find you here," Carter said. "Don't you realize what time it is? You've been going since eight this morning."

"It's only half past seven and I have a few things to finish up before tomorrow." Stacy ignored the mild rebuke in his voice. "Linda and Diane decided to set up the tables tonight instead of tomorrow morning. I thought I'd give them a hand. Did you get the things from Molly that Mrs. Grayson needed?"

"Delivered to her already. She shooed me out before I even got to sneak a taste of her famous barbecue sauce," Carter said. "What's left to do?"

"Nothing, I hope," Stacy answered with a nervous look around at the long row of folding tables. Waving a good-bye to the two women who were walking away, she turned apprehensively to Carter. "Tomorrow will tell the tale. All my mistakes will be blatantly obvious."

"Where's that girl who always rolls with the punches?"

Carter teased with a twinkle in his eyes. Wrapping an arm around her shoulders, he turned her toward the hacienda, adding, "Day's done. Let's go and have something cool to drink."

Stacy laughed in spite of her nervousness. A little relaxation would be in order, especially in the face of the ordeal ahead of her tomorrow. A twinge of pain laced through her as she considered what this week would have been like if Carter hadn't come. Studying his tanned face when he wasn't looking at her, she noticed new lines at the corners of his lips. Outwardly there was no change in his attitude toward her and he'd made no reference to Wednesday's ill-fated evening.

"Regretting the end of all this?" Carter asked, squeezing her arm in a comforting way.

Stacy sighed. "No. I'll be better off when I'm away from here." She didn't want to even think about how haunted she would be by the memory of Cord.

The couple skirted the front entrance, going directly to the patio at the side of the house. While Stacy settled herself on one of the chairs, Carter went in to get the drinks. The fiery globe of the setting sun failed to lighten Stacy's darkening brown eyes as she gazed morosely at her surroundings, her home for the past several weeks.

She kept looking at the rise above the house, hearing the phone inside ring and Carter answering it. Guessing from what he said that he'd be talking for a while, something compelled her to get up and go to the small cemetery she couldn't see from where she was.

She didn't stop until she reached the black, wrought-iron fence that enclosed the graveyard. Ignoring the smaller crosses and markers, she made her way directly to the stone bearing the words *Elena Teresa Harris*. Slowly she knelt in front of the tombstone until a denim knee touched the earth. Her hand reached out tentatively and traced the letters. Two bright tears trickled down her cheeks as Stacy tried to draw comfort from those Cord had loved. Grief and anguish gripped her heart as she leaned against the silent gray stone.

Again Cord's voice echoed in her ear, but this time it sounded so real that she turned her head to look. Her eyes had to be playing tricks on her because there before her stood Cord, an odd light in his eyes.

Suddenly Stacy became conscious of the encroaching shadows among the graves. Looking quickly to where the sun had been, she saw only a crimson glow marking its departure. She wasn't dreaming.

The realization that Cord really was there hit her as she turned back to face him. At the change in her expression, the large muscular arm that had started to extend itself toward her returned to Cord's side as she hastily scrambled to her feet.

"What are you doing up here?" Cord questioned, a hint of the softness remaining in his voice as he surveyed the pained, almost guilty look on her face.

"I came up here to—" The truth of her intention almost escaped her lips before Stacy could stop it. Nervously she glanced to the gray stone that marked the grave of Dona Elena before she looked at the marker beside it. "Your father's grave," she ended lamely, conscious of the narrowing eyes upon her. "I was remembering my father and somehow I thought coming up here would make him seem closer."

Whether he accepted her explanation or not, Stacy couldn't tell. Taking her arm, he steered her out of the small cemetery without any further comment. Uneasily Stacy glanced into his face. Whatever he was thinking wasn't reflected there. The few minutes of silence were unbearable for her.

"How did you know where I was?"

"Your boyfriend saw you walking this way." She didn't miss the edge of sarcasm in his voice.

"Oh," Stacy said faintly as he propelled her before him.

She permitted herself a quick look down at the veranda before concentrating on the uneven ground of the hill they were going down. When they reached the edge of the cobblestones, Cord released her arm as if he hadn't really wanted to hold it. A tight-lipped Carter handed Stacy her drink at last, his eyes examining her face.

"Are you okay? Where were you?" he asked quietly.

Stacy managed to nod an affirmative to the first question before Cord interrupted her. Taking a big swig from his glass, he stated in a mocking tone. "Visiting my father's grave. Wish I knew why. Maybe she was feeling sorry for herself."

Carter's blue eyes studied Stacy intently for a brief second. But Cord wasn't finished.

"Giving in to self-pity is a luxury that this land doesn't allow, not for the people who live here." The coldness in Cord's dark eyes penetrated Stacy's heart, sending the blood rushing to her face.

Cord turned away and started walking toward the area north of the stables where the preparations for the barbecue were going on. Stacy and Carter followed a few steps behind. None of the three spoke on the way. Cord seemed to ignore the fact that they were behind him and Carter only glanced Stacy's way once.

The trio passed the long line of tables gleaming in the waning light and continued toward the red glow emanating from a nearby stand of greasewood trees. Cord slowed his pace so the three approached the fire at the same time.

A long pit had been dug in the grove and a fire started in it. In the hazy glow, an older man moved to shove another log into the fire. Stacy recognized Hank with a smile.

Blinking in the flickering light, she studied the ingenious arrangement of the barbecue with interest. Curiosity overwhelmed the tension that had kept her so quiet. "Are those old bed frames the meat is on?"

"Yup. Army cots," Cord smiled in answer. "We wrap the legs in foil to retain the heat. The hands take turns tending the fire through the night and basting the meat with barbecue sauce."

"Wow," Stacy exclaimed as she saw the enormous cuts of beef and pork on the metal frames. "How is all that going to get eaten?"

Hank snorted. "Us Texans have big appetites. We don't mess around with those tiny sandwiches like folks back east. Now, if you're gonna sit here and watch the fire, I'll get some other things done," he finished. As he turned away from the pit, he added to Carter, "Might as well come along and give me a hand. I ain't as young as I used to be."

Without waiting for an answer, he strolled off into the dark. A twinge of fear clutched at Stacy as she realized that Hank intended to leave her alone with Cord.

She knew Carter was staring at her, waiting for her to say something to indicate that she didn't want him to go. She couldn't think of anything to say. With a stifled exclamation, Carter stalked off through the trees after Hank.

Cord was the one who finally broke the silence, his low voice drawling, "Well, you'll be leaving in another day. I suppose you're starting to look forward to it."

"Not really," Stacy answered truthfully in an unemotional voice. "I've enjoyed my time here."

There was a slight pause as if Cord was mulling over her

reply. "I imagined you'd be glad to be going back where you belong."

Involuntarily Stacy stiffened at Cord's phrase. A flash of her old anger returned at his pompous attitude of always knowing what would be best for her. She quelled the urge to make a retort and continued gazing into the fire.

"Have you and Carter set a date for the wedding?"

"No," Stacy said. "That's something we'll probably do when we get back." She didn't let her hurt seep into her words. Her pride said it was better to let him think that there was going to be a wedding.

"You'll send me an invitation?"

"Of course," she answered, straightening her legs and leaning back on her hands as she scowled into the fire. "Are you going to send me one to yours?"

"Mine?" Cord asked.

"I forgot I wasn't supposed to know," Stacy answered airily. "Though why you wanted to keep it from me, I don't know. It's pretty obvious from the way Lydia acts that there's more between you two than just the burning embers of an old romance."

"I see." Cord sounded almost amused. "I suppose Lydia told you."

"More or less," she replied. Actually, she thought, Lydia had all but written it on the wall. "Now that you're released from your responsibility to me, you can go your merry way and I'll go mine."

Seeing his dark head turn toward her in surprise, she added, "I know about the letter from Carter's father too."

"Really. How did that happen?"

"You left it in one of your desk drawers. I have to say you were careful about keeping an eye on me. It's too bad that you didn't let me in on it. We might've gotten along better if I'd known what was going on."

"It didn't occur to me. You're fairly headstrong, Stacy. I only hope that Carter's more successful with you than I was." Cord seemed to be even more amused, which really irritated her.

"Carter understands me," she answered forcefully, lifting her chin in defiance.

"Oh, I'm sure he does." Cord laughed. "It's too bad the control is all on his side of the equation."

"If that was true, I never would have come here and all this never would have happened." Stacy trailed off, a hint of melancholy in her voice.

"Nope, maybe not."

Cord fell silent with her, until the crackling of twigs and rustling branches announced the return of Hank and Carter.

"Ready to head back?" Carter asked her.

"Might as well," said Cord, rising and extending a hand to Stacy before Carter could intervene. "It's going to be a long day tomorrow."

The ranch yard was packed with vehicles of every description from luxury sedans to beat-up pickups. The auction itself had been over for two hours and the exodus of cars had just begun.

Stacy surveyed the long table that had been heaped with food earlier. So little was left of the vast quantities of meat, baked beans, potato salad, coleslaw, cornbread and biscuits that she sighed with relief that the appetites had been gauged so accurately. Already her group of ranch women had started to clear the tables of leftover food.

"Are you through for the day?" Molly asked, a plump arm reaching out to fill the iced tea glasses.

"I've just been fired," Stacy laughed, "and ordered to join the fun."

"Good. It's mostly all neighbors left now," said Mary, hooking an arm in Stacy's and propelling her away from the table. "You're going to witness a good, old-fashioned hoedown."

"Hey, where are you taking my hostess?" came the questioning laugh from behind them.

Halting abruptly, Stacy paled at the possessive tone in the voice. Her heart beating fast, she felt a masculine hand resting on her shoulder.

"Cord!" Mary cried. "It's about time you got around to your guests. You've been with those horses all day."

"I see you've managed to extricate Stacy," he replied, looking down at her, silent beside him. "You did a wonderful job, Stacy. I'm sorry I haven't had a chance to tell you earlier or give you a hand—not that you needed one."

"Thank you," Stacy said quickly, a flush coloring her cheeks at his unexpected praise. "But everyone has been good to me. I'm sure they covered a lot of my mistakes."

"You're too modest," Molly admonished her. "With someone as sweet as you, people just naturally take you to their heart and do everything they can for you."

Tears pricked the back of Stacy's eyes at the woman's words. Knowing it was her last day at the Circle H, Stacy replied softly, "You've all made me feel as if this is my home and I'll never forget any of you for that."

Cord's hand tightened on her shoulder and the sudden pressure caused Stacy to look into his face. The questioning look in his dark eyes confused her momentarily before he turned to the other two women.

"This evening's party is doubling as a farewell send-off for Stacy. She's leaving us in the morning," Cord said grimly.

In the midst of the barrage of protests and objections, Stacy felt a pang of regret at the ambiguous statements she'd made about leaving, always saying "sometime after the barbecue." If only they knew how little she really wanted to go!

"Why are you leaving so soon?" Mary asked. "I thought you'd be staying at least another week."

"Carter has to be back the first of the week, so we decided to go together," Stacy explained, ignoring the chill coursing through her as Cord removed his hand from her shoulder. "We can share the driving and the trip won't seem so long."

"The two of you are going alone?" Molly asked, frowning a little as she glanced at Cord.

"Why not?" Cord said in a mocking voice. "Remember this is the enlightened generation. Our moral codes are a little old-fashioned for them. Excuse me, I think it's time I mingled with some of the other guests."

Despite Cord's light words, Stacy caught the underlying thread of bitterness in his tone. Embarrassed by the implication, she faced the two women self-consciously, trying not to look at his broad shoulders as he worked his way through the crowd.

"Have you decided to marry Carter?" Mary asked curiously as the sounds of guitars and fiddles drifted their way.

"No," replied Stacy without thinking.

"Speak of the devil," Molly muttered as Stacy glanced around to see the sandy-haired Carter walking toward them. "So you're taking our favorite girl away from us tomorrow," Molly scolded.

"How else will I ever get her all to myself?" Carter wrapped an arm around Stacy's shoulders. "Besides," he said, noting the hidden pain in Stacy's eyes, "a change of scene would do her good."

Stacy missed the glance exchanged between mother and daughter as she looked up into Carter's questioning blue eyes.

"If you ladies don't mind, I think I'll dance with our hostess." Carter smiled and moved Stacy possessively in the direction of the strumming guitars.

At the edge of the dance floor, he turned her into his arms. He got through a few steps before speaking.

"What happened back there? I saw Cord leave before I arrived." He studied the troubled look on her face. "What did he say to make you look like that?"

"It wasn't anything he said," Stacy murmured absently, catching sight of Cord watching them from the fringe of the crowd. "It's me, I guess," she sighed, forcing herself to look at Carter. "I just don't want to leave. I know it's the right thing to do."

"Stacy, are you in love with him?" Urgency crowded out all caution as Carter gripped Stacy's shoulders. "Marry me, honey. I can make you happy, I know that."

"No, Carter." There was agitation and indecision in her tone.

"He's so much older than you. How do you know you're not using him to replace the father you lost?" Carter's voice grew desperate and demanding. "If I hadn't let you come out here, we'd have been married by now. Can't you see that, Stacy? You need an anchor. Let it be me. Say you'll marry me, Stacy, say it now before you regret it the rest of your life."

"No!" Stacy almost shouted, trying to stem the whirlpool of persuasion Carter's words were drawing her into. "No," she repeated emphatically, turning from his arms to face the happy dancing throng before them.

"Think about it. How can you be sure?" Carter pleaded.

"There you are, Stacy," came a masculine voice. "Don't

you know it's not proper for the hostess to run off in the middle of the party?"

Through blurring eyes, Stacy recognized the stocky form of Bill Buchanan.

"Hey!" There was a frantic note in her voice as he grasped her outstretched hand.

"You don't mind if I steal her for a dance, do you, Carter?" Bill asked. "I'm too old to stand in line, and when the rest of the men get a good look at her that's just what I'd have to do."

The doctor whisked Stacy into the clearing where a lively tune was filling the air. As Stacy matched his bouncy steps, she momentarily glanced back to where Carter was standing. Her attention was caught by the tall figure standing steps away from him, separated only by the same trees in which she and Carter had sought seclusion moments ago. Forgetting her partner completely, Stacy stood motionless. Hell. The turbulent emotion in Cord's eyes had to be there because he'd overheard her conversation with Carter. Suddenly Cord was moving through the dancers toward her. Hurriedly Stacy turned to her partner, ignoring his puzzled expression as she maneuvered him among other couples.

It was too late. The firm brown hand was gripping her shoulders as Cord made an abrupt apology to Dr. Buchanan and, without giving Stacy an opportunity to protest, forced her through the whirling dancers. But she tried to pull away from Cord's hold. "Let me go!" she cried desperately.

"Just shut up," Cord replied sharply. "You've done too much talking already."

"It's none of your business what happened between Carter and me." Stacy's temper flashed in her brown eyes.

"I'll decide what's my business." A muscle in his jaw twitched as Cord turned her toward the hacienda.

"What do you want from me?" Her voice trembled.

"Some straight answers for a start." Cord nodded to a couple who crossed in front of them.

Walking on to the veranda, Cord muttered a curse as he caught sight of guests gathered by the pool. Without a hesitation in his stride, he turned her toward the knoll above the house. Realizing they were headed for the cemetery, Stacy glanced back at him suspiciously.

"Why are we going up here?" she demanded, a little winded by the swift pace he was setting.

"It's probably the only place on this damned ranch where there aren't any people," was the curt reply.

Reaching the top of the rise, he moved ahead, dragging her behind him until they were out of sight of the people below. They stopped a few feet from the iron fence. Releasing her arm, he took hold of a breathless Stacy's shoulders.

"Why did you lie to me and let me believe you were going to marry Carter?"

"What does it matter?" Stacy tried to wrench herself free of his hold.

"Do you want to go back? Do you want to leave here?" When she didn't answer, his mouth tightened. "Answer me."

"No!" she sobbed, fighting the answers he was seeking and the truth she couldn't bear him to know. "Please, Cord, don't!"

"Why don't you want to leave?"

"B-because—" she stammered. "Oh, Cord, please let me go."

"Stacy, I can't, not this time." His voice was suddenly tender and pleading. "Not until you tell me what you really feel. This time you've got to tell the truth."

Tears ran unchecked down her cheeks as she gazed into his face with disbelief. Desperately she searched for assurance that the loving tone she'd heard wasn't mockery. He pulled her closer and managed a trace of a smile. He whispered, "Don't look at me like that until you've answered me. Why don't you want to leave me?"

"Because—" she began again, her voice more sure, a flush filling her cheeks as a warm glow spread over her. "Because I love you. Cord, I—"

But his lips silenced the rest of her words. All resistance was gone as suppressed passions were unleashed in a burning embrace. When at last the fiery urgency was satisfied Cord's lips left Stacy's and touched her eyes, cheeks, the curve of her neck as he whispered endearments suffused with the glory of love.

"Oh, Cord, Cord, I can't believe it," Stacy gasped, thrilling at his every touch. "You really love me?"

"Yes I do." His deep voice choked with emotion like hers.

"You were so hateful to me," she murmured amidst another shower of kisses meant to silence her.

"I fell in love with you the day I found you lying unconscious out there on the plains. I knew then that if anything happened to you my life wouldn't be worth living." Cord's voice was husky. "When you recovered and said you were leaving in a few weeks, I knew I had to find a way to make you stay, to make you love this land."

"I do, Cord, I do."

"I know. I've never told you how proud I was of you and the way you took your place with the men on the drive and did your share of the work—uh, except on occasions." He grinned.

"Were you jealous of Jim?" Stacy teased.

"I was jealous of anyone who touched you. Even your letters from Carter irritated me," he confessed.

"Look at the way you paraded Lydia around. She made it pretty damn clear you were going to marry her again." Stacy's upturned face was earnest as she added, "That night on the veranda I thought you were—"

His low laugh interrupted her. "How I wanted you that night, honey." His callused hand traced the curve of her cheek. "When you recoiled from me—"

"Not from you, Cord. Never from you."

"You sure about that?" Cord smiled.

"If you hadn't overheard my conversation with Carter and forced me to admit my love, would you have let me leave tomorrow?"

"I would've shown you no mercy, Stacy Adams," Cord said gruffly.

"No quarter asked." Stacy lifted her face for his kiss.

"And none given, Stacy," Cord murmured, inches away from her lips. "Now that you're finally mine, I'll never let you go. And we're going to be married as soon as we can. You understand that."

"Yes, Cord, yes." Stacy yielded to his embrace, her heart racing with joy. There would be time to talk, but not now. This moment was theirs . . . and it was dedicated to love.

There was nothing sweeter in the world.

FOR BITTER OR WORSE

Chapter 1

Six years later . . .

Stacy paused at the open bedroom door. Her fingers nervously smoothed the side of her hair, pulled back in a clasp at the nape of her neck. A faintly medicinal scent tinged the air as she gazed around the empty room.

The house was quiet in the early morning stillness. Distantly Stacy heard the soft bustle of Maria preparing breakfast. Her eyes anxiously searched the living room and swept the foyer. They stopped at the sight of a wheelchair in front of the veranda doors.

An achingly familiar dark head was resting against the chair back. Black hair in waving disarray shone in the soft light of full dawn. The man in the chair sat unmoving in front of the window.

A quivering sigh trembled through Stacy. It was barely morning and Cord was already staring silently, as if he saw nothing worth looking at in the landscape he'd loved so. It promised to be another one of those days. There had been so many of them lately it was becoming difficult to remember the good days.

Thank goodness their son Josh was staying with Mary Buchanan and her two boys for a while, Stacy thought with weary relief. Cord's black moods were beginning to take their toll on Josh no matter how much Stacy tried to shield him. Unbidden, the admission came that her own nerves were strained to the point of rawness.

Her brown eyes darkened with anguish at the sight of the once proud and vital man confined to a wheelchair. She felt the mental torture and pain almost as intensely as her husband did. Worst of all to bear was her inability to help him.

As if he sensed her presence, a large hand gripped a wheel and pivoted the chair around. Hurriedly, Stacy fixed a bright smile on her lips before she confronted Cord's brooding gaze.

"Good morning, honey," she murmured smoothly. "You're up and about early today."

"Yes." Cord's clipped response sounded harsh.

He propelled the chair forward at her approach. His clean-cut features were rigidly drawn in forbidding lines. As Stacy bent to kiss him, Cord averted his head slightly and her lips were scraped by the roughness of his lean cheek, covered by a shadowy day's growth of stubble. His continuous rejection of any display of affection from her cut her to the quick, but Stacy tried to conceal it.

"You forgot to shave this morning," she chided laughingly, and stepped behind his chair to push him into the dining room.

"I didn't forget. I just didn't see the need."

"You haven't kissed a sheet of sandpaper lately or you might change your mind about that." The forced attempt at light humor made her voice sound brittle.

"No one is making you do it, Stacy."

Cord sounded so cold and insensitive that she had to

close her eyes to remember that he really loved her. It was only his bitterness talking. She couldn't blame him for being bitter.

"True enough," she agreed, keeping the tone of lightness, however artificial it was. "I kiss you because I want to."

She pushed his chair to the head of the table, already set for breakfast. As she released his wheelchair handles and stepped to the seat at his right, she felt the slash of his gaze.

"Since when did my passionate wife become satisfied with a mere kiss on the cheek?" Cord jeered softly.

Stacy flinched inside. "It's enough for the time being." She reached for the juice pitcher sitting in the middle of the table. "It won't be forever."

His mouth quirked cynically and something sharp stabbed Stacy's heart at the action. Maria's appearance with the coffee forestalled any caustic response Cord intended to make.

"Breakfast will be ready in a few minutes," Maria announced, filling the coffee mugs and setting the pot on the table.

"Fine." Stacy smiled, using the break to change the conversation as the plump housekeeper left the room. "Travis will be in shortly," she told Cord. "We want to go over the yearling list with you to get your recommendations on the ones we should keep as breeding prospects."

"Spare me a token involvement." His lips thinned, hardening his expression. "You and Travis operated the ranch this past year without my help or advice. I don't need any magnanimous gestures implying I still have a hand in running things."

Stacy's control snapped, pain lacing her chest. Pressing her lips tightly together, she tried to breathe deeply. She couldn't endure another argument.

"Cord, please. Let's not get into this again," she begged.

"Then don't patronize me!" he snarled.

"We aren't," she protested.

"Aren't you?" His dark eyes flashed like burning coals. "Go over the list of yearlings by yourself then," he mocked. "The Circle H is your ranch. Do what you like."

"It was *your* ranch. It became ours, but it was never mine," Stacy cried out in frustration. "All Travis and I have been trying to do is keep it going until—"

"Until I was well again?" Cord interrupted, a sardonic dryness in his tone. He gave a bark of laughter, if it could be called that. "It's very likely that I'm as well as I'm going to get."

"No."

But it was a whispered word, half choked by an invisible stranglehold around her throat.

"Face the facts, Stacy," he demanded harshly. "It would have been better if Colter hadn't gotten me out of the wreckage of the plane."

She breathed in sharply. "How can you say that?" Her hands were trembling. She stared at them, remembering the agony she had suffered nearly a year ago when she'd thought Cord might not live. Years ago, losing her father the same way had nearly shattered her. "I love you," she blurted out. "How could you possibly think anything would be better if you were dead?"

"Look at me." When she didn't immediately obey, his hand slid over hers until he was holding her wrist. His fingers tightened until her wide eyes met the chilling darkness of his. "Really look at me, Stacy—and tell me if it's love you feel or pity."

Stacy obeyed, slowly inspecting his masculine features. A year's convalescence had paled his sun-browned skin. The chiseled lines had been changed by weight loss, weight that hadn't been completely regained. Yet the rugged leanness only seemed to increase the compelling quality of his looks. Marriage hadn't lessened the physical attraction Cord held for her, only heightened it.

There was nothing about his handsome face to pity, nor the wide shoulders and strong arms. But when her gaze slipped to his long, muscled legs that had once enabled him to tower above her, Stacy was forced to remember that Cord was in a wheelchair.

Her heart cried at the injustice of it. His silence was noble and proud, but his body was still held prisoner.

Yes, it tore at her heart, but that didn't change how she felt about him.

"I love you, Cord," she answered at last.

He sighed heavily and let go of her wrist. His hand closed around the juice glass. There was a suppressed violence about the action, as if he wanted to hurl the glass and see it shatter into a thousand pieces.

Stacy laid a hand on his forearm and felt him stiffen at her touch. "Cord, you have to believe you'll walk again." She leaned toward him earnestly. "It isn't as if the situation's hopeless. The last operation did restore some feeling in your legs. But the healing process is slow—you know that—until the doctors can test you again. There's no telling at this point how extensive the recovery might be."

His impassive gaze shifted to her. "Or how limited," he reminded her dryly. "Forgive me if I'd rather prepare for the worst." He shrugged his arm away from her reassuring touch.

Then Cord released the wheel brake and pushed away from the table. "Tell Maria I'm not hungry."

"Cord, you have to eat," Stacy said as he rolled toward the living room.

"I don't *have* to do anything," he replied without a backward glance.

Stacy started to follow him, then sat back in her chair. Their somewhat embittered discussion had stolen her appetite too.

It revealed so much of the frustration they had known in the past year since the engine of Cord's plane had failed on takeoff from a friend's ranch and he had crashed.

The memory of her father's death had been unbearably vivid when Stacy had flown to San Antonio, uncertain whether Cord would be alive when she arrived. Even when she got there and met with the trauma team that had stabilized him, it was days more before his surgeon and doctors felt confident about his recovery.

The immediate concern had been to stop the internal bleeding and make the necessary repairs to keep him breathing and keep his heart pumping.

The operation to relieve the pressure on the main nerve trunk to his legs had been too delicate and complicated to attempt in his critically weakened condition following the crash, so the decision had been made to wait until he recovered his strength before attempting it.

At the time, Stacy had been too grateful to have him alive to risk losing him on the operating table, so she'd gone along with the medical opinion.

Given a second chance, Stacy knew she would make the same decision. The operation to relieve the pressure on that all-important main nerve had been performed only a short time ago.

It was successful to the point that he now had some feeling in his legs, although he still couldn't walk.

That, the doctors felt, would depend on the healing process, which required time. And hope. For Cord if not for her, hope was becoming threadbare from overuse. He could no longer hold onto it with any certainty that it would be fulfilled.

After being an invalid for nearly a year, his patience was gone. He'd expected immediate results from the operation. Numbed legs instead of no feeling at all hadn't given him much encouragement. After living a life that demanded physical exertion of all sorts, Cord faced the looming prospect of limited activity. Fearful without saying so, he lashed out at everyone and most especially at Stacy.

If he was trying to break her tenacious hold on hope, she wondered how long she would be able to hold onto it under his attacks. The strain of the last months was wearing on her too. Sighing, she reached for the coffee.

"Stacy?" A male voice called her name with quiet concern.

She sensed he must have spoken before, only she hadn't heard him. She glanced up and smiled at the man standing beside the table. It was a haunted smile, a ghost of the animated warmth of her real one.

"Hello, Travis. I'm afraid I didn't hear you come in," Stacy apologized, gesturing toward a chair opposite hers. "Have some coffee."

"I saw Cord out on the veranda. Isn't he coming with us?"

Travis McCrea sat down, smoothing a silver wing in his otherwise dark hair.

Maria walked in, carrying the breakfast plates for Stacy and Cord, enabling Stacy to avoid Travis's question for the time being. Maria frowned at the empty space at the head of the table and glanced at Stacy.

"Where is Mister Cord?"

"He's out on the veranda. He said he wasn't hungry, but you might as well take him a tray in case he changes his mind." Stacy knew that Cord would probably ignore the food or slip it to Cajun, the German shepherd, when he thought Maria wasn't looking.

Maria agreed, clicking her tongue as she headed back toward the kitchen. "He will never be strong again if he doesn't eat."

Stacy sighed, drawing Travis's perceptive gaze. He had to notice the droop to her shoulders. She was pretty sure there were shadows under her eyes too. She hadn't been sleeping well ever since—

"Has he been hard to handle already this morning?" Travis inquired gently.

"Yes." There was a wry twist to her mouth.

There was no point in lying or pretending that she didn't know what Travis was talking about. He'd known Cord much longer than she had. He'd even been there when Cord was pulled from the wreckage. At the time Travis had been the foreman for Colter Langston, Cord's best friend and best man at their wedding.

And Travis had been the one who'd met Stacy at the San Antonio airport and driven her to the hospital where Cord had been taken.

A few days after the accident, he'd stopped by the hospital. It was then that Travis had told her he'd quit his job with Colter and was striking out for parts unknown.

Stacy had never delved into the precise reason that Travis had left after working so many years for Colter, although she had her suspicions. Aware that Cord's convalescence would be a long one, without knowing how long, Stacy had asked Travis if he would temporarily fill the post as foreman on the Circle H until Cord was able to take over again. Almost a year later, he was still here, temporarily filling in.

"I suppose I should be used to Cord's outbursts of frustration by now." Stacy rubbed a hand across her forehead, a gesture of mental tiredness.

"No one ever gets used to it," answered Travis.

"I suppose not." She sighed.

Maria walked through the dining room with an attractively set breakfast tray for Cord. The fluffy omelet on her own plate didn't arouse Stacy's appetite, but she began eating it anyway. There was too much to be done this morning to accomplish it on an empty stomach.

The sound of the sliding glass doors opening to the veranda was just audible. Unconsciously Stacy tensed as she heard Maria's shoes step out.

The musical lilt of Maria's speaking in her slightly accented English carried into the dining room, although her exact words weren't clear.

There wasn't any difficulty understanding Cord.

"Damnit! I told her I wasn't hungry!" His angrily shouted words were followed by a resounding crash as the breakfast tray was obviously hurled away. "Maria, I—"

At least there was an apologetic tone in his voice, but Cord didn't complete the sentence.

Tears burned the back of Stacy's eyes. Even so, she could see the grim line of Travis's mouth. It was all she could do to keep from crying.

"He's in rare form today," Travis commented, sipping at his coffee. "I hope he doesn't explode like that around the colts. They're high-spirited at the best of times and apt to be skittish."

"There's no need to worry. He isn't coming with us," Stacy said tightly, concentrating on the omelet on her plate.

"He's not?" A dark eyebrow flicked upward in a measuring look.

"Nope."

"Did he give a reason?"

"Oh yes," she said wryly. "He said he wasn't interested in a token involvement. He felt we were patronizing him by pretending he still made decisions about how the ranch was run."

"The entire breeding program for the quarter horses is his. Did you mention that?" Travis laughed without humor. "How are we supposed to know what he was trying to develop?"

"I don't think Cord cares anymore." There was a lump in her throat, large and painful. "He essentially said we've run the ranch capably without him and we can keep on doing it." Her eyes were clouded by inner distress as she glanced at the brawny man sitting opposite her. "He's convinced he isn't going to get any better."

"A man like Cord doesn't give up no matter what he says. Inside he keeps on fighting," Travis stated.

"Does he?" Stacy's chin quivered. "Just a little while ago he said that he wished Colter hadn't pulled him out of the plane. I understand how he must feel, but"—she pressed a hand against her throat to check the sob that rose in her throat—"he doesn't seem to care anymore about anything, not even the ranch." *Or me*, she could have added but didn't.

"He denies that because he cares too much."

"I wish I could believe that." Heaven knew that she tried. "It's my own fault that he feels the way he does about the ranch. Whenever there was a problem this past year, I wouldn't let you tell him about it until it was solved. I didn't want him worrying when it was so important that he rest and heal. I let him think everything went smoothly. If I'd listened to you, Travis, Cord wouldn't think I was patronizing him now."

"Stacy, you can't beat yourself up wondering if things would've been easier if you'd decided differently. What's done is done and we have to go on from here. Today we have a crop of yearlings to look at, so eat your breakfast." His voice was gruff, but his smile was understanding.

Stacy returned it. "What you really mean is to get hold of myself." Her mouth curved in a self-deprecating line. "I don't know what I would've done if you hadn't been here to help this past year. And to listen."

"I hope I've been of use as a sounding board. You can't keep everything bottled up inside without eventually breaking." He finished his coffee and set the mug on the table.

"What about you, Travis?" she asked softly, suddenly feeling guilty for burdening him with so many of her own problems without a thought to his. "Haven't you needed someone to listen?"

She undoubtedly knew what was on his mind. Pain flicked briefly in his thoughtful eyes. In his mind danced a haunting vision of a young woman with honey-brown hair and gold-flecked eyes—Natalie, the wife of his former boss, Colter Langston.

Travis breathed in deeply, letting the image fade away. "Doesn't matter if I did. Time has a way of healing most things. Time and hard work."

Stacy left it at that, eating the last forkful of omelet without really tasting it.

"I want to speak to Cord before we get started with the work," she said.

"I'll come along if you don't mind." He rose from the chair, picking up his Stetson. "Maybe I can persuade him to come along with us."

Nodding agreement, she stepped away from the table. She was skeptical of his chances of success, but at this point there was no harm in trying.

The broken glass and plates had been swept up. There was a dark spot on the veranda floor where the liquid, coffee or juice or both, hadn't completely dried.

Cord was sitting silently in his wheelchair as Stacy and Travis walked through the glass doors. His hooded look never wavered from the distant hills, but Stacy knew he was well aware of them.

"We're on our way to the stables," she said quietly.

"So?" Cord's voice seemed to come from a deep, dark place inside, its sarcastic inflection laced with disdain.

It seemed impossible to say that she wanted to be sure he was all right, and that he didn't need anything before she left. Cord was plainly revealing his scorn for any display of concern from her. She glanced hesitantly at Travis, wishing she hadn't felt the need to come out to the veranda.

Travis, with his usual unselfish perception, bridged the taut silence. "Cord, I'm a cattleman. You ask me about Herefords or Angus or Santa Gertrudis and I can discuss their merits with anyone. Ask me about a good cow horse and I'd know about that. But breeding horses and bloodlines, that's not my field."

Cord's aloof black gaze swept to his foreman. The lean look of Cord's face, high cheekbones cut sharp, accentuated the patrician arrogance stamped in each carved line.

"Then you'd better learn." Indifference to the problem chilled Cord's reply.

"Cord!" Stacy breathed his name, frowning at his continued withdrawal from running the ranch.

But the dark head had already turned away, ending further discussion. "Take the dog with you when you go," Cord dismissed them coldly.

Travis went back into the house, but Stacy didn't. Cord's last remark evaporated what was left of her patience. "Cajun can stay here. He's not as young as he used to be, and he doesn't like being in the hot sun." Temper sharpened her soft voice. "After you've driven everyone else away, Cord, you might be grateful for the company of man's best friend."

Her husband's hard profile dipped slightly toward the

black-and-tan shepherd with the graying muzzle lying beside the right wheel of his chair.

"You may have a point, Stacy," Cord replied evenly with the same degree of detachment as before. Then his gaze slashed to her. "A dog never stays with anyone out of pity."

Her lips parted. She wanted to reassure him that she loved him, but the lack of faith Cord had in the depth of her feelings for him just hurt.

"You have a one-track mind, don't you?" she said hoarsely. "I would never feel sorry for you, Cord. You're too filled with self-pity for there to be any room for mine."

Pivoting sharply, she walked from the veranda and looked for Travis. He'd gone out, obviously. If only she had someone else to talk to—someone male, who could understand Cord on his own terms. When she found time to think she sometimes wondered how she'd ended up married and a mom so fast. Six years ago, it had all seemed so right and things had moved so quickly. At least she'd had a chance to see the world before settling here in the wildest part of Texas. Her former life seemed a very distant memory to her now.

Had she even had ambitions beyond being Cord's wife when she'd come here? Stacy paused a moment and surveyed the horizon that had once seemed infinite. Now, in a strange way, it confined her. She sighed and kept on going.

Not much later, Travis's long strides caught up with her on the way to the stables.

"I should have known better." She sighed. "He's always been able to make me lose my temper."

"Well, you can't predict what he's going to do or say."

"But I said the wrong thing—I shouldn't have."

"I don't know if you should have or not." The grooves around his strong mouth deepened. "But if Cord is going to dish it out, he might as well learn to take it."

That sounded all well and good. True, she had turned the other cheek for a long time, but it didn't make her feel better to retaliate in kind. All she knew was that she would feel miserable until she apologized. Cord needed understanding. She should have appealed to his reason, not stoked his anger.

Hank was standing in front of the stables when they came near. His leathered face, browned by the sun, hadn't aged at all since Stacy had known him. He raised a hand in greeting, a glint of respect in the bright eyes when they focused on her.

From the stud pens, a sorrel stallion whickered to her, tossing his flaxen mane and stretching his neck over the rails. When Stacy failed to walk to him, Diablo whirled away from the fence in a display of temper.

Chapter 2

Stacy slid the veranda doors open and stepped through. The setting sun was casting a golden hue on the whitewashed adobe walls of the house. The purple flowers of bougainvillea provided a brilliant contrast. Colorful Mexican pots, suspended by decorative macramé hangings, were overflowing with thick green foliage.

The German shepherd's chair thumped the floor. Cajun rose lazily from his place by Cord's wheelchair to walk to his mistress, thrusting a wet nose against her in an affectionate greeting.

Cord glanced over his shoulder, his gaze raking Stacy from head to toe. There was no admiration, no approval, not even interest in his look.

She could have been wearing sackcloth and ashes instead of the hostess gown in rich colors that did wonderful things for her skin and the highlights in her hair.

"I thought you were doing paperwork in the study," he commented.

Yet his meaning seemed to be that if he'd thought Stacy was going to come to the veranda, he wouldn't have been there.

"Not tonight." She moved nervously to one of the arched columns supporting the veranda roof. She thought she felt him watching her and turned, but Cord was studying the ripples of gold sunlight in the swimming pool.

"Paperwork has a way of piling up if not routinely handled," he said with a shrug. "But then that's your affair."

His hands gripped the wheels of his chair, expertly spinning it around with a minimum of effort.

It was a full second before Stacy realized he intended to reenter the house and leave her alone on the veranda.

"Cord, don't leave." She took a step toward him and hesitated.

He stopped, turning the chair at an angle that would bring her into view. The sad light of sunset bathed his face, changing it into a mask of bronze. A dark eyebrow arched before his arrogant question. "Why?"

"I want to talk to you."

Her voice broke slightly, driven to desperation by the way he'd continually avoided her during the past two days.

"About what?"

His masklike expression didn't change. Not even an eyelash flickered.

"The things I said the other day," Stacy began, running her fingers through her hair, "about your feeling sorry for yourself. I shouldn't have said that. I'm sorry."

The desire to rush to him was strong. She wanted to sit at his feet and rest her head on his lap. If he had smiled even faintly, she would have. But the bronze mask didn't crack and pride kept her standing near the pillar.

"Does that mean you've reconsidered and that I don't feel sorry for myself?" His mouth twisted sardonically. "Or that you're sorry you said it?"

Her chin lifted a fraction of an inch. "To be truthful, Cord, I don't know how you think or feel. You've started shutting me out. Every time I try to get close to you, an invisible barrier goes up and I'm on the other side. I don't know how to reach you anymore."

"I'm not shutting you out," he said evenly.

"Then what's happened?" Stacy lifted her hands up in a beseeching gesture, asking to understand.

"Maybe you haven't adjusted to the fact that now you're married to a cripple. Things can't be the same as they were before the accident."

"Why not?" she protested.

"You can never bring back yesterday."

When Cord wheeled his chair through the veranda doors, Stacy didn't call him back. Her heart cried silently for the man who had once laughed and smiled and swept her into his arms at the slightest provocation. Somewhere behind that barrier of bitterness her man still existed, but first Stacy had to find a way through or else beat down the walls.

She doubted if she possessed the strength for the battering.

She didn't sleep well that night. She tossed and turned alone in her bed, haunted by the memories of the nights she'd spent in her beloved husband's arms and praying for their return.

The fear that Cord might be right and he would never walk again kept reasserting itself. Maybe she should face the possibility, but she refused to give up hope.

When she finally drifted into an exhausted sleep, she was determined not to let Cord give up hope either.

Late the next day, she was in the study with the laptop, catching up on the paperwork she'd let go the night before, when a car door slammed in the driveway, followed by the slamming of another door, and the sound of young voices.

A quick smile lighted her face. The entry was never made in the spreadsheet on the screen as she rose from the desk and hurried into the foyer to the front door. She opened it at the same instant that a small black-haired boy with dark eyes raced toward it.

"Mom!" he cried excitedly.

She reached out, lifting him into her arms. "I missed you, Josh!" she declared, kissing his cheek and hugging him tightly.

He squirmed. He'd informed her a month ago that he was getting too old for that mushy stuff, but habits die hard in mothers and Stacy was no exception.

However, with Jeff and Dougal Buchanan only a few steps behind her son, she let him slide to the ground before she embarrassed him too severely.

"Did you have a good time?" she asked.

He nodded vigorously. "You bet!"

A string of details followed, ranging from Jeff riding him on the handlebars of his bicycle to the collection of rocks he'd found. When he took time out for a breath, Stacy was certain he'd only scratched the surface.

"Hold it!" She held up a hand to stop the flow of words. "It sounds like you could talk all night. But first I think you'd better help Mary bring your stuff to the house, don't you?"

Josh's eyes went all round and innocent. "Bill is helping her and he can carry a lot more than I can 'cause he's bigger'n me."

"I bet there's something that's just your size you can carry," she said with a smile.

Stacy didn't doubt for an instant that her son had charmed his way out of a lot of things he hadn't wanted to do.

She took him by the shoulders and turned him back toward the big station wagon parked in the driveway.

"Go on."

She gave him a little shove toward the car and he moved reluctantly toward it.

A slight frown drew her brows together as Stacy looked at the stocky man unloading Josh's tricycle. In order for Bill Buchanan to be free at his hour of the afternoon, he had to be combining a medical visit with a social call.

A quick mental calculation confirmed that Cord was just about due for another examination. A twinge of unease darted through her.

Her attention shifted to the red-haired woman walking her way, Josh's small duffel bag in her hand. "Hello, Mary," Stacy greeted her. "You seem to have survived a week of Josh with no scars."

"With my two wild Indians, what's one more?" Her friend laughed.

"He wasn't any trouble, was he?"

"None at all," Mary Buchanan assured her.

"Here's my rock collection!" Josh came rushing over. This time he was proudly carrying a paper bag that bulged at the sides. "Where's Daddy? I want to show him."

"I'm not sure. In the house somewhere." Stacy stepped to one side as Josh darted past her without slowing up. The older boys followed, not quite as fast.

"How are you, Stacy?" Bill Buchanan joined his wife.

"Fine, just fine," she answered quickly, perhaps too quickly.

A decidedly clinical eye scanned her face.

"I would say the circles under your eyes got a little darker," the doctor observed. "Part of the plan to have Josh spend a week with us was for you to get some rest. You can't keep on doing everything, you know."

"I meant to rest." Stacy laughed, but it sounded brittle and artificial. "But I keep trying to catch up with all the work. Seemed like the more I did, the more there was to do."

"It's always that way," Mary agreed.

Stacy ignored the look of professional concern in Bill's

eyes. Her problem was more than overwork. Somehow she couldn't bring herself to confide the truth.

Her relationship with Cord was strained—Travis knew it because he saw them together so often.

"Come in and have something to drink. I don't know where my manners went." Quickly she changed the subject. "Maria always has sweet tea or lemonade in the refrigerator. Unless you would rather have coffee."

"Something cold, I think," Mary responded, walking into the house. "What about you, Bill?"

"A cold drink would be great. Where's Cord?" He glanced around the living room. "While you're rustling up refreshments, I might as well see him. How's he doing, by the way, Stacy?"

"The same," she answered noncommittally. "If the boys are with him, by the sound of their voices, he's on the veranda."

"Probably buried beneath the pile of Josh's rocks." Mary laughed softly. "Whoever said little boys were made of snips and snails and puppy-dog tails forgot to include rocks!"

"And toads and lizards and worms," Stacy added. "You two go ahead. I'll go to the kitchen and let Maria know you're here."

"I'll be on the veranda with the boys," Mary replied.

A few minutes later Stacy carried a tray of lemonade and cookies to the veranda. Neither Cord nor Bill was there.

It was several minutes before the three boys were situated with their lemonade and cookies. Stacy sank onto a chaise lounge near Mary's chair, out of earshot of the boys.

"From the looks of you, I should've kept Josh another week," the redhead commented. "Bill is genuinely concerned about you, you know," she added gently.

"If you had done that, I would've started worrying about Josh." Stacy smiled, trying to make light of Mary's remark.

"Seriously"—Mary shook her head—"how long do you think you can keep up this pace? You're trying to run the ranch, your home, take care of Josh, be a practical nurse for Cord, and probably a hundred other things I haven't mentioned."

"I have a lot of help," Stacy pointed out. "If I didn't have Maria and Travis, I would have collapsed a long time ago. But it really isn't so bad, just hectic."

"Well, you should take a break and get away—for a little while if nothing else," Mary said.

"Cord needs me." A bittersweet smile played at the corners of Stacy's mouth. "If Bill was in a wheelchair, would you leave him?" She paused. "Even for a little while?"

"No." She gave a rueful grimace as Mary made her point. "They would have to come and drag me away by force."

"Who would drag you where?" Bill pushed Cord's wheelchair through the opened veranda doors.

A warning glance from Stacy checked Mary's initial reply.

"If you didn't hear the first part of the conversation, then I'm not going to tell you." The redhead switched her attention to the impassive man in the wheelchair. "Now that my husband is finished poking and prodding at you all over, would you like something cold?"

"Yes, I would," said Cord, but Stacy noticed the brooding darkness in his eyes.

"I'll get it," she offered quickly when his gaze swung to her, piercing and searching.

"No, I'll do it," Mary insisted as Stacy started to rise. "There's no need to stand on ceremony with us. Sit down and relax—heaven knows you don't have that many chances to."

"Okay then." Stacy leaned back.

When Cord asked in a low voice, "Feeling overworked?" she wished she hadn't given in so easily.

"Who doesn't?" She ignored the unspoken taunt in Cord's question.

"In one way or another, the spouses generally go through as much as the patients do," Bill said almost absently.

Stacy tensed. Was it an idle remark or had Bill caught the sting in Cord's voice? She glanced warily at her husband. A muscle was twitching along the strong jaw.

He was upset about something; she knew him too well not to recognize the signs.

A glass of iced lemonade was held out to him. Cord stared at it for several seconds before taking it and setting it on a wrought iron stand near his chair. He impatiently waved aside the plate of cookies and let his gaze slice to Bill.

"How much longer is it before someone finally admits I'm not going to walk again?" he challenged.

Bill's blue eyes narrowed thoughtfully in the crushing silence that followed. "That depends," he said at last.

"On what?"

Cord tipped his head back, aggressively thrusting his chin forward.

"Partly on whether you've decided that you can't walk," was the calm reply. "Miracles are in short supply, like everything else. A doctor can't snap his fingers and have you on your feet. It takes a combined effort of doctor and patient, with a bit of grace from God thrown in."

"Which doesn't answer my question." One corner of the hard mouth quirked cynically, as if he'd expected the question to be dodged.

"Clinically speaking, the odds are still good that you're going to walk, but it isn't going to happen overnight."

A sound, something between laughter and contempt, rolled from Cord's throat. "That's a relief! For a minute there I thought you were going to tell me this paralysis was psychosomatic."

"If I believed that," Bill said briskly, "I would've suggested a psychiatrist, not a—"

"Of course," Cord broke in sharply. His hands gripped the wheels, knuckles turning white under the strain of his hold. "Excuse me."

Before any of the three could speak, he was rolling his chair away.

The rudeness gave Stacy an uncontrollable shudder of dismay.

Unruffled, Bill turned to look at her, all business. "How long has this been going on?"

"Since shortly after he came home from the hospital this last time, almost constantly this last month," Stacy admitted. Her eyes smarted with tears as she looked in the direction Cord had gone.

"This ordeal would be rough on any man. As self-sufficient and independent as Cord's always been, I should have realized it would be even more difficult for him," the doctor murmured grimly.

Swallowing, she asked the inevitable. "You, ah, suggested something to Cord. Was it more surgery?" She wasn't sure she could go through the anxiety of another operation and convalescence without losing her sanity.

"No, I suggested a physical therapist," he replied. "The simple exercises he's been doing have probably taken him as far as he can go on his own."

"What was Cord's reaction?"

She held her breath.

"Shall we say, less than enthusiastic?" Bill answered dryly.

"I'd like to shake him until his teeth rattle!" Mary declared. "Either way I don't envy the person who has to work with him. He knows exactly how to cut a person down to size."

"That's why I'm arranging to have Paula come." A faint smile of agreement with his wife's opinion curved his mouth. "She's the best I know."

"Paula? Paula Hanson?" Mary was suddenly alert. With an approving toss of her red hair, she turned to Stacy. "You'll like her."

"The question is—will Cord?" Stacy sighed.

"I doubt it," Bill chuckled. "But don't worry, Paula will be able to handle him. She not only knows her job, she also has an uncanny knack of knowing what tactics to use on her patient."

"Tactics? Is this a war?" Stacy asked.

"In a way, it is, yes," the doctor said. "And she's worked with returning vets, even some multiple-trauma victims, and really helped them."

"I see," Stacy said. "Well, I hope she's strong-willed, because he's just about impossible at this point."

"She is," Bill said. "And incredibly capable, considering she's only twenty-eight."

"Is she married?" Stacy couldn't help asking.

"So far, only to her career. She specializes in difficult cases, which is why I want her," Bill explained. "Paula once told me that every success makes her want to take on another patient so she can apply what she's learned, and learn more. You can tell that she finds her work very rewarding."

"I guess she'll have to live here with us. We're really too far away from anywhere for her to rent and drive in each day. Not with gas prices high as they are." For some reason the thought of having a newcomer—female—out at the ranch was unsettling. Stacy couldn't say exactly why.

A frown creased Bill's forehead as if he'd considered

that a foregone conclusion. "It would be easiest if it's not too much trouble for you."

"No, of course not," she hastened. "I was only wondering what you'd told her."

"I'm sorry. I guess I wasn't thinking of much else besides her availability," Bill said. "I should have consulted with you first before telling Paula she could stay here. It wasn't very considerate of me."

"I'm in favor of anything that helps Cord," Stacy assured him.

"Hey, I was thrilled when she called me this morning to say she was released from the case she was on and would be available to come here after a few days off. I never gave a thought to calling you first to clear things," he said ruefully.

"Bill, it really doesn't bother me. She's more than welcome to stay here." Yet she felt an uncomfortable twinge of doubt. "I'm sure we'll get along."

"Don't judge her too quickly," he warned. "Sometimes she comes on a little tough and blunt. But if the saying was ever true that someone has a heart of pure gold, it's Paula. She'll take some of the load of caring for Cord off your shoulders."

"Of course." Stacy smiled.

Inwardly she realized she was suffering from the pangs of jealousy. It was foolish and selfish to resent a woman she hadn't even met because she would be doing all the little things for Cord that Stacy was doing now.

It was difficult to get close to him. Paula Hanson's arrival might deny Stacy the few chances she had for intimacy.

Recognizing the reason for her resentment also enabled Stacy to remember why Paula was coming. She was willing to sacrifice those moments with Cord if it would make him well again.

Mary and Bill Buchanan stayed for another hour. The conversation shifted from Cord to Josh and his visit.

Cord didn't return. When Stacy walked the Buchanans to the front door, she noticed the door to his bedroom was closed.

He was still in there when Maria announced that dinner was ready. Stacy knew if she went to the door he would simply say he wasn't hungry, so instead she sent Josh.

Cord wouldn't refuse his son.

The ploy worked and the three of them sat at the table together. Josh's nonstop chatter couldn't cover the brooding silence of his father, although Stacy was the only one to notice it.

"We played baseball too," Josh declared, intent on relating everything he'd done while he was gone. "Bill says I can hit pretty good. One time I hit a ball clear across the yard. That's a long way, huh?"

"It sure is," said Stacy, hiding a smile.

"Will you play ball with me tomorrow, Dad?" Bright dark eyes looked longingly at the man in the wheelchair. "I'll show you how I can hit the ball."

Cord looked down at his plate, turning a little pale. "It's difficult to play ball from a wheelchair, Josh," he responded with remarkable calm.

"I have an idea." Stacy spoke up quickly trying to divert the sudden frowning look Josh was giving his father. "Why don't you and I play ball tomorrow? Daddy can watch while you show him how well you can hit the ball."

"I guess so," Josh agreed. He pushed the peas on his plate around for several seconds, and then he frowned again at Cord and tipped his head to the side. "Dad, don't you get tired of watching all the time?"

Cord's fork clattered to the plate at Josh's question and

Stacy rushed to answer. "Of course he does, but it can't be helped." Hoping to distract him, she said, "Eat your dinner."

"I'm full." The small shoulders shrugged indifferently. He set his napkin on the table and leaned back in his chair, swinging his legs in a rhythmic motion. "How much longer is it going to be before Daddy gets better?"

Casting a sideways glance at Cord's grimly silent face, she dodged the question.

"I don't know. If you're through eating, you may be excused from the table. Ask Maria if she'll fix you an ice cream cone to eat on the veranda."

Josh slid from his chair and walked unenthusiastically toward the kitchen. His departure left the room charged with tension. Stacy picked a small dried leaf off the floral centerpiece and then, pushing thick chestnut hair behind one ear; she looked at Cord.

"He's just a little boy. He doesn't understand about these things," she said uneasily, not knowing how to soften the pain their son's innocent remarks had caused.

"Doesn't he?" His gaze pinned her. "I thought Josh summed it up well. I am bored and tired of watching all the time." Cord crumpled his napkin and tossed it on the table. "Excuse me."

"Cord, the therapist who's coming—" Stacy began as he pushed himself away from the table.

But he interrupted her attempt to restore hope. "I don't want to talk about it," was his caustic reply.

Chapter 3

Stacy lifted her head from the pillow and listened. She was sure she heard something. She waited. Had it been Josh crying out for her? There wasn't a sound in the quiet house.

She glanced at the luminous dial of her clock. One AM.

Nibbling at her lower lip, she waited a few more seconds, then slipped out of bed with a sigh. It was no use.

She wouldn't go back to sleep until she was sure Josh was all right.

It was crazy but all the while he'd been staying with the Buchanans, she hadn't woken once during the night to check on him. Yet this was only his first night back at home and she was already instinctively listening for him.

Her peach-colored robe was lying near the foot of the bed. Throwing it around her shoulders, Stacy walked barefoot to the hall door. Silence greeted her as she entered the corridor. She relied on her memory to make her way in the darkness to Josh's room across the hall from hers.

She opened the door quickly, stepping in to see him sleeping peacefully beneath the red and blue bedspread. Moonlight streamed in from the window, touching his black hair and magically lacing it with silver.

As she started to close the door, she heard what sounded like a low moan. Was it the wind rubbing a branch outdoors against the house? But there wasn't a strong wind, only the gentlest of breezes.

Then it came again. From downstairs, Stacy thought. Was it Cord? Her heart skipped a beat in fear that he might have fallen and was unable to pull himself back up.

Her feet barely touched the steps as she raced down the staircase to the master bedroom she'd shared with Cord until the accident. A low, deep moan sounded on the other side of the door and she flung it open.

A small night light illuminated his long shape in the bed. The black of his hair contrasted sharply with the white pillowcase.

His head rolled to one side. A tortured sound came from his throat, escaping his lips in the low moan that Stacy had heard. Swiftly she moved to his side, pausing for a frightened second when she saw the sweat beading his face. Again his head moved restlessly to the side.

Stacy realized with relief that he wasn't ill or fevered. He was dreaming; it was a nightmare. Lightly she laid a hand on his shoulder.

"Cord, wake up," she whispered. "You're dreaming. Everything's all right. It's just a dream. Wake up!"

His face was twisted as if in pain. He shook his head as though trying to chase away the image that troubled him. Her hand tightened on his shoulder. "Cord, wake up," she repeated.

Sooty lashes raised as Cord stared at her blankly. His fingers closed over the wrist of the hand resting on his shoulder. She could feel him trying to fight through the misty waves that still gripped his consciousness.

"Josh?" He frowned harshly. "Is he all right?"

"He's fine," she nodded, smiling to reassure him.

"Are you sure?" Cord lifted his head from the pillow.

"I'm positive," Stacy said. "I just looked in on him before I came downstairs. He's sound asleep."

Cord was back against the pillow, breathing shakily. "My God!" He shuddered. "I had this nightmare . . ."

His fingers were biting into her wrist so tightly he was nearly cutting off the circulation. Stacy leaned against the bed, half sitting on the edge. With her free hand, she took a tissue from the bedside table and began wiping the sweat from his forehead.

"It was only a dream," she repeated.

Cord sighed heavily. "He was in the swimming pool and he couldn't swim."

"You know that Josh swims like a fish," she chided him gently.

"I know, but this time he couldn't. I don't know why." Cord shook his head wearily and gazed into a dark corner of the room. "He kept crying for me to stop watching and save him. But I couldn't move. I—"

"Sssh." She touched a finger to his lips and he turned to look at her. His dark eyes showed the tormenting anguish that consumed him. "Forget about the dream."

Cord loosened the grip on her wrist without releasing it.

With his other hand, he stopped her from wiping his forehead, bringing her palm to rest along the hard line of his jaw. Sighing from the depths of his soul, he seemed to banish the last remnants of the nightmare.

As if he needed her nearness to keep it from coming back, he slowly slid his arms around her and pulled her down to his chest. Her head was nestled near the hollow of his throat.

"It was so real," he murmured, wrapping his arms around Stacy to hold her there.

"I know." There was a slight catch in her voice.

Beneath her head, she could feel the uneven thud of his heart. The dark, curling hair on his chest tickled her cheek. Her arm was thrown over him, her hand resting on the silken hardness of a bare shoulder.

The heady male scent of him was heightened by the sweat his nightmare had brought on. It filled her with sensual intoxication.

Her heart skipped several beats at the caressing warmth of his breath stirring her hair. Almost of its own volition, her hand began lightly exploring the smooth muscles of his shoulder and the strong column of his neck.

A large, pleasantly rough-textured hand moved down her spine, drawing her closer to him. Then lazily it began rubbing the curve of her waist. A searing contentment swept through her and Stacy sighed. There was no barrier between them now.

Cord pressed his mouth against the side of her hair for an instant, then rubbed his stubbly cheek against the silken strands.

"Sometimes," he said huskily, "I lie awake nights remembering how it was when you lay all soft and warm beside me."

He slid a hand beneath her tousled hair, curling it gently on the side of her neck. His thumb moved in a rhythmic circle on the sensitive skin. Shivers of joy danced over her as her heart quickened its pace.

"I remember how good your hair always smelled. Clean. Like flowers." Cord nuzzled the side of her head. "And the way you trembled when I touched you, your breasts swelling hard in my hand. I can still see the golden glow of your skin when you lay naked beside me, waiting. Your eyes shimmering with the fire we'd kindled."

Stacy was trembling now, the same liquid fire racing again through her veins. The seductive pitch of his voice was arousing more than just a memory. Her head was tipped back over the curve of his arm. Her lashes closed as Cord softly brushed his lips over her eyes, teasing the corners and kissing the gold dust of freckles over the bridge of her nose.

"And your lips." He pressed his mouth to hers, but only for a few seconds. "I would taste and taste and come back for more. I always wanted more from you."

A soft moan of aching desire rolled over her tongue, his words teasing and stimulating her until her mind was reeling. She felt the crook of his smile against her skin.

"Most of all I remember those little cat noises you made. Deep in your throat, halfway between a mew and a purr. But what I don't remember"—there was a note of amused mockery in his low voice as he slid a gentle hand to the neckline of her robe—"is you wearing so much to bed."

"That's because my nightgown was never on long enough for you to notice," Stacy murmured with a sighing laugh.

Her fingers wound into the raven strands of his hair. Arching in response, she welcomed the exquisite torture of his teasing mouth. Her heart rocketed under the commanding urgency of his kiss.

His mouth opened over hers, tasting the sweetness of her lips before parting them to explore her mouth. Deftly Cord untied her robe and cast it to the floor.

The narrow straps of her nightgown left her smooth shoulders bare to his caress.

The passionate embrace was a catalyst that released all the pent-up longings they'd held in check for so many months. The intimate touch of his hands made her feel more alive than she had in ages.

The days, the months, the strain of being together yet

apart vanished as Stacy gave herself up to the joy of a moment that transcended a mere physical response.

Holding a handful of her hair, Cord tipped her head back to expose her throat to the ardor of still more kisses.

Stacy shuddered as he moved inexorably closer to the shadowy cleft between her breasts. She strained against him and her fingers dug deep into the hard muscles of his arms.

In the next second, Cord was pushing her away from him with a groan.

Her bare foot touched the cool tile of the floor to keep her balance. Still quivering from his expert lovemaking, she gazed at him numbly, her eyes luminous and very soft.

"I love you, Cord." Her voice trembled.

His breathing was labored and Stacy knew he was as shaken as she was. In the dim light, she could see the frown creasing his wide forehead. His eyes were tightly closed as if . . . as if he was trying to shut out the sight of her.

With a nearly inaudible moan, she glided back to the broad chest, sliding her arms around his shoulders to cling to him.

But his hand closed punishingly over the soft flesh of her upper arms and he shoved her away.

"Stacy, don't," Cord demanded with a tormented groan.

Her fingers trailed over the rigid muscles in his arms as they held her away. She wanted more than anything to lessen the distance between them.

"I want you to hold me," she protested in an aching murmur. "Just hold me for a little while. It's been so long since I've had your arms around me or known your kisses."

"And what about the agony of an unfulfilled embrace?" he taunted in half-anger. "Don't torment me with that—or yourself."

"You're wrong, Cord," Stacy cried softly. "I can be satisfied with kisses. It's better than going without touching you or feeling you caress me."

"I know you better than that," Cord breathed. "We've spent too many nights together for me to forget that core of passion inside you. A touch—a kiss—isn't enough for either of us, not ultimately."

His words made her feel cold all over.

"What are you saying?" She looked at him warily, almost afraid to hear his answer.

"That I don't accept half measures," he answered. "I would always want all of you. And I want to be everything to you."

Stiffening, Stacy pulled away from his iron grip. "What about what I want? What I need?"

"Damnit, Stacy," he swore softly in frustration. His jaw was clenched, the line of his mouth set. "I can't come to you half a man."

Her chin quivered as he straightened away from the bed. "So you won't come to me at all, is that it?" she asked tightly. "And I'm not supposed to touch you or kiss you no matter how much I want to, is that what you're saying?"

"What I'm saying," Cord snapped, "oh, hell. This is hard to explain. What it's like for me—try to understand, Stacy. If you go without food long enough, you stop being hungry."

"Do you, Cord?" flashed Stacy. Her heart was nearly bursting with pain. "Or do you just die?"

A muscle leaped in his jaw. "Not entirely." He scowled and looked away from her, his gaze again seeking the dark corners of the room. "Although I've wished for it." He rubbed a numb thigh with his hand. "Now I know how a wild animal feels when it's caught in a trap and can't escape."

"But you aren't going to be trapped forever," she retorted. "You will walk again. Why can't you accept that? Why can't you believe that?"

"And why can't you accept the possibility that I may never walk again?" Cord growled.

"If I did, then what? Do you expect us to go on for the rest of our lives with you sleeping in one room and me in the other? Never touching? Never kissing? Never showing our love for each other?"

"I expect you to understand," he said impatiently. "My God, can't you guess what it's like, remembering what we once shared? How can you ask me to make love with virtually half of my body dead? I would prefer endless nightmares to that."

"It isn't dead," Stacy protested angrily.

Naked as he was, the faint glow from the night light brought out his physique. Cord had always been leanly muscled, but there was now a sinewy look about him, a result of the weight loss he'd suffered.

It didn't detract from his dark looks. He was still strong, still possessed an aura of virility, a touch of annoying arrogance, and a dozen other indefinable qualities that marked him out as a real man.

One corner of his mouth lifted in a cynical sneer. "Are you denying that I can't use my legs?"

"You can't use them now, but—" She brushed her hair away from her face, helplessly searching for words to make her argument. "That doesn't mean it will always be that way."

"And it doesn't mean that it won't," Cord countered.

"The physical therapist Bill is sending—he wouldn't have her come if he thought you were beyond help. Don't you realize that?" Stacy pleaded in a desperate kind of anger.

Cord breathed in deeply, a brooding look in his eyes.

"Sometimes I have the feeling that I'm a jigsaw puzzle that was put together the wrong way. The pieces don't fit anymore, but that doesn't stop people from trying to force them."

The weary despair in his voice touched her. Stacy couldn't help flinching at the strong undercurrent of monotonous pain that made his tone sound dull and flat.

"You mustn't give up," she said at last.

"Really?" A dark eyebrow lifted in dry amusement. "For nearly a year I've listened to one person after another telling me how good my chances are that I'll walk again. I keep hearing it and hearing it, but I'm still either in a wheelchair or in a bed. My hope is wearing thin."

"Maybe the therapist will try something new," Stacy offered weakly.

"There goes another maybe." He laughed without humor. "Maybe the therapist. Maybe the operation," Cord mocked. "Maybe, maybe, maybe."

"But what's the alternative?" she wanted to know. "Not to try at all? Don't you want to walk?"

"That's not the point." His mouth thinned.

"Forgive me, but I don't understand." Stacy walked to the end of the bed, her fingers gripping the bedrail until her knuckles were white. "What is the point?"

"I'm tired of having hope build up like air in a balloon, then watching it slowly deflate when it comes to nothing. Not just my own, but yours and Josh's, everyone's. I don't want you to be hurt anymore because of me." Cord stared at her for a long time, a heartrending ache in his eyes. "I've seen it happen and I've seen the way you try to hide it so I won't see. But I do."

Stacy shook her head. "Forget about what it's doing to Josh and me. Look what it's doing to you!" she argued. "You've become bitter. I can't even come near you these days. You don't want me to touch you or kiss you. You just keep retreating farther and farther away, living in your own little world. It must be terribly lonely there. Maybe you're tired of fighting, tired of trying and failing—I don't know."

"You haven't listened to anything I've said," Cord declared irritably.

"Oh yes I have. You're trying to tell me that the chances are you won't walk again. You want me to admit that. All right, I do." Anger was building inside her again, an anger born because he persisted in looking at the negative side. "You call yourself a cripple, then that's what you are. Do you hear?" Suddenly Stacy wanted to hurt him with words as he had hurt her. "You'll always be one. If that's the way you want to look at life, that's the way I'll look at it too!"

Her cheeks were damp and Stacy realized that she was crying. Her vision had blurred to the point where she could only make out a dim shape of him.

She swallowed a sob of pain and pivoted sharply around. "Stacy!"

But she was flying from the room, sobs wracking her with each racing, stumbling step. In her room, she threw herself onto the bed, soaking her pillow with tears.

She had held them back for nearly a year, but now the deluge had begun.

The ravages of the storm were visible in her face the next morning. Maria clucked anxiously at her, sure that Stacy's red nose, swollen eyes, and paleness were the symptoms of an oncoming cold. Stacy insisted she was fine, but her gaze kept straying to the closed door of the master bedroom.

Only Josh shared the breakfast meal with her. Cord remained in his room. On her way out of the house, she paused at the door, wanting to go in and apologize but not knowing what to say. Finally she left to meet Travis.

There was so much that had to be done in preparation

for the annual quarter horse sale at the ranch. Stacy wished she'd broken with tradition and postponed it.

She was a trembling mass of nerves, unable to concentrate. She kept remembering that first sale she'd organized for Cord. It had been that day—the day of the auction—when she had been on the verge of leaving that he'd told her he loved her and asked her to marry him.

Eventually Travis told her he would take care of the rest of the duties and suggested that she take the morning off. Stacy couldn't bring herself to go back to the house.

She didn't want to face Cord until she was in control of her emotions. If anyone looked at her crooked, she felt like she would burst into tears all over again.

Not once had she broken down when she learned of Cord's plane crash, nor during her flight to his side, nor during the harrowing hours and days after his stabilization and surgery. When he'd regained consciousness, Stacy had rejoiced with laughter and warmth. Now it had finally caught up with her and it seemed she couldn't stop crying.

A tear slipped from her lashes. She wiped it away with a shaking hand. Releasing a sobbing sigh, she turned away from the house and walked toward the stables.

Hank ambled forward to meet her, his sharp eyes missing nothing.

"Hi, Hank." Stacy greeted the old cowboy with forced brightness. "Would you saddle my mare for me? I thought I'd take a ride and chase the clouds for a while."

"Sure will."

Minutes later he led the chocolate-brown mare from the stable, saddled and bridled and ready to go. The breeze stirred the horse's mane as it nosed Stacy affectionately.

With Hank holding the bridle, she stepped into the stirrup and swung up into the saddle, gathering the reins in her hands. Hank remained at the horse's head, his wizened face turned up to her.

"The boss don't like for you to go out ridin' by yourself," he said quietly.

"I promise I won't go far."

Stacy smiled but her voice broke at the end of the sentence.

There was only one person that Hank ever referred to as the boss, and that was Cord. She touched her heels to the mare's flanks and reined it away before Hank saw the shimmer of tears in her eyes. The sorrel stallion in the stud pen whickered forlornly as she rode away.

Chapter 4

A Texas spring was impossible to ignore. After leaving the ranch buildings, Stacy had given the mare her head.

They cantered through the flowering meadow where the brood mares with new colts were pastured. Colorful bluebonnets, Mexican hats, and prickly poppies nodded and bowed their heads as Stacy and the mare went by.

Bees buzzed from blossom to blossom while bright butterflies lazily flitted along. The creak of the saddle leather and the dull thud of cantering hooves were soothing sounds to Stacy's jangled nerves.

To the west were the mountains, once the stronghold of the Mescalero Apaches. A dusty haze obscured them.

Raised all over the world, Stacy thought of herself as a Texan now. The land rejuvenated her—especially this land where she lived with Cord. It was her home and she loved it. She could ride for hours over its vast reaches.

Sighing, she reined the mare in and turned her toward the ranch yard. Unfortunately she didn't have time for such indulgences. There were a hundred and one things to be done at the ranch today. Stacy decided that she had better get them done while her eyes were dry and the pain in her chest had been reduced to a funny little ache.

Hank was waiting at the pasture gate to let her through.

She guessed he'd been watching for her for some time, although it seemed to her that she'd barely left. His concern touched her.

"You see, I made it back all in one piece." Dimples appeared in her cheeks as she teased him affectionately.

"You sure took your time about comin' back," he declared with mock gruffness. He took hold of the mare's bridle and held her while Stacy dismounted. "I was about to send someone out to look for you when I saw you in the meadow."

"You're worse than a mother hen," she chided.

"Yeah, well, it'd be my back the boss would climb on if anything was to happen to you."

"What could happen riding Candy Bar?"

She handed the reins to him, patting the mare's neck.

"I was beginnin' to wonder that myself," Hank grumbled.

"Would you mind walking her out for me?"

At his agreeing nod, Stacy angled toward the ranch house sitting on a slight rise above the other buildings. Josh was playing in the front yard with Maria keeping an eye on him through a window as she did the housework. When he saw Stacy coming, he hopped on his tricycle and rode down the driveway to meet her, varooming all the way.

"Where have you been, Mommy?" he asked as he wheeled alongside of her.

"I went for a ride."

Josh immediately scowled at her answer. "I wanted to go too!"

"Another time, maybe," she suggested.

"That's what you always say," he complained. "You'll forget, I know you will."

"How could I possibly forget you?" As they started up the driveway, Stacy slowed her steps. Josh's small legs pedaled harder to keep up.

"Will you play softball with me?" He glanced up at her, the scowl leaving his face. His foot slipped off a pedal and he nearly rolled down the hill before Stacy could grab the handlebars. "You said you would," he reminded her.

"I can't now, Josh." She shook her head ruefully. "I have work to do. Later, okay?"

"Promise?"

"I promise."

Stacy crossed her heart with her fingers and he was satisfied.

"I hit grounders best of anything," he told her importantly.

"I'll bet you do." She gave him her biggest smile. They had reached the sidewalk to the house. "You stay outside and play until lunchtime, okay? But don't go out of the yard."

The level front offered a perfect straightaway and Josh was already careening down it as he shouted his answer. "Okay, Mommy!"

Stacy opened the door. Walking in, she turned to close it, darting a last, tenderly maternal glance at her son.

"It's about time you got back!" a harsh voice growled behind her.

Her shoulders tensed under Cord's piercing gaze—it seemed to drill right through her jeans jacket. She turned around slowly. Her barely healed nerves were suddenly fraying again, considering the sharpness of his tone.

Cord's wheelchair blocked the foyer door into the living room. His clenched jaw made his lean features taut and forbidding. She felt pinned to the spot by his narrow gaze.

Somehow she managed to close the door.

"Were you looking for me?" she asked with forced calm.

"No, I wasn't," he informed her in a steely voice. "I was listening to everyone else tell me how ill you looked."

His eyes raked her mercilessly, nearly stripping away the thin veneer of composure that she had attained. Her mouth tightened, guessing that Maria was the talebearer and wishing the woman had kept silent.

"I hardly think it was everyone," she murmured, avoiding his gaze.

"First Maria, then Travis, then Bill," Cord said tersely.

"Bill?" Stacy frowned.

"The good doctor phoned a little while ago to let you know that this Hanson woman will be arriving on Friday." The explanation was snapped out.

"How did he know about me?"

Immediately she wished she hadn't worded the question that way.

It was an admission that she hadn't been herself when she'd gotten up that morning. Despite her heated statements last night, Stacy didn't want Cord becoming concerned about her.

Because right now he needed to concentrate on his own recovery and nothing else.

"Maria answered the phone," Cord explained. "By the time I talked to him, he was more worried about where you were."

"I went for a ride."

Stacy flipped her long hair away from her neck, striving for a nonchalance that she just didn't feel.

"Alone."

It was an accusation.

Her head jerked slightly. "Who told you?" Surely Hank wouldn't have.

The strong, male line of his mouth tightened. "I saw you leave the stables." With suppressed violence, he swung the wheelchair around toward the living room. "Damnit, Stacy, you already know how I feel about you wandering out on the range by yourself!"

Stacy winced. "Yes, Hank reminded me," she said in a low voice.

"Suppose your mare fell or you were thrown. Do you want me to start having nightmares about you lying unconscious in some remote place? Is that why you did it?" he challenged her.

"No." Stacy followed him, her hands clasped nervously together. "I had to get away for a while, to be by myself and think."

"Alone on a horse?" he jeered. "I didn't realize that was a necessity for thinking."

"You don't understand. I had to get away," she began desperately.

"No, I don't understand!" Cord interrupted. "If you wanted to be alone, you could've just as easily gone to your room."

"Like a misbehaving teenager? Listen to yourself, will you?"

Cord shot her a glare.

"I couldn't stay in the house, Cord. Everything was closing in around me. I had to get away from—" She stopped abruptly, glancing at him.

A sardonic eyebrow went up.

"From me?" Cord finished the sentence for her.

Stacy hesitated, then admitted, "Yes, from you. Last night—"

She wanted to say that she regretted some of her outburst, but her tongue tied itself in knots over the words.

"What about last night?"

His dark head was tilted to one side at a watchful angle.

She couldn't meet his alert gaze and turned her back to him. Her stomach was churning. There was a throbbing pain in her temples as her poise began to splinter.

"I can't take much more of this fighting," she began. "I need to get away from these crazy emotions—they're toxic, I swear. Oh, Cord—"

A sob rose in her throat and she had to stop to swallow it. She didn't want to break down in front of him again.

"I thought that was what this was leading up to," Cord declared, exhaling harshly. "I should probably be surprised that it's taken you so long."

Stacy pivoted to look at him blankly. The disgust etched in his drawn features nearly took her breath away.

A smoldering fire darkened his eyes to the shade of hard black diamonds, just as sharp and cutting.

"There's no need to look so puzzled," he said sarcastically. "Bill's already paved the way for you. Did you cry on his shoulder last night?"

"I don't know what you're talking about."

She frowned in genuine confusion.

"Don't you? Didn't you just say that you needed to get away?" he countered.

"Yes, but—"

"It was Bill's medical opinion that you needed a few weeks rest, away from me and the ranch." Cord breathed in deeply, as if summoning his strength. "He seemed to think you were under too much stress. And that you'd reached your limit."

Stacy opened her mouth, wanted to deny it, yet secretly she feared the same thing. At this moment, she couldn't explain that. It was a good thing that Bill had done the talking for her.

"It hasn't been easy for me," she murmured finally.

"Did you stage that outburst last night so I would be convinced when Bill talked to me today, knowing all the while that he would call?" Cord asked.

"No!" she gasped in wounded outrage. The accusation bordered on paranoia. Cord was going too far.

"And you made sure this morning that others saw how upset you were," added Cord, totally ignoring her denial.

"You were the one who had the nightmare," Stacy reminded him indignantly. "You woke me—that's why I came to your room. And you were the one who started the entire argument with your stupid pride and self-pity, and your insistence that there couldn't be any physical contact between us. Did you expect me to just bow my head and say *whatever you wish, my lord*?"

"Don't pretend with me, Stacy!" There was a savage note in the controlled anger of his reply. "I should've known that it wouldn't last."

"Oh, please—"

"I should have guessed why you kept clinging so desperately to the hope that I would walk again. I have to give you credit for trying."

"Pretend? Trying? What are you talking about?" she demanded, now thoroughly confused. "Everything I've said is the truth. I didn't ask Bill to tell you I should have a few weeks' rest. When he suggested it to me, I told him no."

Cord laughed coldly. "Whatever you do, don't mess up the image of a loving wife," he said bitterly. "Be sure to twist things around and make it look as if you're the injured party."

"I never claimed to be the injured party," Stacy cried helplessly.

"Plenty of people seem to be willing to do it for you." The grooves around his mouth deepened with cynicism. "Why?" She ought to know better than to argue with him in this irrational mood, but hell—she was feeling fairly irrational herself.

"Throw yourself a pity party. Ask for all the sympathy you want, because you're married to a cripple. You'll get it," Cord replied.

"You're not bitter or anything, are you?"

"Yes, I admit that I am," he said grimly. "As for the rest of it—just tell me that what I'm saying is true and we'll call it even."

"But I don't understand what you're saying and I'll be damned if I'll bargain with you—"

"You've finally become bored with ranch life, haven't you?" Cord studied her with freezing aloofness.

"What?" She was stunned.

"It wasn't so bad before the crash, was it?" he asked. "We traveled a lot, took some fun horse-buying trips or odd weekends to shop in Dallas or Denver. Josh kept you busy when he was a baby. And the ranch was still a new experience for you at first. Then"—he reached down and gripped his leg, his mouth quirking with pain—"the accident happened."

He lifted his gaze from his legs to her. Stacy was so shocked by what he was implying that she couldn't speak. She stared at him in disbelief.

"This past year, it's been different. You've been either at the hospital or at the ranch," continued Cord. "No side trips to break the monotony. No social events, because you wouldn't go without me. No nothing. You're bored and wondering where the hell the magic went. Sorry about that."

"Cord, don't talk crazy. I mean it."

He was on a roll. "You're young, Stacy. I can understand, in a way. You want to see and do things that I can't, just have fun once in a while."

"My father took me all over the world with him,"

she protested. "Freelance photographer, footloose single dad. Remember?"

"Yeah. So?"

"I've seen everything. I'm happy here with you and Josh."

"Really? I don't think you're ready to settle for the same-old, same-old routine around a ranch." For all the sudden lack of emotion in his voice, the cold glare of his eyes was condemning. "You don't want to accept the possibility that I might be an invalid for the rest of my life because that would mean the boredom would never end. No trips, no vacations, no dancing, no fun. Just a lifetime of taking care of me."

"I don't mind," Stacy insisted.

"For how long?" he questioned. "Right now you feel guilty about leaving me alone. That's why you stage-managed an incident where someone else suggests you go away for a rest. It wouldn't be your idea that way."

"I didn't do anything of the kind." He was irrational, she knew, and there wasn't any use getting angry with him. What Cord was going through was the result of many things. Worry. Not eating. Not sleeping. And not being able to walk. It might take more than just physical therapy to get him back on track, she thought. She would ask Bill about antidepressants—and about someone Cord could talk to. Not her.

"Just admit it," he was saying. "You think that if you leave me for a few weeks, it won't be so bad when you come back. But in six months, you'll be bored again and want to take another short break. A couple of months after that, you'll want to go again until finally you won't want to come back at all."

"That's not true," she said evenly. "This is my home." Best to keep him talking for now, even if he was just about ranting, she thought. Let him get it out of his system. Then maybe he'll feel better.

You won't, said a small voice in her head.

"It is true," Cord insisted. He was close to shouting now, his deep voice rolling like thunder over her. "You're forgetting my mother—she was just as high-maintenance as you are. She liked the ranch at first too—it appealed to her adventurous nature, I guess. But she got sick of it and went back to the so-called civilized world—"

That was too much. She forgot all about humoring him and responded heatedly, "I'm not like your mother was!"

"Aren't you?" he said. "I'll bet you didn't even intend to take Josh with you when you went on Bill's medically recommended vacation. You would leave him the same way my mother left me—"

"I would not leave him! And I'm not going away on any vacation!"

"That's right," Cord began.

"Listen to me, Cord! I get that you're scared and in pain, but you need serious help and I can't give it to you—"

"You listen to me, Stacy." His hands gripped the armrests of the wheelchair, the muscles in his forearms rippling. It was difficult to believe he wasn't able to get out of the chair and have those long strides of his carrying him to her side. "You made a vow to me. If you love me, you'll keep it. Remember what you said? In sickness and in health—"

"We got one wrong." Her voice was starting to break, an uncontrollable anger trembling on the edges. "It should have been for *bitter* or for worse!"

Stacy was about to run from the room, when a small, dark-haired boy appeared in the doorway to the veranda.

His rounded eyes were sad and troubled as he looked from the glowering face of his father to Stacy, gone suddenly pale.

The awful silence lasted only a few seconds, but they seemed much longer when both Stacy and Cord realized Josh had overheard their heated argument. Stacy recovered her wits first, taking a step toward her son.

Josh immediately started to retreat, half turning as if to run.

"Joshua!" Cord's commanding voice checked the boy's flight. He darted a frightened look at his father. When Cord spoke again, the bite of anger was out of his voice. "Come here, Josh. It's all right." Although said calmly, it was no less imperative.

Josh hesitated, glancing at his mother. "It's all right." Stacy added her reassurance to Cord's and held out a hand to the little boy.

With obvious reluctance, he walked toward her, his feet dragging. The silken black head was tilted downward, but he managed to watch both his parents, peering at them warily through thick, curling lashes.

There was a scalding ache in Stacy's heart when he stopped in front of her, not taking her outstretched hand.

Kneeling, she placed her hands on his small shoulders. They were stiff and he seemed to resist her touch.

"It's okay, Josh," she reassured him again in a shaky voice. "We were arguing, that's all. You've heard Mommy and Daddy quarrel before."

"You were yelling at each other," he muttered, his lower lip jutting out slightly.

He could tell this time that it was different, more than a mere disagreement.

Biting at her lower lip, she glanced at Cord. His expression was grim, his mouth clamped shut in a tight line.

He had clasped his hands in his lap, gripping them with punishing fierceness.

"Y-your daddy was upset with me," Stacy began, trying to give Josh an explanation he would understand.

It was difficult. The emotionally charged scene with Cord was still whirling in her mind. The strange things he'd said preoccupied her and dulled her thinking.

"Why?" Josh prompted in an unconvinced tone.

"Because—I'd gone riding by myself." She smiled weakly, running a hand over the sleeve of his shirt, wanting to draw the little boy into his arms. "You see, Daddy became upset because I might've fallen and got hurt. Since I was all by myself, no one would know. And sometimes, when you're very upset because you care about someone, you start yelling."

Josh looked at Cord out of the corner of his eye, seeking confirmation of her words. Cord breathed in deeply, relaxing the fierce grip of his hands.

"That's true, Josh," he agreed.

Turning back to Stacy, Josh studied the brittle calm of her expression. He didn't seem very sure of himself.

"Are you going away, Mommy?"

"Of course not." She got busy straightening the collar of his shirt and smoothing his hair. "If I went away, who would tie your shoes?" she teased softly.

"Daddy said you were, though."

"Daddy said"—she swallowed the lump in her throat—"that I was going to stay here with you and him forever and ever and ever. Because we're a family."

He blinked. "Are you sure?"

"Yes, I am. Never been more sure about anything in my life."

"Okay." Josh grinned in satisfaction.

"Say, I have an idea." She brushed a playful finger across the tip of his nose.

"What's that?" His eyes were again bright and clear as he cocked his head.

"Instead of waiting until this afternoon, why don't we play ball now?"

"Yeah!" he said excitedly. "And Daddy can come outside with us too, huh?"

"Ask him." Stacy smiled stiffly.

There was a time when she could have answered for Cord. But after the things he'd said to her, he seemed practically like a stranger. She had a feeling she didn't know him at all.

Josh turned eagerly to Cord. "Will you come watch us?"

"Yes," he said with a curt nod.

Straightening, Stacy ruffled her son's soft hair.

"Go and find your bat and ball," she said. "We'll meet you outside in a few minutes.

Not needing a second invitation, Josh was off with a rush. Stacy's gaze followed him, watching the doorway for several seconds after he had disappeared from view. Wearily she slid her fingers through her hair, lifting it away from her face, and turned to walk toward Cord.

She felt drained.

"I'll help you outside," she muttered, heading toward the back of his wheelchair.

As she came nearer, his hand closed over her wrist to stop her. She glanced down, stoically meeting his hooded look.

"I owe you an apology," Cord said quietly. His next statement was not as welcome to her. "You could've easily used Josh as a weapon against me, but you didn't."

Stacy twisted her wrist away from his hand. "That's a hateful thing to say." Her voice was choked with emotion. "He is *our* son, not just mine or yours. I would never make him take sides."

"I did apologize for thinking it," he reminded her.

"Lately I don't know you." She stared at him almost fearfully. "I feel like I'm living with a stranger. No matter what you're going through—and I know it's a lot—I don't see how you can imagine for one minute that I would do what your mother did."

Cord studied her silently for a long moment. "But you were the one who told me yourself that you couldn't take much more and that you needed to get away. I didn't imagine that."

"But—" The beginnings of another argument formed in her mind. Stacy paused and shook her head hopelessly. "Don't start this all over again."

"We won't," he said with finality. "I only want to remind you that you're my wife and I'm never letting you go."

Stacy bridled at the ring of possession in his voice. It was the same tone that had once thrilled her when it was spoken with confidence and love instead of needy desperation. So much had changed.

"We'd better go outside." She suppressed the urge to make a cutting retort and got behind his wheelchair. "Josh will be waiting for us."

Chapter 5

"Maria." Stacy stepped into the kitchen, adjusting the wide-brimmed hat on her head.

"Si." The plump housekeeper was standing in front of the sink, washing the breakfast dishes. She glanced over her shoulder at Stacy without pausing in her work.

"I'm leaving now with Travis to check on the cattle the boys are moving to the summer range," she told Maria. "I should be back shortly before lunch if anyone calls. Josh is playing out front."

"I will keep an eye on him," the older woman promised.

"Thanks, Maria." Stacy was on her way out, then she turned back. "Oh—Paula Hanson, the physical therapist Dr. Buchanan got for Cord, should be arriving sometime today. If she comes while I'm gone, you can put her things in the room down the hall from mine."

"I have it all aired and cleaned for her," Maria assured her.

"Good. I'll see you later." Stacy waved briefly and hurried down the hallway to the front door.

As she passed Cord's room, she heard the radio playing, but she didn't stop to tell him she was leaving. If he wanted to know where she was, he could ask Maria.

The barrier between them was growing higher. Truth be told, she felt safer with it.

Even though she knew much of what he'd said was irrational, Cord's embittered accusations had wounded Stacy deeply. She wasn't able to shrug them off. It was impossible to ignore the things he'd said by chalking them up to his sorry state of mind and physical misery, her feelings had been hurt too severely to do that.

If he believed any portion of what he said, he couldn't possibly love her as she loved him. And that was the cruelest blow of all. Pride wouldn't let her go to him one more time—why did she always have to do the forgiving?

If he didn't know how, he would have to learn. He too had to try and undo the damage their heated argument had done.

And she wasn't going to pretend that the traumatic scene hadn't taken place. No, if the barrier was going to come down the first move would be made by Cord, not by her.

The music coming through the closed door followed Stacy as she walked out the front of the house, stopping when she shut the main door firmly behind her. It wasn't as easy, unfortunately, to block out the painful memory of Cord's unfounded accusations.

The pickup truck was parked in the driveway. Travis was kneeling beside the red tricycle on the sidewalk and Josh was beside him supervising the tightening of the handlebars.

Both had glanced up at the closing of the front door. Stacy forced the strained line of her mouth into a smile of greeting.

"Hey, you two."

"Hey, yourself," Travis called amiably.

"If you start adjusting all of Josh's toys to his personal satisfaction, Travis, he'll never give you a minute's peace," she declared, teasing her son's near obsession with getting things to operate smoothly, a trait of his father's.

"I don't mind," Travis insisted with a slow smile, straightening to his full height. He ruffled the mop of black hair on Josh's head. "After all, a kid can't steer a tricycle properly if there's too much play in the handlebars, right?"

"Right." Josh bobbed his head emphatically.

"It's no wonder he's becoming a little spoiled." Stacy sighed but with loving indulgence. "Everyone on the ranch caters to him."

She looked pointedly at her son. "Have you thanked Travis for fixing your trike? He wasn't obliged to do it."

White teeth bit into his lower lip as Josh cast a quick sideways look at the tall foreman. "Thank you, Travis."

"You're welcome," Travis answered, winking at Stacy.

Stacy took a deep breath of the morning air. "We'd better be going." Then she said to Josh, "You behave yourself."

He frowned. "Can't I come along?"

"Not this time." She shook her head in a definite refusal. "And you stay right here in the house yard so Maria won't have to worry about where you are."

"Fooey!" Josh grumbled, making a face. "Travis said there were two new colts in the barn. Can't I even go down and see them?"

"No, you can wait until after lunch and we'll go down to see them together. In the meantime, you stay here where Maria can keep an eye on you, like I said. Do you understand?"

"Ye-es," he mumbled.

"Yes what?" She prompted a more respectful reply.

"Yes, ma'am, I'll stay here," was his unenthusiastic response.

"I'll be back around lunchtime. Love ya," she told him and walked toward the pickup with Travis following her.

"He's a great kid," Travis commented as he slid behind the wheel.

"Yes, he is," Stacy agreed quietly with a note of pride in her voice.

At the starting of the engine, she waved goodbye to Josh. The sight of the small figure wistfully watching her leave made her heart ache all over again. For Cord to think she wanted to leave him because of his long, difficult recuperation was one thing, but him accusing her of wanting to leave their son as well was unforgivable.

Was it hopeless? She had no way of knowing. Stacy's shoulders slumped as her elbow rested on the rounded metal below the open window. She stared out, her mind registering nothing that her eyes saw.

"I wish you hadn't let Cord talk you out of getting away for a few days," said Travis after several minutes of silence.

"What?" Her head jerked toward him in surprise and confusion.

Briefly his dark gaze left the rutted track to meet her stunned look. "Josh told me about it while I was his fixing his tricycle," he explained. "I filled the odd parts in myself."

"How . . . how much did he tell you?" Stacy faltered.

"That he happened to hear the two of you arguing the other day about your leaving." They were approaching a fence gate and Travis geared the truck down. "Josh said that his daddy didn't want to let you go."

When his gaze again swung toward her, Stacy averted her head, unwilling to meet his eyes. He was much too perceptive.

"I see," she murmured.

"Forgive me for poking my nose in what's none of my business," he said bluntly, "but that was one time you should have stood your ground, Stacy. You need a break from the pressure of the ranch and Cord. Everything in general."

Stacy had two options. One was to deny that she'd been the one to suggest to Cord that she wanted to get away for a few days. But that would mean explaining how Josh had misunderstood the argument. The second choice was to let Travis believe that she'd asked Cord and he had refused to agree to a short vacation. She chose the second, not wanting to discuss the real argument that was still so very painful.

"I suppose I should have." The deliberately indifferent agreement was offered as Travis braked the truck to a stop at the fence gate. Immediately she lifted the door handle. "I'll open it."

Hopping down from the cab of the truck, she walked to the gate, unlatched it and swung it open for Travis to drive through. When the rear of the truck cleared the gate, she closed it securely and went back to the passenger side. With her fingers crossed that the subject was ended, she climbed back into the truck. For nearly a mile there was silence.

"You didn't ask Cord if you could go away for a few days, did you?"

It was more of a statement than a question. Travis stared at the road ahead.

Out of the corner of her eye, Stacy studied his strongly etched profile and the silvery streak of hair under the brim of his Stetson. When his keen gaze swung to her, she looked away.

"What makes you say that?" She tried to sound casual.

"You've been too adamant about leaving Cord," he replied. "And if you had changed your mind, you can be as stubborn as he is. You wouldn't have let him talk you out of something you really wanted to do. That means Josh didn't understand the argument, did he?"

"Does anyone really understand arguments or how they get started?" Stacy responded ambiguously.

"Very seldom," Travis admitted. "Do you want to talk about it?"

Her shoulders lifted in a shrug. "Cord was just a little more unreasonable than usual, that's all."

"Was it his suggestion that you should leave?" he asked quietly.

"Something like that," she answered, again noncommittally.

His thick brow arched. "Don't tell me he gave in to a crazy impulse to say that you should leave him permanently? And did he add that you shouldn't be tied to a supposed invalid for the rest of your life?"

"Actually," her mouth twisted wryly, "he believed that was what I felt and what I wanted. He reminded me in no uncertain terms of our marriage vows. In sickness and in health"—her own paraphrase slipped out—"for bitter or worse."

"I don't believe it!" The words came out in an explosion of disgust.

"Unfortunately, it's true."

"How—" Travis began with controlled anger.

"Please," Stacy interrupted in a strained voice. "I really don't want to talk about it. It won't change anything."

"I could go and talk to Cord and straighten him out on a few facts," Travis declared.

"No." She refused his suggestion immediately. "I shouldn't have told you about the argument."

"You didn't—Josh did. In all innocence."

"That's a moot point, since I explained what it was really about," Stacy said ruefully. "I shouldn't have. Our personal problems are something that Cord and I will have to work out alone."

They both lapsed into silence. It wasn't broken until they reached the noon holding ground for the cattle drive. Then the talk centered on the spring calf crop, the drive, the condition of the pastures, and the water levels of the various wells.

When the main herd topped a distant crest. Stacy's mind wandered from the conversation between Travis and Ike, the trail boss. The dusty haze that obscured the cattle and their faint lowing held Stacy in the trap of nostalgic memories of other drives. She remembered her first one, when she and Cord had been virtually at war with each other.

After they were married, they had sentimentally spent at least one night on the trail during the drive. Sharing a big bedroll, they'd settled in beside their campfire at some distance from the main campground. They had laughed and teased each other about that first drive, when she'd accused him of being arrogant and he'd declared that she was just plain spoiled.

Closing her eyes, Stacy could remember the way their laughter and soft voices had inevitably faded into silence. For a few minutes they would simply gaze into each other's eyes. In the few seconds before Cord would draw her into his arms, the stars had always seemed to grow brighter, just as if they knew what was on the minds of the two lovers below.

They had been so close, spiritually and physically. An invisible knife twisted inside Stacy at the knowledge that they were further apart now than they had ever been.

Suddenly she wished she hadn't felt the necessity to personally check on the cattle drive. The bittersweet memories from previous ones were just too overwhelming.

Moving away from the windmill and its watering tank, Stacy joined Travis and the trail boss, needing to lose herself in the present in order to forget the past. It was not an altogether successful attempt, she realized; when Travis suggested some time later that they should be getting back to the ranch house, her relief was too great.

Travis reversed the pickup onto the ranch road as the

remuda vans arrived with fresh horses for the riders. During the drive back to the ranch house, Stacy felt his gaze dwelling on her several times. Yet when he spoke, it was invariably about ranch business.

A small economy car was parked in the driveway when they arrived at the house. Stacy looked at it curiously, not remembering for a brief instant that Paula Hanson, the physical therapist, was expected today. She felt an odd mixture of anxiety and hope that the woman was actually here at last.

"Do you suppose that's Miz Hanson's car?" Travis stopped the pickup behind it.

Stacy nodded. "I imagine so. I don't know of anyone else who was expected today."

Her hand gripped the door handle but she hesitated before opening it. "Why don't you join us for dinner, Travis?"

Kind eyes studied her thoughtfully. It wasn't uncommon for Travis to have dinner with them. Stacy had invited him often.

"How does Cord feel about her?" He ignored Stacy's invitation for the moment.

There was no sense hiding the truth. Cord would be quick enough to tell it if the occasion arose.

"He's nearly convinced himself that it will be a waste of time." She was afraid Cord's opinion was more definite than that.

"So you want me to act as a buffer tonight?" There was an understanding quirk to his mouth.

"If you could, that would be great." Stacy smiled faintly. "I'd like to make her first night here as cordial as possible."

"She isn't married?" Travis asked.

"No."

"Then I'll be there," he said, winking.

Despite his teasing, she sensed a lack of real interest in the woman's single status. Stacy thought of the heartbreak Travis concealed, but she knew better than to mention it, ever.

"Thanks." She opened the cab door and stepped out. "Is seven too early for you?"

"I can make it," he assured her as he shifted the truck into gear.

With a saluting wave of one finger, he pulled around and drove toward the ranch buildings beyond the house. Stacy glanced again at the lime-green economy car and walked to the house. Unconsciously, she squared her shoulders as she went through the front door.

In the living room arch, she paused, looking at the woman seated on the sofa. Her hair was ash blond and long, swept away from her face and secured at the nape of her neck with a knotted scarf in a blue silk print.

Blue pants covered her long legs. Cajun's graying muzzle was resting near the toe of her white sandals. A sleeveless knit top in the same shade of blue as her pants revealed wide shoulders. Paula Hanson could definitely be described as statuesque.

"Well, Mrs. Harris?" The therapist spoke clearly when Stacy's slow study was completed. "Do you think I can handle him?"

Stacy swallowed, hoping that she hadn't seemed rude.

The other woman only smiled and the action made Stacy notice that the blonde's features were not very feminine. The line of her brow was too straight. There was a slight crook in her nose and her chin jutted out from a strong jaw.

The smile was just as strong. However, it animated Paula's face, and her blue eyes even seemed to sparkle a bit.

"What?" Stacy asked, forgetting the question that had just been put to her.

Paula Hanson's expression immediately became serious

again as she rose to her feet, confirming Stacy's impression that she was tall.

"You are Mrs. Harris, aren't you?" She tipped her head to the side, an end of her silk print scarf trailing over one shoulder.

"Yes, I'm Stacy Harris," she said with a quick smile, feeling a little stupid. She walked into the living room, extending a hand toward the therapist. "You obviously are Paula Hanson. I'm sorry I wasn't able to be here when you arrived."

"It's all right. I understand." Long fingers firmly clasped Stacy's hand. "Maria showed me my room and helped me settle in. She indicated that you'd be back for lunch."

"Great. I hope everything's all right." But Stacy noticed the omission of any reference to Cord. Hadn't they met yet?

"Everything's fine," Paul was saying.

She sat back on the sofa and reached for a glass filled with red liquid and ice cubes that was sitting on an end table. "Tomato juice with a dash of Tabasco." She identified the drink with amusement in her voice. "Maria wanted to fix me something stronger, but I didn't want you to think you suddenly had a lush living in your home."

Stacy's smile became genuine and relaxed, her faint wariness toward the stranger vanishing. "You're welcome to have something stronger if you'd like," she assured her.

"Do you think I'll need it?"

She nodded in the direction of the master bedroom.

"You haven't met"—Stacy breathed in deeply—"my husband yet, have you?"

"No." Her gaze ricocheted from Stacy to study the clear cubes in her glass. "I have the feeling he would like to ignore me as long as possible in the hope that I'll go away."

Stacy didn't attempt to deny the comment. "He's aware that you've arrived, though, isn't he?"

"Oh yes," the therapist confirmed. "Maria knocked on his door and told him, but he seemed less than thrilled."

That was probably putting it mildly, Stacy thought with chagrin. "I'm sorry—"

"No need to be." The woman sipped at the tomato juice. "He has to come out of the room sooner or later."

Looking over her shoulder at Paula, Stacy felt confused by her attitude of unconcern toward her patient.

"I thought you'd want to meet Cord as soon as possible."

"There's time enough to beard the lion in his den. I'd just rather not do it on an empty stomach," Paula Hanson declared. "By the way, I tend to be blunt, Mrs. Harris."

"Call me Stacy." She studied the other woman's no-nonsense expression. Paula might be just what Cord needed.

Paula nodded. "I don't mean to offend, Stacy, when I say that all I've learned so far about your husband makes me believe that he intends to be difficult. It happens more often than not. So I don't mind putting off meeting him for a few hours."

"I think you might be right." Stacy's lips twitched with amusement as she pivoted back toward the woman.

How long had it been since she'd found humor in the situation? A very long time, if ever, she was sure. She had the feeling that she needed Paula Hanson's bracing forth-rightness and wit as much as Cord needed her professional help.

The blonde leaned over and scratched behind the ears of the German shepherd lying near her feet. "I love this dog. What's his name?"

"Cajun." As she spoke, the dog thumped his tail against the floor and gazed adoringly at Stacy. "He seems to like you, Paula."

Paula gave her an odd smile. "All kinds of beasts end up liking me."

The sly reference to Cord wasn't missed by Stacy. Paula's remark was also a prophetic-sounding statement that Stacy hoped would come true. Now that she'd met Paula Hanson, Stacy didn't feel any of the jealousy she'd expected to feel about someone else seeing to his needs. Already the presence of the physical therapist in the house seemed like a breath of fresh air in a house that really needed it.

Maria bustled into the living room. "Lunch will be ready in a few minutes," she announced.

"Thanks." Stacy smiled, then glanced toward the dining room. "Where's Josh? Did he wash up yet?"

"He is outside. I fixed him a picnic lunch," the housekeeper explained. "What about Mister Cord? Is he coming to the table or should I fix him a tray?"

"You'll have to ask him. I haven't spoken to him since I came back," Stacy answered.

As the housekeeper's rolling walk carried toward the master bedroom, Stacy turned to the blonde sitting on the sofa. "It's a good thing that I made it back for lunch or you could have been eating your first meal here alone. Have you met our son Josh?"

Paula Hanson nodded. "He was playing outside when I drove up. That boy is going to be breaking women's hearts soon enough. He's a real charmer."

"Like his father was." The smile suddenly faded from Stacy's lips as she realized she'd used the past tense. But it had been a very long time since Cord had been charming about or toward anything.

"Don't worry about your husband's behavior, Stacy."

Whew. Paula Hanson understood a lot without needing embarrassing explanations, and thank God for that, Stacy thought.

"Like I said, it happens in my line of work, especially

with men. I'm accustomed to the snarling and growling," Paula chuckled. "It's my job to change them back to what they were."

Stacy couldn't respond to that. Too many of her prayers were riding on those same thoughts.

"Tell me a little about your husband, Stacy. Right off the top of your head, how would you describe him? I don't mean his appearance, of course."

"Ah—" Stacy hesitated, a little puzzled by the question and not about to reveal anything emotional or intimate. "He's—he's the practical type. Cord can't stand it when things don't work right and he won't give up until they do. Does that give you some idea?" The words came out in a rush, but they seemed to be about all she could safely say. Despite her first impression of Paula, the therapist was still a stranger. Stacy smiled weakly.

"Yes, it does. Thanks very much."

Stacy got up, hoping there would be no more questions. It would be up to Cord to answer them if so. "Would you excuse me, Paula?" She held up her hands. "I'm dusty from the drive. I'll wash up and join you at the table in a few minutes."

"Fine," the blonde agreed.

Stacy was climbing the stairs to her room when Maria stepped out of the master bedroom, closing the door behind her. Stacy didn't pause to ask if Cord was going to show for lunch.

As Paula had said, he was trying to ignore her presence in the house, and the best way to do that was to remain in his room. Stacy sighed at his stubbornness.

Chapter 6

As she started down the steps to rejoin Paula, Stacy saw the back of Cord's wheelchair as it disappeared into the dining room and she paused in surprise. She'd been sure that he would insist on having a tray in his room. Her heart quickened at the thought that he might have changed his mind about the new therapy.

Hurrying down the stairs, she entered the living room just as Cord wheeled the chair into the dining room. He stopped inside the archway, obviously gazing at Paula Hanson. For some reason, Stacy hesitated for a moment, wanting to witness the meeting unseen. She held her breath, watching his set profile.

"So you're the miracle worker," he said in a low, flat voice. His skepticism obviously hadn't lessened one bit and Stacy's feeling of hopefulness vanished. "I'm the cripple," he added.

"So I see."

Stacy drew in a silent gasp at the therapist's reply. Paula made no attempt to talk him out of the self-pity that the harsh term sprang from.

"Do you?" Cord snapped. "Then you can also see that I'm likely to stay that way."

She shook her head, unperturbed. "Dr. Buchanan didn't seem to think so," Paula replied smoothly. "He went over your medical history with me in detail."

"So you know it all."

She raised her eyebrows. "No, probably not. I'm sure you could give me an update. I'd like to hear what's going on directly from you."

Cord snorted. "Are you trying to gain my confidence? Won't work."

"It will if you want it to."

Cord fell silent and Stacy held her breath. "So what do you think you can do that's going to make a difference?" he asked at last, and not in a nice way.

"I start with a complete assessment of what *you* can do, for starters." Paula looked him over. "And it's probably more than you think."

"Hah."

The short sound held only contempt. But it didn't seem to bother Paula.

"I'm ready when you are. Of course, we should probably have lunch first. Maria's set out a plate of appetizers already. We should get to know each other, don't you think?"

"Forget it," he said acidly. "I'm not going to bond with you over stuffed celery sticks, if that's what you mean."

He just wasn't able to get her goat. "We don't have to talk," Paula said. "I brought some reading material that you can look at. There's a lot of new research on spinal-cord injury that has practical applications, especially in cases like yours. New treatments are being developed every day, and the traditional methods can be fine-tuned as well."

Completely professional. Neutral. And informative. That approach took him off-guard.

Cord scowled all the same, but he didn't argue with her.

Not right away. "That may be, but not every broken thing can be fixed," he said sharply. Paula didn't answer right away.

Stacy had to hand it to Paula. At least she'd gotten Cord to begin to talk to her about physical therapy. Maybe the trick was to get him to see himself as a machine that needed fixing, and let him take it from there. He was quite capable of tinkering with a truck engine until he got it going. Maybe, just maybe, if he stopped thinking of himself as tragic, misunderstood, and useless, he could get it together and help himself get better.

"Why not try?" the therapist asked in a cool voice.

"Because I'm about as broke-down as a man gets, and about as fixable as a rusty pickup in a ditch."

She smiled at his fierceness. "That doesn't faze me."

"It should. I'm surprised you came all the way out here, but now that you have, you can turn around again and go home." He gave her a mulish look. "Eat lunch if you want to. Maybe my wife will join you."

Paula eyed him speculatively. "You're not a hopeless case, Mr. Harris. Not in Dr. Buchanan's judgment, not in the opinion of your surgeon, and not in mine." She grinned. "Give me half a chance."

Stacy saw Cord shift uncomfortably in his wheelchair. "No," he said finally. "I don't want to talk to you."

Paula rose and gathered up her things without a word, heading for the dining room.

Stacy couldn't stand it another second.

"How could you?" she whispered when Paula was well out of earshot, walking in front of him.

"Where the hell did you come from? Were you listening all this time?"

"Yes," she hissed, not caring if he thought she'd snooped. Right now Stacy didn't want to lose the tiny advantage she instinctively knew the therapist had gained.

"I'm sorry that I did. I saw you go in and knew that she was there—and yes, I listened. Please, Cord," she begged him. "Don't throw away this chance. She's here. Let her work with you. What do you have to lose?"

Cord looked down at his legs, seeming a little ashamed and a lot angry. "Not a goddamn thing," he said under his breath.

"Exactly."

He shook his head. "So you two women are going to gang up on me?"

"Is that so bad?"

"I'm the one who can't escape," he muttered.

"It's not like that—"

"When are you going to admit that this whole therapy thing is a waste of time?"

"When did time become such a valuable commodity?" Fire flashed in her brown eyes. "All you do all day is sit in that chair and watch the second hand move on that old wristwatch. Since you have nothing better to do, you might as well try the therapy."

He slammed his hands down on the armrests of the chair. "Why?" The agonized question was almost inaudible.

"Because you owe it to—" She wasn't going to say *me*. "You owe it to Josh. And to yourself."

He didn't answer, just hung his head. Then he grabbed the wheels and turned the chair so fast he almost ran over her feet.

"Where are you going?"

"To have lunch," he snarled. "You coming?"

"Yes." She followed one step behind, not pushing the chair.

Paula was munching on a pimento-cheese-stuffed celery stick when they got there. Stacy noticed there were only two place settings, and smiled at Maria, who was coming in with a third.

That was a battle won, Stacy thought. A small but significant one.

Cord rolled up to the place that was already set opposite Paula and took a celery stick for himself, pointing it at her, about to speak.

Here we go. Showdown at the OK Corral, Stacy thought for a fleeting second, almost wanting to laugh. With celery instead of pistols.

"All right. I'm here. And you can stay. But I don't intend to talk over lunch."

Paula finished her celery and patted her lips with a napkin. "Look at it this way, Mr. Harris. If after a few weeks of therapy, you're able to get out of that wheelchair, think of the satisfaction you'll have in throwing me out. Something to look forward to, am I right?"

"It would be a joy," Cord declared through clenched teeth.

"Good. That's settled. You're the boss."

"Not any more," he snarled, forgetting that he didn't intend to talk.

"Do you want me to be the boss, then?" Paula inquired.

"Hell, no." He looked from one woman to the other, as if realization had just dawned. "Did you two set me up? I have a feeling I'm being led around by the nose."

Stacy shook her head vehemently. "No. We didn't. And that's the truth."

Cord thanked Maria as she slid a plate of food in front of him. "Then I guess I'm here because I want to be."

"It's a start," Paula said evenly. "Now let's eat."

Cord chowed down in silence, not entering into the discussion of the new research as Paula shared the articles and extracts she'd brought for him to read with Stacy instead.

She asked most of the questions and got a lot of very interesting answers he pretended he wasn't listening to.

Whatever. He ate more heartily than he had in weeks. Stacy didn't comment on it, nor did she remark about his having two pieces of strawberry pie. He slurped a cup of coffee, muttered a not very gentlemanly goodbye to her and Paula, and rolled out.

"Whew!" Paula breathed a silent laugh when she heard his bedroom door slam. "I thought I was going to need a whip and chain to keep him at bay. He's a hell of a man."

The long ponytail of ash-blond hair swished back and forth between her shoulder blades as she shook her head in admiration. "My problem will be to challenge all that ferocity and spirit into the exercises."

"He likes a challenge," was all Stacy said.

Sighing, Paula folded her napkin and pushed her dessert plate away, resting her elbows on the table and her chin on her hands. "There goes my resolve to stop falling in love with my patients."

Stacy stared at her incredulously. "I beg your pardon?" She couldn't have heard correctly.

Round blue eyes returned her look. "Figure of speech— don't take it the wrong way. Yikes, I should have phrased that differently."

Stacy made no reply.

"But you might as well know up front that I couldn't do what I do without getting emotionally involved," Paula added. "Believe me, I set clear boundaries, even though I have to get physical with people. You have nothing to worry about— outside of the fact that I don't always think before I speak." Paula paused. "I really shouldn't have said that, huh?"

Stacy shrugged, still searching for the right comment to make.

"Oh, boy. I blew it. Do you want me to not take the case,

Stacy? I'll understand if you do. I would certainly be jealous of any woman who came near him if he was my husband."

Stacy's mind ran through a whole gamut of thoughts as she hesitated before answering. There was appreciation for the blonde's honesty, for one, and her professionalism. She reminded herself that Bill Buchanan had recommended Paula. Stacy instinctively liked her, and felt confident that she had the ability to help Cord.

But she couldn't quite ignore the fear that Cord might fall in love with her. Patients fell in love with nurses and doctors all the time—why not a physical therapist? Stacy wasn't feeling all that secure, not after the last few weeks.

"Don't be silly," she said finally. "I want you to stay. And he does too."

"I'm glad you thought about that before answering," Paula stated decisively. "Because I'm going to need your trust as much as I need his. I don't want to divide my energies by fighting for it from the two of you."

"Don't worry." Stacy smiled faintly. "Besides, I've invited our foreman to dinner tonight. He happens to be a tall, rugged, handsome bachelor. Maybe we can channel your emotions to him instead of Cord."

"That's an idea." Paula laughed good-naturedly. "Ah, here comes Maria with more coffee. And I think I'll have more pie." She held out her cup. "Thanks very much."

Maria nodded and refilled Stacy's cup next.

"As well as being strong as a horse, I'm afraid I have the appetite of one."

True to her word, Paula polished off another piece of pie with the gusto of someone who loved good food. Josh wandered into the dining room for a few minutes, looked curiously at Paula, and poked a fork at his mother's piece of pie.

"Tastes better when it's on my plate, hmm?" Stacy said. She drew him close to her. "Go ahead. Finish it."

He took another bite before he spoke again. "You promised you'd take me to see the baby colts, Mommy."

"As soon as we've finished lunch," she said.

"Want to come, Paula?" he asked the therapist. "They just got borned."

"The colts were just born," Stacy corrected his grammar.

"That's what I said." He looked at her blankly.

"And did you ask Miss Hanson's permission to call her by her first name?"

"She said I could." He glanced at Paula for confirmation.

"I did tell him he could."

"Okay then." She scruffed up Josh's hair until he protested. "You're a fast worker, kiddo."

Paula laughed out loud and Josh gave her a devil-may-care, five-year-old grin.

"You're welcome to come to the stables with us if you'd like to," Stacy repeated Josh's invitation.

"I would like to," she agreed. "I'm a native-born Texan but I've never been on a real ranch before. A few ranch-type farms, sure, but nothing ever of this size."

"Josh and I will give you a grand tour."

"You bet!" He picked up the last of the pie crumbs from his mother's plate with a finger that he stuck in his mouth. "We can show you everything. We've got sheep and goats and horses and cattle and—can you ride?" He interrupted his list with a quick question.

"Sorry. I don't know the front end of a horse from the back." The blonde lifted her hands palm upward, smiling at his excitement.

He frowned importantly. "The back is where the tail is."

"You'll have to show me." Paula offered him her hand and he grasped it quickly, eager to be off on the tour of the ranch. "At a walk, though, Josh. I'm not as young as you are."

"You two go ahead." Stacy waved them on. "I want to have a word with Maria. I'll meet you outside in a few minutes."

During the tour of the ranch, Paula continually expressed her amazement at the size of the operation. Seeing it through a newcomer's eyes, Stacy was actually a little stunned by it herself. It had become so familiar to her over the years that she'd come to take it for granted.

"You're really in charge of all this?" Paula asked again as she paused on the rise leading to the house. She looked back at the ranch property sweeping to the horizon.

"Yes," Stacy said, bemused by the fact as well. "With Travis McCrea, our foreman. I don't think I could run it without his help."

"Oh, I didn't mean I thought you couldn't do it on your own. I guess I was just wondering what your husband thought about it."

"Cord? I'm not sure I follow you."

"It must have deflated his ego to find out everything could run smoothly without him. As proud and as independent as he is, I bet he wished it had fallen apart— secretly, at least."

Was that something else Stacy should have been worrying about? "I hope not."

Paula's thoughtful gaze swung to Stacy. "Has he taken part in some of the decisions?"

Remembering how Cord had pretty much accused her of patronizing him, Stacy shook her head and looked away. "Travis and I have tried to involved him in the running of the ranch, but he refuses to take any interest."

"I see," Paula mused absently.

"Aren't you coming?" Josh was waiting impatiently at the sidewalk, anxious to enter the house and have the afternoon snack of milk and cookies he knew Maria would have waiting for him.

"I appreciate your taking the time to show me around," Paula said as they accompanied Josh into the house. "What a wonderful place. Hope the tour didn't interfere with your work schedule."

"Not at all," Stacy assured. "The hot part of the afternoon I generally spend in the office doing the paperwork and data entry, ordering feed, and things like that. After devoting a couple of hours to Josh, of course." She glanced at her watch. "I still have time to get a lot done before dinner. Incidentally, I asked Travis to come at seven and Maria is planning dinner for seven-thirty."

"While you're working, I can take all the time I need to get ready for dinner." The blonde gave a big laugh. "So maybe I can impress your bachelor foreman. What do you think?"

The door to the master bedroom was ajar. As she was about to respond to Paula's comment, Cord's voice barked her name.

"Stacy!"

Paula rolled her eyes. "The imperial beast is roaring. I believe you have been summoned before the throne."

Stacy had to smile, but she hoped Cord hadn't heard.

"I think you're right," she murmured. "See you later."

"Where have you been?" Cord demanded when she entered.

"Josh wanted to see the new colts after lunch. And since Paula had never been on a working ranch before, we took her on the grand tour." Stacy found it difficult to reply calmly. If she had to put up with much more of this childishness from Cord, she would have to slap a muzzle on him and go find a psychiatrist for herself.

"She rubs me the wrong way."

"Really? I thought she was remarkably polite, considering how rude you were at first. After all, you knew she was coming."

"I don't know—the reality of her being there was just different. Hit me all of a sudden that it wasn't my choice."

"It is," Stacy said wearily. "All I was asking was for you to give her a fair chance."

"I sat down. I ate. I listened to you talk about my proposed course of treatment like I wasn't even there."

"You could have joined in anytime."

"Well, I didn't," he said grumpily. "How did Josh like the colts?"

"He liked them fine."

"And how did he like Paula? If she's going to stay, I hope she doesn't mind a little boy who never stops moving."

"They got along well. I wish you could have seen how easy she was with him, more natural than a lot of parents are with their kids. Paula knows exactly how to handle children."

"Is that a not-so-subtle endorsement of her ability to handle me?" He frowned.

"No," Stacy said. She refused to be baited and drawn into a ridiculous argument.

"Look, Stacy, just so long as you both understand that I get the final say in anything that involves me. It can't be the two of you against me."

"Of course not. And no one is against you. That's all in your imagination."

He wheeled his chair to the window and, apparently unable to come up with a valid counter-argument, changed the subject instead.

"Nice that you two can pal around out there."

She could guess at what he didn't say. *While I'm stuck inside.*

"I'm too busy for that," Stacy sighed. "Paula Hanson is a working guest, after all. I hope you're not going to skip dinner, by the way. Travis is coming."

"Well, whoop de doo. We haven't had company for a long time."

"And you're not going to spoil it. I don't want to quarrel with you anymore—I have more constructive things to do with my time. Travis will be here around seven and dinner is at seven-thirty."

"I'll polish my hubcaps," Cord said dryly.

"You do that. No reason you can't be presentable. It would do you good to be in civilized company instead of listening to cry-in-your-beer songs on the radio so much."

"Now I embarrass you." There was a mixture of scorn and amusement in his voice. "What comes next, Stacy?"

"You getting better, I hope. Just be nice to Paula tonight, okay?"

"Sure thing," he said. "But tell me why you invited Travis. Is he to provide Miss Hanson with male companionship or to keep the conversation on safe topics?"

She gritted her teeth. "Both."

For an instant there was silence.

Then Cord sighed wearily. All the sarcasm and bitterness seemed to flow out of him. He rubbed the back of his neck for several seconds. "Ah, hell. I didn't call you in here to give you a hard time, Stacy," he muttered. "I don't even know how it got started. I lash out at everyone these days."

"Why *did* you call me like that?" she asked, trying to adjust to the abrupt shift in his mood.

"I was worried about you. You were gone longer than I thought you would be and Maria said Josh was with you. I—"

Cord hesitated, still staring out the window. "Don't worry about tonight. I'll be pleasant to your miracle worker."

"Thank you, Cord," Stacy said, controlling her own temper. "If you need me, I'll be in the study. I have work to do before dinner."

The congenial atmosphere that dominated the evening meal was a welcome change. It was due in part to the immediate rapport between Travis and Paula, who showed an instant and mutual liking and respect for each other.

The talk at the dinner table was mainly between them, in fact, with Stacy joining in occasionally. Paula's brief tour of the ranch that afternoon had sparked a curiosity to learn more about the operation and especially the cattle drive being carried out. Travis obligingly explained it to her.

Cord, who had grown to detest any discussion of the ranch, showed exemplary restraint and stayed silent during much of dinner. Stacy sometimes glanced his way, trying to discern some small crack in the polite mask. Nothing revealed that he listened as eagerly as Paula did to the account of the latest activities.

He didn't show a glimmer of interest, but at least he was keeping his promise to be pleasant this evening. More than that Stacy couldn't read into his silence no matter how much she wanted to try.

She attempted to feel grateful that he wasn't irritable or wary with Paula, but there wasn't much comfort in that. Stacy was becoming as difficult to satisfy as Cord. She sighed inwardly as Maria cleared the dessert dishes and brought in the coffee.

A cup was set in front of Cord.

"No," he said. The word seemed to explode softly from him, not tempered with a thank-you. He pushed himself away from the table all of a sudden. "I mean, I'll have my coffee on the veranda, Maria."

He didn't invite anyone to join him as he wheeled toward the sliding glass doors. The omission was too blatant to be missed.

Paula made a slight face and said, "Why didn't he come

right out and say he didn't want our company? I could've taken the hint."

Travis chuckled softly. Stacy only smiled. There was no point in apologizing to them or making excuses for Cord's behavior. Yet something inside her wouldn't let him exile himself to the veranda alone.

Glancing at Maria, who was setting Cord's cup back on the tray, she made a mental note to send the housekeeper on an all-expenses-paid trip to Mexico for a month when Cord got better, just for putting up with him so patiently for so long. She felt guilty for asking her to do one more thing.

"I'll have my coffee on the veranda too. Thanks, Maria. I owe you."

"*De nada*," Maria said.

Stacy nodded to Travis and Paula as she rose. "Excuse me, please," was all she said.

Chapter 7

The night air was sultry from the afternoon's heat. The star fire shimmering from the sky cast soft shadows on the whitewashed arches of the veranda.

Cord murmured a genuinely appreciative thank-you when Maria set the tray on a table near his wheelchair. His gaze was riveted on the two cups sitting on the tray. He recognized the significance of them and knew he wasn't alone.

Stacy paused beside him, feeling the invisible crackle of electricity in the still air. Her shoes clicked loudly as she ignored his silent demand that she leave him alone and walked to a chaise beside him.

"What are you doing out here?" he muttered impatiently, then continued without allowing her an opportunity to reply. "If you came to tell me that I shouldn't have left, save your breath." He heaved a sigh. "If I'd stayed inside, I doubted I would have kept my promise to be a good boy. So be grateful for a small show of bad manners."

"I am." Stacy sat back in her chair and sipped at her coffee.

His tightly clenched jaw twitched. "Shouldn't you go back inside to be with our guests? One of us should be in there to entertain them."

"Travis isn't exactly a guest," she replied. "He can keep Paula company for a while."

"You make it sound as if he's practically a member of the family instead of the foreman."

"I guess I do think of him in that way," Stacy admitted. "I don't think you realize how much help he's been to us through all this."

"To you, you mean," he corrected her. His mouth turned down. "Do you confide all your troubles to him and cry on his shoulder?"

"I don't cry on anyone's shoulder."

She was too independent to do that and Cord knew it. But there were certainly times when she'd wanted to. "What I meant was that Travis has shouldered the bulk of the ranch operation, not that he'd helped me specifically."

Travis's knowledge of her problems was gleaned from what he witnessed or guessed, and not from any confessions from Stacy, regardless of Cord's accusation to the contrary.

"And you're so grateful for his assistance that you've left him at the mercy of Paula," Cord said.

Stacy breathed in deeply. He seemed determined to incite an argument and she was just as determined not to oblige.

"Cord, I came out here for some fresh air," she said slowly and distinctly. "If you don't want to enjoy the peace and quiet with me, then I'll move to another part of the veranda."

His cup clinked loudly in its saucer. Stacy's heart thudded rapidly in the heavy silence that followed. It wasn't a desire for fresh air that had brought her outdoors but the feeling that Cord had wanted her company. She wanted his, but not if it meant arguing. For a wonder, he let her alone, absorbed in his own thoughts.

Gradually Stacy relaxed, resting her head against the chaise cushion. Miles away, a coyote yipped and howled. The sound echoed clearly in her ears.

Her thoughts drifted to the cattle drive as she gazed at the starry sky. Somewhere out there a night rider was watching over the herd, taking his turn while others slept in bedrolls around the campfire. A lump entered her throat as Stacy remembered again the nights she and Cord had camped out.

Eager to rid her mind of the poignant memory, she focused her attention on Travis's recounting of the drive's success so far this year. It had been almost unbelievably smooth and without incident.

"It's a relief that the cattle drive is going so well." The absent comment was out before Stacy realized that it was her voice that had broken the silence.

Darting a sideways glance at Cord, she held her breath. There was no sudden tightness in his expression, and there usually was whenever any mention of the ranch's operation was made.

He appeared relaxed and calm as he gazed heavenward at the stars.

The tensing of her nerves eased. Stacy decided he hadn't heard her inadvertent remark and she breathed a silent sigh of relief. She let her gaze drift back to the stars.

"I can almost smell the smoke from the campfire," Cord murmured softly.

The stars seemed to glow more brilliantly, filling her brown eyes with hopeful light as his warm voice rolled caressingly over her. Hesitantly, she glanced at him, wondering if he too was remembering the nights they'd spent alone on the trail. The affirmative answer was in the glittering darkness of his gaze on her face.

No words were spoken as they looked at each other. Sometime during the eternity of seconds, his wheelchair glided silently to the side of her chaise. Stacy wasn't aware of the actual movement. She wasn't certain that Cord knew he had done it.

He was simply there. Near enough that she could have touched him with only the slightest movement of her hand.

But she didn't. His previous rejections of physical contact with her were too painfully branded in her heart. Any touch or caress would come first from Cord or not at all.

As he remained motionless for several more seconds, Stacy quivered with the aching longing to be in his arms. He leaned forward, his hands clasping her middle to draw her toward him. She didn't need the assistance to move to the hard male line of his descending mouth.

The searing possession of his kiss burned the softness of her lips. Fire rocketed through her veins as she responded to his hungry demand. Her hands cupped the powerful line of his jaw, resolute and firm beneath her fingers.

Too soon, his hands were decisively but slowly pushing her away from him. Her own hands retained the shape of his face, suspended in air, as Cord set her back in the chaise. Unwillingly her lashes fluttered open. His eyes were black, fathomless pools of agony.

"Stacy, my life," Cord said in a tortured whisper. "What am I doing? I'm destroying both of us. For bitter or worse, you said. But how much bitter can either of us take?"

He turned away, his profile hardening into an unrelenting silhouette in the starlight. "God help me, I can't let you go. I'll never let you go!"

"Cord, I don't want to go," she murmured huskily. "I only want you to stop shutting me out. I want to share in your life."

His groan was laced with deep pain. "I can't share. What is there for me to share? This wheelchair is my prison." His mouth twisted in sardonic amusement. "This wheelchair is my prison, but I'm your jailer. I'll never let you go free—not willingly."

"I don't want to be free," Stacy protested with a faint catch of pain in her own voice.

"Do you know what I'm afraid of?" There was no humor in his cold smile. "That some day you'll say that so often I'll finally believe you, even though I know it's not the truth."

"No." It was an inaudible denial, lost in a choked sob that Cord didn't hear.

There was the quiet swish of his wheels turning. Stacy's head was bowed so she didn't see him reenter the house. Her hands were clasped in front of her in desperate prayer. Pain reverberated through her body, wracking her muscles until she wanted to cry away the hurt, but she held her tears in check.

It was several minutes before she was in sufficient control of herself to join Travis and Paula in the living room. Her hand wearily pushed the hair away from her forehead as she walked into the house.

The sight of Cord in the living room brought her to an abrupt halt. She'd been sure he would retreat to his bedroom after pulling his disappearing act from the supper table.

But no. There he was.

The impregnable hardness of his gaze swept over her, noting the ravages of her storm within. Not a sound had betrayed Stacy's entrance into the living room, yet Paula glanced up, as if sensing a change in the atmosphere. Her blue eyes looked Stacy over, noting the wan cheeks. A split second later a warm smile brightened the blond woman's face.

"You're just in time, Stacy," Paula declared, darting a glance at Travis. "I was just trying to find out more about this annual horse sale you have. He said you were in charge of that, and that it'd been your personal project for the last several years."

"That's true."

Stacy started forward, grateful for the safe topic of conversation and the lack of any comment about where she had been. "What did you want to know about it?"

"Well, I—"

"Isn't there something else we can discuss?" Cord interrupted her.

The physical therapist gave him a disapproving look.

"I was only going to ask Stacy what she was doing now—in connection with the sale."

"What difference does it make to you?" Cord met her look and returned the challenge.

"Not any, really." Paula shrugged. "I was just interested, that's all."

"Well, I'm not," he retorted.

"Do you mean you're not interested in what goes on here at the ranch?" she asked in a considering way.

"That's precisely what I mean," Cord said sharply.

"I understood it was your ranch," Paula said.

"It was," he agreed, stressing the past tense. "Since my accident, Stacy and Travis have taken over the operation of it. And that's that."

"Really?"

Cord seemed dangerously annoyed. "They make all the decisions. So be it."

"Why don't you, if it's your ranch?"

"In case it hasn't occurred to you, Paula, it's difficult to oversee an operation of this size from a wheelchair."

"Difficult but not impossible," Paula mused.

"Uh-huh. As a veteran of a two-hour tour, if that, of the Circle H, you apparently know everything."

Paula narrowed her eyes at him. "I was speaking in general terms. Just about anything can be done from a wheelchair, given determination and ingenuity. And that's something I do know a lot about."

"Good for you. It doesn't necessarily apply to me."

Travis and Stacy exchanged a look. Paula was obviously getting a rise out of Cord, and that wasn't necessarily a bad thing.

"Your wife can't go it alone. She needs you. Time to rejoin the human race, Cord," Paula forged on. Stacy wondered if she'd been at the whisky. She seemed fearless. "And your family. And your friends. I can help."

Stacy breathed in sharply when she saw Cord lean back in his chair, as if Paula's words had made a physical impact on him.

"You're not opposed to hitting below the belt, are you?"

The grooves around his mouth deepened as his gaze honed in on his blond adversary.

"Why should I be?" Paula countered. "You don't seem to be bothered when you hurt people who care about you."

Just in case Cord didn't get it, she cast a meaningful look at Stacy. Cord followed it. There wasn't even a glimmer of guilt or remorse in his expression. He turned back to Paula, a suggestion of arrogance in the tilt of his head.

"Say what you want," he replied calmly. "It doesn't bother me in the least. As for my wife, Stacy and I understand each other."

No, Stacy thought. Not true. But she was staying out of this confrontation. His moods were so volatile—mostly withdrawn, sometimes angry, and a few precious moments of tenderness that kept her hoping—she didn't want him to feel ganged up on.

"I'm aware of what she wants from me," Cord continued. "I doubt you do, and it's not your job to psychoanalyze her. Got that?"

Paula only nodded.

"It is your job, though, to get me walking again. Good luck."

"Maybe I crossed a line by bringing her into this, but the look on her face when she came back in here after being alone with you told me a lot," Paula said with spirit.

"Mind your own business," Cord said vehemently.

"Hey now, Cord," Travis began.

"You too."

"I didn't mean no harm, Cord."

The man in the wheelchair was the center of all their

attention for a charged second. "So now it's three against one? I'm outnumbered. Better call the cavalry."

"You did. Or Dr. Buchanan did," Paula said. "Think about it, Cord. We are the cavalry—me, Stacy, and Travis. To the rescue."

He folded his arms over his chest.

"Go rescue someone else. To hell with all of you," he said with disgust. "I'm going to bed."

A silence followed his swift departure from the room.

"That was interesting," Travis said, looking at Paula. "Do you always speak your mind like that?"

"Sometimes. He's a hard case. He doesn't want help, but he's not all that disabled. I was watching him carefully. He has the potential for more mobility than he knows, which is just as I thought. I'm working on his motivation."

"But what if he ends up hating you?" Stacy said.

"They often do at first," Paula said philosophically. "I'm pushing him to respond and he doesn't like it."

"But he is responding," Travis said thoughtfully. "Paula, if you can get him to walk, all I can say is that you'd better be prepared to run. He really doesn't like to be bossed."

"I can see that." Paula was thinking hard and not looking at Stacy, who felt like her world was turning upside down. There seemed to be nothing she could do or say to put it right. Alone under the stars, Cord had called her his life and given her a kiss that was soul-deep. But even so . . . he'd said again that he didn't believe her when she vowed she would never leave him. It didn't make sense.

And now Paula was saying that his case might not be that bad. Well, maybe not physically. But what was going in his mind was just as paralyzing to him as the numbness in his legs.

Stacy walked away from the other two and looked out the window. The timeless landscape was shrouded in darkness. But that wasn't what chilled her.

It was her own inability to help him. She'd failed completely—and in the process, failed herself.

Paula seemed to have figured out her husband in less than a day—and she had the expertise to rehabilitate his suffering body. If what Cord needed was a challenge, Stacy hadn't offered one.

He'd seemed so beaten down for so long—she'd been afraid to make demands on him, afraid to ask too much. And now she had to step to the side, and let someone else take over. Let go.

A stranger could do better than Stacy. The thought rankled her. Paula had known what to do, just like that. In so many ways, Cord had become a stranger to her, his wife. She just didn't know him anymore.

A lump rose in her throat. Her stomach churned sickeningly and rubbery legs threatened to give way beneath her. She swayed unsteadily, pressing a hand against the flat of her stomach to quell the convulsing muscles.

She turned around to find Paula and Travis both looking at her.

"I—I think I'll check on Josh."

She needed to escape. It was a believable excuse.

"Stacy."

Paula's voice checked her first awkward step from the room. "Before I forget, will you be here at the house tomorrow morning?"

"I—" She couldn't think. Tomorrow was an eternity away and her mind couldn't seem to focus on it.

"You mentioned something about going into town in the morning," Travis prompted gently.

"Oh, yes, of course." Stacy managed a brittle laugh. "I have to take the yearling list for the sales catalog to the printer. Almost forgot." Her nerves were threadbare. "Was there something you wanted, Paula?"

"No." Paula gathered up the articles she'd brought to the

dinner table. "I was going to start your husband with some basic mobility exercises and I just wondered where you'd be."

"I can postpone going into town until the afternoon if you'd like me to help."

The offer was made almost desperately as Stacy turned, her chestnut hair swinging around her shoulders. She wanted to maintain any link with Cord regardless of how rusty the connection might be.

"Don't do that." The blonde shook her head.

"I don't mind. I—I want to help. Like you said . . . we're the calvary."

For the first time, Stacy noticed a look of uncertainty in the woman's face. The blue eyes looked in her direction without looking directly at her.

"Actually, Stacy, it would be better if you weren't here— at least in the beginning," Paula added hastily. "You would be more of a distraction than a help, however good your intentions. The therapist-patient relationship is very important, especially in your husband's case. Besides, the first few days or more will probably be pretty rough on Cord. Caring about him the way you do, your instinct would be to try to make it easier for him. I'm sorry, but it's nothing personal."

"I understand."

Did she though? Stacy didn't know. There were so many things she didn't know or understand anymore. Not the least among them was Cord.

"Excuse me," she murmured, "I do think I hear Josh. He has bad dreams sometimes." This time she made her exit from the room.

The next morning Stacy had genuinely intended to be gone from the house before Paula started her exercise and therapy program with Cord. But one minor interruption after another kept her in the study until half past nine.

With the list in her hand of the yearling colts and fillies to be sold, Stacy walked out of the study. The door to the master bedroom was ajar. It drew her gaze like a magnet.

"Damnit, that hurts!" she heard Cord mutter savagely. Stacy wondered what hurt and then Paula spoke briskly.

"It's supposed to," was her unruffled but not uncaring response. "And it's going to hurt a whole hell of a lot more before we're through."

"I don't like it when a woman swears," he retorted with a muffled grumble.

"For once we share a similar viewpoint, Cord," Paula declared. "I find it offensive when a man swears."

Suddenly Stacy realized that she was eavesdropping. That realization was followed by a nagging doubt as to why she'd allowed herself to be detained at the house when she could have left earlier as planned.

With a guilty start, she hurried toward the front door before her presence was discovered.

The next day Stacy made sure that she succeeded in leaving the house early in the morning, not returning until lunchtime. She brought Josh with her. He was delighted to have extra time with his mother. Even with his sweet, little-boy-eager company, she still felt insecure and a little jealous of Paula's close physical contact with Cord. She decided to overcompensate by staying away rather than turning into a suspicious, prying wife.

True to Paula's prediction, the first week was miserable. Stacy's self-imposed exile in the mornings—sometimes with her son, sometimes not—had begun to make her feel like an intruder in her own home, as if she should ask permission whenever she wanted to spend any length of time there during the day.

The physical and mental exertion left Cord even more short-tempered than before. His moodiness increased, falling on a spectrum anywhere between brooding silence to snarling sarcasm. It seemed to Stacy that she was his favorite target, although Paula came in for her fair share of scathing remarks.

Maybe it only seemed that Cord singled Stacy out because her love gave him such an overwhelming power to hurt. Inwardly she cringed, not knowing what he would say when they happened to meet. She tried to emulate Paula by pretending his acid comments didn't bother her at all.

As her fork played with the tuna salad stuffing of her tomato, Stacy searched for something to say. The atmosphere at the lunch table was oppressive, induced by Cord's gloomy silence. The tines of her fork made a scraping sound on the plate.

His dark eyes flashed at her. "Are you going to eat that or just keep pushing it around on your plate?" Cord said irritably.

His sudden attention disconcerted her. Awkwardly she set the fork down and clasped her fingers in her lap, out of sight of Cord's penetrating gaze.

"I'm not very hungry," she answered with forced calm. For a fraction of a second, she contemplated throwing the tuna-stuffed tomato at him and decided not to. It wouldn't be fair. He had already eaten his and couldn't retaliate.

"Then stop playing with your food," he growled.

Silence descended again. Stacy looked at Paula, who had also polished off her stuffed tomato. How could she be so indifferent to this constant tension? Or was she simply used to it?

"How is the—the therapy coming along?" Stacy faltered over the question, again drawing Cord's dark gaze.

"Don't ask me, ask Paula." His nostrils flared with scorn. "She's supposed to be the expert."

The physical therapist buttered a slice of bread, and waved the knife at him. "It's going great. When he cooperates."

"I'm trying," Cord said. "I hate every minute of it. And I'm beginning to really hate you."

Paula munched her bread slice. "Can't be helped. Lately I couldn't say that I like you very much. I wouldn't go so far as to say hate. Strong word."

Cord coughed. "Whatever. I don't particularly care whether you like me or not."

"Whatever," Paula said with a saccharine smile. When her blue eyes turned to Stacy, they held a twinkling light of mock despair. "To answer your question, Stacy, it's slow when you have to fight every inch of the way."

"Translated, that means a lot of pain and little progress," Cord said dryly.

"When did you become such an optimist, Cord?" Stacy's mouth curved in a humorless smile.

"What?" He looked at her blankly.

"You just admitted there was a little progress, which is better than none at all."

He exhaled a short, angry breath. "Damned little," he muttered in a savage undertone. Almost instantly, a black eyebrow arched in Paula's direction. "Pardon me, Miss-Harris-Who-Doesn't-Like-Men-Swearing."

"I'll be damned. I shouldn't, but I will, Mr. Harris-the-Hypocrite." A smile twitched at the corners of her full mouth.

The exchange of insults didn't hide the rough affection underneath. Stacy felt jealousy flame inside her like emerald green fire. Before it consumed her with its destructive force, she pushed her chair away from the table. The suppressed violence of her action nearly tipped over the glassware.

"Excuse me, I have work to do," she muttered as she started to flee from the surprised glances.

Inside the study, she shut the door and leaned against it. If she hadn't overheard their conversation the other day, she wouldn't have understood the teasing about swearing between Cord and Paula. They hadn't expected her to understand and they hadn't bothered to explain.

So. Now they were sharing secret jokes. In the green

throes of her misery, she wondered what else they shared during all the mornings she decamped with Josh and left them alone. Were they taking advantage of that, too? A curious little kid who had the run of a house and opened any door he wanted to was a sure deterrent to fooling around. But most mornings, Josh wasn't there either.

Cord could not . . . *would not* . . . do something like that in their house. She'd always trusted him. Always loved him.

She walked to the desk. At this time she knew she wouldn't be able to concentrate on paperwork. Her mind would be wondering what was going on in the house.

Her wide-brimmed Western hat was sitting on top of the letter basket where she'd left it this morning. Picking it up, she hurried from the study and out of the house.

At the stable, Hank stared at her in astonishment. "Saddle the mare? You want to go ridin' in the heat of the day?" He peered at her closely, his weathered face crinkled with perplexity. "Are you all right, Miss Stacy?"

"Of course," she answered sharply. She bit her lip for a second to check any further venting of her frustration on Hank. "If you're too busy, though, I'll saddle Candy Bar myself."

"I'll do it," he said reluctantly, and shuffled toward the corral. But Stacy heard him mumble as he left, "Somebody around here is tetched in the head, and it ain't me!"

Chapter 8

The green pickup truck rumbled down the lane toward the stables, slowing down as it approached Stacy, walking to the house. She waited until it stopped beside her and smiled tiredly at the man behind the wheel. His arm was crooked over the open window of the cab.

"Hello, Travis," she greeted him. "Seems like I haven't seen you for ages." He was the one person with whom she didn't feel she had to always be on her guard.

"We've both been pretty busy lately," he agreed. He kept the truck in gear, the engine idling eagerly. "How are the preparations for the horse sale going?"

"Fine." Stacy gave him a wry smile. "I think."

"And Cord?" His eyes were thoughtful as they ran over her wholesomely attractive features, drawn and tired, the hollows of her cheeks visible. "Paula's been there almost two weeks now. Has there been any improvement?"

"None that I know about." Stacy glanced self-consciously away.

No information had been volunteered to her regarding Cord's progress, or lack of it. She wanted several times to put the question to Paula, but the very fact that Stacy hadn't been kept in the loop held her back.

"It takes time, I guess." Travis shrugged.

"Yes, of course," she agreed. "I was just going up to the house for lunch. Would you like to join me?"

He frowned curiously. "Won't Cord and Paula be there?"

"Sure." She smiled nervously. It had been a slip of the tongue to say "me." The truth was that Stacy felt like the unwanted third at the table. The thought of Travis joining them for lunch had been a means of being included for once instead of feeling left out. She realized that it was all in her imagination, but she still felt uncomfortable.

"I'd like to," Travis hesitated, "but—"

"I understand," Stacy said, stretching her mouth into a smile. "Work," she offered him an excuse. "Another time."

"I'll hold you to it." He smiled and the truck began rolling forward.

If only something had developed between Paula and Travis. Stacy sighed wistfully. But it hadn't. They were friendly to each other, but nothing more.

When her path was clear, she started toward the house again. The closer she got, the more taut her nerves became. Her throat and mouth were dry. The food would be tasteless again.

Lately she'd had to force herself to eat, but the portions she'd succeeded in swallowing had been small.

"Hi, Mom!"

Josh came racing down the sloping lawn toward her. Water glistened on his small chest. His red swimming trunks were plastered to his body. Shining wet hair gleamed as black as a raven's wing in the sunlight.

"You've been playing with the water hose again, I see." Stacy smiled indulgently.

"No, I've been swimming."

Her smile vanished completely.

"Joshua Stephen Harris!"

She grasped his shoulders and held on despite his squirming. "You've been told and told and told never to go swimming by yourself! You are not to be in that pool unless"—Stacy had been about to say "your father or I" but she quickly changed it—"there's an adult in the pool with you. Now you can spend the afternoon in your room."

His dark eyes flashed resentfully at her. "But Daddy and Paula were in the pool with me!" he declared.

"I don't like it when you lie to me, Josh," scolded Stacy. Her frayed nerve ends had armed her temper with a short fuse.

"I am not lying. It's the truth!" Josh insisted. "We all went swimming together."

Her head tipped to one side in doubt. "Your father too?" she asked skeptically.

"Paula said it was 'ther'py'"—he mispronounced the unfamiliar word—"to make Daddy stronger. They've been swimming a lot and today Paula said I could come in, too."

The brisk nod of his chin added a very definite "so there!" to the end of his explanation.

"I—" Stacy was flustered. She'd heard of swimming used in physical therapy, of course, but she hadn't realized Paula was employing it. "I didn't know. I'm sorry, Josh."

He accepted her apology somewhat sullenly, his lower lip jutting out in a pout.

She should have realized he wouldn't deliberately disobey her. Or if he did, he wouldn't brag about it. She was just too keyed up. She shouldn't have jumped on him without allowing him to make an explanation.

"I was wrong and I take back everything I said. Naturally, you don't have to stay in your room this afternoon." Then, trying to change the subject, she said, "Do you suppose Maria has lunch ready yet? Shall we go and see?"

A bare toe dug into a clump of grass. "I guess so," he agreed without enthusiasm.

But he didn't walk beside her. Instead he raced ahead, a faint droop to his shoulders. Her unwarranted anger had taken his enjoyment out of the swim, and he wasn't going to let her forget it immediately. Knowing that she'd been wrong only made Stacy feel worse.

If only Paula or Cord had mentioned the swimming, Stacy defended her reaction silently, none of this would have happened. Resentment smoldered, as it had done in Josh.

Entering the house, Stacy walked directly to the master bedroom. It was time she found out all that was going on in her house. She had a right to know what was being done, when, where, and why.

The door was open. One step through the frame and Stacy halted, stopped by the sight of Cord lying nearly half naked on a sheet-draped table. A blue towel was wrapped around his waist. The narrow towel revealed the rippling muscles of his shoulders and back, and the dark, curling hair on his thighs and legs. Cord was lying on his stomach, head resting on his hands, face turned away from the door. Dampness had changed his hair to midnight black, inclining it to wave.

Stacy's view was blocked by the tall figure of a woman whose strong hands began to spread massage oil over Cord's back. Stacy just gaped at her.

Paula's ash blond hair was swept on top of her head in a disheveled coil. Wet tendrils had escaped to curl attractively on the slender column of her neck. A white lace beach jacket veiled a two-piece swimsuit, revealing the stunning length of golden legs.

Her long fingers expertly massaged Cord's back, polishing his skin with the oil. Stacy noticed that his tan had returned—no doubt they'd been spending a *lot* of time in the sun. How unobservant she had been these past days, Stacy thought silently. Not once had she noticed the deepening color. Her pulse stirred at the virility of the totally male body. There was an ache in the pit of her stomach, a yearning emptiness that wanted to be filled.

Envy crushed her heart into a painful ball as Stacy watched Paula's hands moving with familiar intimacy over his naked back and shoulders. A cry of jealous anger rose in her throat that Paula was the one touching him, caressing him. Not her. Smothering the tortured sob with the back of her hand, Stacy retreated from the doorway.

It was either that or race into the room, screaming and clawing at Paula. The strength of her raging emotions dazed her. Not even with Lydia, whom Stacy had once thought Cord might marry, had she ever wanted to start a spitting, hair-pulling fight. It was crazy, because she had despised Lydia while she actually liked Paula. But not with Cord—never with Cord.

Three steps backward into the hall, she heard Cord speak and stopped to listen, despising herself for doing it.

"You could make a fortune with your hands, Paula," he murmured in the husky, warm voice that had so often quickened Stacy's heartbeat and sent flames of desire shooting through her.

"I'm not interested in making a fortune," the therapist replied quietly.

So . . . was she doing it for love? A searing pain plunged through Stacy's heart, nearly doubling her over.

"What do you want?" Cord spoke again. His languid but decidedly interested tone indicated that the question was more than idle curiosity.

"What a lot of women want. A satisfying and rewarding

career, a home and a man." An instant of silence followed before Paula added, "Not necessarily in that order."

Not Cord. You can't have Cord, Stacy cried silently.

"Are you hard to please?" he mocked.

"Very." Paula's tone sounded deliberately light.

"The man who gets you will have his hands full." His voice held amusement.

"But he'll be man enough to handle me." Despite the smiling sound in Paula's answer, it carried an inflection of complete seriousness.

Cord chuckled. "That sounds like a challenge."

"Are you going to pick up the glove?"

Stacy couldn't tell whether Paula was teasing or trying to make her interest in Cord apparent to him. And hadn't Paula warned Stacy the day she arrived that she always fell in love with her patients?

Her eyes burned, but they remained dry as Stacy hastily stumbled into the living room. She was afraid to hear one more word. Dread of what might be froze her senses to everything but the image of the two semi-clad people in the master bedroom and the feminine hands that so freely touched Cord's body when he had denied Stacy the right.

She sank onto the couch, hugging a pillow, then flinging it away. She stared out the glass doors of the veranda at the blue sky outside. Something inside her shattered, splintering into a thousand pieces. What was it? Her heart?

Mostly unaware of the world around her, Stacy realized she was not alone in the room when she finally heard Maria repeat her name several times. She turned to the housekeeper, staying calm.

"What was it you wanted, Maria?"

"There is a phone call for you."

Stacy shook her head. "Take their name and phone

number and tell them I'll call them back. I don't want to talk to anyone right now."

"I will tell them you call back this afternoon."

"Not this afternoon. I won't be in this afternoon," Stacy replied in the same emotionless tone.

"You are never at the house anymore," the housekeeper chided her.

"No, I'm not." It seemed to be a pronouncement of her fate.

Stacy roused herself a little. Routine. Stick to the routine. "Is lunch ready?" she asked.

"A *momento* only," Maria answered.

As Maria left the room, Stacy got up from the couch to mechanically go through the motions of washing up for the meal. She felt very much like a robot sitting at the table, silently eating the salad of avocado and grapefruit sections in a tangy dressing. Her tongue tasted neither sweet nor sour.

Yet it wasn't her silence that Paula, dressed in casual pants and a baggy T-shirt, noticed. The blonde glanced curiously at the unnaturally silent little boy seated across the table from her.

"You're very quiet, Josh. Are you tired?" she asked lightly.

His small dark head moved in a negative shake, his gaze never leaving his plate.

"You usually chatter like a chipmunk," Paula teased. "Something must be bothering you."

"I scolded him for going swimming this morning," Stacy explained blandly when Josh didn't reply. She kept her face expressionless. "I wasn't aware until after I did that you and Cord were using the pool for physical therapy, and that Joshua was supervised and not swimming alone as I'd assumed. My apologies haven't been fully accepted so far."

"I'm the one who should apologize, Stacy. I'm sorry. I thought you knew," Paula said.

"It doesn't matter." Stacy shrugged. "I know now. Has the, er, swimming been helpful?"

She glanced up in time to see the brief look Paula and Cord exchanged and felt her stomach do a sickening somersault. The look implied private, intimate secrets.

"It hasn't done any harm," the therapist replied diffidently.

An inadvertent shudder quaked through Stacy. "Excuse me," she said suddenly. "I just remembered there was an important phone call—Maria said I was supposed to return it immediately."

It was a feeble excuse, but it was the only one she could think of to leave the table in the middle of a meal. Her retreat was haunted by the idea of how many other secret glances they'd exchanged when she wasn't looking.

She cursed her vivid imagination, but it was fed by the vague look of contentment in Cord's eyes and the ever so slightly softer contours of his mouth.

Slipping out through the front door, Stacy knew she would never be able to share another meal with them without wondering what silent message was being transmitted. She resolved not to subject herself to that.

Over the next few days she began leading a different life. Travis became her link with sanity and she used him shamelessly as a buffer. Since Paula had arrived, she'd invited him over several times each week for dinner. Now she scheduled their ranch meetings at lunchtime. If Travis thought her behavior was odd, he took care not to mention it, treating her almost constant demand for his time as natural.

The question Stacy kept ignoring was a simple one. Where would it all end? This day-to-day strategy couldn't continue forever.

How long could she avoid acknowledging the not-so-hidden relationship that was developing between Cord and Paula?

But what was the alternative? Should she confront Cord with her suspicions and look like a fool if she was wrong? Or should she accuse Paula and kick her off the ranch?

Being passive never got a woman anywhere worth going. Sighing dispiritedly, Stacy tucked her chestnut hair behind her ears. She couldn't leave. Her boots didn't seem to be made for walking anywhere except to her own house, which was where she was headed right now, her troubled eyes looking mostly at the ground.

A squeal of childish delight came from that direction, followed by a resounding splash of water. Nearing the rise that permitted her a view of the pool area on the west side of the hacienda, Stacy paused. The red-tiled roof gleamed dully against the whitewashed adobe walls.

Two more steps and she could see the swimming pool and the three people in it. Cord's rolling laughter carried across the distance. Her chest contracted as she tried to remember the last time she'd heard him laugh with such happiness. It must have been shortly after the accident when he'd been simply glad to be alive.

She could see Paula's blond head in the water near Cord's. When she turned and said something to him, Cord laughed again. Stacy bit her lip until the salty taste of blood was in her mouth. She hadn't been able to make him laugh like that, but Paula had.

Jealousy scored another hit. The scene of man, woman, and child playing in the swimming pool was an ideal picture of a family. But there was something wrong with it, very wrong, because Stacy should have been there to portray the mother, not Paula. *Why do they have to look so happy together,* she cried silently.

"Looks like they're having fun, doesn't it?"

The male voice made Stacy's head jerk around, alarm registering in her wide eyes and in the sudden draining of color from her face. Concern darkened Travis's gaze.

"Sorry. I didn't mean to startle you."

"I . . . it's . . . okay. I just didn't hear you walk up."

Stacy fought to regain her composure with limited success. "You're early. I wasn't expecting you until lunch."

Awkwardly, she started toward the house, anxious to take his attention away from the occupants of the swimming pool. She didn't think she could talk about them with any degree of poise.

"I can't make it today. That's why I stopped now on the off chance that I would find you." Travis fell in step beside her. "If you aren't busy now, I thought we could go over those grain invoices together and see if we can find the reason for the discrepancy with our records."

"I'm free." Stacy was grateful she would be deprived of the time to brood on the scene she'd witnessed.

Unfortunately the office work didn't prove to be the distraction she'd hoped for. Somewhere part way through the stack of papers, none of which had been entered in their system software, she forgot to concentrate on what she was doing. Her gaze wandered to the window and the driveway beyond it. The laughter and voices from the pool area had stopped some time ago, yet the sounds echoed endlessly in her mind.

"Stacy, what's wrong?"

Her reaction was in slow motion as she turned to Travis. "What?" she asked blankly, hearing his voice without hearing his question.

His frowning gaze inspected her face. "I said, what's wrong? Why are you crying?"

Stacy lifted a hand to her cheeks, surprised by the moistness she found there. Hurriedly she wiped the tears away, only to feel more trickle down, retracing the paths of the first. In agitation and embarrassment, she rose from her chair, turning her back to Travis.

"Nothing—really." Her voice quivered, revealing her lie, and more tears slipped from her lashes.

A chair leg scraped as Travis straightened. Stacy knew she hadn't deceived him. She wiped frantically at the tears and tried to laugh. It was a choking sound.

"I don't know what's the matter with me. I'm sorry, Travis." She muffled the words through her hands, trying to calm herself. "You must think I've lost my mind." It was what Stacy was wondering.

"Well, I think something is wrong. Will it help to talk about it?"

"Yes—no." She slid her hands behind her neck, letting them rest there for an instant. "I'm so mixed up." A sigh accompanied her admission. "I'm such a fool, I know, but you saw them out there."

"Cord and Paula?"

"Did you hear him laugh?" Stacy glanced at Travis's handsome features and the wings of silver hair lacing the sides of his black hair. She turned away from his thoughtful gaze. "I wanted to be the one to make him laugh again. It . . . it sounds selfish, doesn't it? Selfish and jealous?"

Again she wiped at the tears on her cheeks. "I am jealous." Her voice was low and defeated. "It's just that they've become so close—so friendly. I know . . . I'm sure they . . ." Stacy couldn't put her suspicions into words.

Her throat tightened and silent sobs shook her shoulders. Breaking down like this in front of Travis was too humiliating.

His large hands closed over her shoulders and brought her to his chest. The sight of the inviting expanse snapped what little remained of her control, and she buried her face in his shirt and cried. Travis rocked her gently, like a child, stroking the silken length of her hair. Over and over again, Stacy sobbed that she was sorry.

"Ssh," Travis soothed. "You've been living like this for too long, bottling everything up inside. This was bound to happen."

"I didn't want it to," Stacy mumbled brokenly.

He smiled slightly. "That's beside the point now."

"If only I didn't think that Cord . . . Paula . . ." She shook her head, pressing her lips together.

"If you think something is going on between Cord and Paula, then you're letting your imagination run away with you," Travis scolded gently.

"I want to believe that." Desperately—oh, how she wanted to believe that.

Travis crooked a finger under her chin and raised it to smile into her face. "It's just a matter of time."

The little breath she exhaled was wistful. Tremulously, her lips curved into an answering smile. She did appreciate his encouraging words and, God, she hoped he was right. But uncertainty lingered in her tear-wet eyes. Tenderly he wiped the tears from her left cheek, a soothing roughness to his callused hand.

Blinking, she glanced from his roughly hewn face to the hand that caressed her. Halfway there, she saw something else. The study door was opened and a tall figure stood within the frame.

Cord? Standing?

The jubilant light in his jet dark eyes flamed into fury, piercing Stacy to the heart.

Her mouth opened as she stared incredulously at Cord. He was upright, leaning heavily on a walker. But he was standing! She wanted to cry for joy, but she couldn't speak.

At the shining change in her expression, Travis turned

around and instantly he mirrored the same surprise and gladness as Stacy.

But he noted, too, the chiseled coldness in Cord's strained features. Stacy was still too overwhelmed by Cord's recovery to be anything but happy.

"First it was Colter's wife, now it's mine, is that it?" Cord jeered. "Can't you find a woman who doesn't belong to someone else?"

"You've made a mistake, Cord," Travis replied quietly.

Stunned by the violence in Cord's voice, Stacy finally registered what he must be thinking. Unhurriedly Travis moved her away from himself.

"The only mistake I made was being fool enough to trust you!" Cord snapped. "Get out of here, McCrea!"

Lifting the walker that supported him, he set it inches forward into the room, half dragging his legs after it. A few more times, and he'd cleared the doorway.

"What you're thinking—that's not true," protested Stacy as he continued to glare savagely at Travis.

"It's all right, Stacy." But she could see Travis was controlling himself with an effort. "I'll leave for now."

"You're damned right you will!" Cord growled in agreement.

With smooth strides, Travis walked from the room. When the front door had clicked shut, Cord shifted his diamond-black gaze to Stacy. She shivered at the contempt in his expression.

"I was upset," she said defensively. "Travis was only trying to make me feel better, that's all."

"Do you expect me to believe that?"

"It's the truth."

She shook her head helplessly, her gaze running over him. "Oh, Cord, you're out of that wheelchair! I can't get over it." She moved blindly toward him, wanting to forget the stupid misunderstanding over Travis and rejoice in Cord's recovery.

"It was meant to be a surprise. Some surprise!" His mouth thinned bitterly.

The darkening fire in his eyes made Stacy realize that he was only seeing the scene with Travis when he'd opened the study door.

"It wasn't what you think—not at all. Let's not argue," she pleaded softly.

The tips of her fingers hesitantly touched his hand on the walker. Cord made no answer.

"This is a time to be happy you're on your feet again. How long? When did it happen?"

Cord shifted his hand away from her touch. "Does it matter?" he mocked. "Tell me, Stacy, how did it feel to have a man's arms around you?"

His rejection of her tentative caress stung. Stacy drew back, tilting her chin forward. He towered above her, aloof and wounded.

"Tell me how it feels when Paula touches you, rubbing your shoulders and neck. And your back." There. She'd said it.

"That has nothing to do with what we're talking about!" He became angry at her question. "Don't try to justify your cheating with that."

"Where's the difference?" She stood stiffly in front of him. Her heart longed for him to deny it all, for him to speak the few words that would tell her she'd simply been imagining that something was going on between him and Paula.

But he ignored the question. "I knew you'd become bored with ranch life and with being tied down to one place. But I never suspected for one minute you'd take the easy way out—in the arms of another man," he declared in disgust.

Stacy flinched uncontrollably, then recovered. "Would you believe me if I told you that Travis and I are only friends?"

"I'm not blind!" The hard line of his mouth crooked cynically. "I saw the two of you in a clinch when I opened the door!"

"And you believe everything you see? So do I, then! I guess there's nothing more to say, is there?" She sounded quite calm as she walked toward the door, but she was seething.

"I want Travis off this ranch within the hour," he snapped.

Her hand rested on the doorknob. She turned, meeting the freezing blackness of his gaze. "I'm the one who's running this ranch, Cord, not you," she replied softly to keep her voice from betraying the quaking of her body. "I was the one who hired Travis and I'll be the one who tells him to leave. Except I have no intention of doing so."

Without another word, she walked into the hall. She could hear Cord cursing under his breath as he tried to follow her, laboriously dragging each leg a step at a time. She was truly frightened at the raging anger she had sparked—and yet . . . she understood it. She had to get away, for her own safety and his. Quickly she closed the front door and hurried from the house.

Chapter 9

Travis was leaning against the fender of the pickup, his dusty Stetson pushed back on his head. A cigarette was cupped in his hand as he watched Stacy approach.

"Did you explain?"

His brown eyes moved over her grim expression and the defiant thrust of her chin.

"Cord was too convinced of his own conclusion to listen," Stacy replied.

"I'm sorry." Travis flipped his cigarette to the ground and then crushed it beneath the heel of his boot.

"Neither of us has done anything to be sorry about," she retorted with a rush of indignant pride.

"I know that." He stared down the winding lane leading through the broken Texas hills to the main road. "But just the same I think Cord was right when he told me to leave. It'd probably be best all the way around. With me out of the picture, he'd be more likely to listen to you."

"No!" Stacy didn't want to consider the idea, not for a second. "Under no circumstances do I want you to leave unless I personally ask you to go."

Shaking his dark head, Travis looked back at her and

sighed. "You're only complicating a difficult situation. His jealousy pretty much proves there's nothing going on between him and Paula. You were only imagining it."

"That's where you're wrong," she said emphatically.

His mouth tightened in exasperation. "Stacy, you can't still believe he'd do something like that to you, in your own house, with his son never far away. Come on!"

"I confronted Cord with it." Tears burned the back of her eyes, and she bent her head so Travis wouldn't see them. "It's the old twist on what's sauce for the gander isn't sauce for the goose. It's one thing for Cord to be unfaithful, but it's unforgivable in his eyes that I should be."

Travis frowned, studying her intently. "I don't believe it."

"It's the truth." Swallowing hard, Stacy lifted her gaze. "Travis, I want your word that you'll stay."

He hesitated, carefully considering her request. "I'll stay for the time being." His reluctant agreement told her that he thought she was making a mistake by asking him to remain.

"Thank you," she murmured gratefully. Pausing for a second, she added, "And I'm sorry about the reference Cord made to Natalie."

Travis took a deep breath and stared into space again. "I love her."

His mouth crooked wryly. "I'm afraid I haven't got to the point where I can say it in the past tense. Maybe I never will. But there was never anything physical between us. She was always Colter's. She was never mine to take. They're happy now and I couldn't wish any more than that."

Abruptly he turned and walked to the driver's door of the pickup. "Since I'm still on the payroll, I'd better get to work."

Stacy didn't attempt to stop him. "I'll see you later, Travis, and thanks—for everything."

When she returned to the house at lunchtime, Stacy expected another confrontation with Cord, but there was nothing but glacial silence as they faced each other over the table. Before the meal was over, she wished there had been a volcanic eruption instead.

His chilly attitude didn't change one degree during the next three days, and Stacy didn't make any attempt to begin a thaw. She had tried to explain once and Cord wouldn't listen. She was too stubborn and proud to try again.

Cross-legged on the end of the bed, she methodically brushed her long hair, electricity crackling through the silken strands.

Once she had thought things couldn't get any worse between herself and Cord. How very wrong she had been.

There was a light rap on her bedroom door, and she tensed, her heart quickening in hope.

"Who is it?" She hadn't heard the labored sounds of Cord's footsteps, but the carpet might have muffled them.

"It's me, Paula. May I come in?"

"Sure." It seemed almost like admitting a traitor into the camp. As the door opened, Stacy resumed the rhythmic strokes of the brush through her hair, not glancing up. "What was it you wanted, Paula?" she asked briskly.

"I hoped you weren't in bed yet. There was something I wanted to talk to you about." There was no indication that Paula had noticed the absence of welcome in Stacy's voice.

"What is it?" Deliberately she didn't suggest that the physical therapist take a seat in the velvet-covered chair in the corner.

"It's about Cord."

Paula didn't wait for an invitation and settled her tall frame on the chair.

"Yes?" Stacy prompted coolly.

"Lately he's reverted to his old snarling self."

Uncurling her legs from beneath her, Stacy walked to the vanity table and stood in front of the mirror.

"So I've noticed," she responded indifferently. Actually Cord hadn't spoken a word to her, but she'd heard him snapping at everyone else.

"In a way, I expected it," Paula said.

She rose from the chair and moved until her reflection joined Stacy's in the mirror. "He's on his feet again and replaced the walker with crutches, but he's not as mobile as he wants to be. When I first came here, I had to bully him into the therapy. Now he's trying too hard."

"I see," Stacy murmured, but she kept all of her attention on fluffing her hair into its style.

"If I don't find some way to distract him, he'll overdo it."

There was a second's pause as Paula waited for Stacy to comment, but she didn't. She sensed that the therapist had a suggestion to make and she was waiting to hear it. "There's no reason why he can't begin taking part in the operation of the ranch. I want you to talk to him about it."

"No!" The word exploded from Stacy as her flashing gaze swung to Paula's reflection. She wouldn't seek Cord out for any reason. Placing the hairbrush on the table, she moved toward the window. "It wouldn't do any good. Travis and I have tried many times before."

"You have to try again," Paula said firmly.

"He wouldn't listen to me," Stacy argued. "You would be much better off to suggest it to him yourself."

"I can't do that, Stacy—that's going too far. How the ranch is run or who runs it isn't something I could or should dictate."

"Glad to hear it," Stacy muttered.

"The suggestion has to come from you, that's all I'm saying. But he does seem to think that you really don't need his help and he hates feeling patronized."

"Sounds like he tells you everything."

Paula shrugged. "He's opened up a little."

"Glad to hear that too." But Stacy wasn't, as unfair as it seemed. It rankled that Cord would confide in another woman, one he hardly knew.

"Anyway, Stacy, anyone looking at you can see that you're overworked and overwhelmed. All you have to do is say that you can't cope with all of it anymore. It's a fact."

Stacy had seen the signs of exactly that in the mirror. There were shadows around her eyes, and even their warm brown seemed dull. Her face looked drawn and a little thin, and there was no happiness in her face. Even the gold-dust sprinkle of freckles across her nose seemed to have faded.

Although Paula's words were valid, Stacy couldn't bring herself to agree, and she felt mean to refuse point-blank, so she made no reply.

"Stacy, what's the matter with you?" Paula demanded. "You almost act as if you don't want Cord to recover completely."

"That's not true!" She spun to face Paula.

"Something has happened between you and Cord, hasn't it?" Blue eyes watched Stacy alertly. "What is it?"

Stacy turned away from the scrutiny. "You'll have to ask Cord," she answered stiffly.

"I have. He told me to mind my own business."

"Then that's my answer too."

"I won't accept that from you," Paula responded. "I don't care whether you think I'm sticking my nose in where it doesn't belong or not. My only concern is Cord and what's best for him. I thought you'd think the same thing."

Staring at her clenching fingers, Stacy cried inwardly at the unfairness of being blackmailed by her love for her husband.

"I am concerned." Her voice was barely above a whisper.

"If you are, then talk to him," Paula said. "Persuade him

to take some of the work off your shoulders. Give him something to do other than brood all day long."

"All right." The reluctant agreement was made through gritted teeth. "I'll talk to him tomorrow."

"Tonight," Paula stated unequivocally. "Putting it off until tomorrow won't make it any easier."

Stacy pivoted, meeting the other woman's direct blue gaze. The angry protest rising in her throat was checked by her tightly compressed lips. Without a word, she swept past the tall blonde through the door and down the stairs to the master bedroom.

There her courage faltered. She stared at the closed door for a hesitating second, her hand clenching nervously. Quickly she knocked once and opened the door without waiting for permission to enter. Cord was standing freely at the end of the bed, a hand clutching the sturdy carved post. His expression was grim with determination as he glanced up. At the sight of Stacy, he drew his head back in a wary way.

"What do you want?"

Avoiding his cold gaze, Stacy glanced at his crutches some distance away. "What are you doing?" she breathed, alarmed by the obvious unsteadiness of his legs.

Half dragging and half lifting one leg forward to put himself at a better angle to face her, Cord took a deep breath.

"Don't you recognize the movement?" he asked. "It's called walking."

"But you could fall," she said worriedly, realizing what Paula had been talking about. Cord was trying to push himself beyond the limit of his capabilities.

He leaned a hip against the bed railing. She could see by the strained muscles in his arms the effort it was costing him to remain upright. He was wearing only pants, his shirt tossed somewhere. Sweat curled the dark hair on his bare chest.

"I'm not impressed by your show of concern," he said. "Get to the point and tell me why you're here. I know it's not your burning desire for my company."

Stacy's mouth opened to deny his cutting remark, but she closed it without speaking. It would be a waste of breath. He wouldn't believe her.

"I need your help," she finally said.

A black eyebrow arched in arrogant disbelief. "For what?"

"The ranch work has become too much for me. I can't handle it all anymore," Stacy said all in a rush.

There was more than a grain of truth in the statement. Managing the ranch was a full-time occupation without the added burden of the coming horse sale.

"What's the matter?" Cord asked harshly. "Don't you have enough free time to sneak off to meet Travis for some cowboy-style comforting? Are you expecting me to provide it?"

Stacy flinched as if she'd taken a physical blow. His sarcasm was too extreme to respond to. Agitated, she moved with no direction to her steps beyond a release of the frustration and pain that consumed her.

"Travis has nothing to do with my asking you for help," she said in a low voice.

"Doesn't he?" Cord snarled. His fingers suddenly closed around her wrist and yanked her to him. The force of the contact with his hard male body momentarily took her breath away.

Her eyes widened at the fire in his gaze. Her heart pounded like a hammer in her chest. All she saw was him—and his gaze centered on the parted moistness of her lips.

"Is Travis a good lover, my passionate Stacy?" His gaze

traveled down to the exposed curve of her neck. "Do you make those kitten sounds in your throat for him?"

Relentless, he kissed the sensitive cord of her neck over and over as if to obliterate any trace of another man's caress or touch. He paused near her ear to nip hard at its lobe.

Hot fire raced through Stacy's veins as her fingers spread over the hard flesh of his shoulders, muscles bunched and flexing beneath her palms. The scent of his body was musky and warm, arousing her senses with rekindled desire. But desire wasn't what was driving Cord, only an overwhelming need to claim what he thought of as his.

"Don't do this, Cord. Please," Stacy begged.

Her protest was muffled by the sensual, demanding pressure of his mouth. Yielding against him, she knew she couldn't deny him. The truth was that she wanted his caresses no matter what drove him.

As she leaned against him, her knees buckled. He was forced to release her to let his arms grip the bed, taking his weight away from his still weak legs. Instantly Stacy reached forward when she realized what had happened, anxious to lend him her support.

"Let me help you," she pleaded.

Cord turned away from her, struggling to keep his balance. "I don't want your help," he said savagely. "Just get out of here!"

Stacy took a step backward. Then she turned and hurried blindly to the door.

His voice followed her. "And you can tell your precious Travis that you weren't able to trick your husband into allowing you more time for a rendezvous!"

Stacy stopped cold. "For the last time, Cord, Travis had nothing to do with my coming here." Her voice quivered with pain. "The quarter horse auction is only a week away. I can't cope with everything there is to do."

She made one last attempt to fulfill the purpose that had brought her to the room. "I talked to Paula and she said that your helping with the ranch probably wouldn't interfere with the therapy."

Her back was to him as she reached for the doorknob. It turned beneath her hand before he replied to her statement.

"When did you talk to Paula?" he demanded quietly.

A frown marred her forehead. "A few minutes ago. She's upstairs." She released the knob and faced him. "What difference does that make?"

"Was this her idea or yours?"

"It was Paula's idea," she answered truthfully. "But it doesn't change the fact that I do need help, Cord—your help. I once said I would ask for no quarter from you, but now I'm begging for it. I can't make it without you."

Stacy meant that in every sense of the word, but she qualified it almost instantly out of pride when he didn't respond. "At least you could do the bookwork and data entry if nothing else."

He seemed to weigh her appeal, testing its sincerity, then nodded grudgingly. "All right. I can do some of that. Now go away and leave me alone."

He began the slow task of walking by the bed, his arms bearing most of the burden as he made it clear that the dismissal was final.

Knowing any offer of assistance would be summarily rejected, Stacy left his room. Listlessly she climbed the stairs, walking past her room to Paula's. The door was opened and she paused in its frame.

"Cord has agreed to help," she said simply.

"I knew you could persuade him." Paula smiled.

Stacy didn't feel like smiling back. She felt that Paula's name had carried more weight with Cord that her own plea for aid. She made no reply to the comment as she turned and retreated to the emptiness of her bedroom. Her body still tingled from being held so passionately against Cord's. There would be no rest tonight. Nor the next two nights.

Wearily she pushed the front door open, wondering why she had bothered to come to the house for lunch. She was too tired to eat and felt as brittle as an eggshell.

There was a rustling of papers from the study. The door stood open and Stacy guessed that Cord was in the room working. She started to go silently by, not wanting to see him when she was so vulnerable to his barbs.

"Stacy! Come here!"

His imperious order checked her in mid-stride. She hesitated then moved into the doorway. He was sitting beside the desk, an angry expression on his face.

God, she was tired of his anger, above and beyond everything else that made her tired. And just why he, like way too many men, felt so entitled to take it out on the nearest female or underling was beyond her comprehension. If he hadn't been struggling so hard to get better, she would've walked up to him and tipped the desk, the chair, and him right over.

"What do you want?" Her brisk question was intended to hide the oil-and-water mixture of anger and compassion that she felt. And she hoped it would get across that she was busy and impatient to be on her way.

"I want an explanation for this." Lifting a handful of papers, he tossed them to the front of the desk for her inspection.

Stacy paused, wanting to flee. Resolutely squaring her shoulders, she walked to the desk and picked up the papers. A quick glance identified them as the catalog of the yearlings to be sold.

"What do you want explained?" She frowned, seeing nothing that was in error.

"Why are the two stud colts sired by Lije Masters's stallion listed for sale?"

Stacy shrugged, confused. "Neither Travis or I saw any reason to keep them. We already have three two-year-old stallions for stud prospects as well as the proven stallion you bought last year. That's not even mentioning the two we already use for breeding."

His mouth tightened. "You knew I wanted to add the Malpais bloodline to my stock. This one yearling out of the Cutters's mare I especially wanted to keep."

"How in the world could I know that? Am I supposed to read your mind?"

"You could've used common sense. Is that too much to expect?"

"Hey, I asked you to help choose the yearlings to sell!" she shouted in defense, her raw nerves unable to tolerate his high-and-mighty tone. "Travis told you he didn't know anything about horses, only cattle. You refused to help, so don't blame me if there are horses listed that you don't want to sell. It's your own fault!"

"How was I to know you would do something as stupid as this?" Cord waved the catalog at her.

Hot tears spilled over her lashes, flaming her cheeks with their scalding warmth.

"I can't do anything to please you anymore!" she declared with fury. "If you think I'm doing such a lousy job of running things, then you can do it all from now on! I'm handing in my resignation as of this moment!"

She raced from the room, putting a hand over her mouth to stifle the sobs that wrenched her throat.

"Stacy, come back here!" Cord shouted.

She slammed the front door behind her. Her headlong

flight took her down the sloping grade to the stables. Throwing open the door to the tack room, she pulled a bridle from the walk and her saddle and blanket. Indifferent to the weight, she walked swiftly to the corral, but there was no sign of the chocolate-brown mare.

From a sturdy enclosure apart from the others came a whinny of greeting. Stacy glanced in its direction, seeing the sorrel stallion at liberty. His elegant head was over the top rail, luminous brown eyes returning her look, pointed ears pricked forward.

"Diablo," Stacy murmured with decision, and moved to her corral.

Docile for a change, the red horse nuzzled her arm, playfully nipping at her blouse as she entered his corral. He bent his head without misbehaving to accept the bridle and swished his flaxen tail contentedly as she laid the saddle blanket on his back.

Minutes later, Stacy was swinging into the saddle, mentally thumbing her nose at Cord's longstanding order not to ride the high-spirited stallion. With her on his back, the stallion pranced eagerly. His four white feet stirred up the dusty ground.

Running a soothing hand over his arched neck, Stacy turned him toward the corral gate. From the corner of her eye, she saw the wizened figure hurrying to intercept them. She leaned forward and unlatched the gate only to have Hank reach it before she could swing it open.

"You get down off that horse!" He held the gate shut as he frowned at her, certain she'd gone way past "tetched" and lost her senses.

"Get out of the way, Hank," she ordered.

"You know you ain't supposed to ride that stallion."

"He's my horse and I'll do what I want."

Stacy nudged the sorrel forward until his shoulder was

pushing against the gate. Her hand joined the effort to swing the gate open. "Move, Hank," she warned.

"The boss gave strict orders none of us was to let you ride that horse!" He strained to keep it closed, but the combined strength of horse and rider was more than he could stop, especially when the sorrel saw the narrow opening and pushed to enlarge it.

"I don't care what the boss says!" Stacy declared.

Hank was knocked to the ground as the horse burst through. Stacy had only a second to glance back to make sure that the old man was getting to his feet unharmed. After that, all her efforts were directed to controlling her mount.

Reining him away from the fenced enclosures of the other horses, she guided him toward the house and the winding lane that would take them to the open range. In a lunging canter, the sorrel threatened to bolt with each stride. The leather reins bit into her ungloved hands as she tried to hold him.

Cord was outside when the stallion plunged by the house. One look at Stacy fighting to hold the horse and he began shouting orders to the stable hands emerging from the buildings. A smile curved her mouth, guessing his anger at seeing her astride the horse he'd forbidden her to ride.

Her pleasure was short-lived. She had to concentrate on mastering the spirited steed beneath her. It had been so long since Diablo had tasted freedom and he wanted to drink his fill. Lack of sleep and loss of weight had depleted Stacy's strength, and the muscles in her arms began to tremble at the effort of holding the stallion in a canter.

With a determined shake of his head, the sorrel loosened the hold on the reins and gained the bit between his teeth. In one bound, he was at a dead run, breaking away from the ranch yard to veer across the rolling plains racing toward the mountains.

The wind whipped Stacy's breath away. A blackness swam around her eyes as she buried her face in the flaxen mane and gripped the saddle horn to stay on. Dodging patches of prickly pear cactus and skimming over the top of sagebrush and range grass, the stallion ran with ecstasy.

Somehow Stacy managed to stay in the saddle, at one with the runaway, heedless of the wild ride. Not until he slowed to a bone-jarring trot miles from the ranch house did she take notice of her surroundings. His flanks heaved as he blew the dust from his lungs and finally obeyed the pressure of the reins when she drew him to a stop.

Weakly she slipped from the saddle, a death grip on the reins. Her knees buckled beneath her and she slumped to the ground. Diablo was content to munch the long grass. For the moment, Stacy didn't care if he broke away. She lay there on the ground, strength gradually flowing back into her limbs.

But it was nearly an hour before she climbed back into the saddle and turned the horse toward home.

Chapter 10

Both Stacy and Diablo were hot and tired by the time they gained sight of the ranch yard. Pausing beside the wrought iron fence enclosing the family cemetery west of the house, Stacy watched the activity below. The circuitous route she'd taken had been necessary in order to get her bearings after the wild ride.

Travis's green pickup truck was parked in the driveway in front of the house. The door to the driver's side was opened. The broad-shouldered figure sitting half in the cab and half out was undoubtedly Travis.

There was also no mistaking Cord, leaning on his crutches and gazing in the direction Stacy had originally gone. Paula was there too, her hands on her hips conveying an attitude of troubled concern.

A search party had obviously been organized for her. Stacy guessed that Travis was probably in contact with it now, via the radio in his truck. She supposed she hadn't run into it because of the different route she had taken back.

Touching a heel to the sorrel, she started down the small hill toward the truck. She gave no thought to Cord's anger at her deliberate disobedience that would await her return. She felt invulnerable to everything but her own tiredness.

She was a hundred feet away before Travis glanced around and noticed her approach. He got quickly out of the truck, saying something to the other two. With a jerk of his head, Cord looked at her, a taut alertness about him like a lion about to spring.

It was Travis who moved forward to intercept her, his hands grasping the reins near the cheek strap. Diablo tossed his head, disliking the touch of a man's hand.

Travis ignored the stallion, his gaze taking in Stacy's disheveled appearance instead. Dirt clung to the shoulder and sleeve of her blouse where she had rested on the ground.

"Are you all right, Stacy?"

"Yes," she smiled wanly.

Looping the reins around the saddle horn, she swung her right leg over it, kicking her other foot free of the stirrup to slide to the ground. But Travis's hands were around her waist, lifting her down. For a brief instant, she stumbled against him before regaining her balance.

Almost absently she looked into Cord's blazing dark eyes, blistering hotly over her. She stepped away from Travis's supporting hands.

"Get that stallion out of here, McCrea," ordered Cord. "As for you, Stacy—" His voice was ominously low.

Paula placed a restraining hand on his arm for just a moment. "Let her be, Cord," she said. Her blue eyes looked sympathetically at Stacy's exhausted expression. "She's hot and tired. She needs a shower and a lie-down, not a lecture."

A muscle worked in Cord's jaw as if he wasn't entirely convinced of Paula's statement. Before he could complete his interrupted sentence, Paula dodged him and curved an arm around Stacy's shoulders, turning her toward the house. "Come on, Stacy."

In other circumstances, Stacy would have resented her intervening unasked. At the moment, though, she was too tired to care. It didn't even matter that she'd been rescued from Cord's wrath. She was numbed beyond emotion.

The sting of the shower spray eliminated that protection. Wrapped in a cotton robe, Stacy stood at her bedroom window watching the search party that had just ridden in, recalled by either Cord or Travis. Guilt nagged at her at the amount of work undone or abandoned because they'd had to search for her. Riding Diablo had been a childish gesture of defiance.

An odd thudding sound came from the stairs and Stacy frowned in absent curiosity. The thuds stopped outside her door, and a wave of certainty washed over her that Cord was on the other side. A second later he opened the door, a stormy look on his face.

"Did you think by staying in your room you would avoid facing me?"

She shook her head without verbally answering and stared out the window, assailed by a complex mix of painful sensations.

"You deliberately rode that horse knowing how I felt."

"Yes."

"You realize you could've been seriously hurt, don't you?"

"Yes," she said again. She didn't want to think about the possibility that she had wanted to hurt herself. Or why.

"If you don't care about yourself or me, then think about our son, Stacy. He needs both of us—and I almost bought it a year ago in that damn plane crash. He doesn't need you to tempt the devil on that horse of yours."

"His name is Diablo, in case you've forgotten it. Fits, doesn't it? But I can handle him."

He wasn't in the mood for banter, clearly. "Don't take that tone with me," he warned. "And don't pretend you had control of him for one second, because he was running away with you."

"But I wasn't hurt," she said with forced evenness.

"That's beside the point," Cord snapped.

Irritated, she moved away from the window. "There's no reason to go into all of this. It's over and done with and I admit it was foolish. I was . . . I was just upset."

"You're right," he said. "It is over and done with. And it won't happen again. Diablo will be off this ranch before nightfall."

It was a full second before his statement hit home. "What do you mean?" Stacy demanded.

"I'm selling him," Cord declared flatly. "Never again am I going through what I did this afternoon."

"He's not yours to sell!" Temper flashed in her brown eyes. "Diablo belongs to me!"

There was a complacent curve to his firm mouth. "The ranch belongs to me—you even handed the running of it over to me this morning. And I refuse to have a dangerous horse on my property. You can fight the sale, but you can't fight that."

"How can you do this?" She shook with anger.

"How could you do what you did?"

"I told you I was upset!"

"And I'm insuring the next time you get upset, you don't go riding off and breaking your foolish neck!"

"You can't sell him. He's mine," Stacy repeated.

"He'll not stay another night on this ranch," Cord reiterated just as forcefully as Stacy.

"If he goes, I leave with him!" she threatened.

To add credibility to her words, she pivoted away from Cord with a defiant flourish, but before she could take a step, his hand encircled her wrist and spun her back.

"You are not leaving here!" He wouldn't let go.

Needing a hand on a crutch to stand up, Cord couldn't check Stacy's free hand as it swung toward his cheek. It struck its mark, and his tanned skin turned white, and then filled with red. For a shocked instant, as much at herself as at him, she thought he was going to retaliate in kind.

Stone-faced, Cord released her wrist and maneuvered himself in awkward steps to the door. There he paused, his furious eyes pinning her.

"No matter what you do, I will never want to let you go. So quit trying to make me hate you." It wasn't a warning. It was an unequivocal statement.

As the door closed behind him, Stacy slumped onto her bed, rubbing her wrist.

After several minutes she went to the bedroom window and waited to see if Cord was really going to get rid of Diablo.

If he did, she had no idea of her next step. She was afraid that mutual anger had brought them to an impasse and pride wouldn't allow either of them to back down.

There was no activity in the driveway below, no movement of horse trailers or vans. Perhaps Cord had reconsidered, she thought hopefully.

Then an almost imperceptible click of the doorknob turning got her attention. Very slowly the door swung partway open. Stacy watched it warily. Josh peered around the corner.

His round dark eyes found her and he asked, "Are you sick, Mommy?"

"No, I'm not sick." She managed a maternal smile. "Come in."

Still he hesitated. "Maria said I shouldn't bother you and I thought you were sick."

"I was just very tired and decided to hang out in my bedroom for a while," Stacy explained more fully to her doubting son.

"Are you all rested now?" Josh asked, stepping just inside the door. His expression was expectantly bright.

She inclined her head toward him in amusement. "Why?"

"'Cause." He shrugged. "I got nothing to do. I thought you might think of something."

Gazing at the hopeful look in his eyes, Stacy knew she'd spent little time with her son lately. There wasn't any reason not to make up for it now.

"Any suggestions in particular that you wanted me to make?"

An impish smile lit up his face. "We could play ball."

"How about something less strenuous, like—like swinging?"

"Okay," Josh agreed readily.

"Give me five minutes to get dressed and I'll be down," Stacy promised.

With a nod of his head, he darted into the hall. She wasted no time changing into a pair of shorts and a cool top.

At the door, she glanced to the bedroom window, then left. There would be plenty of time to find out what Cord was doing about Diablo. She didn't mind postponing her own decision.

The rest of the afternoon was actually carefree, as Stacy played with Josh, pushing his swing high in the air and enjoying his shrieks of delight. She ruffled his hair affectionately as they went back to the house.

"Quit it," he said.

Stacy looked down at him. She had succeeded in tiring him out—not easy for a kid as active as Josh. "Why don't you see if Maria has anything cold to drink?" said Stacy.

"And cookies?" Josh added.

"You bet. We'll have it out here on the veranda. You can help Maria carry it out."

"Yeah. I'm strong."

She watched her little man dash to the sliding glass doors and she settled contentedly on a chaise lounge. The glass door wasn't completely closed by Josh, and with a sigh at his impatience, Stacy rose to close it.

The loud impact of something falling stopped her hand from sliding the door shut. Identifying the location of the sound as the study, she pushed the door open and ran inside the house. Her heart kept skipping beats at the thought that Cord might have fallen.

She was not alone in her fear. Paula was already racing from the living room to the study. Stacy followed her with no hope of reaching Cord first. As she entered the hallway, Paula disappeared through the study door.

"Honey, are you crazy?" Stacy heard Paula exclaim in mock reproof. "What on earth were you trying to do?"

The endearment, consciously used or not, slowed Stacy's feet. A cold chill ran through her veins, reducing her pulse to a dull thud.

"I was trying to get some papers from the file." Cord muttered his answer. His voice was low and strained as if from making a supreme physical effort.

"Yeah, you were trying to get them without your crutches," Paula reprimanded him. "When are you going to learn that you have to take things by stages? You'll walk soon enough if you don't break a leg first. Are you hurt anywhere?"

Stacy paused near the door, giving herself a limited angle to view the room. Jealously she watched the tall blonde kneel beside Cord, the contrast between his dark looks and Paula's fairness crushing the life from her heart.

What an attractive couple they made. And how nice they were to each other. Not like two married people who only found fault and fought too often.

"I'm only suffering from wounded pride," he answered, levering himself into a half-sitting position with one arm, and struggling to persuade his uncoordinated legs to shift him to his feet.

"Let me help you," Paula said.

Without waiting for his agreement, she hooked his arm around her neck and shoulders. The physical effort they both made brought Cord upright, and he wavered unsteadily for a few seconds, trying to regain his balance on his own.

Razor-sharp jealousy sliced at Stacy's heart. Paula's height brought the top of her head even with Cord's dark eyes. The fullness of her lips was just below the jutting angle of his chin.

They stood so closely together with Cord's arm again around her shoulders that breathless, impotent rage welled in Stacy. When Cord looked so warmly into the therapist's bright eyes, Stacy had to put a hand over her mouth to keep from crying out in pain.

"You're one in a million, Paula," he said.

"I'm glad you finally recognize that," she said lightly.

Cord nodded. "Oh, I've known it for a long time." A half smile played at the corners of his mouth. "I just haven't gotten around to saying anything until now."

Paula's head moved downward as if glancing at the floor. Stacy knew the impact of Cord's charm, especially that close. Cord placed a thumb and forefinger beneath Paula's chin and turned her face toward him again.

"Do you know something?" he asked rhetorically. "I don't think I'll throw you out of the house when all this is finished."

"Careful," Paula warned huskily, "or I might make you live up to that statement."

Cord shook his head and smiled. "You're welcome to stay in my home as long as you want."

Paula seemed to catch her breath, then laughed, a brittle

sound to Stacy's ears. She no longer felt guilty about spying. Sometimes you had to. And this was one of those times.

"What do you want, a harem?"

"The stallions have them."

Paula tsk-tsked. "Stacy might have something to say about another woman taking up permanent residence here," she went on.

His handsome features immediately hardened, the line of his mouth straightening. A guarded look shadowed his gaze as he released Paula's chin. "Yes," he agreed quietly, "if Stacy is still here."

Definitely here. And closer than you know. Moving quickly away from the study door, Stacy stumbled back toward the veranda.

Jumbled thoughts assailed her. His enigmatic statement echoed in her mind, its meaning no clearer than when he'd said it. The only certainty in it was that Cord considered it a distinct possibility that she, Stacy, would be gone. The unanswered question was would she leave at her instigation or his?

For two days, Stacy wandered aimlessly through each waking hour, in automatic-mommy mode with Josh and uninvolved with everyone else. Diablo was still in his corral. She hadn't found the courage to ask Cord if he'd reconsidered his vow to sell her horse. She feared the result of such a confrontation.

The entire ranch was bustling with preparations for the quarter horse auction on Saturday, just two days away. Only Stacy and Paula had nothing to do. Stacy couldn't tolerate the company of the woman who was stealing Cord's love and boosting his ego to unheard-of heights. That, Paula would regret someday, Stacy thought sourly. And how.

The lovely old hacienda with its whitewashed adobe and red-tiled roof became a stifling prison, which she had to escape for some part of each day. The shopping expedition that had brought Stacy into McCloud, Texas, had merely been an excuse to escape from the uneasy atmosphere of the house.

Josh tugged at her hand. "I'm hungry, Mommy."

Catching back a sigh, Stacy glanced at her watch. It was nearly time for lunch. She knew Maria was expecting them back, but she had no desire to return yet.

"Why don't we have something to eat here in town instead of going home?" she suggested with forced brightness.

"Yeah!" He gave her a huge grin and a thumbs-up approval that he'd learned from Travis.

As they entered the restaurant, one familiar face stood out from the townsfolk.

Speak of the devil. Or a very lonely angel, Stacy thought.

Josh saw him at the same moment his mother did.

"Look, there's Travis!" His loud voice turned heads, including the foreman's.

Travis straightened from the table as Josh withdrew his hand from Stacy's and rushed forward to greet him. She would rather have avoided the discerning eyes, but she followed her son.

"Hello, Josh." Travis held out his hand for the boy to shake, which pleased him no end, then lifted his gaze to Stacy. He nodded a greeting. "Stacy."

"Hello, Travis," she said, hoping her voice sounded calm. "We didn't expect to see you in here."

"I had an errand to run in town and thought I'd have something to eat before going back. Would you care to join me?" He gestured toward the empty chairs at his table.

It would have been rude to refuse. "Of course." She felt uneasy about it all the same.

Travis had already ordered before they arrived. After the waitress took their orders, Stacy fiddled a little with the cutlery until she realized Travis was watching her. Quickly she hid her hands in her lap and tried to fill the growing silence.

"How are things at the ranch?" It seemed like a strange question for her to ask, but Stacy'd had no contact with the operation of the Circle H for nearly a week.

"Running smoothly," Travis replied. "Cord has taken charge as if he'd never been away."

"That's good." Hesitating, she asked, "Has he said any more about you—leaving?"

"Not directly." He lifted the coffee mug and held it in his hands, swirling the brown-black liquid. "He said he needed my legs for the time being."

"I'm sorry for not warning you in advance that I was turning things over to him." Stacy looked down at the table top, feeling self-conscious.

"I guessed it was a sudden decision." Travis sipped the coffee. "How is it going with you two?"

"We haven't talked much." That was an understatement. "Before I was busy at the ranch. Now Cord is."

She watched Josh flipping idly through the coloring book she'd bought for him, as she avoided the gaze of the man seated opposite her. "And he still has to spend a lot of time with Paula," she added.

"You don't still believe—" The waitress arrived, interrupting Travis's comment.

The hot food brought Josh's attention back to the table and Travis wasn't able to reintroduce the subject, to Stacy's relief. Her son's chatter covered her lack of participation in the small talk.

"Are you going to the ranch now, Travis?" Josh wanted to know as the three of them lingered outside the restaurant.

Travis adjusted his dust-stained Stetson on his head and nodded. "I have to go back to work."

"We're going back now, too," Josh said with certainty.

Stacy couldn't agree with his statement. They'd killed the morning wandering through stores and Josh's interest in the outing had waned. She couldn't expect her son to understand that she wasn't eager to return to the ranch. It was his home, even if she had begun to feel uncomfortable in it.

"Where is your car parked?" Travis asked.

"Over by the lumberyard." She motioned in that general direction.

"So's my truck." He winked at Josh. "How about a piggyback ride to your car, Josh?" At the boy's eager nod, Travis hoisted him onto his shoulders. "Watch the hat," he warned Josh's clasping hands, "and my neck."

With Josh giggling, Travis started walking toward the lumberyard. His large hands firmly held the small legs dangling across his chest.

"Giddy-up, horsey!" Josh laughed, moving back and forth across Travis's shoulders to urge him to go faster.

"Careful or I'll buck you off." Travis tipped his head back in a pretend threat.

Stacy laughed at the wide-eyed look on Josh's face as his hands clutched the strong neck before he realized that Travis was only teasing. As they were about to step off the sidewalk into the street, a small lime-green car slowed to a stop in front of them, blocking their way.

In disbelief, Stacy stared into the cold mask that was Cord's face. He was sitting in the passenger seat, his tall frame looking cramped in the economy car. His unrevealing gaze was narrowed on the man carrying his son.

"I thought you were at the ranch, Travis," he said flatly.

"I had an errand in town," was the calm reply as Travis swung Josh down from his perch.

Stacy silently marveled at the way Travis ignored the underlying accusation in Cord's statement. The ruthless set of Cord's jaw made her shiver, yet nothing seemed to ruffle Travis, a quality he had probably developed through years of working for Colter Langston.

Her thoughts were pulled back to the present as Cord's gaze sliced from Travis to her with condemning force, as if he was mentally accusing her of keeping an assignation with the foreman.

"Josh and I ran into Travis at the restaurant when we stopped for lunch," she explained, hating herself immediately for feeling like she had to explain at all.

Paula bent her head to look past Cord at the threesome standing on the sidewalk. "You were in town shopping, weren't you, Stacy?" she asked.

"Yes."

"What did you buy?" Cord glanced pointedly at the flat, thin paper bag in her hand.

Stacy's fingers tightened on it instinctively. "A coloring book for Josh."

"And you've been gone all morning?" Cord's tone was unpleasant.

"I—I couldn't find anything else I wanted," she said defensively, knowing that she hadn't looked at anything except in the most absent-minded way.

"How disappointing," he said in a bored tone. "And how lucky you accidentally ran into Travis and didn't have to eat lunch alone."

"Yes, it was." Stacy agreed, shaking back her head in a proud way and sending her silken chestnut hair dancing around her shoulders. Her defense was shaky, so she tried to attack. "If I'd known you and Paula were going to be in town, I would've met you for lunch."

"It was time for Cord's checkup," Paula explained. "And

Bill was too busy to get away and come to the ranch for a house call."

"Then you haven't eaten," Stacy commented, glad the image of them sharing an intimate lunch could be banished from her mind.

"Actually Mary talked us into eating with them," she said.

A fingernail broke through the thin paper bag as Stacy clenched it tightly in her hand. Now Paula was even usurping her position with Mary, one of her best friends. The thought was infuriating.

"I see," she responded, tautly soft.

"We'll be on our way back to the ranch after that," Paula said.

"We're leaving now." Stacy aligned herself with Travis in deliberate defiance, not caring about the diamond-sharp look it got her from Cord.

"See you there." Paula lifted a hand in goodbye, which Stacy managed to return.

With their way across the street cleared, Stacy took hold of Josh's hand. As they stepped off, Travis stood for an instant on the curb, staring after the car.

"When Cord gets an idea in his head, he doesn't let go," he muttered.

Stacy knew he was referring to Cord's irrational belief that she and Travis were having an affair, but she didn't comment. There wasn't anything to say.

Chapter 11

There was a tired movement of her mouth into a smile. The shining dark head on the white pillow looked so peaceful and happy. Long, curling lashes lay against Josh's tanned cheeks. He had been so adamantly opposed to the suggestion of a nap, yet he had fallen asleep before she had reached the last page of a storybook.

Quietly she closed the door to his room. She thought how blissful it would be to have the sweet, untroubled sleep of a child for one night. But then there were times when they had nightmares too.

Halfway down the stairs, Stacy heard the thump of Cord's crutches in the hallway below. Freezing for an instant at the sound, she was motionless when Cord frowned up at her.

"Do you know where Travis is?" he demanded curtly.

"No." She started down the stairs.

"I thought you kept track of him," Cord mocked.

"You think a lot of things that are just plain wrong."

"You're all sweetness and innocence, aren't you?" His mouth quirked.

"Just as much as you are," Stacy flashed.

"What's that supposed to mean?"

"You figure it out." Impatient that she had allowed herself to become involved in a squabble, she started to walk past him to the living room.

"Don't walk away from me!" Cord snapped, grabbing her arm and spinning her back. The action unbalanced him and he fought to stay standing.

Stacy's temper flared. "Of course not! That's unthinkable! I'm one of your possessions, right? Do you keep me around for decoration or for the sake of appearances?"

"It certainly isn't for decoration." His gaze raked her thinning figure with scorn. "I can feel your bones beneath my hands. You're turning into a scarecrow!"

His contempt for her appearance hurt. "Starving for love from you." The words were blurted out before she could check them.

"Pining for your freedom is more like it." Cord dismissed her truthful admission with more scorn. The crutches beneath his arms supported him as he reached out for her, taking her by the upper arm.

She endured it. She didn't want to see him fall under any circumstances.

"Admit it, Stacy. You want to be free, don't you?"

Free from what, her whirling mind wondered. Free from the agony of wanting his love and knowing it was no longer hers to have? Free from the torture of wondering what he and Paula did when they were alone? Free from the pain of a broken heart?

"Yes. Yes! *Yes!*" The admission rose to a crescendo of emotion as her head moved insanely from side to side in denial.

His grip tightened until her arm throbbed with pain. Then his hold suddenly loosened and he shifted back onto his crutches. Stacy buried her face in her numbed hands to smother the sobs that racked her.

"I told you I would never want to let you go." His voice was ominously low, rumbling like thunder in the storm-charged seconds. "But if I don't, it will destroy both of us. My father was right when he sent my mother away. Why ruin two lives? You're free, Stacy, I won't hold you here."

"Wh–what are you saying?" She raised her wet eyes, trying to read the granite-hard lines in his expression.

"I'm saying that you're free," Cord repeated coldly. "You can leave whenever you want. Today, tomorrow, this minute, I don't care."

With painstaking carefulness, he pivoted on his crutches to leave her. Uncertainty assailed her. Even in her darkest moments she'd never really believed that Cord would send her away.

His back was to her, broad and strong. With laborious steps, he began walking toward the study. Stacy couldn't let him go without knowing for sure what he meant.

Her fingers touched his arms to stop him. He halted immediately, his muscles stiffening beneath her hand, but he didn't turn to face her.

"I gave you what you wanted," he growled. "What is it now?"

"I—I . . ." She faltered, studying him with an anguished look. "I want to know if it's what you want."

His jaw was clenched for an instant. "Stacy, you're free to do what you want. You can go or stay. But don't make me look at you again."

Her hand fell away from his arm, the nails digging into her palm. Stacy lifted her chin in an attempt to react with dignity to his final, cutting statement.

"Well, then," she said numbly. "I'll start packing my things. Guess I should let Maria know where I want them to be sent. Or you can tell her. It's all the same to me."

"I will," he agreed tersely, and began heading for the study again.

Stacy watched him for a painful second, then pivoted to race back up the stairs. She threw a few essential items into an overnight bag and hurried out of the room. Cord had made no reference to Josh and neither had she. She was leaving, but she was taking Josh with her.

In his room, she quickly added his things to the overnight bag. When it was bulging at the side and sitting by the door, she went to the bed to wake the slumbering boy.

He rubbed his eyes sleepily when she shook his shoulders. "I'm tired," he grumbled.

"You have to get up now," she coaxed, lifting him to a sitting position. "We're leaving."

The statement got his attention. "Where are we going?"

Stacy hesitated. This was not the time to tell him the truth, not when she wanted to get him out of the house without Cord being aware of what she was doing. She tucked the tails of his shirt into his pants.

"We're going on a trip." It was half true.

"Where?"

Stacy had no idea. It didn't seem to matter where they went. "You'll see." She tried to make it sound like a mysterious adventure.

Taking Josh by the hand, she hurried down the stairs, carrying the overnighter. Silence came from the study. She didn't know if Cord was there or not and she didn't pause to find out.

Outside, Josh gave her a confused look. "Isn't Daddy coming with us?"

"Not this time." Her throat constricted and she bustled him into the car.

Stacy didn't look back at the house as she reversed out

of the driveway onto the lane. She didn't dare or she wouldn't have had the strength to leave.

Chaos reigned over her thoughts, scattering them to the winds and leaving her without conscious direction. Road dust billowed from the tires of the accelerating car. She drove in a daze, not knowing or caring where she was going. Her eyes were dry, parched by pain that was beyond tears. Staring straight ahead, her mind registered no details of the landscape, fixed on the endless road. She was barely aware that she'd stopped the car.

"Mommy, why are we stopping here?" Josh laid a hand on her shoulder. Her hands were still gripping the steering wheel as she tried to shake off the stupor she was in. "Mommy, why are we at Mary's house? Aren't we going on a trip?"

Mary's house. The words pierced the fog. With an effort Stacy focused on the familiar ranch-style house of the Buchanans. Something inside her began to crumble. It suddenly became imperative that she reach her friend before that "something" caved in.

"Come on, Josh." She switched off the engine and stepped out of the car.

Not noticing her son's bewilderment as he unclicked his seat belt and scrambled out, Stacy walked to the front door and rang the bell. A few seconds later it was opened and Mary's smiling face greeted them.

"Stacy, this is a surprise!" the redhead exclaimed in delight, swinging the door open wider. "Come in. You'll have to excuse the house. It's a mess, but I'm in the middle of—"

Stacy's hand tightened around Josh's. "Can you put us up?" There was a note of despair in her voice.

Astonishment made Mary stare. "Well, of course, but—"

"I've left Cord," Stacy answered the question that had been forming in her friend's mind.

"You did what?" Mary exclaimed incredulously. "Stacy, you can't mean it! Why, for heaven's sake?"

Then came a shuddering collapse. A black voice swirled in front of Stacy's eyes. Dimly glad that she didn't have to answer the question, she slipped into unconsciousness.

The dark world wrapped her in a protective cocoon, insulating her mind from the pain it couldn't bear. Occasionally a haunting image of Cord would drift into the blackness. Her lips would form his name and she would call out to him. The masculine vision would only look at her sadly and then fade away.

The last time his ghost, if that was what it was, appeared, he took her hand and looked at her gravely. "I'll always be with you, Stacy," the image told her. "I'll never leave you."

"No . . . no . . ."

"Ssh, angel," the familiar voice soothed. "You have to rest."

Then the apparition dissolved into a mist and oblivion claimed her again. She welcomed it, seeking the darkest corners of the voice to escape from Cord's specter.

For a long time Stacy remained safe in that world, untouched by outside forces. Then a hand took her arm and lifted it, almost physically drawing her back into reality. Her lashes fluttered in protest, resisting the attempt to bring her back to the world she couldn't endure without Cord.

"Have you decided to rejoin us, Stacy?" a voice she knew inquired gently.

A frown creased her forehead. It wasn't Cord's voice. She struggled to focus on the stocky figure standing beside her. Bill Buchanan. Bewildered, she stared at him for a minute as he held her wrist in his fingers, checking her pulse.

"Wh–what happened?" she murmured, disoriented. Was she ill?

"You collapsed," the doctor informed her, "as I predicted you would if you didn't get away for a while." He let her arm lie back along her side when he was done.

"I don't understand." Stacy gave a confused shake of her head.

"It was a case of complete exhaustion," he explained. "When you wouldn't give your body the rest it needed, it took over. That's why you blacked out."

A movement near the window got her attention—and Stacy's heart constricted at the sight of Cord leaning on his crutches. Sunlight streamed through the window behind him, blinding her to the expression on his handsome face.

"What are you doing here?" she breathed, her emotions swinging wildly between fear and hope.

Bill Buchanan glanced from Stacy to Cord. "I'll leave you alone for a few minutes." He addressed the statement to Cord. "But only a few minutes. She still needs to recover."

There was a curt nod of agreement from Cord, followed by silence as the doctor left the room. Stacy's gaze searched her husband's face.

"Why are you here?" Stacy repeated. Instantly the answer occurred to her. "You've come to take Josh, haven't you?" She thought that subconsciously she'd known that Cord would come after their son.

She couldn't blame him. Not if she wasn't capable of caring for a child or herself.

"That's why, isn't it?" Pain throbbed in her voice.

Cord moved out of the sunlight. His expression was an inscrutable mask that told her nothing. He stopped beside the bed.

"Mary called me to let me know what happened. I came

because I wanted to make sure you and Josh were all right."

Stacy turned her head away.

"What difference would it make to you?" she murmured, disliking the note of self-pity in her voice.

"I haven't stopped caring about you, Stacy," he declared with a hint of impatience.

No, she supposed he hadn't. He might have stopped loving her, but they had shared too many things for him to stop caring. A broken sigh quivered from her.

"You won't take Josh, will you?" she asked weakly.

Cord let out a sigh of his own. "No, I won't. But I do want to see him." He seemed to hesitate. "You're welcome to come back to the ranch until you're better."

"I won't go back there!" Stacy violently rejected the suggestion and the thought of seeing Paula and Cord together.

"Okay. If that's what you want." He nodded grimly and turned on his crutches. "I have to be getting back to the ranch. There's a slew of things that have to be done."

"Yes." There was a poignant catch in her voice. "The horse sale is tomorrow, isn't it?"

Cord paused, not quite looking over his shoulder. "You've been out of it for a long time, Stacy. Tomorrow is today. The auction is going on right now."

Had she been unconscious that long? The discovery startled her.

"I'll see you later," he offered distantly and opened the bedroom door.

"No," Stacy responded abruptly. His concern for her welfare wasn't enough, not when she hungered for his love. "There's no need for you to come back," she added stiffly.

His shoulders squared. "Maybe not," was his noncommittal answer. "I'll let Josh know you're okay. The kid's been worried." He moved out of the room. The door closed and Stacy turned her face into the pillow. Shutting her eyes tightly, she held back the tears. Rest, Bill Buchanan had decreed. It seemed impossible. Yet within minutes, her exhausted body had fallen asleep.

The opening of the door awakened her. Through half-closed eyes, she glanced at her visitor, not welcoming the interruption of her heavy sleep. At least asleep she stopped thinking and feeling. When she saw that it was Paula, she was even less glad.

"How are you feeling?" Paula smiled sympathetically.

Stacy ignored the question. "Why are you here?" To rub salt in the wounds, she added silently in resentment.

"I brought some things in for Josh," the blonde explained, "I thought I'd look in to see how you were, that's all."

"I'm fine." Stacy sat up a little, raking the fingers of one hand through the sides of her hair. "Please go away. You've done enough damage already." Bitterness surfaced with a rush she couldn't hold back. "Unless you're here to gloat."

Paula frowned at her. "What on earth are you talking about?"

"Stop the innocent act, Paula." Her voice was choked with emotion. "You know I'm talking about Cord. He's yours. I've conceded. Now get out of here!"

A charged moment of silence followed Stacy's outburst. Then Paula came a little farther into the room, her blue eyes narrowing.

"I don't like what you're saying, Stacy. Mary told me some nonsense about you telling her you'd left Cord just before you fainted on her doorstep yesterday. Or was it nonsense?"

"Hardly." Stacy blinked furiously, trying to hold back her tears. "He's all yours now."

"That's wonderful!" exclaimed Paula with obvious

amusement. "Do you actually mean you left Cord because of me? Oh, geez—"

"You didn't expect me to stay there while you two carried on your little affair, did you? I do have some pride left," Stacy declared.

"An affair? Me and Cord?" Paula's mouth gaped with astonishment.

"I saw the two of you together." Stacy hated Paula's faked surprise. "Laughing and smiling and sharing your secret jokes. And that's not all—"

"The joke is on you, honey." Paula shook her head. "Not that I wouldn't give my eyeteeth to have an affair with your husband, because I would. Two things would stop me, though. One is that I happen to like you. And the second and more important reason is that Cord and I are just friends. If you don't mind a cliché, he thinks of me as a sister."

"I don't believe you," Stacy said, because she wanted to believe it so desperately.

"Cord is a one-woman man and that one woman is you, Stacy."

"But he said—" Her head spun. Could it be true? "I thought—"

"How much more proof do you need?" Paula sighed. "The man never left your side the whole time you were unconscious. Mary said it was like he was possessed, sitting beside the bed staring at you."

It hadn't been a dream. Those visions of Cord that had haunted her when her mind was wandering really had been him.

"But—" Stacy pressed a hand against her temple in confusion. "Why did he tell me to leave?"

"Probably because he thought you wanted to go." Paula shrugged. "It sure wasn't because he stopped loving you.

In fact, it was probably the reverse. He loved you too much to keep you against your will."

It was all too possible that everything Paula said was true. She'd never been able to convince Cord after that argument that it wasn't about the ranch at all. And most likely he still mistakenly believed that she cared for Travis.

Throwing back the bedcovers, Stacy started to rise.

Bad move. The room began spinning and she reeled back against the pillow. When the dizziness stopped, she tried to rise again.

"What do you think you're doing?" Paula was at her side, trying to stop her. "You're still too weak."

"I have to get to the ranch." Determined, Stacy tried to sit up. "I have to see Cord."

"I understand that you have to straighten things out, but—"

The bedroom door burst open and Cord came swinging in, barely using his crutches. Joy made Stacy's eyes glow brightly as she looked at him.

"Cord!" she cried, flinging open her arms as Paula discreetly moved to the side.

He stopped just short of her reach, his dark eyes scanning her face. "I just talked to Travis." He glanced over his shoulder at the foreman standing in the doorway. "He said—"

Stacy guessed what Travis had said. He had obviously cleared up the matter of her supposed affair with him and her fears that Cord had been fooling around with Paula.

She interrupted him with a laugh. "I've just been talking to my rival for your affections. She straightened me out in a hurry. Oh, Cord—"

In the next second he was sitting on the bed, crushing her against his chest. Stacy clung to him without restraint as he buried his face in the curve of her neck.

"It is true, then." His voice was muffled by the ardent kisses he trailed over her neck. "You love me?"

"I love you," she whispered achingly against his ear.

Cord trembled against her, raising his head to gaze at her upturned face, animated and blushing with emotion. A mixture of tender feelings and fiery passion blazed in his dark eyes.

"I never thought it was possible to love you more than I did in the beginning," he murmured only for her to hear. "But I do, honey."

Rapture coursed through her body, held so close to his. Her lips moved inexorably closer to the sensuous line of his mouth, hard and firm.

Their contact was prevented by a third voice dryly asking, "What's going on here? This looks like a lovers' reunion."

With an embarrassed start, Stacy pulled away but only by a few inches. She saw Bill Buchanan standing behind his redheaded wife in the doorway. Mary had a tray in her hands.

"Ya think?" Paula asked with cheerful bluntness. "Travis and I were just wondering how we could disappear before it got too warm in here to breathe."

"I was bringing you and Stacy some hot tea." Mary smiled at Paula. "I thought it would perk Stacy up. Obviously she doesn't need it."

Cord smiled at Stacy, stealing her breath with the sheer charm of it.

"Your timing is terrible, Mary." He wrenched his gaze from his wife. "But since you went to the trouble, serve it up. I want my wife to get all the tender loving care she's entitled to."

"TLC, coming up." Mary smiled.

"We're intruding," protested Paula. "The two of you should be alone."

"Bill warned me this morning about overexciting Stacy

when she came to." The light in Cord's eyes danced over the sudden flush in Stacy's cheeks. "So I think you all should stay or I'll forget about his advice."

"Okay, for a few minutes," Bill agreed. "Long enough to drink to your happiness."

Minutes later they were lifting the extra cups Mary had scurried to get in a toast to the happy couple. As Cord touched the rim of his cup to Stacy's, he gazed into her eyes.

"I'm the luckiest man in the world," he murmured. "To love and be loved by you with no end in sight."

His head dipped slowly toward hers, tasting her lips ever so briefly, barely controlling his desire for more. Stacy felt positively weak when he lifted his head. Somehow she raised the tea cup to her mouth and sipped at the reviving liquid, unable to look away from Cord as he did the same.

"This should be champagne," Cord declared regretfully.

"Isn't it?" She smiled, feeling giddy.

"When you can't tell tea from champagne, you're definitely in love." Bill laughed. His hand slipped under his wife's elbow. "I think it's time we made our exit, Mary."

"Me too," Paula said.

This time Cord didn't protest. Only Travis lingered after the others had left. His hat was in his hand.

"I'll be leaving too," he said when Cord looked expectantly at him. "Now that the quarter horse auction is over, the ranch work will be back to normal. You and Stacy can handle it."

"Do you mean you're leaving permanently?" Stacy breathed.

"You don't need me anymore. Nope, not at all." He shook his head and smiled.

"But we want you to stay," she protested, glancing at her husband. "Don't we, Cord?"

"Definitely."

"Thanks, but—" Travis broke off to study them for a long moment. "I never planned to stay as long as I did anyway. I started looking for a ranch of my own. It's time I found it."

"Travis." A seriousness came over Cord's face. "I was wrong about a lot of things that I'm sorry for now. I've never thanked you for all you did for us."

"It isn't necessary. You had your reasons at the time, so there's nothing to forgive. And as for thanks, well"—he grinned as he placed his wide-brimmed Stetson on his head—"I've had that today."

"Won't you stay at the Circle H just a few days more?" Stacy asked as Travis strode to the door.

"Nah. I'm not one for long goodbyes." But he paused in the doorway.

"When you buy that ranch," Cord told him, "let us know. I have a seed bull and thirty cows that I'm gonna give you."

"That isn't necessary," Travis began firmly.

"It's a bonus," Cord announced. "You earned it five times over. And you don't have to thank me. I'm giving you thirty-one headaches on the hoof!"

The grooves around his mouth deepened as he met Travis's gaze. A smile lit up the foreman's face. He raised a finger to his hat brim and walked into the hallway, closing the door behind him.

"That was generous of you." Stacy beamed at him.

"Generous?" Cord looked at her in a bemused way. "I'd give him the ranch for opening my eyes to the truth—if the Circle H wasn't going to belong to our son someday."

He took the tea cup from her hand and set it on the bedside table. It left her hand free to lightly caress the powerful line of his jaw.

"Oh, Cord," she whispered. "We almost blew it."

"I've been such a fool about so many things." He caught her fingers and kissed the tips. "Can you ever forgive me for the terrible things I said to you?"

"Of course." Stacy sighed.

"I loved you so much that I couldn't stand the thought of you staying out of pity for me." Cord frowned at the memory of their bitter arguments. "Each time you came near, I doubted that it was because you loved me. That's why I kept pushing you away, why I kept hurting you and destroying myself each time I succeeded."

Stacy slid her fingers inside his shirt, feeling the warmth of his body and the pleasant tickle of chest hair on the palms of her hands. She tilted her head back, her lips moist and parted.

"Try pushing me away now, honey," she said huskily.

Beneath her hands, she felt his heartbeat stop for an instant. Then he was pushing her—not away, but back against the pillow as his mouth closed over hers.

"Mommy!" Josh's voice called from the hallway.

Stacy moved in a faint protest beneath his commanding kiss and Cord smiled against her trembling lips. "Mary will find something for him to do for a little while. Let her distract him."

Reassured, Stacy heard Mary's voice in the hall saying something about cookies and the sound of retreating footsteps. She wound her arms around her husband's neck.

"I think we're alone now," she whispered.

"And I intend to take full advantage of that fact," he whispered back.

And he did.